WHERE WE BELONG

An EVERMORE novel

N.S. Perkins

To anyone who's ever felt like things can't get better.

They will.

Chapter 1

Lexie

I feel like I've been run over by an eighteen-wheeler.

Or at least my body does. I'm used to always being in pain, one way or another, but this has to be one of my worst days. I only have myself to blame, though. Going on a cross-country drive alone while barely taking any breaks was dumb. I can see that now. Gymnastics—and the countless injuries it has given me—has transformed my twenty-five-year-old body into that of an elderly woman.

Down the quiet country road, my headlights catch on a large sign, and when I squint, I see it reads *Evermore Christmas Tree Farm*. Thank freaking god. I put my blinker on, and a groan escapes my lips as I turn onto the gravel road that leads to my rental. I'm not sure what the sound is for, if I'm honest. Relief at finally being here? Despair that this is what my life has come to? Who knows. I'm too exhausted to even understand myself.

I drive for another two hundred yards through a thick canopy of fir trees before coming across a small wooden shack that resembles the one I've seen on the rental website. If I continued even farther down the road, I would reach a bigger house that resembles a giant version of the cabin, with similar wooden beams and a huffing chimney. The lights in what I assume is the owner's house are on, and fairy lights are hung all over the front porch, creating a holiday-like vibe, even in September.

Once my car has come to a halt in front of the cabin's front door, I rest my head back and let my eyes fall shut. This is it. The place I'll be living in for god knows how long. I can't think too much about what that implies, or else I might break down into a full-on panic attack. Instead, I force myself to exit the car.

My back cracks in fifty different places as I stretch and take a look around. Even in the darkness, the cabin looks cozy and safe. Sure, it's kind of in the middle of nowhere, but it doesn't feel like the kind of place I'll get attacked in overnight. At least, I hope not. That would just be the cherry on top.

Faint music is emanating from the warm house at the end of the road, but otherwise, everything is utterly quiet. No busy intersections with honking cars and rushing drivers. No planes flying overhead or sirens going off or shouting matches from balconies.

Peace.

After inhaling another deep breath of pine-scented air, I pop the trunk and pull out the three duffel bags I'd packed before leaving the house in Phoenix. Once again, a rush of dread fills me as I'm reminded that this is everything I have in this world. Some clothes, a few pairs of running shoes, a dozen leotards, and a few trophies I brought with me as mementos. That's it. My whole life, able to fit into three bags.

Don't go there, Lexie. Self-pity has never done me any good. The only thing that could help right now is training until I can barely keep my eyes open... Or tequila. Tequila would definitely help.

Closing the trunk and locking the doors to my run-down Kia, I walk to the out-of-place garden gnome, where the guy I'm renting from said I'd find the keys to the cabin. Balancing my stuff on one shoulder, I bend down and lift the little man. *Bingo.*

Steps creaking under my weight, I reach the freshly painted, deep-brown wooden door. Once it's unlocked, I walk inside and turn on the lights before dropping everything onto the hardwood floor. I then take a look around, humming. It's cute. The entire space is one big room, with furniture and decoration I'd dare call vintage, but it's clean and smells of lemon disinfectant and fresh air. I'll take that any day over the cigarette-and-beer smell I've had to endure on a daily basis since I was a kid.

Directly in front of the door is a kitchenette with a two-burner stove and miniature fridge. To its left is the small living room, with a couch sitting in front of a gorgeous bay window and old-school fireplace, and the far end of the cabin is occupied by a double bed, onto which a burgundy wool cover was thrown. I walk straight to it and sit down, finding the mattress surprisingly comfortable. To be honest, I wasn't expecting much when I responded to the ad and asked if this cabin could be rented long term. So long as I had a place that wasn't too sketchy, where I could sleep in between work and practice, I'd take it. It's not like I'll have much free time to spend here anyway. With the schedule I'm about to have, it'll be a miracle if I end up not sleeping at the gym every night.

The cable box under the small television shows it's almost midnight. Untying my short ponytail, I drag a hand through my hair, eyes shut. If I'm lucky, I can aim for six hours of sleep to get rid of the driving fatigue before I have to be up and functional. No matter how much I love my sleep, I won't allow myself to be a second late tomorrow. I need this gig.

With one last face rub, I get up and head toward the bathroom on the opposite side of the cabin, then rid myself of my tight leggings and sweatshirt. I don't remember the last time I changed my clothes, but it very well might have been two days ago, at the truck stop between Saint Louis and Indianapolis. It's not like there was anyone with me to complain about the smell.

Is this what rock bottom feels like? Yep, I think it is.

Once naked, I jump into the shower and spend a good twenty minutes scrubbing the four days of gas station bathrooms and greasy breakfast sandwiches from my skin. The owner of the cabin kindly left toiletries in the bathroom, which I'm thankful for since I haven't even considered going shopping for groceries and supplies yet. Tomorrow. I can barely keep my eyes open anymore, and my bad shoulder is screaming for a good night's rest.

Turning the water off, I walk out and grab one of the white fluffy towels that were left on the bathroom counter. Without giving a single thought to skincare or hair brushing, I walk to the bed with my eyes half-closed. If I could fall asleep upright, I would.

Bending to retrieve one of my bags, I open it to find my pajamas.

And that is when everything goes to hell.

The second I drop my towel to the ground, the cabin's front door opens, and a tall man with a buzz cut and a flannel shirt bursts in, yelling, "Who's there?"

The high-pitched scream that comes out of me would be embarrassing if I wasn't certain I was about to get killed.

So this is it. A life of shitty days interspersed with rare good ones, always waiting for the other shoe to drop and hopelessly wishing for the tide to change, only to get murdered after just having turned twenty-five in an AirBnB in the middle of nowhere, Vermont. Just my luck.

"Jesus fuck!" the guy shouts as he spins in my direction and jumps so hard, he trips onto the edge of the welcome mat and falls onto his ass. Meanwhile, I continue screaming. I can't seem to stop. That is, until I notice that the guy is staring at me from his spot on the ground.

Because of course my murder had to happen while I was buck naked.

In a flash, I bend down to grip my towel, all the while screaming, "Get out! I'm calling the cops, you freak!"

"The hell you are!" the guy says with a huff as he gets back to his feet. "You're the one trespassing!"

"Trespassing?" I say, wrapping the towel around my body as tightly as I can. "I rented this place. *You're* trespassing." My heart is beating so erratically I can barely hear anything over the rush of blood in my ears. "And being a total creep."

"A creep?" the guy repeats, but this time, there's a trace of humor in his voice, which does calm me down, even the tiniest bit. He doesn't appear to have a weapon on him and hasn't made a move to rip my head off yet, which also helps.

"What else do you call a guy who walks in on naked girls inside their homes?" I reply, still huffing and puffing. Maybe this isn't the moment to argue, but I'm riled up, and when that happens, I tend to not be able to stop myself from sputtering stupid shit.

He lifts his hands in defense. "Okay, that's not what I—"

"Then leave!" I say, pointing at the door with the biggest eyes I can make.

He stammers an answer, but I only make my eyes rounder.

"Fine, jeez," he ends up saying as he takes a step back. "But meet me outside once you're decent."

Decent my ass.

I groan like a fire-breathing dragon as I watch his every step until, finally, the door closes behind him and I'm alone.

I blink, staring at the door. What in the world just happened?

As I rush into a pair of clean jeans and a T-shirt, all the while cursing my poor luck, my mind starts spinning. A stranger just saw me naked. Something's clearly wrong with this rental. Where will I live all year if I can't have this place? Usually, I'd start hyperventilating from the anxiety of it all, but I think I'm past that stage. Instead, in a state that's almost trance-like, I walk to the door, then down the porch steps, where the man is leaning against the railing, arms crossed in front of his broad chest.

Now that I'm dressed and only half-frightened, I take a second to study him. He's young—maybe late twenties or early thirties—and has one of the sharpest jaws I've ever encountered.

Straight nose, strong cheekbones, and deep-set eyes, although in the darkness, I can't quite tell the color. He's standing in the shadow of a tall pine tree, and although I can't make out every detail of him, he feels familiar. Like I've seen him before. Or maybe that's just my post-trauma brain playing tricks on me. I'm still not a hundred percent sure I'm getting out of tonight alive.

I clear my throat, bringing his attention from his unlaced boots to my face. "So, are you going to explain what's going on here?"

He snickers. So he finds this funny now? "How about you start?" he says.

Fine, then. "I'm renting this place," I repeat, also crossing my arms.

"Impossible. I'm the property manager, and the cabin's free this week."

"Well, I don't know what to tell you. I *did* rent it." Cocking my head, I add, "Although if barging in on guests while they're fresh out of the shower is how you manage this place, then I want a refund."

His jaw ticks. "I told you, it was supposed to be empty. I thought someone had broken in when I saw the lights turned on in there." Shifting position against the railing, he asks, "Who'd you talk to for the rental?"

"I don't remember." When he looks at me with expectant eyes, I keep my smart-ass comment to myself, and I grab my phone from my pocket, ignoring the text from my mom asking me if I paid the electricity bill last month. I scroll through my emails until I find the rental confirmation. "Some guy named Aaron, I think."

The stranger closes his eyes and throws his head back, this time with a smile skimming his lips. Under his breath, I'd swear I hear a "fucker."

I don't know what else to say, so I stand there with the still-warm September air ruffling my wet hair. Now that I know this was some kind of mix-up and not some murder plan, I feel kind of bad about yelling at this guy. Although he *did* ogle me.

"Look," he says, "I'm really sorry about this whole thing. It was a misunderstanding. I'll talk to Aaron in the morning."

I nod. "So I can stay?"

He rubs one large palm over his eye, seeming almost as tired as I am. "Yeah, you can stay."

"And no more creep moves?"

He laughs, the sound deep and clear. "I promise. Plus, I didn't see anything."

"I'll pretend you didn't just lie to my face," I say with a small smile.

He laughs again, then takes a step my way. The moonlight catches his face at another angle, allowing me to get a better glimpse at him, and I have to say, he's good-looking. Very good-looking. I usually prefer the long-haired type, but his close crop fits him well. Again I'm hit with the feeling that I've seen this grin before, but I can't quite put my finger on where.

"Can we start over?" He extends a hand my way. "I'm Finn."

My smile drops instantaneously, a gasp escaping my parted lips. "You!"

I *knew* I'd met him before.

Letting his hand drop back to his thigh, he says, "Me?"

"Yes, you!" I lift a hand to point in his direction, as if we weren't the only two people here. "You thief!"

"I'm sorry?" he says, face half-amused, half-confused. That bastard. He doesn't even have the decency to remember me.

"Rome, seven years ago? You and your group of dumbasses spent the night with me and my friends, only to steal from us and skitter away? Ring any bells?"

I never could've forgotten that night, or that name, no matter how many years passed. I'd been having a rare night out with the girls on my team during a three-day competition abroad. Our coaches expected us to stay in because we had an early start the next morning, but Lacey, our team's balance beam specialist, convinced a few of us to enjoy the city for the night. At one of the bars we went to, we met this group of guys with whom we spent the night, and when we went to the bathroom and stupidly left our purses at the table, they stole all the euros we had and proceeded to escape in the taxi we'd called for ourselves. We ended up having to walk back to the hotel, and by the time we showed up, one of our coaches had been alerted of our escape and made our lives at practice a living hell for the following six months.

Nothing like gymnastics to make a group of grown women feel like children.

But that's beside the point. All this happened because of him. The guy with the blood-drained face standing in front of me.

"Oh, I..." He blinks. "I'm—"

"An idiot? A criminal? A shithead?" I could go on and on. I don't think there exists a limit to the number of names I could find to describe him.

"I'm sorry," he corrects. "We were young. And dumb, clearly." He scratches the back of his head. "Never thought I'd see you again."

"So that makes it okay?" I say, fuming from the inside. And to think I'd been having a good time with him that night. That I'd felt a little flutter of something in my chest while we'd been talking. Really, *I* was the dumbass.

"No, of course, not, I—"

"Wait." Another thing comes back to me from that night. The guy I'd been talking to all night had an English accent. He was dressed in a nice dress shirt and slacks, just like his friends, who'd all said they were from Manchester. "What happened to the accent?"

He winces, then rubs the back of his head again. "It's something we did for fun, back then." His eyes drift to the ground when he says, "Fake lives for the night."

I roll my eyes. Of course. What else did I expect? That anything he'd said to me that night, save for his name, had been true? "A creep, a thief, *and* a liar," I count on my fingers. "This just keeps getting better."

"I thought we'd cleared the creep part," he says, at least having the decency to look sheepish.

"Well, guess what? I changed my mind." My shoulders are tight as a drawstring, and it gets worse the longer I stare at him. "I actually kind of want to punch you in the face a whole lot right now, and I'm not in the mood to get arrested, so I think I'll just walk away and hope for your sake you make sure I never see you again." With one last glare at his slack jaw, I say, "Goodnight, creep." Then, without skipping a beat, I climb the stairs and slam the door behind me.

I make sure it's locked this time.

Chapter 2

Finn

Aaron answers on the second ring when I finally find the time to call him the next day. That prick had better.

"Hey, what's up?" the man I've considered my best friend ever since I can remember says, his tone too unbothered for my liking.

"Oh, not much," I answer as I pace in front of the Sonder Hill Gymnastics Center, the pavement under my feet darkened from the recent bout of rain. The air is still chilly, dampness going straight through my windbreaker. "Except for the part where I might get arrested for voyeurism, but other than that..."

"You what?" Something rustles in the background, like bedsheets or clothes, accompanied by a soft whine, likely from one of his and his wife's two dogs. "Finn, what the hell did you do?"

"What the hell did *you* do, you mean. Renting the cabin without telling me? Didn't want to give me a heads-up so I wouldn't walk in on a naked girl thinking it was that damn Cameron bastard again?"

The moment I saw those lights turned on in there all the way from my office window, I almost went batshit. The memory of the last time someone unexpected had been in there was still too fresh in my mind, and the last thing I wanted was a repeat of that night.

Although now that I know what happened next, I think I'd rather have taken my chances on a second fight with Cameron.

"Ah, shit, man. Totally slipped my mind. Was trying to help you with the workload one night, but then Wren came home and—"

"Yep, I don't think I need to hear the rest of that."

Aaron chuckles.

"And I told you to stop helping anyway." My job used to be Aaron's, although he never actually wanted it. His family has owned the Evermore Farm for generations, but two years ago, Aaron's dad had a stroke, and neither he nor his wife, who happens to be my mother's best friend, were able to handle the farm anymore. Aaron took over for a while, but eventually, I offered to do it, and he was more than happy to give me the job so he could go back to Boston and his graphic-design job. "I don't need your gracious help," I say.

"Finn..."

"No, stop it. I'm serious. I like it. I'm not doing it for you." At least not anymore.

At first, I *did* start to work at Evermore to help him and his family out. Once I learned that Aaron would be taking over the farm after his father's stroke, I immediately booked a one-way ticket from Thailand to Vermont, the place I'd always called home. I knew my best friend would be having his hands full, and I also knew he'd be too prideful to ask for my help, so I pretended it was my plan all along to return, and Aaron bought it. Traveling the world without a purpose had gotten old anyway. And while coming back was originally to lend a hand, I came to love the job. Spending time outside, working with people, seeing smiles on customers' faces... It was all more than I'd hoped for.

"And I definitely don't need you getting involved in booking the cabin if you're going to fuck it up anyway," I add, not wanting to get into another emotional conversation. We've had enough of that for a lifetime.

Aaron laughs again. "I'm really sorry. Totally my fault."

"Damn right it is." While Aaron's family lives in the main house on the farm, they don't use the cabin, which is a bit down the road from their place, so they rent it to tourists, usually during winter. Or, I guess, to random girls from my past too. Under my breath, I mumble, "And out of all the people in the world, it had to be *her*."

I'd be lying if I said I'd recognized her right away. The last time I'd seen her, she had long brown hair and heavy going-out makeup, and I was definitely drunk. But the second she recognized me, it's like the connection happened in my mind too. And goddammit, if the earth could've swallowed me whole at that moment, I would've taken it gladly.

"What was that?" Aaron asks.

I sigh. I could lie, but then again, Aaron always ends up learning everything, and I'm really fucking bad at keeping secrets. "The girl I walked in on?" I close my eyes, trying hard not to let the image of her naked body invade my head. It'd be disrespectful, and getting a boner while I'm waiting to pick up Aaron's little sister from gymnastics class would be a thousand kinds of fucked up. "She wasn't just a random stranger. I know her." Or rather, I met her once. *Stacey.* It's not like I'd gotten to know her all that well during that night in Rome, but it was enough for me to feel like I'd just spent an evening with one of the coolest girls I'd ever met. Enough for me to still remember her name after all these years.

"Okay… And?"

"And I was kind of a dick."

"Tell me something I don't know."

"Fuck off," I retort, making Aaron laugh once again.

"All right, so what did you do?"

I wince, wishing I could erase that entire night from my brain. "It was a long time ago, while I was still in Italy. I was with a bunch of other dickheads, and we decided to pretend to be some British douchebags for the night. It was stupid, but whatever. And then we met this group of girls, and when they weren't looking, the guys thought it'd be funny to take a few things from their purses and run, and I didn't stop them. I laughed like a motherfucker, and then I ran with them."

"And let me guess, that girl was one of them?"

I hum my answer, all the while cursing karma for doing its thing.

"Well…at least things can't get any worse?" Aaron says.

"That's so stupid," a feminine voice adds from the other side of the line. "Give me the phone."

"Wait," I say, "was I on speakerphone?"

"Hello, Finn," Wren, Aaron's wife, says at the same time Aaron apologizes.

And karma keeps on striking.

"Hey, Wren. Enjoying my public humiliation?"

"It was very much deserved," she says in that no-nonsense way of hers, as if I didn't already know that. "But you want some advice that's better than 'at least it can't get any worse'?"

Laughter comes through the phone, and I don't even want to imagine what's going on in their home right now.

"Sure," I say, scraping my sneakers against the pavement. Another gust of cold wind brushes my scalp, the sign of more rain coming. I walk toward the front door and step inside, hit instantaneously by the smell of sweat and lemon carpet cleaner that's as familiar to me as the scent of my own place. I'll wait inside for a while. Callie should be done soon anyway.

"You were stupid, but we all know you've changed since then, so just apologize and show her that you're not a shithead anymore," Wren says.

Right. Because I definitely am not the same little shit I was a few years back, but Stacey couldn't possibly know that.

I sigh again. "Yeah, I guess that's the only thing I *can* do."

On the floor section of the gym, a group of girls stretch into splits, one of them shrieking as the coach adds a block under one of her feet, the sight so painful I look away.

"Where are you?" Aaron asks, probably because of the level of noise inside the gym.

"Nowhere," I answer a little too fast.

"Finn."

"I offered to pick Callie up for your mom, okay? And you know I don't mind." Aaron's family has gone through so much in the past years, so helping them out from time to time is the least I can do, and I don't want Aaron to move back here to help out, because I know he would, and he deserves to live his life. I don't have anything else. No girl waiting for me at home, no passion project I can't live without. I've always lived by the seat of my pants, so this is fine. "Callie's like my little sister anyway. Now that I think about it, she actually told me she preferred me to—"

"I'll hang up, now," Aaron says, and I laugh. "For real, though. Thanks, Finn."

"No big deal."

"Okay then," Wren says with more sheet rustling, "we were kind of in the middle of something, so we'll let you go now. Bye Finn!"

I shake my head, smiling wide. I'm happy for my friend. He deserves this life. "Bye, lovebirds."

I hang up just as the group of girls get up from their stretches and head toward the locker room to the left of the gym. A couple of parents are sitting in the reception area with me, waiting for their kids to finish. I notice the gym isn't as packed as it was a few years ago, but there's still a few groups going for lessons, spread out and practicing on the different events.

"What. Are. You. Doing. Here?"

I look up to find the last person I'd want to see towering over me, her strong arms crossed in front of her chest, dark eyes glaring. Thank god looks don't kill, because I'd be six feet under right about now. Her small size doesn't make her any less intimidating.

I realize I haven't answered when she adds, "Is this some kind of stalker situation? Should I actually call the cops now?"

Don't imagine her naked, you dickhead.

I stand up, feeling a little too much like a scolded child. I lift my hands in defense—something I seem to be doing a whole lot with her—and say, "Coincidence, I swear."

"And I'm supposed to believe that?" Her wide brown eyes, which I should've recognized the second I saw her, stare me down.

"Yes, actually. I'm here to pick up my friend's sister."

That doesn't seem to make her believe me any more.

She's wearing a tank top and sports leggings, which are skintight, showing her toned body. She's not tall, maybe five two, but she's still terrifying. I wholeheartedly believe she could make good on any threat she gives.

Which is why I'm infinitely grateful that Callie chooses this moment to come out of the lockers and meet me out front.

"Hey, Finn," she says, a bored look on her face. She's only thirteen, but her teen attitude is definitely there. Before, she would've thrown herself into my arms and given me a big hug, which always made me smile, but I guess we're past that now.

Stacey looks at us with pursed lips before she asks Callie, "You know this guy?"

I snicker with a roll of my eyes as Callie says, "Yeah, he's family."

My number-one hater hums, still eyeing me like I'm some kind of rabid beast.

"Finn!"

I look to my right to find my mother walking toward us, the gym's SHGC logo printed on her zip-up vest. Her blond hair is pulled up and held in a bun with a yellow pencil, the way I've seen it time and time again when she didn't have the time to go find a hair tie.

"Didn't think I'd catch you here tonight," she says with a quick side hug. Meanwhile, I throw Stacey a look with raised brows like, *See?* She doesn't seem to appreciate it, or maybe it's just that she hates me too much to care.

"Yeah, just grabbing Callie," I say.

"You talk as if I'm some kind of object," Callie says.

"A really pretty one." I pull at the end of her ponytail, and despite herself, she gives me a corner of a smile, which I count as a win.

"So, Finn, you've met our new coach, Lexie?" Mom says.

I look around, confused. That is, until I realize who my mother is pointing at. My brows lift high as I repeat, "Lexie?" Meanwhile, the tips of Lexie's ears redden as she fakes a smile.

"Yeah, we've met," she says, not elaborating any further.

"Good," Mom says. "Well, I gotta go, but I'll see you guys later! Great first day, Lexie." She grins at her with a thumbs-up, then leaves toward her office. I don't look her way, though. My gaze is fixed on the girl standing in front of me, with her red cheeks and a tilted-up chin.

"Callie, do you mind going to wait for me in the car for a sec?" I ask as I give Aaron's sister my keys while maintaining my staring contest with *her*.

"Don't be too long, I have homework," Callie answers before she thankfully listens, leaving the two of us alone.

"So, *Stacey,* huh?"

Her jaw tightens. "We were with a group of random boys in a foreign city. It would've been dumb *not* to use fake names."

I tilt my head. "So you can lie, but I can't, is that it?"

"That's not the same thing."

"Seems pretty similar to me," I add with a smirk. That little heathen was making me feel two inches tall for using a fake accent when she gave me a fake name for an entire night.

"I used another name, I didn't steal from your pocket and ensure you had six crappy months to follow."

My grin disappears. I'm not sure what the second part of her statement means, but she does have a point about the first. Just imagining some guys doing this to Callie or to my own sister makes me grit my teeth. I'm not blame-free just because I wasn't the one to do it.

"Look—"

"My name doesn't matter anyway," she interrupts. "We don't have any reason to interact again."

"You live on the property I manage," I point out.

She gives me a smile that's bordering on creepy. "I'd rather not be reminded."

I frown. Not to sound conceited, but I'm used to people liking me. I've always been an easygoing, people-pleasing man, and starting on such a bad foot with someone is making me more uncomfortable than I'd have thought. Plus, I can't imagine why she'd still be *this* mad after seven years have passed.

She turns as words escape my lips. "Don't you think you're taking things—"

I don't have the time to finish my point before she's stomping back to me. "I wouldn't finish this sentence if I were you." Her nostrils flare. "I've had a really crappy week—month, year, you name it—and I don't think I can handle dealing with yet another asshole. I'm just asking for one day of peace. Just. One." Her voice cracks on that last word, and she pauses before adding, "So please, walk away."

My lips twist to the side as I watch her. Her breaths are coming in and out fast, dark circles underlining her beautiful eyes, and I don't like that I might be responsible for this. I don't mind riling women up when we're fucking around, but this isn't the same. She's hurt, or at least she has been hurt, and she's counting me among the people that are making her life hard.

I fucking hate it.

But I won't make things better by staying and trying to explain that I've changed, that I'm a much better person than I was at twenty-one and that I'm deeply ashamed of a lot of things from my past. Maybe another time, I'll be able to convince her, but now's not the time.

So I give her a nod and walk outside and drive Callie back to the farm before burying myself in work.

But no matter how much I exhaust myself, the distraught look in her eyes stays with me all night.

Chapter 3

Lexie

I should be sleeping.

I don't need a doctor to tell me my daily routine is unhealthy. However, I also think doctors often forget that healthy schedules are not for everyone. Having time to work, exercise, cook dinner, spend time for yourself, *and* go to bed at a reasonable hour is only possible for rich people who have their lives together. Or maybe just for people who don't have a stupid dream like mine.

It's almost 1:00 a.m., and I have to be up in about six hours, but I can't leave until I get myself to do this one thing. My gaze drifts to the multiple sets of uneven bars looming from the shadows of the gym, almost like the villains of a horror movie. And the worst part is they don't just look like it. To me, they *are*.

I didn't always see the uneven bars as my nemesis. Before last year, I'd even enjoyed them. They'd always been a challenge, but a good one. When they almost break your neck, though, you start looking at them from another perspective.

I've gone through all my other events for the night, so I can't stall any longer. I've waited long enough. Nostrils flaring, I take another gulp from my water bottle, one that still wears the logo of my old gym in Phoenix, then get to my feet and head toward the bars, turning on the lights in this section of the gym as I go. I know I should always leave all the lights on during practice, for safety, but I hate how a bright, empty gym feels. In the dimness, I can pretend I'm not entirely alone in this place.

The neons flash up one by one, and once again, this feels like the final confrontation of an action movie.

I shouldn't be feeling shivers all over my body just looking at the bars. Technically, they didn't bring me to the brink of death. I did that all by myself. As Andy, my old coach, would say, "You master the apparatus, not the other way around." But that's much easier to say than to actually make my brain believe.

Wiping the sweat from my forehead, I put on my grips, the sequence of movements as familiar as breathing. The moment I'd heard the sound of Velcro tearing for the first time, after so many months away in physical rehab, felt heavenly. That is, until I'd realized I didn't master the bars any longer.

I spray water and scrub chalk over my hands and grips as I stare at the apparatus, going through the routine I want to do in my head. I'll start easy. A few release moves, two basic transitions, and a simple dismount. Something I could've done at twelve years old.

My heart starts beating quicker as I walk in between the two bars, facing the lower one, and as if on cue, a twinge of pain pops into my neck and shoulder.

Don't get into your head, kid. Andy's old adage resonates through my head, a sentence I've heard countless times over the years, but even more so after I came back this year. I try not to let myself focus on what happened the last time I heard it, which was only a few weeks ago. He told me not to overthink, so of course, I did just that and choked my dismount, and that was the final drop for him. He didn't even spare me a glance, only turning back toward his office and saying we were over. *Uncoachable.* The word still hurts, even weeks later. Who knew an injury followed by a major mental block was going to be what ended me? After years of pain and sacrifice, my freaking head got the best of me.

"You're not done," I say out loud even though I'm alone, just because I need to make myself believe it. It doesn't matter if I don't have a coach, or if there isn't a single person on this planet who believes my dream is achievable. If *I* believe it, then not everything is lost.

Now, I just need to remaster this bitch.

Eyes closed, I breathe in once, nice and slow. Then, I let my muscle memory take over, and I jump to catch the lower bar.

The first part of my old routine goes well. I don't have to think through most of it, Andy's corrections coming back to me naturally. My wrists are killing me, especially after two hours of floor training, but the pain is good. It means I'm doing the thing. Getting one step closer to being ready for New York in five months.

God, five months. Andy was right. This *is* crazy.

I go through my Maloney transition, a movement that almost feels like flying backward as I move from the low bar to the high one. My grip isn't as strong and confident as I'd like it to be when I catch it, but I'm still good. Still safe.

I go through one giant, where I complete a full rotation around the high bar, my posture nowhere near close to perfect. My head's stretched in a hundred directions at the same time, which means I can't do a single thing right. I try to focus on tightening my core and making sure my hands are at the right width when I catch the bar after a ray—yet another release movement I used to be able to do in my sleep—but the only thing that fills my head is images of falling. Of not catching the bar the right way and seeing my life flash in front of my eyes. I didn't believe in that concept until I found myself falling through air and seeing flashes of a little girl pulling at the loose strings of her mom's jean shorts, begging her to come outside to play, and of a teenager hiding in her closet because her half-brother was back home and had had a drink or twelve, and of a young woman who wanted to win more than anything in the world, because winning would mean it had all been worth it.

Nothing like a near-death experience to make yourself realize how much your life has sucked.

I try to catch my breath as I go through the motions, but the blur of fearful thoughts has thrown me off. As I'm rotating, I lose track of where I am in space, until I can't tell what's up and what's down, or even where I'm supposed to be. Gritting my teeth, I blink, then push through and force myself to transfer to the low bar with a sequence of kip cast and bail, except my proprioception isn't right. I let go of the bar a millisecond too late, which is enough to mess everything up.

Palms not close enough, it's the tips of my fingers that snap against the low bar instead as I fall. I hit the mat, which I'd thankfully put under the apparatus, face first, feeling the impact from my neck down to my toes. And don't even get me started on my fingers.

"Fuck!" I shout across the empty gym, the sound of my voice echoing through the equipment, only silence answering me.

I don't know how many times this exact outcome has happened to me since I returned to training. A hundred? Two? It starts well. I think I can actually do the motion. And then I mess something up, and I can't get back to where I was, which leads to me falling one way or another, always afraid that the body part that will hit the ground first is my neck, and that this time, I won't get as lucky.

Biting my tongue, I flip onto my back and stare at the neon lights as I run through the last minute in my head, all the while massaging my poor bruised fingers.

What would Andy say if he were here?

You got lost inside your head. You don't listen when you get this way. Your technique was horrible. Your grips were all over the place. You waited too long to get back to it, and now you're fucked. Fear's ruling over you now, and there's no way you'll ever win a competition again.

I wish I didn't have to think about what his feedback would be, but I don't know how else to reflect on my routines. I'm so used to hearing his voice the second I dismount, telling me all the things I did wrong and all the things I did *really* wrong, it's like I'm not me without him.

I'd thought practicing alone wouldn't be so bad, but I might've underestimated this thing.

I scrub a hand over my face, probably smearing chalk all over my skin. At this point, it doesn't matter since my thighs and simple black leotard are already covered in white too.

This has got to stop. It doesn't matter that I'm great on the floor or have a solid balance beam routine. There are two types of athletes that can make the US Olympic team. Either you are great all around, which means you have good chances of having competitive scores in all disciplines, or you are the best at one event and have a pretty sure shot at medaling for it. Unfortunately, I'm not option B, which means I need to be good enough in all four disciplines to have a chance at even the Olympic trials. In simple words, if I don't get my shit together at the uneven bars, I can wave goodbye to the dream I've carried with me throughout the years.

Pushing myself to my knees, I crack my neck left and right, staring at my most hated equipment again. At least things *could* be worse. Two weeks ago, I didn't even have a gym to practice at. I had no coach, barely enough money in my bank account to make it through the end of the month, and no opportunity to even try and get back to where I was before my accident.

And then I saw Shelli's ad, offering a position as a full-time gymnastics coach in a small town in Vermont, and I knew this was my opportunity. I negotiated rights to use the gym whenever it was empty, and she must've been desperate enough to find someone, because she agreed right away.

As much as I don't want to, I get back into my starting position in front of the low bar. I run through the routine in my head again, and just as I gulp air in before starting, the sound of my phone ringing from my bag on the floor section stops me in my tracks. Not many people have my number, and even if people from here did, I don't see why they would call me this late at night. That can only mean it's someone from another time zone, which means I have to take it. Might be Josie.

I jog to my bag, answering immediately when I see my little sister's name on the screen.

"Hey, Jos, what's up? Everything okay?"

She doesn't answer right away, which gives me all the warning I need.

"Hey," she says in a low voice. "Are you busy?"

"Not at all," I say. Words I wished I could've heard throughout my childhood, especially at her age. I remember well enough asking my mother for a glass of milk or for help with my homework and being answered with a "Will you shut up for once?" Josie probably hasn't even thought that it's late here for me, but it would never occur to me to make her feel bad for it.

"You haven't answered my question, though," I say. "Everything okay?"

She clears her throat. Goosebumps rise on my neck.

"He's back."

My stomach clenches, causing bile to rise inside my throat. "Who is?" I ask, but it's not necessary. Based on her tone, on the element of fear in her voice, I know who she's talking about.

"Kyle."

I close my eyes, resisting the urge to repeatedly hit my head against the wall next to me. After cursing under my breath, I ask, "Did he do something?"

"To me? No. He just got here."

I shouldn't have left. A few days away, and this happens. My asshole of a half-brother comes back home, and I'm not there to act as a buffer between him and Josie.

The urge to leave Phoenix had become something close to survival instinct in the last year. Growing up, I never felt completely safe inside my own home, either because of Kyle, Mom's boyfriends, or Mom herself, but these last months, it had gotten to a point of no return. I felt like if I didn't leave, I'd end up getting into a fight where one of us wouldn't come out alive, and I didn't want to risk it.

But I guess that makes *me* the asshole, because I left my little sister to deal with it—no escape option for her.

"I'm so sorry, Jos. I honestly didn't think he'd be back so fast." A month ago, he left the house after finding "the next big thing to invest in," but that likely flopped, just like his projects always do. If I've learned one thing about my brother over the years, it's that he's a lazy bastard who will drop whatever he's doing the second it takes a minimum amount of effort or time. However, he's never bounced back this fast. It usually takes a couple of months for him to abandon his quests.

"Me neither," she says. At eleven years old, she's had to grow way too fast, and even though she's a tough kid, I can hear the treble in her voice. It breaks my heart into a thousand pieces.

"I'm coming back," I declare, getting to my feet. If I leave in an hour, I could be home in three days, maybe less if I don't stop for more than a few hours at a time. Then, if it's too bad out there, I'll just take Josie with me and leave. Anywhere would be better than there.

"No," she says. "You can't."

"Damn right I can."

"No, you can't. This is your dream. You need to do it."

I bite my bottom lip so hard it starts bleeding. What kind of person am I, prioritizing gymnastics over everything, to the point where my own sister thinks it's more important than she is?

"Jos—"

"I don't want you to come back. I swear. It'll just cause more drama and more fighting."

Another jab. While Josie usually lets things slide and locks herself in her room most of the time to avoid trouble, I'm always smack dab in the middle of it. It never occurred to me that I might've been as much of a bother to her as the rest of my family was.

"I'm serious, Lex. I didn't call you for that. I just thought you should know."

I wipe a bead of sweat running down my temple with the back of my hand. "Let me at least call Mom and talk to her," I say. Our mother has put us through enough shit. The least she can do is make sure her son doesn't make Josie's life a living hell.

"All right," my sister ends up saying.

"Thank you."

"But you're going to stay in Vermont, right?"

"Yeah, if that's what you want."

"Good." I hear the squeak of the springs in her bed that used to wake me up every time she moved at night. I can imagine her, lying over the pink comforter I handed her down, her feet in the air, leaned against the wall and crossed at the ankles, her thin lips twisted to one side. "You deserve to be happy, Lexie."

My throat tightens. She's too young to be this mature.

I don't like the emotions overwhelming me, so I clear my throat and say, "I love you, Jos. You call me whenever you need to, no matter the time. Can you promise me that, at least?"

"I promise. Love you too."

"All right. Take care."

"Bye," she says, then hangs up.

I drop my phone in my bag, then let my head fall back. "That motherfucker," I mutter. I don't even have it in me to shout anymore.

I glance back up at the other end of the gym, where the bars still gleam under the glow of the neons, but at this point, with my head all over the place, it'd be plain stupid to get back to it.

Grabbing my stuff, I head outside, locking the gym behind me. My phone tells me it's close to 2:00 a.m. now. If I skip a shower, I could get a good five hours of sleep.

As I drive back to the cabin, which is thankfully less than five minutes from the gym, I run over what I'll tell my mother first thing tomorrow morning. She needs to make sure Josie's safe.

Throw Kyle out on his ass if she needs to. After all the shit he's pulled over the years, he more than deserves it.

I knew coming here was selfish. My entire Olympic dream is selfish. But fuck me, I can't get over it. No matter the injuries, the shitty lifestyle, the loneliness on the other side of the country, I need it like I need air. I need the wins. I need the thrill I get when I finish a routine and the roar of the crowd in the stands zaps me up like a shot of lightning, making me burn from the inside. It's stronger than any drug.

I stand by my choices now. I just hope I won't come to regret them.

Chapter 4

Lexie

"Push! Squeeze that butt! More!"

My voice is hoarse from how much I've screamed today. On the balance beam, Gerty, an eleven-year-old with tremendous potential, is trying to perfect her routine before her competition in two weeks. However, today doesn't seem to be her day.

Welcome to the club.

She lands her acro series on shaky legs, arms flailing.

"Fight! Fight for it!"

She does as she's asked, tightening every muscle in her body and succeeding in staying upright by sheer determination alone.

"Good." I watch with my arms crossed as she resumes her motions. Sweat is curling the dark hair at her nape, and her lips are pressed in a tight line. "You can do it. Point that foot!"

I wish I could say I was a sweet, quiet coach, but the truth is, I don't think that exists in the world of gymnastics. We only know loud and extra loud. Andy was always rough on me, but his tough love brought me to where I am now, as much as I wanted to wring his neck every time he put me through an extra set of burpees after I'd missed a landing or a skill.

Still, I don't think I'm that bad all the time. Poor Gerty and her teammates caught me in a mood, and they have nothing to do with it. No, that would be my mother, who never answered my seven calls this morning and afternoon. Clearly, she didn't mean it when she promised to stay in touch.

"Tighter!" I shout once more as she goes from her handspring to her dismount.

She lands on her foot at the wrong angle, but she does everything in her power to stick it, no matter how much her eyes scream in pain.

She's a fighter. I'd recognize that look anywhere. How many times have I battled through pain to make a landing or to get through a routine with a competitive score?

I walk to her with my hands up in the air. "Good job," I say.

She returns my high five but doesn't smile. "I was all over the place."

I don't want to lie to her and say she's wrong, because she's not. I wouldn't be a proper coach if I told her whatever she wanted to hear. Instead, I put a hand on her shoulder and say, "We all have harder days, but you gave it your all, and that's good enough for me. Tomorrow, we start from scratch. Good?"

Her nose twitches as she redoes her ponytail. "I should have this by now."

"And you do. You just can't have it a hundred percent of the time."

I'm such a hypocrite. Do what I say, not what I do.

"Don't overthink this," I add, tipping my head toward the reception area. "Go home, and we'll get it tomorrow."

My words clearly haven't convinced her, but I didn't expect them to. Again, a fighter. Still, they get her to nod at me and head out, which is what I was hoping for.

The rest of the girls are already in the locker room since their practice officially ended ten minutes ago. I should probably go home too. I'm beat after the crazy week I've had. I've barely spent any time in my new home, the vast majority of my days—and nights—spent in the gym. Thank god Shelli doesn't mind. In fact, I'm not sure she's noticed.

I realized quickly after I got here that Shelli didn't just wish for an extra full-time coach; she *needed* help. Not all classes are full, and the gym's schedule has holes that need to be filled, but it doesn't matter. There isn't enough staff. Shelli is too busy with administrative stuff to coach, and finding competent people to train the competitive-level groups isn't easy. I've assisted Andy enough times to know all about it. Coaching has always been a good option to help pay for competition fees and team gear, so I've been at it on and off for years.

While cracking my neck, a bad habit I can't seem to shake, I head to the staff room to grab my things. With the way my shoulders and neck are screaming in pain, I should probably take the night off. Maybe stream something or go to bed early. I'm still on schedule, I think. Hard to say without a coach telling me exactly what I need to be doing every single day to be ready for the Winter Cup in New York in four months.

Without allowing myself the time to feel bad about going home and changing my mind, I grab my bag and coat, then sit to change from my tennis shoes into beat-up sneakers I'd throw away if I had even a few bucks to spare on things like shoes. My back cracks loudly as I stand up.

"Jesus," I mutter before chuckling to myself. How old *am* I?

I walk out of the room, but just as I reach the reception, my phone rings, stopping me in my tracks. I answer the second I see the name on the screen.

"What took you so long?" I ask by way of greeting. I wish I didn't have to don armor and prepare for battle every time I speak with her, but she's taught me too well.

"Hello to you too, Alexandria," my mother says in that raucous voice of hers before she breaks out into a wet coughing fit. I can imagine her, sitting on the cracked and rusty swing on the front porch, a cigarette dangling between her index and middle fingers and a glass of Captain Morgan in the other hand, the phone held between her bony shoulder and cheek. I hear her drag an inhale. "I'm guessing you're not calling to talk about the weather?"

I grind my teeth together. *Calm down.* Riling her up usually makes things even worse.

When I feel I'm as calm as can be, I say, "Josie told me about Kyle."

She hums. "So?"

"So?" I press two fingers at my now-throbbing temple. "So you know how he is. How it turned out last time." Aka, him scaring the hell out of the entire house with every one of his outbursts, including one episode of a fist punched through the wall after I asked him to pick his socks off the floor. "Do you really think it's a good idea to let him come back home?"

Ever since my sister called me yesterday, my mind has been filled with all kinds of horror scenarios. Kyle busting the data plan so Josie can't do her schoolwork any longer. Kyle getting mad about Josie putting her music too loud in her room and throwing something heavy at her head. Kyle inviting friends over, and them somehow finding a way into my little sister's room during the night. It wouldn't be the first time.

Mom chuckles. "You're one to talk. Aren't you the one who was still living here last week?"

I exhale slowly. Of course, she skips over the part where I helped pay the bills and took care of chores at home, but she has a point. She did help me for a few years when I wasn't able to afford moving out because of hospital fees and gym fees.

I swallow thickly. "Just... She's young. He scares her. If you could just—"

"I know my own daughter's age, Jesus Christ."

I don't bother answering.

I'm not sure exactly why my mother had three children with three different men when she clearly would've preferred to have none. I don't remember a single instance when she made me feel wanted. No hugs exchanged, no kisses blown from the school parking lot, no hair braided on competition days. In fact, she always seemed to work her hardest to keep us out of her way.

Probably why she got me into gymnastics in the first place.

"Anything else?" she barks.

"No. Just... Please keep him and his friends away from her. *Please*." My eyes close briefly at the feeling of phantom hands on my shoulders, on my arms, on my legs. I bite the inside of my cheek hard enough to draw blood, fighting the shivers running down my body.

"Don't worry. We'll be fine without you," she says.

I'm not sure whether that's an actual reassurance or a dig at me, but exploring it further would be a bad idea. "Thank you," I grit out.

"All righty then. Talk to you later."

She hangs up before I can get a word out, and by the time I've put my phone back into my bag, I'm fuming. There's no way I can make sure she actually does something to protect Josie from that dumbass, and I'd bet what's left in my bank account that she hasn't heard a word of what I just said.

I'm restless. I can't stay away from them, but I also can't go back. Everything I've worked my entire life for is here, and everything I've spent years trying to escape is there.

Which means I'm stuck in the middle. Neither here nor there, nowhere truly home.

Pressure builds in my chest, in my throat, and I know I can't relax now. When I'm this amped up, there's only one thing that can calm me down.

I head back to the staff room and drop my stuff. I guess I'm not going home tonight after all.

The music resonates in my bones.

A remixed version of a tango classic, the song has inhabited my head for the past two years. The choreographer Andy had hired created it specifically for the World Championships that happened last year. I was ready for them. Aced every single one of my routine runs. I thought that would be my year. A gold medal, with a clear path to the Olympic trials two years later.

And then I got cocky on the bars one day, and everything went to shit.

But today, I don't think about the competitions or the challenges ahead. The music is blasting from the speakers, and I let it control me. I'm panting as I go through the motions, my hardest tumbling pass coming next.

The floor has always been my element. I can hold my own in the rest of the gym, but here is where I've always shined. There's also no place like it to exorcise all the feelings you're holding inside through raw power.

The rest of the gym is bathed in darkness as I turn to face my diagonal. Andy's corrections barge through my head—*shorten your steps, straighten your back, don't choke on that last twist.* I take an inhale, and on the beat, I start running. The movements come naturally, although the difference since my injury is obvious. I've lost strength in my shoulder, which means I've lost height in my flips, which means the ground comes too fast at the end of my rotation, and when I land, I have to take three steps back to catch my balance. By the time I get my body to stay in place, I'm out of the floor's boundaries.

Motherfucker.

I go through the rest of the routine, but my mind is out of it. Those three steps would've cost me the tenths of a point needed to get above the others. At this level, the difference between placing on the podium and a loss can be this small.

How can I be ready to compete again in five months when my performance is shit and I don't have a coaching team behind me?

Maybe Andy was right. Maybe my career was over the second I fell from those bars onto my neck. Maybe what this is is simply obstinacy.

I get into my final pose as the song comes to an abrupt end, limbs lose and despair written all over my posture.

I *wish* I could give up. Be smarter about this. It'd be so much easier for me, for everyone. Take my geriatric ass out of this and move on. Sadly, I don't have it in me.

"You won't win with this."

I jump to my feet with my hands balled into fists at the sound of the deep voice coming from the opposite end of the gym, my pulse jackhammering from fear rather than exertion. That is, until I realize who it is.

"Je-sus," I shout, unable to catch my breath. "Two times I could believe, but three? That's actual stalking."

Finn comes out of the shadows, large headphones wrapped around the back of his neck, wearing a black crewneck and sweatpants. His hands are in his pockets, and his lips are curled into a smug smirk.

"Are you always this bubbly?" he teases.

"Are you always this shady?"

He snickers. "Why am I being shady now?"

"Uh, I don't know, because it's past midnight and you've followed me here to watch me practice when I thought I was alone?"

"Are you serious?" He snickers. "Of course I didn't follow you here." With a movement that's so casual it's annoying, he leans against one of the balance beams and crosses his arms. "In fact, if anyone's invading the other's space, it's you."

I lift a brow.

"This is my mother's gym. I help her with the cleaning sometimes." His eyes widen in delight.

Well. That would explain why Shelli was so familiar with him last time.

"You still could've let me know you were here instead of hiding in the shadows like some kind of murderer."

"Scared?"

"It's not like you've given the best first impression," I say, avoiding the question, because the truth is, I'm not scared. I probably should be, but as annoying as this guy is, I don't think he'd hurt me. He doesn't give off that vibe, and I've learned to have a good radar for that type of thing.

He sighs, his smirk disappearing. "About that. I want to set the record straight. That wasn't me."

I fake gasp. "Do you have a twin brother I didn't know about?"

He rolls his eyes. "No, it *was* me in Italy, but I didn't steal from you. I just...didn't stop them. The other guys."

"Is that supposed to make a difference?"

"I hope it does?" he says before taking a step forward. Reflexively, I take one back, which stops him in his tracks. His jaw shifts. "Look, I'm not a bad person. I swear. I did some dumb shit when I was younger, but that's not who I am anymore."

My lips twist to the side. "They didn't just take my money. They stole my ID too. Do you know how much I hate going to the DMV?"

He chuckles, still looking stricken with regret. "I'm really, really sorry."

As much as I hate to admit it, he seems honest. Plus, I've spent a lot of time with Shelli since I got here, and she's as good as they come. I don't see how she could raise an outright bad person.

"Okay," I say.

"Okay?"

"Yes, okay." I go to grab my water bottle. "What else do you want from me?"

"I don't know? For you to accept the apology?"

I twist the cap open and take a large gulp. "Fine, I accept it." Putting the bottle down, I say, "But just so you know, I'm as petty as they come, so don't expect me to become *bubbly* anytime soon."

He lifts one of his shoulders. "I'll take it."

I watch as he stays there, not taking his eyes and his too-energetic smile away from me. Finally, he claps his hands and says, "So, as I was saying: you're not gonna win with this."

It takes me a second to figure out what he's talking about, and when I do, I wish I hadn't. "I'm sorry, did you get a coaching accreditation in the past five minutes and I didn't notice?"

"My mother's been bringing me to women's gymnastics competitions since I was a baby. I know a good deal about it, and you're obviously really fucking great, but I'm telling you, that routine won't get you where you want to be."

My jaw clenches, and I keep myself from telling him the thought had already crossed my mind. In the time since that routine was made, trends have changed. Skills have evolved. It's probably not up to par with what other people are doing out there for this year's season, but what am I supposed to do? It's not like I can afford choreographers and additional coaches when I don't have a gym backing me. Plus, as Andy said, I'm "uncoachable" and "too old for this." Fucker.

"Well, thanks for all that precious advice," I say, "but I'm good."

He hums in answer, then continues standing there, watching me.

"Can I help you with anything else?"

"Don't like having an audience?" he asks, not moving an inch, that infuriating grin still there.

"You know what? I was actually done for the night."

"Please, don't stop on my account."

"Don't think that highly of yourself," I say as I walk past him on my way toward the staff room. "You know the way out, I assume?"

He snorts. "I don't think I've ever been dismissed that many times by a girl."

Without looking back, I say, "There's a first for everything. See ya."

His laugh resonates behind me, and by the time I come out of the room, he's gone.

Chapter 5

Finn

I need to focus.

I've been bouncing the tip of my pen on top of my knee for the past ten minutes, the numbers on the computer screen blurring in front of me as my mind keeps drifting off.

Or rather, drifting toward *her*.

I don't know why I can't get the image of her in that ruby-red leotard and those skintight shorts out of my head. It's been days. I've seen enough half-naked women in my life to know I'm not that easily affected by them.

The thing is, I'm not thinking about her body. Or not only, at least. I'm mostly thinking about the way she looks when she goes through her routines.

She might think that night four days ago was the first time I'd seen her, but truth is, I *have* been the tiniest bit of a creep. I helped my mom out with cleaning a few times over the past two weeks, and every time I went to the gym, no matter how late, she was still there, practicing. That night was simply the first time I found the guts to say something.

But all those times I watched her, I couldn't look away. Not wouldn't. *Couldn't*. It felt like watching a comet, knowing you'd get burned and still not moving an inch, the sight too wonderful to miss.

Throughout the years, we've had a few good gymnasts practice with us. One that went on to qualify in the World Championships a few years back, and the others performing well in one event or the other.

But Lexie? She's in a league of her own.

She's not good. She's exceptional. And with the right training, she could make it big. I assume that's her goal too. If not, she wouldn't be practicing until god knows what time every night after work.

With my feet on the desk, I stretch back and look around. The office—my office—is decorated with all kinds of memorabilia I've collected over my years abroad. When you spend the majority of your twenties lounging on a beach chair in Bali or couch surfing in Europe, you don't get to collect that much furniture or, let's be honest, that much money. But trinkets that serve as memories, I have those by the dozens. When I first got the job, there was no official office for the farm's manager, but ever since I took over and worked on some expansion, Martina and Dennis—Aaron's parents, and my parents' closest friends—have given me the okay to build one for myself in one of the barns, and I personalized it the moment I stepped inside.

The spreadsheet continues calling to me from the computer, but I know I won't be able to focus on anything before I settle this.

I pick my phone up from the desk, then dial my mother. She answers on the third ring.

"Hey, you."

"Hi. Got a minute?" I ask as I get up and start walking around the office. It's not large, but it's a place I love spending time in, with its bright-orange accent wall that reminds me of Tuscan rooftops and the soft linen couch I've taken a few naps on when I've woken up early for one task or another.

"Sure. Give me a sec." I hear voices behind her, so she's still at the gym. "Everything okay?" she asks.

"Yeah, why?"

"It's not like you call me often," she says, clearly aiming to make me feel bad.

"Mom, I see you more in a week than any respectable twenty-eight-year-old should see their mother." Whenever she makes too much of one recipe for dinner, she invites me over, and more than half the time, I accept her offer.

What can I say? I'm a homebody these days.

She laughs. "Yeah, maybe." A door closes in the back, then the voices disappear. "So, what's going on?"

"I wanted to ask about that new girl you hired," I say, as if I didn't already know her name. As if I hadn't alienated the girl already. I'm not delusional enough to believe Lexie will actually get over what happened in Italy that easily. If she were my sister, I wouldn't want her to.

"What about her?"

"Well, I've seen her practice, and she's good."

"I assumed so. She has Olympic goals."

"Wow." So I was right. She *is* great. "So why's she training here?"

"She answered the job offer for full-time coach, but her one condition was that she could practice in the gym whenever she wasn't working."

"So she doesn't have a coach?" I ask as I scratch the back of my head. Maybe I just haven't seen them around. Someone she'd have hired from another gym, maybe? That would make more sense than the other option. You can be a damn good athlete, but without a coach backing you, it's almost impossible to get far, or at least far enough.

"Not that I know of, no." Mom tsks. "Poor girl, getting dropped by her coach like that."

So she's truly coach-less. *Dropped.* She must've done something pretty bad to be getting dropped at that level, and a year away from the Olympic trials.

"Anyway, why are you asking? Did she catch your eye?" I'm sure she's wiggling her brows to herself now.

"Nah, it's not like that. I just... I was wondering what was up with someone being in the gym at midnight." No need for my mother to know about the Italy incident. I've been embarrassed enough about it. Plus, it's not like I have a true good reason for asking. I'm nosy, and she's the first new person this town has seen in a while.

"Oh. Well, there, you got it."

I walk to the yoga ball I sometimes use as a chair when I'm feeling antsy and bounce on it once, twice. "This could be good for the gym, you know. If she makes a name for herself, then she'd make a name for you too."

"You're right. And she's a nice girl, so I'm rooting for her anyway."

"Yeah, me too," I say, already coming up with ideas for the gym, if this actually came to fruition. It would bring young girls from all over the state. We could host clinics and meet-and-greets and fundraisers. I might already have a job here, but I'd never hesitate to throw in some hours at the gym too if it could help my mother.

"All right, then. Have a good day, Mom. Love you."

"Love you too," she says before hanging up.

I bounce a little more before returning to my chair, still feeling jittery. I might have gotten some answers, but I feel even more intrigued than before.

And if there's one thing any person who knows me would say, it's that when I get stuck on something, there's no way to pull me away.

I barely have one foot out the barn's door when I'm hit by something, the force strong enough to propel me on my ass.

"Jesus. Again?" I grunt. It'd be very appreciated if I could stop falling to my butt every time our paths cross.

"Oh god, are you okay?"

I look up to find Lexie lying in a position similar to mine on the ground, her face flushed, large brown eyes on me.

"I'm so sorry," she says. "I was running. I didn't expect anyone to come out of there."

I push myself to a kneeling position, groaning at the pull in my back. "Are you made of steel or what?"

She tries not to laugh, but the twitch of her lips gives her away. It's the first time I've seen so much as a hint of glee in her face since she figured out who I was, and it's enough to make my lips curl in response.

"Maybe that's a sign you need to bulk up," she says.

I bark out a laugh. "Bulk up?" My gaze drifts down my own body. At six one, I might not be the largest man alive, but I've never thought of myself as needing to gain some mass. This body allows me to chop and lift tree after tree during the holiday season, and I've never had any trouble with it either.

"Why not?" she says, now also in a kneeling position. With October right around the corner, the ground is cold and the air crisp, but she doesn't seem to mind one bit. "Maybe you would have been able to stay on your feet if you'd had a stronger core."

I chuckle, then get to my feet. "You're funny when you want to be."

"I wasn't joking."

I offer Lexie a hand, and she goes to take it, but midair, she freezes, then shakes her head and gets up by herself.

As she wipes her leggings-clad butt, I say, "You didn't make me fall because you're stronger."

She blinks. "Oh, was it my invisible aura that made you fall, then?"

"I don't know what it was," I say.

She stares at me for a long moment before she shakes her head. "I can't believe it. You don't believe I'm stronger than you?"

I close an eye and wince. "Sorry, but I know you're not." She's what, five two, 130 pounds? I could probably bench-press her.

Her pink lips part, and I'd swear her face reddens. With a jerk of her head, she says, "Plank."

"I'm sorry?"

"Plank. Come on. Let's see who can last the longest."

I look around, at the ground covered in pine needles and rocks, surrounded by thousands of fir trees of all sizes. "There's no mats out here."

"Afraid that'll make you lose?"

I chuckle. "Darling, I'm not going to lose."

That gets her to grit her teeth. Am I playing with fire? Maybe, but she's so damn fun to rile up.

"Then get on your forearms and pray you don't die."

"Fine," I say, watching her as I get into position, ignoring the dig of the rocks against my forearms. I've seen my fair share of competitive people in my years of playing hockey, but I'm not sure I've ever met one like her.

"Ready?" I ask.

"Already in position."

I shake my head, then join her in the exercise.

A crow caws in the trees as I start counting. I'm not sure why I do it since it's a last-one-standing kind of thing, but I hope it'll help time go faster.

Except the only thing it succeeds in doing is making me see just how slow time passes when you're in a fucking plank.

Ninety-eight, ninety-nine, a hundred...

I look up from the ground, my abs on fire, pulse throbbing in my throat. Meanwhile, Lexie looks like she's going for a walk in the park. Not a single bead of sweat on her flawless skin, cool as a cucumber.

How is that even possible?

With her head facing the ground, she says, "I don't even need to look up to know your position is shit. Lower that butt."

I keep silent but do as she says. No way will I admit she had a point.

What a dumb fucking thing I signed myself up for. When was the last time I did some proper abdominal exercises? I might be in good enough shape because of my often-active job, but I'm no athlete. Who was I kidding?

I'm not giving up, though. Not yet.

Another full minute passes, and my condition goes from bad to worse. Sweat is dripping down my nose, I can't feel my elbows anymore, and I'm fairly certain I'm a few seconds away from throwing up the lunch I ate five hours ago.

"I've been doing weekly drills of these since I was four years old," Lexie says, her voice not even strained. "I can do this all day if I need to."

Fuck.

Twenty drawn-out, never-ending seconds pass, and yep, that's Martina's enchiladas coming up.

In the end, I don't make the choice to give up. My body does it for me, arms giving out under me, making me fall face first into the ground, rocks embedding themselves in my cheek, the cherry on top of the humiliation.

"Done already?" she says, humor clear in her voice.

I grunt. Everything hurts.

"Well, glad we were able to settle this debate," she says as she gets up and wipes her hands against her thighs, gravel crunching under her feet. "Let me know if you ever need another piece of humble pie." She ends the sentence by giving my shoulder two little taps. "Have a good evening, *darling*."

I remain on the ground for longer than I care to admit.

What. A. Dumbass.

Chapter 6

Lexie

Fall has always been my favorite season.

In Arizona, summer is never anything less than flaming hot. It doesn't matter how much AC there is in a gym; you always end up fighting for your life at the end of your practice session. When October hits, you can finally begin to breathe without feeling like you're living in Satan's armpit, and I don't know anyone who wouldn't feel blessed about that. Plus, the weather is usually good, so you don't have to spend too much time inside. At home, I always dreaded winter time. Having to spend the coldest days inside the house with my older brother, my mother, and her man of the hour felt like sitting on a ticking time bomb, counting down the seconds until I could finally escape the place where making a noise could mean the start of World War Three.

Fall's also the time when we truly start getting ready for the new competition season, and since I wasn't able to participate last year, I feel extra thrilled to be here now. Or scared shitless. The feeling changes from one hour to the next.

I'm sitting by the large bay windows in the cabin, which gives me an unobstructed view of an infinity of Christmas trees. Fall has truly set its hooks into Evermore, giving the leafy trees interspersed between the pines an auburn tint, something I never witnessed growing up. It feels so special to see the seasons blur into the next instead of living in constant summer. I think I'll enjoy this fall even more than I usually do.

This morning's sight is the only thing brightening my mood, though. I look down at the notebook in my lap, which has been open for half an hour, and still no progress in sight.

I need a plan. A concrete one. What I'm doing right now, aka, practicing stuff left and right without a tight schedule or a clear idea of the direction I want to be headed in, makes no sense. I'm not sure what I was thinking—or actually, I do. I wasn't thinking at all. I wanted to practice, I wanted to go out there and win competitions, so I got straight to it as if all the hope in my heart and the fire in my chest would lead me there. And while that has helped me regain a couple of my skills in the month since I've been here, I'm nowhere near competition ready, and I won't ever be if I continue down this path.

I don't need to look online to know what this year's competition schedule looks like. I've been in this rodeo since before I could read a book. Usually, the big competitions making up the elite gymnastics season start around February with the Winter Cup, and the season ends in October with the World Championships. A dozen large events take place during that period, and getting good scores, especially at the World Championships, will allow me to qualify for the Olympic trials. There are also smaller competitions scattered here and there throughout the year, but I haven't participated in those since I started competing at a higher level. Andy has always made his schedule so that we wouldn't waste our time with the "small fish," but this year, I'm not in the same boat. For now, *I* am the small fish.

It's been too long since I've competed. The last time, I was this twenty-three-year-old girl who thought she had as much of a chance as any other to win the whole thing. The previous year had been an Olympic year, and I hadn't been *quite* there yet, but at that point, I was better and ready to kill it until I could make my way to the top. I was older than most of the girls competing that season, but it didn't matter. My skills were on par. People viewed me and my team as actual adversaries. Most importantly, I felt confident.

And then I fell, and my shoulder and my neck got messed up, and I had to get through rehabilitation, then PT and then I had to start from the ground up, except this time, I had the constant fear of death in the back of my mind every time I had to throw a skill.

Andy's demeanor toward me changed the minute I came back after my accident. As soon as I started showing signs of nerves, he looked at me like I wasn't his prized cattle any longer. If I was scared, it meant I wouldn't be able to win for him, and what was the point in helping me then? I was too old and too stubborn to be worth the trouble. He didn't seem to have any remorse when he dropped me as easily as letting go of an old rag.

I force my jaw to relax when I realize I'm almost grinding my teeth to shreds and try to loosen my body into the window-side cushions.

Less thinking, more working.

I look back down at my notebook, where I've scribbled the names of the competitions I could potentially attend in the next year. I can't go to all of them, not with my finances. The vast majority of my coaching salary is currently going to my year-old hospital bills, so it's not like I'll accumulate much over the year.

As the embers of the fire I lit this morning crackle in the fireplace, I rub one of the sheets of paper between my thumb and index finger and in a low voice, ask myself, "What would Andy do about it?"

As soon as the words are out, the answers come to me. He'd start by saying I need to attend at least half a dozen of those events to get used to the feel of competitions again, to the chaos of sounds and flashes and people everywhere. He'd want me to start rebuilding a reputation for myself in order to get some of my old sponsors back. I'm sure he'd also say to go to at least one event before the official elite competition season starts in February so I can assess the competition and readjust my strategy and routines based on what I see, before the big events begin.

So that's exactly what I'm going to do.

I get up and pad to the kitchen table, where I've left my antique of a computer. It makes the sound of a plane engine about to take off when I turn it on, but it still works for the moment, so I'll take it. In a few minutes, I find a competition that takes place in Mississauga a little less than two months from now, which will be the perfect test before New York in February. I sign up, pay the fee, then get back to my spot by the window, where I go take a look at my social media. I've been MIA ever since I made a post almost a year ago, explaining my injury and my need for a time-out. The post shows no picture, only a dark block of text. I scroll through the comments, most of which I never read. At the time, when I didn't know whether my dream would ever be a possibility again, the last thing I wanted was to receive people's pity. I felt like I'd lost the only thing I'd ever had for myself, and people's kind words were only going to remind me of it.

Going through some of them now, seeing old teammates and gymnastics fans wishing me well and asking when I'd be back, my stomach fills with a mix of warmth and dread. All these people I barely know who were showing support, while my own family never once asked me if I was okay. Mom was angry I'd had to quit my part-time coaching job so I could focus on my recovery, which meant less money for rent, and I don't think Kyle even noticed something was different. Thank god Josie was there during that whole year. I don't know how I would have survived it without her.

I go back to my main page, where I see I've lost many followers, as expected. But now I need the sponsors more than ever. My credit line is already maxed out, and competitions, coupled with the necessary travel and apparel, are expensive.

I'm not someone who likes to share on social media. People can be nasty in the comments, and if it were up to me, I'd keep all of my life private. Unfortunately, my privacy ends today.

Selecting a photo I took of the empty gym last night, I post it, with a simple caption:

Let's do this.

Once I finally felt like my plan for the next months was solid, I got ready for my run, expecting to do a simple four miles through the trees, hoping not to get lost.

What I did not expect was to see someone sitting on the front porch stairs when I opened the front door.

"You're just everywhere, aren't you?" I say, making Finn turn around and get to his feet.

"A real roach," he says.

A corner of my lips begs to inch up, but I force it down. "What are you doing here?" As the question leaves my mouth, I notice what he's wearing. Basketball shorts, a sweatshirt, and a beanie. He looks like he's getting ready for training.

He also looks really, really good.

I'm not sure how I didn't notice it before, but now, standing in the early morning light, traces of lavender still coloring the sky behind him, I cannot deny it. The guy might have his faults, but he's a stunner.

And the smirk he sends me tells me he knows it all too well.

"Last time's embarrassment clearly proved I have some work to do if I want to get back in shape," he says as he stretches an arm behind his back. "And I was hoping I could get a tip or two from you."

I fight another smile. After the little plank contest, I thought he'd go lick his wounds in private and never speak of it again.

That's what most men would do after losing to a woman—one he felt confident he could beat, no less. But here he is, grinning and admitting his defeat without a hint of shame or anger.

Some male athletes could learn a thing or two from this guy.

"Get *back* in shape?" I bend down to tie my shoes, full of caked mud from my years of outside runs, rain or shine.

"I used to play hockey. Never got to the big leagues, but I wasn't bad." He shrugs.

"Huh." It makes sense, with his build. I'm standing three stairs above and am still barely taller than him.

Finn looks at me expectantly, as if he actually wants to do this. And honestly, I don't understand it. Don't understand *him*. With the way we met—and re-met—I would've thought he'd be a complete dick, but from what I've seen of him since arriving at Sonder Hill, he seems more of a happy-go-lucky type of guy.

I look toward the forest, then decide to make him work for it a little. I hate to admit it, but he's fun to mess with. "Are you going to complain the whole time?"

"I won't."

"What if you're too slow?"

"I won't be."

I raise both brows and blink, which makes him release a deep laugh, the chilly morning air clouding in front of his mouth. "Fine. I don't *think* I will be too slow, but if I am, feel free to abandon me to fend for myself."

I stare for a second, but before I can say anything, he kneels and says, "Please let me come with you, oh great master."

Laughter bubbles out of me before I even realize it.

"Oh my god, please stop," I say as I pull on his shirt so he gets back up. "All right. Let's go."

His only answer is a grin.

We stretch in silence for a minute, the smell of pine and wet leaves thick in the air, and when I start running, he falls into pace beside me.

I like to run in complete silence. The gym is always bursting with all sorts of noises, so my runs are the one moment in my day when I can hear myself think. Normally, I don't even record my times or try to meet a distance goal. I just run to clear my head.

Except someone didn't get the memo, because a couple minutes in, Finn clears his throat and says in a breathless voice, "So, have you thought more about what I told you?"

"That you're in perfect shape?"

"Har. Har. I'm talking about your routine."

It takes me a second to figure out what he's talking about, and when I do, I only throw him a quick glance and return my attention to the gravel path ahead. "I told you, I'm good."

He fakes a cough, into which he says, "No, you're not."

I roll my eyes. "Why do you even care?"

"Cause I think your success could help the gym, and working together could be mutually beneficial."

Ignoring the second part because, yeah, not happening, I say, "I thought your job was to manage this farm." Every time I'm not at the gym during the day, I see his truck is parked at the main house. Even though I'm not sure what his job entails exactly, this place is ethereal—whether during my early morning runs, when mist rises from the small pond against the marigold light, or in the evening, when the gigantic trees are bathed in the end-of-day sun rays catching their last breaths—so he must be doing it well.

He sniffles, his breaths more ragged. "It is. I just like to help out as much as I can. The gym is literally my mother's baby."

"Hm."

I wish I could say yes, if only for Shelli's sake, but I don't see how he could help me with new routines, no matter how involved he is in the gymnastics world. Plus, with a competition in less than two months, it'll be easier to perfect the ones I already have than to learn something new. "Thanks for offering," I say, "but I still think I'll manage."

He turns to look at me, and while this pace is clearly too fast for him, he doesn't let up. I'll have to give it to him, he's tough. Even though he looked ready to have a one-on-one with death when planking, he resisted dropping down until the very last second. I admire that.

After a moment of silence only interrupted by his panting and mine, he says, "You're not used to accepting help, are you?"

I stay silent because I don't want to lie, but the answer isn't easy to say. Not because I'm not used to accepting help, but because I'm not used to it being offered to me. I've been a nuisance most of my life. To my family, to the teachers who'd get mad when I couldn't figure out the right answers to their questions no matter how many times they tried to explain the theory, to the friends who thought it was annoying that I always wanted to have sleepovers at their place instead of staying at mine.

"It's okay to do it, you know."

God, will he ever drop this?

"I'm good," I grunt, praying we can finish this run in silence. The more I think about this, the more I feel like there's something wrong with my life. With me.

"Let me at least—"

The root comes out of nowhere, or maybe it was very obvious and I was too distracted to see it. One second I'm on my feet, and the next I'm falling on my hands and knees, the rough ground digging into my palms faster than I can brace them for.

Finn's feet slide against the gravel as he comes to a halt next to me. "Shit, are you okay?"

Concern etched onto his face, he drops to his knees, and he clasps his hand on my shoulder. Before I can stop myself, I flinch, hard enough that I feel him jump back.

Fuck.

I blink quickly, shoving myself up and wiping my palms on my thighs. I ignore the tears at my legs and the roughness of the gravel embedded in my skin. This is so embarrassing. I don't think I've reacted this strongly in years, even when Andy would come up to me from behind to spot me for a movement and I wasn't ready for it. He really caught me by surprise.

Even without looking directly into his eyes, I can feel the questions written all over him.

"What's—"

"You know," I interrupt, keeping my attention on the small cuts on my skin, "I think I'd rather finish that run by myself, if you don't mind."

I don't wait for his answer, and the only thing I hear as I jog away from him are his confused stutters. I try to ignore them—to ignore everything that just happened—and to focus on each new step. I up my speed, hoping for the pain and exertion to clear my head. Except it doesn't matter how fast I run. My demons always catch up.

Chapter 7

I don't like days off.

It's 4:00 p.m. on a Saturday, and while I work all weekends starting November, when the Christmas season truly begins, there's no need for that in October. It's something I wish I could enjoy but usually don't, especially today. When I woke up, I felt this urge to do something with myself, only to remember I had a whole day ahead of me and no clear plans. After tossing and turning in bed, unable to sleep late, I decided to show up at the farm to see whether there was work I could do to help for the coming weeks, but I came up empty and returned home, honestly disappointed.

There's something wrong with me.

Since I came back home, I cleaned my entire apartment, went on a long walk while listening to a podcast on managerial skills and wider goals, meal-prepped for the week, watched one of those superhero movies, and completed a third of a new puzzle.

Even so, here I am, still as antsy as I was first thing this morning.

There is something about having an entire free day that makes time feel endless. I can almost feel the clock ticking, second by slow, painful second, the small needle reminding me of a car stuck in a

Boston traffic jam. When I'm working, I don't notice it as much, but here, the emptiness in my life is blaring.

I'm sitting at the kitchen table in front of a puzzle that's supposed to represent an abstract painting of a bowl of fruits, my fingers tapping the wooden surface. I guess I could go on another run to use up some energy. Alone, this time.

Running is something I barely ever do, so I can't say for sure why I decided to go yesterday. It almost didn't feel like a conscious decision. One second, I was standing in my small kitchen, drinking coffee and scrolling through my phone, and the next, I was getting dressed in training clothes. There was the possibility that Lexie could've left for work already, but I'd seen her running around the farm at dawn earlier in the week, so I knew she might have decided to do so again. As to the reason why I wanted to go on a run with her specifically… I also don't have an answer for that. She clearly doesn't like me much, and I've never been one to run after people who don't want me. Mom always used to say that the only people you should want in your life are those who want you in theirs. But yesterday, I felt like being a masochist, and fuck if I know why. I wanted to go, so I did.

I shouldn't have. Clearly, she didn't want me there. At first, when she ended up letting a smile slip, I'd thought maybe she didn't mind. But then she became stiff when I talked, and she jumped away when I just touched her shoulder, and the next thing I knew, she had left me there, alone in the woods and fighting for my next breath. That girl isn't just strong. She has cardio for days, and once again, I could barely keep up.

Maybe I did something wrong. I was trying to make her feel like she could talk to me, to get to know the girl who lives on my land and yet is so mysterious I barely know a thing about her after a month, but even that must've been too much. I pushed too hard.

Joining her for her run yesterday was a wild shot, but going back today would just be dumb. I'm not *that* much of a sucker.

I get back to my puzzle, but fifteen minutes later, the only thing I've been able to do is fit two pieces on the peach and get even more restless.

Giving up, I stand up, then pick up my phone and call Aaron.

"Hey," he says as he picks up. "What's up?"

"I'm bored. Wanna do something?" He lives two hours away, but I'll make the trek to Boston, no problem. We could go out. Maybe Wren would even want to come with us.

"Can't," my best friend says, bursting my balloon. "Will and Violet are in town, and they're staying for a few days. You can join if you want, though," he says, and although I'm sure he means it, I also know he rarely sees his cousin, and that time must be precious to them.

"Nah, I'm good. Actually, I just thought about that thing I have to do, so never mind. Have fun!"

"You sure? Wren's cooking enough for ten people—although I can't promise it'll be any good."

"You prick," I hear Wren say in the background, followed by Aaron's chuckles.

In a faint voice, he says, "I'm kidding, *cariño*." He gives her a loud kiss, and while in public, I'd roll my eyes at how sickeningly sweet they are, here, in the privacy of my apartment, I can say I'm so fucking jealous it hurts. Not that I'm not happy for Aaron and Wren; they deserve it a thousand times. But this just reminds me of how lonely I am.

"Yeah, I'm sure. Say hi to Will and Violet for me."

"Will do."

I hang up, feeling even worse than I did before the call. How horrible of a friend does that make me?

Walking in circles around the living room, I scroll through my contacts. My only other real friend around here is Lilianne, but she's likely busy with that boyfriend of hers.

I could always ask my folks if they want to come over for dinner—no, I'm not above hanging out with my parents as a social activity—but they're having a date night at a fancy restaurant a few towns over.

There's one last person I could reach out to, who might actually want to spend time with me. Francesca might often ignore me, but maybe today, she'll want to see me.

My younger sister has always been some sort of enigma to me. She's only a couple years younger, but it's like there's a world dividing us. When we were kids, she'd look up to me, ask me to go on drives and to tell her all about my high school life. She liked when I made her feel included. She had the biggest crush on Aaron for years, and while I teased her relentlessly about it, I still let her hang out with us whenever she wanted.

And then she turned sixteen, and everything changed.

Me: Hey, wanna come over for dinner tonight? I'm making those pork chops you like.

I wasn't planning on it, but if she says yes, I'll just go to the grocery store and make them. I'm not above bribing.

Mom would be happy if she came over. Ever since Fran started dating this Cameron guy, she's been scaring us, and it only got worse after I asked her to stay away from him and he retaliated by breaking into the cabin one night and wrecking some of it. Since then, she's been keeping her distance even when we both find ourselves at my parents' place, and as much as I want to physically get her away from him, I know it would only alienate her.

I wait five minutes, then ten. Fifteen. No answer.

After thirty minutes, the "seen" message appears on screen.

And still, nothing.

I throw my phone down on the couch, letting myself fall onto my back next to it, my head hanging off the side. A TV show is on in the background, but I barely hear it. It's not like I was watching it attentively in the first place.

This day reminds me of why I decided to leave, back when I was twenty. How trapped I felt here. How it felt like I knew everyone around this small town, and yet I had no one. I also have the same urge to pack up and buy the first plane ticket out of here, going wherever it takes me and go from there. Lose myself in a new culture and place, and forget about real life for a while.

Obviously, I can't do it. I have responsibilities here now, and I'd never walk away from them, but that knowledge doesn't tame my wanderlust.

Back then, Chrissy had just dumped me, and I was so heartbroken I'd gotten numb.

You're a good time, Finn, but you're not forever material. I can still hear her words, casually spoken over the phone like she wasn't making me question everything I was.

The next day, I was on a plane to Taiwan. Staying in a town where no one saw me as anything worthy felt like living in a cage, and I'd had enough. I was just a good time? Sure, why not. I'd never settle down? Right on.

I stayed away as long as I could. And now here I am, with a job I love and family around me, and still I feel like escaping the life that keeps tugging me back.

What the fuck is wrong with me?

I drag a hand over my scalp, feeling patches of thinner hair through the buzz cut. I've noticed I tend to get more of those when I'm back home than when I'm away. Maybe a sign that I should never have offered to manage the farm in the first place. I should have stayed untethered. Maybe a settled life simply isn't for me, and that experiment only proved Chrissy's statement from years ago.

But I'm still needed here, and the need to help is stronger than my feeling of suffocation.

For a nanosecond—really more of a passing thought than an actual idea—I think of going to the gym. Maybe Lexie's there. It's crazy I'd even think of going to see her when she's the furthest thing from a friend I have, but she's also the only person in this godforsaken town who doesn't see me in a way I hate. She dislikes me, sure, but in a different way than others.

I'm sure a therapist would have a field day with me.

Not wanting to think more about it, I stand up, then go to my bedroom and change from my sweats into a flannel shirt and jeans. I won't wait around for Francesca to deem me interesting enough to answer, and I won't go to the gym either. That would probably be the definition of pathetic.

No, I'll drive around and find a good place to hang out for the night. Maybe a bar or a pub. If I'm to be alone, might as well just go ahead and show some girl a good time. After all, that's what I'm good at.

Chapter 8

Lexie

A lot of things have suffered from my dire financial situation over the years.

With all the gymnastics-related expenses I've had, my life has been lived counting pennies. My summer jobs and after-school gigs allowed me to practice my sport, but I never had any money left for anything else. My clothes were always too old or too cheap to win me friends at school. The handmade cards I brought to birthday parties always earned me side eyes. But since my injury, things have only gotten worse. My current grocery basket is a prime example of that.

I should be eating all kinds of lean proteins and nutritious meals if I want to get my body where it's supposed to be, but sadly, adulthood includes realizing just how expensive vegetables are. I don't meet the eyes of the cashier as I pay for the ramen noodles and half a dozen packs of frozen chicken breasts that were on sale.

I catch a few glances thrown my way as I fill my grocery bags. I'm not sure why, but I think it has to do with being new in town. I've never lived in a place as small as Sonder Hill, and based on the way everyone greets each other everywhere I go, I'd say it's custom to know everyone in town.

Once again, I feel like a puzzle piece that's *this close* to the right shape, almost fitting, but not quite.

"Thanks," I tell the teenage girl manning the register before I grab my bags and head out. My car waits for me in the parking lot in all its rusty glory. It might be old and make weird sounds every now and then, but as long as it can carry me where I need to go, I'll keep her.

"Lexie?" I hear as I put the last of the bags inside the trunk. Not a lot of people know me in this town, much less by name. Anyway, I'd have recognized him by voice alone.

I turn to find Finn standing on the sidewalk closest to my car, but rear back when I realize he's not alone.

A beautiful, tall, slim blonde stands next to him, a large smile adorning her lips.

Why am I surprised? Of course, he has a girlfriend. He's a good-looking man, and as much as it would've pained me to admit it at first, he seems like a pretty good guy. Arrogant? Sure. But he also has a way of making me laugh, even when I try my hardest not to.

It takes me too long to answer. Why does it take me too long to answer?

"Oh, hey," I say.

I meet his eyes, finding them to be a bright green today. I've noticed they change color depending on what he's wearing or the time of day. Right now, they remind me of grass on dewy mornings, when the farm is still asleep but the trees feel alive.

They also remind me of how much of a bitch I was to him two days ago.

I didn't want to leave him hanging like that, but survival instinct took over. My natural response to a situation of discomfort has always been to run. You don't grow up in the kind of household I did and turn out any other way.

"What are you doing here?" he asks with a grin, but even if I haven't known him for long, I see it's not his usual fun one. It's stiff.

I let out a single awkward chuckle, lifting the paper bag I'm holding. "What does it look like I'm doing?"

He laughs, and this time, I see a hint of true humor in it.

To his right, the girl lifts her pale eyebrows at him, which makes him say, "Uh, right. Lexie, this is Lilianne. Lil, this is Lexie."

"Pleasure to meet you," she says in a sweet voice, and I'm pretty sure I catch her pinching the skin behind Finn's elbow. He winces.

"You too," I answer.

A silence ensues, where the girl—Lilianne—stands there, smiling at the both of us, her hands buried inside the pockets of her fluffy pink coat, and Finn licks his lips, staring at me. He's probably also thinking about how shitty I was to him last time, and that only makes me feel worse.

I swallow, then pull the trunk door back down. "Well—"

"We were going to get ice cream," Finn interrupts. "Wanna come with?"

I look around, at the almost-naked trees and brown leaves on the ground, then at the empty ice cream stand that sits right next to the grocery store.

A gust of wind hits me as I say, "Isn't it cold for ice cream?"

"Tell that to this girl," Finn says with a tip of his head to the side.

Lilianne tips her chin higher. "There is never a bad time for ice cream."

My lips twist up.

I'm tempted to say no. I need to use my only day off judiciously, mostly for stretching exercises and for boring domestic tasks like meal-prepping and cleaning. But when I meet Finn's eyes, I see something there that tells me he might like me to say yes. He seems like the kind of guy who'd ask just to be sure no one feels left out, but I don't think that's what this is, and I don't want to disappoint him yet again. I'm not sure why. I've been a disappointment to most people I've crossed paths with. I should accept it at this point.

Except maybe this place could be a fresh start. Allow me to expect something different.

"Okay," I say.

Lilianne smiles even wider. Strange. What girlfriend has ever been happy to have their boyfriend invite another girl on their date?

We walk the short distance to the ice cream parlor, where Finn says, "All right, what can I get you two?"

"Oh, I'm good. I'll get mine," I say.

Finn doesn't budge, only throwing me a glare. "I said, what can I get you?"

 I glare right back.

"We'll both take a cookie dough cone," Lilianne interrupts, grabbing my arm like we're old time friends. "Thanks, Finny."

"You got it," he says with a wink before walking away. Meanwhile, Lilianne brings me to a seat around one of the neighboring tables.

"So, tell me about you," she says, fists propping her head up. She reminds me of some Disney princess, with her mischievous grin and girly colored coat against the bleak background of the not-quite-winter, not-quite-fall weather.

"There's not much to tell," I say. "But can I ask you something?"

She nods, eyes wide, as if she can't wait to hear it.

"Was 'ice cream' a code word for some kind of threesome thing?"

She looks at me with pinched lips for all of a second before she bursts out laughing, the sound loud enough to make Finn glance over his shoulder in our direction.

"Oh my god, is that what you think this is?" she guffaws.

Her laughter is contagious. "I don't know!"

She laughs even harder. "Oh god, wait until I tell him that."

"Please don't."

She must see the urgency in my eyes even though I'm still laughing because she says, "All right, I won't. So long as you don't say stuff like that again."

"I won't. Scout's honor."

She shakes her head, stealing a look in Finn's direction. Even though there's no line, his order seems to be taking a long time. Maybe the parlor didn't expect anyone to actually show up today.

"I can't believe you thought we were together," Lilianne says, still snickering.

"You're not?"

She swats my hand on the table. "I thought you said you wouldn't say stuff like that again."

"I don't know!"

"No, we're definitely just friends." Her nose scrunches. "Not interested in being 'one of his girls,'" she says with air quotations. I'm sure I don't want to know what that even means.

"So where'd you two meet, then?'

"Hospital."

"I'm sorry?" I say with a cough.

"We were on dialysis together for a while," she says without a change in her tone, as if talking about the weather.

I blink. Open my mouth, then close it.

Dialysis? Like what people do when they're really sick? Reflexively, I turn toward the man who's now leaning against the counter of the parlor and chuckling, as if he's just become best friends with whoever's inside serving him.

"Is... Are you..." I start.

"We're good. Well, good-ish." She points in Finn's direction. "His thing was only temporary. Lucky bastard."

I let out a deep breath, then say, "And you...?"

"I'm still on it." A shadow crosses her face, but it only takes a moment before her bright smile returns. "But I'll get my transplant one day. It's coming."

I nod and give her what I hope is a reassuring smile. I almost lean forward to squeeze her hand, but I refrain, knowing all too well how it feels when someone crosses a boundary you didn't want them to.

It's at that moment Finn comes back with three cones between his fingers, some of it dripping down his skin despite the cold outside.

"Ladies," he says as we pick them up from him.

"Thanks," Lilianne says as she takes a bite—yes, an actual bite—into her ice cream and groans. "God, this is good."

I'm about to thank him when my words freeze in my mouth at the sight of him licking the ice cream off his fingers. I blink, but can't force myself to look away. How does he make this look so pornographic?

He answers my question when he looks up and, still licking his finger, winks at me.

Shameless.

I shake my head, which makes him laugh, the sound crisp as the morning air.

"So, what were you talking about?" he asks while taking a seat next to Lilianne.

"Lexie thought we were together," she says simply, ignoring my glare.

Finn laughs again. "You wish," he says, bumping his shoulder with hers.

The whole scene is light, yet something in my chest dims at the sight. I can't believe someone like him could be sick. Even if Lilianne says he's not on dialysis anymore, needing it is no small thing, at least from what I've heard, which means that at least for a while, he was severely ill.

It makes all my problems pale in comparison to what these two have gone through already.

"What's up with you?" Finn asks with a nudge of my foot under the table.

"Nothing," I say, taking a lick of ice cream. Damn, this is good.

"You're even crabbier than usual," he says.

"I'm not crabby."

Glee twinkles in his eyes as he shifts and says, "Darling, you're the crabbiest."

I'm getting out of the door five hours later, with my gym bag thrown over my shoulder, when Finn's ATV passes by the cottage.

"Finn, wait!" I jog down the stairs and wave a hand just in time for him to come to a stop. He turns the engine off, then meets me on the gravel road.

"Hey, what's up?" he asks, hands in the pockets of his faded blue jeans. He's changed since this morning, now wearing a honey-colored flannel shirt open over a white T-shirt.

"Here." I pull a five-dollar bill out of my front pocket and hand it to him. I was going to drop it in an envelope under his office door later, but this is even better.

"What's that?" Finn asks, not moving to take the money.

"Do you need your eyes checked?"

He looks up, as if asking the heavens to grant him mercy. "What is it for?"

"The ice cream." I shake the bill. He still doesn't take it.

"I don't want your money," he says matter-of-factly.

"Well, I don't want to be indebted."

He throws his head back again, this time with a snicker. "Oh my god. It's not a debt. I just paid for an ice cream cone."

"Still." I extend the money again. I've met so many men who did everything they could for you to owe them something. Coaches, boyfriends, stepdads. I'm not doing it ever again.

Finn shakes his head. "Pay me back by allowing me to train with you sometimes." His eyes drift toward the spot where we had our plank competition a while back, and his brows climb his forehead. "Can't have you beating me forever."

I snicker. Fun times. "I can do that *and* pay you back."

"No."

"Finnegan, take that money."

"Finnegan?"

"Isn't that what your name's short for?"

"My name's just Finn. Why, is Lexie short for something else?"

"Not to you, it isn't."

He laughs. "You really are something else, aren't you?"

"Take the money, please."

"Not a chance in the world. I can buy you a damn ice cream cone if I want to." He winks. "See you later."

He turns to leave, and unease returns to my chest. This morning's hangout was fine—fun, even—but without Lilianne acting as a buffer, I'm reminded once again of how crappy I was to him during our last run.

"Hey, Finn?"

"Yeah?"

"I'm sorry about being rude last time. It wasn't about you."

His face sobers for a second. He dips his chin, then brings his smirk back when he says, "Not the first time you were rude."

I fight an eye roll, which he seems to find immensely funny. "Just shut it and accept the apology," I say.

"I do. Thank you."

With a nod, I say, "All right, well—"

He nudges his chin in the direction of my bag. "I thought today was an off day?"

"It is. I'm, uh, going to take pictures for my social media." It sounds even more stupid when I say it out loud. "Sponsors like it, and I kind of need them right now," I admit.

"You're going to take pictures of yourself by yourself?"

"I'll build a makeshift tripod."

"I'll come with you, it'll be way easier. And don't—"

I beat him to the chase. "Thank you, but I'll be fine."

He sucks air through his teeth with soft shakes of his head. "One day, you'll accept my help. I swear it."

I smile. I don't think I ever will, but I also don't think anyone has ever tried this hard.

"I appreciate the offer. Really."

He watches me for a moment. I've noticed this man has no sense of embarrassment when doing so. If he feels like staring at you, he will, brazenly so.

"I'll get through to you," he says, then turns around to walk back to the ATV.

As I focus on his departing silhouette—if he can stare, then so can I—my thoughts drift back to what Lilianne revealed this morning. For a moment, I want to ask him to turn around and tell me all about it. I want to know if he's completely healthy now, or if there's more to the story. I want to know what happened.

I don't think he'd like that, though. If he hasn't mentioned it to me, then he likely doesn't want to. We all have things we'd rather keep hidden. If people don't know about them, they kind of stop existing, if only for a moment.

I let him go, but not before I run up to him and put the five dollars in his back pocket. When he spins around, I'm already walking toward my car.

"Darling, if you wanted to touch my ass, you just had to say so."

I bite my cheek to keep my smile in check, then walk backward as I shout, "You're impossible, Finnegan."

"I return the compliment, Crabby."

Chapter 9

Lexie

"**G**ood job, girls!"

My last group of the day gives me high five after high five, the ten preteens walking off the floor mat where we were stretching a minute ago. They're not at a competitive level yet, but I'll suggest a couple names to Shelli that I think could make it to the more advanced group for the next season.

I crack my neck left and right as I watch them get their things from the lockers, all the while trying to kick my own ass to get to work myself. It's been a long week. Now that I'm settled on what competition I'm going to attend, I need to get my skills back to a pristine level, and I haven't given myself much leniency. I don't have that privilege. The first of the small competitions I registered for is less than a month away, and the last thing I want is to embarrass myself out there. I could use a win, especially since I haven't had much luck with sponsors yet. A few of the ones I had when I was still in Phoenix messaged me to let me know they'd be watching my comeback and cheering from the sidelines, but they haven't offered to take me on. With a medal, maybe I could tip the balance.

I wave goodbye to the last of my girls still here, and because I'm too lazy to start training right away, I take my phone out of my back pocket and open my Instagram account. As much as I hate it, I need to check it more frequently now that I'm looking to get something out of it.

I have notifications of likes and comments on the photos I've posted recently. The majority are nice, but some of them are nasty. It was the same thing a few years back, but it never becomes easier to read.

Who are you again?

Can't wait to see you back Lexie! Rooting for you from AZ!

No guy wants a girl with shoulders like that.

She has thicker thighs than The Rock LMAO

My muscles tense as I read the last two. As if my body's only use was to look good to others.

I don't think I'm the prettiest girl out there, far from it. I do have large thighs and broad shoulders. But those large thighs and broad shoulders allow me to do the impossible. To fight gravity and fly for as long as a human being can. I may not have the best looks, but I love my body for all it gives me.

I continue scrolling past, not bothering to read the rest of the comments, good or bad, until something stops me in my tracks. I back up, confirming what I just saw.

@Finnthegreat is now following you

I stare at my phone longer than necessary. I'm not sure how I feel about him being here. On Instagram, he'll see me not as Lexie, the girl who's renting the cabin on his land, but as Lexie Tuffin, two-time silver medalist at the Gymnastics World Championships and, according to my old coach, "geriatric gymnast." He'll see the pictures I feel forced to take. He'll see my body in poses that show my ass and legs and that attract comments comparing me to gigantic male actors.

Oh, whatever. I push the phone back into my pocket, forcing myself to ignore it. So what if he thinks I'm ugly? It shouldn't mean anything. It doesn't.

"Lexie," I hear a millisecond before a hand clasps my shoulder from behind, making me jump and jerk forward, a shiver going down my spine.

I spin with a yelp, and immediately, my shoulders loosen. *Shit.* That's two times with him.

"Hey," I say with a smile I'm sure looks fake, because really, when have I smiled this big to him? "Ready for me to wipe the floor with your ass again?" I joke, hoping it'll be enough to make him forget my overreaction. He's been coming to the gym a few times this week after-hours to exercise, and every time, we have the same routine. He tells me he can beat me at one thing or another, and every time, I prove him wrong. I think at this point, he's looking for embarrassment.

Finn shakes his head, and it's at this moment I notice just how wrong he looks. His skin is pale, jaw tight and gaze hard. He's lost all the humor that usually inhabits him.

"What's wrong?"

"Have you seen my sister anywhere around?" he asks while looking over my shoulder and quickly scanning the gym.

"Your sister?" I wasn't even aware he had siblings. "I don't know, what does she look like?"

"A lot like me, in her twenties. Long brown hair? Maybe she was here with her boyfriend?" He's speaking fast, and I don't miss the way his jaw shifts at the last word.

"I..." I rack my brain trying to remember something, but I was focused on my girls throughout the day. "I don't think so, but I might have missed her."

His upper teeth are chipping at his bottom lip as he sighs loudly. In a quick motion, he removes his beanie and rubs a hand over his short hair.

"What's going on?" I ask, voice stern.

It's throwing me off-balance to see him like this. He's never looked this concerned over anything before. It's unnerving. I find my heart rate increasing in response, which is stupid since I don't even know what's going on. "Can I help with anything?"

"So she can offer the help but not accept it, huh?" He smirks, but even then, there's no humor in it. He looks emptied out.

"Finn, not the time," I say. "What can I do?"

"Nothing. It's..." He looks over my shoulder again. "Complicated. But thanks, though."

"Do you think she's in danger?" I ask.

"Probably not. It's not the first time this has happened. We just..." He drags a hand over his jaw, then puts his beanie back on. "Anyway, I have to go."

"Are you sure you don't want me to come with you?" I don't like anything about this. I don't know my way around town yet, but if he gave me any indication on where she might be, we could split up.

He starts walking away, and over his shoulder, says, "I'm sure. But thanks, Lexie. I appreciate it."

In four strides, he's out of the building.

This isn't working.

I'm lying flat on my back, eyes on the high bar, out of breath and *this* close to blowing a fuse.

I can't do it. My old bar routine is too rough for my current body. Even with all the PT in the world, I'm still not back to where I used to be. Every time I go through my final full rotations around the bar, I remember the feeling of hearing something crack as I fell onto my neck, of lightheadedness overcoming me as I wondered whether I could still feel my feet, of waiting to see if I'd lose consciousness and possibly never regain it. And then my shoulder gives out, and I get to where I am now. Sprawled on my back, ribs screaming in pain, breath stolen out of my lungs, and quite literally, pathetic.

Which is to say, this is a recipe for disaster in a competition.

With a groan, I push myself into a sitting position. I don't have enough time before my first one to get this routine right. No way. I'd need at least four months to get this right, not a meager four weeks, and certainly not on top of all the routines I have to perfect. Dusting my hands on my thighs, I pull my legs onto the low bar so I can dangle upside down, knees holding me in place and arms falling loosely over my head. When I was younger and felt confused or angry or sad, I'd get into this position and wait until blood rushed into my head and I could focus on something other than my worries. It always worked.

Already starting to feel my head getting heavy, I run through my old routines. There's one I did a few years ago, when I attended my first world championship in France. It didn't win me a medal, but it also wasn't that clean. If I get it perfectly, I might not get the highest score for difficulty, but I'd be able to master it, at least. The dismount is a double layout, which I know I could do any day. I've been doing those since I was fourteen, and they never came close to killing me, which is a nice point in their direction. Maybe I could add a full twist in it to make the dismount a little harder while still knowing I can perform it, even under stress. With the time I have left, it's pretty much the only good option I have. Then I'll use my current floor and beam routines, and I'll need to think more about what I want to do on vault. Usually, I'd do an Amanar, which is a back handspring onto the vault table followed by a straight salto with a two and a half twist. However, with the way my shoulder is hurting right now, I'd probably be better off choosing a slightly easier skill so I don't risk messing it up because I'm exhausted from my other routines. My orthopedist told me a few months ago to start slow, and that's pretty much as slow as it could get for me without throwing in the towel.

I swing myself so I can land on my feet, then stand in front of the set of bars. I could start working on my old routine right away, but I'm bone tired. I glance at the clock, which shows it's past 1:00 a.m. Probably a sign to go home. Tomorrow, I'll start working on it.

I go grab my stuff in the staff room, then exit the gym, careful to lock the door behind me. The parking lot is empty—obviously—so I rush to my car while constantly checking over my shoulder, just in case. I don't waste time entering my car, but just before I pull the driver's door closed, my phone rings in my bag. I pull it out, seeing Josie's name on it.

"What took you so long!" I say as a greeting while locking myself into the car.

"I'm sorry," my little sister says. "School has been keeping me busy."

I twist my lips to the side, not wanting to say how it feels like a knife to the gut every time she goes days before calling me back. Sometimes it feels like she's the only person I have in the world, and while it wouldn't be fair to put that on her, I can't stop myself from feeling hurt by it.

"It's fine," I say. "So long as you're good, I'm good."

"Yeah," she says in a voice so low it's suspicious.

"What's wrong?"

"What? Nothing."

"Jos. What's wrong?" Goosebumps cover my skin from the frigid air inside the car, so I turn the engine on and put the heat in full blast. "Is it Kyle?"

She hesitates before she says, "Mom asked me not to tell you."

I grind my teeth and count to three before speaking. I know Josie doesn't see our mother the same way I do, and I don't want to influence her one way or another. She'll grow to form her own opinion of her. But Jesus, what kind of an idea is it to ask her youngest daughter not to tell her older sister what's bothering her?

"You can still talk to me."

"Promise you won't tell Mom."

"I promise," I say.

Josie sighs loudly. "She has a new boyfriend."

This time, I have to move the phone away from me so Josie doesn't hear me swear. Repeatedly. When I bring the phone back to my ear, I ask, "Is he...nice?" I hope my voice doesn't sound as raw as I think it does.

"I haven't seen much of him with school, but he's moving in tomorrow, so—"

"What?" I shout before clearing my throat. "What do you mean he's moving in?"

"Apparently he doesn't have a job right now, but he's working on some big project and just needs a place to stay for a while."

Of course. Of fucking course she'd do that.

Fighting with all I have to keep my calm for the sake of my sister, I ask, "But he's been okay to you for now?"

"Sure," Josie says.

"Okay. Good. Now listen to me, Jos, okay? You don't forget to use the lock I put on your bedroom door. Ever. You hear me? You need to be careful about it."

"Yeah, okay," she says breathily. Then, "Should I be worried?"

"No, honey, no, you'll be okay. It's just a precaution. Okay?"

"Okay."

I hear papers rustling in the back before she says, "I have to get back to my homework, but I'll call you soon."

"All right. Be safe, Jos. I love you."

"I love you too."

Once she's hung up, I let the phone drop in my lap, noticing my hands are shaking. My whole body is, actually.

So now there's Kyle, his friends, *and* this new boyfriend to worry about.

I hate it. I hate it with everything in me. I also hate how scared I've made my little sister. Maybe there's nothing to be scared of and my own childhood experiences have tainted my view of things. Maybe I'm the one traumatizing Josie now by making her afraid of things that likely won't happen.

Still, I'm part of the "better safe than sorry" crew.

I go to start the car, but I'm still shaking too hard. Fisting my hands and bringing them back into my lap, I exhale slowly. My gaze roams over the empty parking lot, going over the streetlights and the letters showing the gym's name. Far away to the left, a truck is parked in front of a row of apartments, one that looks a whole lot like the one I always see in front of the office at the farm.

I wonder what ended up happening with him. If he found his sister after all.

The expression he had when he entered the gym was actually pretty similar to the one I'm probably wearing now. Whether he wanted to or not, he showed me yet another side of him today. One that reminds me a lot of the way I am with Josie.

He wasn't there for his cleaning gig later during the evening, so I wasn't able to ask him anything about it. And strangely, I found myself glancing around a few times. I wanted to see that smirk back on his face, as annoying as it is.

I hope everything turns out okay for them. Along with worry, love for his sister was painted all over his face, and I know well enough what that feels like.

I misjudged this man. I've been seeing it for a while, but what he's shown me tonight just confirmed it. There are more sides to him than what meets the eye. Sides that remind me of the charming man I'd initially met in Rome.

And I have to admit, I don't dislike those sides of him. Not at all.

Chapter 10

Finn

I love Halloween.

Ever since I was a kid and discovered the magic of dressing up as a superhero and becoming someone else for an entire day, I've loved the holiday. For the past month or so, I've been working on making it a big event at Evermore so we could start shifting the place from a Christmas-only location into a year-round profitable enterprise, and I couldn't be more excited about the final result.

The sun is slowly making its descent, creating a halo of marigold over the trees as I look around the main area of the farm. My staff and I have been hard at work for the past two weeks, building a haunted house and a maze throughout the forest, decorated by yours truly. Next to the haunted house, which takes place in one of our bigger barns, two food trucks are setting up for the evening, the smell of fried dough and popcorn filling the air. I'd planned on going to grab some for myself before the beginning of the event, but my stomach feels a little queasy.

This is Sonder Hill. It can't get smaller than this, there's not much to do on a Saturday night, and I've advertised this event everywhere, so chances are, people will show up. Still, I can't help wondering, *what if?* Maybe they know I'm the person in charge of the event, and they only remember me as the guy who accidentally burned down Mr. and Mrs. Montgomery's pool house with a cigarette butt while hooking up with their daughter in my junior year of high school. It may have been ten years ago, but that's not the kind of thing people quickly forget.

With one last look around, I jump back into my office to change into my homemade James Bond costume, then walk back out with my hands in my pockets so I can stop wringing them together.

Everything will be fine. It's Halloween. My favorite holiday.

I cross the main driveway and go set up at the entrance of the farm, where I left the little bags of candies I woke up early this morning to pack. Hopefully, we'll get a few trick-or-treaters too.

With my toy gun in my right hand and my satin bow tie glowing in the end-of-day light, I take a seat next to the box of candy and wait for people to show up.

Without anyone in sight, I take the opportunity to check whether I've received any texts. After what happened with Francesca, I can't stop myself from being on edge.

We ended up searching for her for a full day before she finally called us back and admitted she was with Cameron, her thirty-five-year-old boyfriend, at some kind of party. Even when Mom pleaded with her to come back home, she refused and said she was fine where she was.

Last year, when she dropped out of college, everyone in the family freaked out, but I tried to rationalize things with my parents. She was a smart girl, and we should trust her to decide what was right. Fran was happy when I took her side and thanked me. I felt confident she was doing the right thing for herself. And, after all, I didn't go to college either, so I wasn't one to talk.

Except now I really fucking regret not seeing something was wrong the minute she dropped out of school. I should've suspected something was up with her. Immediately after making the decision, she told us she'd found this job with a guy named Cameron, but when we started asking her about it, she closed off and gave vague answers. Then, a month later, she told us she was actually dating the guy. I looked him up, and when I found out how old he was, I blew a fuse. It was a mistake—made her step away from me and stop confiding—and while I've tried to keep things to myself since then, I've always known something was wrong with that guy. My sister has been different ever since they met. She's on edge, always asking me to stop worrying and to stay away from the two of them.

And then there was the time she called me in tears, asking me for help. I drove to the guy's place faster than I ever had, but when I got there, she acted as if everything was fine. I confronted him, obviously, but he kicked me out, and the next day, the cabin was trashed.

I don't know what goes on when she's with him, but I can tell it's bad. Worse than that, when she finally came home for dinner a few days ago, she had dried blood under her nose. I'm not sure whether it was from drugs or from being hurt, but either way, I hate it, and there's not a single fucking thing I can do about it.

I rub a hand over my scalp. *It's Halloween. Your favorite holiday.*

I need to stop thinking about this. I can't do anything about it now, and as much as I'd like to help Francesca, if she doesn't want to help herself, there's nothing I can do except be there for her when she decides to leave him.

Once I've put my phone back in the inside pocket of my jacket, I lift my head to find an old sedan approaching the entrance. One I've gotten accustomed to seeing a lot in the past few weeks.

Lexie slows down beside me and rolls her window down.

"Are the Oscars now taking place in Sonder Hill and I didn't know?"

"Ha, ha," I say. "It's Halloween. This is my Halloween costume."

"And you're supposed to be...?"

"Bond, obviously." I pull my fake gun out.

Her brows lift as she rakes me up and down, then blinks. "Right."

"Want some candy?" I ask, hand already plunged in the bowl next to me.

She shakes her head. "No, thanks."

"All right." I look left and right, the rest of the lot still empty. My stomach dips once again at the thought it might remain this way. When I return my attention to Lexie, I find her staring. I clear my throat, then say, "I'm still missing a Bond girl, if you feel like hanging around."

"I think I'll pass." She smirks. "But as the only woman around, I feel honored that you thought of me."

I laugh as I watch her drive away and then turn into the cabin's parking spot. My gaze snags on her as she gets out of the car, her leggings and coaching jacket hugging every single curve on her body.

"Trick or treat!"

The high-pitched voices bring me out of my daze. Three little boys stand in front of me, all dressed as Ninja Turtles, a pillowcase open in front of each.

"Hey, guys. Aren't you missing a friend?"

I fill their bags as one of them says, "We're a trio now."

"Good to know." I fill the last bag, then put a hand on my heart and say, "Thank you for your service, ninjas."

They chuckle as they run back toward where their parents are waiting for them, and I don't miss the "What was his costume?"

Ah, kids.

I take my spot on the stool but don't wait long before more people arrive. Car after car turns onto the gravel road leading to the main farm, where my colleagues will be waiting for them and directing them toward the different activities. More kids also show up while trick-or-treating, each making me smile more than the last.

Halloween really is the best.

It's almost fully dark out when I hear footsteps on the gravel behind me. I turn, then feel my jaw fall to the ground.

I've never seen Lexie like this. Granted, she's mostly in training gear when we cross paths, but not even when we met in Italy and she was wearing that short navy dress did she leave me this wordless.

Lexie's a beautiful woman. There's no denying it. But right now, in her long red gown with a low neckline and sequins all over, she looks...

I swallow as she comes even closer and the smell of her shampoo fills my nostrils, like fresh pears and vanilla. I rarely see her with any makeup on, but now, she's wearing a dark smoky eye—at least I think that's what my sister calls it—and bright red lips that match the exact color of her dress. The almost full moon is reflected in her dark eyes, and I find myself unable to look away.

As she takes a seat next to me, she says, "Thought you were missing some feminine presence."

I grin. "So you're my Bond girl after all?"

"If you ever repeat this, I'll have to end you," she says with a straight face.

"Oh, look, Crabby's back."

She rolls her eyes, but can't hide her soft grin when she says, "Never left."

I smile too as I look at her. She came. It shouldn't make me this happy that she decided to come hang out with me after all, but it does. And when she looks up and finds me happily gazing at her, she doesn't comment on it.

She glances behind her shoulder at the space where music is coming from, children shrieking while running with potato donuts held between their sticky fingers and teenagers screeching inside the haunted house. I tried it yesterday when the actors were rehearsing, and I will neither confirm nor deny that I almost peed my pants once or twice.

Lexie clears her throat. "So, uh, how's your sister?"

"Good. She's..." I bob my head a few times before turning toward her. "Actually, no, she's not. Or she is, but I think she's in a bad spot, and it's killing me a little."

She chews on her lip. "I'm sorry. That must be hard."

"Yeah. It's fucking me up, to be honest. I just can't figure it out. Why she'd decide to stay with a man that's bad for her."

Lexie's skin pales. One of her hands starts scratching at an already raw patch of skin on her other wrist. "I really wish I had the answer to that."

I lean forward. "Did you..."

"My mother had a lot of boyfriends when I was younger," she spits out, almost too fast for me to catch. "I spent most of my time asking myself the same question." She doesn't look at me when she finishes, playing with the short curls framing her face.

I want to answer something, anything, but I come up empty. I never expected her to actually give me information for free.

"No, you say it," a little voice whisper-hisses, forcing me to look away.

"Oh my god, how did you escape prison!" I say in a frightened voice before I cower and drop candy into the bags of two Marvel villains, which makes them laugh out loud. "I promise I won't tell anyone you were here, my lords."

The two boys try making scary faces, but fail when they break out into grins.

"Happy Halloween," I say. They don't answer, but I hear their laughter as they run all the way back to their moms.

When I take my seat again, I find Lexie smiling wide, no snark present. No trace of her previous confession either.

I like having this kind of smile directed at me.

"They were pretty cute," she says.

"Don't you mean *we* were pretty cute?"

"I didn't misspeak."

I snort with a shake of my head. "Can't you give a guy just one compliment?"

"I guess I can say you have a very nice scream."

"I'm sorry?"

"I heard you when you tried the haunted house yesterday." She tilts her head. "I think all of Vermont did."

"Oh, shut up," I say, laughing.

Now that we're in complete darkness save for the fairy lights strung through the trees lining the driveway, the place feels more remote from the rest of the farm. Colder too.

"Shit, you must be freezing like that," I say, finally noticing her arms are bare.

"I'm fine."

"Here." I remove my suit jacket—I don't think we'll have any more trick-or-treaters at this hour, but I keep that quiet. I'm not ready to leave yet. I go to drape the coat on her shoulders, but she shuffles out of the way, taking it in her hands.

"Thank you," she says, wrapping herself in the too-large jacket.

I nudge my chin toward her dress. "Where'd you get that any-way?"

She looks down and drags a hand down the skirt of her dress. "I got it for the end-of-year gala at my old gym a few years back."

I want to tell her it's gorgeous—*she's* gorgeous—but I have a feeling that would make her close up. Talking with her feels a little like playing with fire sometimes. Instead, I say, "Do you miss it there? The gym, I mean."

"Yes and no." She shrugs. "I liked my team, and I liked practic-ing there, but no one believed anymore."

"Believed what?"

She turns to me, her irises blending with her pupils. "That I could do it."

"And why would they think that?" You'd have to be dumb not to see this girl's talent.

"It's complicated."

I hum. "But you're going to prove them wrong, I assume?"

"Hopefully." She starts scratching her wrist again. "First com-petition of the unofficial season in two weeks. I guess we'll see." A heavy sigh escapes her lips, one that sounds like she's carrying the weight of the world on her shoulders.

"You sound ecstatic."

She huffs. "The stakes are high, and I haven't always thrived under pressure."

"Why are you going then? You look like you're in pain just talking about it."

"Being a gymnast is kind of like being a martyr."

"Yeah, I've heard that before. So I repeat my question: why do it?"

She leans forward, her weight on her hands. "Have you never asked anyone else at the gym?"

"I don't care why other people do it. I want to know why *you* do it."

She licks her lips, gaze lost in the stars above us. "That sport gave me stability. A reason to get up in the morning. Discipline." Her gaze falls to my hands splayed on my knees. "It's been the biggest pain in my ass, but it's also been my salvation."

She falls silent, and I remain still for a moment, waiting to see if she'll give me more. It feels as if I've just opened a Pandora's box, and now that I've gotten some information, I can only want more.

Lexie exhales loudly as she gets to her feet. "Anyway, I think our service is no longer needed here."

She's right. The street is now silent, no kids in sight.

I shouldn't be this disappointed.

"Right. I should get back to the maze anyway."

She nods. "Good night, Finley."

I laugh. "Night."

Even though I do need to get to the rest of the activities at the farm, I stay seated, and for a moment, do the same thing I did before: watch her make her way toward the cabin. This time, though, I find myself thinking back to what happened tonight. She came to me. I don't know what made her change her mind, but she did. And more than that, she opened up. Let me in, if only for a moment. Somehow, it makes me feel like I've just won the lottery.

When was the last time I felt grateful to be let in by someone? It makes no fucking sense.

And yet I can't stop myself from smiling the rest of the night.

Chapter 11

Lexie

I'm nervous. That's a first.

The air smells faintly of sweat and chalk. Music is blaring from the floor area, where a girl who doesn't look like she's hit puberty yet is performing her routine with extra sass in all her movements. I lift my upper body from where it's resting on the floor as I continue stretching. I was assigned to an area next to the balance beams, which gives a perfect view of the floor in this gym. She's good. Really good.

I wasn't expecting today's event to be this big. With the start of the official elite competition season still a few months away, I'd thought the sports center would only be half full, but all the seats are filled and the roster packed. Apparently, I'm not the only one who wanted to assess the competition before our first real event in February.

Noise is coming from every corner, and with the wide space worsening the echo, it's a cacophony in here. It always amazes me when I watch sports like golf and I see players who expect the crowd to be silent. It couldn't be farther from us. If you can't focus while loud music is playing and people are cheering for multiple athletes competing at the same time, then it's too bad.

It never used to bother me before, but today, the mix of sounds overwhelms me. Breathing slowly, I get to my feet so I can stretch my shoulders and run through my routine one last time, gazing down at my leotard. It's my favorite, made of carbon black material and decorated with onyx rhinestones. As I pull one of my arms behind my head, I touch my hair to make sure my short ponytail is still in place.

It'll be fine. I'm ready for this. Or, as ready as can be. It's been more than a year since my injury. If I can't come back now, I never will.

To my left, a group of girls wearing the same team leotard is talking in a circle with their coach, as if finalizing their plan for the day. One of them seems familiar, and when I squint, I recognize Laura, a gymnast I used to train with a few years back in Phoenix. She was nice, always letting me room with her when I couldn't afford rooms on my own during competitions.

When she glances my way, I wave, getting out of my splits to say hi, but before I can move in her direction, she waves back and returns her attention to her team. I freeze for a moment, then move into another stretch, as if this was the plan all along.

I don't blame her for not wanting to catch up. I wasn't the best teammate, always having to find excuses for not hanging out with the other girls. With work and everything going on at home, I couldn't stay after practice, so it's only natural that the five girls on my team became close, in a way only other people who share your hardships can, while I remained on the side.

I try not to focus on how I wish I could be the type of person old acquaintances are happy to see again or how envious I am of Laura for having a coach and a team by her side today.

Dragging my tongue over my teeth, I look away. I need to get used to being alone. It's not like it's going to change anytime soon. At least not until I make it onto Team USA.

Another incentive for the end goal.

I finish stretching, and when my turn is up, I walk to the warm-up mat, where I run through my routines and practice a few movements. I do two simple tumbling passes, feeling my pulse starting to thrum with adrenaline. Yes, the thousands of things happening during a competition can be distracting, but the energy is also palpable. It fills everyone. I feel it in my muscles, in my bones. The nerves don't go away, but they're accompanied by anticipation now. I'm here. I'm actually back. Something I wished for but thought would be impossible for months last year.

Everyone is called to move ahead to the next station, where I have to wait for someone else to perform on the floor before I can go. I watch as a girl who must be in her early twenties steps onto the floor, salutes the judges, and starts her routine.

I jump in place as I watch her performance, keeping my blood flowing. This feeling, right before going in? It's like a drug. There's so much possibility ahead. A chance to prove something to people. To feel like the best.

I could never have let that go even if I'd tried.

The girl performing is good. Not the best I've ever seen, but her tumbling is solid and she's graceful through every movement. Her music is a cha-cha that gets everyone who's watching clapping to the rhythm. Her routine has a good level of difficulty, but if I do mine perfectly, I think it will be worth more.

A routine lasts a minute and thirty seconds, but the clock ticks so incredibly slowly. I want both to be performing already and to delay it for as long as possible.

But then she's done, and the stadium is music-free for a moment. As people applaud, my hands fly once again to my head, making sure every stray strand is tucked where it's supposed to be.

"Alexandria Tuffin," a presenter calls.

I inhale and exhale slowly. Then, I step onto the mat, a bright smile on my lips. They won't see my nerves today. Not on the outside anyway. I salute to the table where two women and a man are sitting, then get into my starting pose.

I hear every smashing beat of my heart as I wait statue-like for the music to start.

One beat. Two.

Get it, Lexie.

And then the song I know like the back of my hand begins, and all my thoughts disappear.

Muscle memory takes over as I go through my first motions, then run into my first tumbling pass, which ends with a double arabian salto. It's one I love doing, and by the cheers I hear when I land, I'd say I executed it well. I then have a sequence of dance and jumps, which I go through easily. My second tumbling pass comes next, which is my favorite one. I wasn't sure whether I wanted to do it since it's rough on my shoulder, but I wanted the points. Plus, if I want to prove the floor is still my best element, I have to do it. I push through the straight-backward salto with triple twist, and on the last rotation, I land a little sideways, which makes me take one step back before I regain my balance. Thankfully I'm still within the lines, so it'll only count as a small deduction.

I'm already out of breath, but I still have one pass to go. I gulp air as much as I can while I do a ring jump, bringing my feet right up to my ponytail, then do another sequence of jumps, and finally, I run through my last tumbling pass. It's a little rough around the edges, and I don't gain as much height as I'd like, but I still land it nicely.

Cheers and applause ring from the seats, pumping me with energy to go through my final motions and twists, and then the music ends with me on my knees, head thrown back, my weight on my hands.

My lips curve in a wide grin. I did it.

Was it perfect? Not at all, but I fucking did it.

I get up and salute the judges once again, then wave at the people clapping before stepping off the mat. I head toward the spot where Andy usually waited for me, but realize halfway there that I'm alone. Brushing it off, I walk to where I left my water bottle, gulping half of it down as I catch my breath. I definitely need to add more cardio to my daily routine if I want to finish this season in one piece.

Two minutes later, I realize I'm still smiling and tone it down. This was just one event. I still have three to go. Still, it was an encouraging start.

Maybe my dream isn't that out of reach after all.

I have twenty minutes to get down from the adrenaline of my floor routine before it's time to get ready for the balance beam.

Once again, I wait in front of the beam for the gymnast before me to finish, all the while running through my movements one last time in my head.

The balance beam is not my best, but not my worst apparatus either. I'm a power and strength gymnast first, so the floor and the vault fit me better, but I can always do somewhat okay on the beam.

I'm still reeling from my first routine when my name is called.

I walk with my chin held high and shoulders tucked back, more confident than I was an hour earlier. I salute the judges, then stand in front of the springboard and force myself to breathe, something I often forget to do. Then, I drown out the music. There's just me and this beam.

When I feel fully focused, I jump on the board and use a front salto to mount, then begin my routine. Under my foot, chalk sticks to the leather of the beam, anchoring me as I go through the motions I've been practicing for more than two years. I then move into a split jump followed by a side aerial. My breaths are in rhythm with my movements when I enter the acrobatics section, where I chain a back handspring with a back layout. A few claps come my way as I transition into a series of jumps, which go perfectly. I exhale. This is going okay too. I'm almost done.

I crouch on the beam so I can do a double turn on one foot. This is a movement I've always aced, so I move into the spin easily.

Maybe too easily.

Something in my balance isn't right. I can't pinpoint it, but as I turn, I feel like I won't make the second rotation completely. I end up slowing too fast, and can only complete the first half of the second turn. Regaining my balance, I stand back up, shoulders straight. No one noticed, I'm sure. They don't know what I was supposed to do in the first place.

Except *I* know, and I can't brush it off. I think of the points I lost by modifying the movement and only doing a one-and-a-half turn. It might bring me down a position. Maybe even off the podium.

The music from the floor suddenly feels louder, like it's invading my ear canals and deafening me. I go through a jump while breathing loudly, my landing wobbly.

Fuck.

Fuck, fuck, fuck.

I need to refocus. It doesn't matter how many points I've lost. I'll lose even more if I don't get it together.

But as much as I try, thoughts are racing through my head. I replay the spin. I hear the loud shouts from someone in the audience. The smell of too many bodies in one place fills my nose. I taste bile.

I get into position for my front aerial. After that, I'll barely have anything left. I get through the arm movements that were choreographed into the routine, all the while subtly cracking my neck. I can do this.

Once my feet leave the beam and I feel my body lift off, I try to focus on every muscle I need to tighten to get through the aerial, but the only thing that fills my head is the memory of how it felt to see the ground coming at me when I fell last year. The fear. The nausea. The cracking noise.

That's when everything truly goes wrong.

What hits the beam first isn't my feet, but my ass, followed by my back, and then there's sharp pain everywhere. Still, I don't realize what just happened until I look around and see I'm on the ground.

Oh god.

I fell.

I haven't fallen from the beam during a competition in years. Wobbled, sure, but never fallen like this.

I blink fast once again, this time chasing away tears of shock. No matter how much I want to run away and disappear from this moment altogether, I can't *not* finish. That's not what sportsmanship is. So I get back up and climb on the beam, a few awkward claps resonating around me.

Everything hurts as I finish my routine, and while, technically, I do fine, there's no life in it. It's useless to pretend this matters anyway. I know I fucked up, the judges know I fucked up, and everyone watching does too. Somehow, the humiliation hurts worse than my physical pain.

I dismount with a double tuck, landing it roughly. I feel the reverberation from my heels all the way to my scalp. With my exhale, I let all the frustration and disappointment out, then I turn to the judges and salute again. I force a smile, but at this point, I'd probably be better not to. It must look pained anyway.

I don't wave as I walk away like I did at the floor, but I don't allow myself to break either. The only thing I want to do right now is run to the bathroom and let myself feel whatever it is I'm feeling, but that's not who I am. I registered for a competition, and I'm going to finish it, no matter how badly my heart is breaking.

After all, my sports ethics might be the only thing left of my career in gymnastics.

Chapter 12

Lexie

It's barely 8:00 a.m. four days later when I leave my place and come face-to-face with a half-naked man chopping wood right in front of my front porch, grunting with the strain of his movements.

My feet stall as I stare. And stare.

Did I mention he was shirtless?

Finn wasn't lying when he said he didn't need to buff up. Sure, I can best him during plank contests, but that has nothing to do with his physique.

Because what the...

I never wondered what he looked like under his flannel shirts and loose hoodies, but now that I've seen it, I don't think I'll ever be able to forget the image. The way the muscles in his back contract as he lifts the hatchet in the air before dropping it into the log, breaking the piece of wood in two. The drop of sweat sliding down between his bunched shoulder blades. The part of his lips as he cracks yet another log in two, then in four.

Something clenches in my belly at the sight of all that man standing in front of me, my grip tightening around the plastic handles of my laundry basket.

Stop it. I'm the creep, now. He hasn't even noticed I've come out of the cabin.

I clear my throat. "This looks an awful lot like the intro of a shitty porn movie," I tease by way of a greeting.

He jerks at the sound of my voice, but quickly recovers. "And wouldn't you like that." He drops his hatchet to the ground then stands tall, not even trying to hide himself. "Plus, I'd lean more towards the high quality shit." He smirks then, the move dripping with self-confidence.

"And here I was, thinking you couldn't sound more like a douche."

Finn laughs as he walks toward the pile of discarded clothes on the ground, then puts on a white T-shirt, followed by his coat. All the while, I trace the outline of his chest, regretting for a second that I said something and made him dress back up.

What the hell is wrong with me?

"I thought you might need more wood for the fireplace," he explains as he gathers some of the logs and walks up the cabin's stairs. Pointing to the door, he asks, "Can I?"

"Oh, sure." I open it for him, then go grab a pile of logs for myself and bring them next to his. "Thanks for that. You didn't have to."

"Course."

We return outside and bring the rest of the wood inside. Once we're done, Finn doesn't linger inside, so I follow him out onto the porch.

"What's that?" Finn asks, his eyes on my laundry.

"You have a way of asking very obvious questions, don't you?"

He gives me the stink eye. "I meant, where were you going with that?"

"Laundromat.

"Why?"

"Because there's no washer in here?" I say, brows high. "Shouldn't you know that?"

"I do, I just...didn't think about it."

 "Clearly," I say with a grin, then lean down to grab my basket. "I need to get to it before it gets too crowded, but thanks for the wood."

The smell of moss and clean sweat emanating from him makes me grit my teeth a little tighter as I cross his path.

"I wouldn't do that if I were you," Finn says as he walks up to me.

"What?"

"Go to the laundromat. Mr. Gervais hasn't cleaned the place in at least fifty years. It's nasty."

"Well, since there's no magic washing machine in the forest, I don't have many other options." Although he has a point. The first time I went to the laundromat in town, I gagged once or twice at the grime that had clearly spent decades accumulating on the appliances.

"Just come to my place."

I freeze halfway to my car. "I'm sorry?"

"Believe it or not, I do have a washing machine. Just come do your laundry there."

Go to Finn's place? After I had the weird belly jitters looking at him just minutes ago? I don't think so.

"Thanks for the offer, but I'll be fine."

I finish my walk to my car, but as I put the basket on one hip to manually unlock the door, someone steals it from my arms.

"What are you doing?" I ask Finn's retreating back.

"If you're not going to accept my help, I'm going to force you to."

"Finn."

He doesn't answer, only continues to walk toward his truck parked in front of the main house.

"Finneas!"

"Continue playing that name game, darling. I don't mind. It just means you're thinking 'bout me!"

This man. This goddamn man.

I run after him, and when I reach him, I try to wrench the basket out of his hands, but clearly his arms are stronger than his core, because it doesn't budge.

"You're a brute," I say as he puts my stuff in the back seat of his truck.

"And you're a brat. Now hop in."

After lots of huffing and puffing, I end up listening to him, but my frown doesn't budge.

"See?" he says as we clip our seatbelts. "Wasn't so hard?"

"This is, like, half kidnapping."

He laughs out loud as he starts the truck. "Sure thing."

We make the short drive to his place—which really is right opposite the gym—in silence, soft country music playing from the radio. Once he puts the truck into park, I jump out to grab my laundry basket first. I don't need him to sneak a look into my stinky training clothes any more than he probably already has. Thankfully, he doesn't fight me on this, instead walking straight to a door on the first floor that opens right onto the street and unlocking the door.

"Make yourself at home," he says as he holds the door open for me.

I take a few careful steps inside, unsure of what I'll find in there. The few guy apartments I've seen in my life belonged either to crappy one-night stands or to guys from the gym who'd hosted parties, and throughout all these occasions, not one man has proven to be clean.

But surprisingly, this place is. The apartment is all open space, and while there's a pair of socks in front of the couch and a few plates in the kitchen sink, it's...neat.

"Wasn't expecting that," I blurt out.

"What did you imagine? A live-in baboon?"

"Something like that, yeah."

He chuckles. "Washer's right there."

I walk toward the kitchen, noticing once again how tidy the place is. But the more I look, the more I see it's not just clean; it's empty. The living room only holds a gray two-seater and a television stand. Same thing for the kitchen, which only has the bare minimum. All the basic furniture is there, but there's barely anything personalized about the place. It almost looks as if it hasn't been lived in. There's even a couple cardboard boxes stacked next to the kitchen table.

"Did you just move in?" I ask.

"If by 'just,' you mean 'more than a year ago,' then yeah, I did."

I hum, then continue exploring the kitchen space. The only items that don't seem like they were already here when he moved in are the few trinkets spread across the windowsill above the sink. Some sort of wooden mask. A tiny music box. A clay sculpture. Russian dolls.

"What's all of this?" I ask, dragging a finger over the dolls.

"Just things I picked up while traveling."

He must've traveled a lot, then.

Finally, I make my way toward the door he pointed at earlier, and sure enough, inside are a washer and dryer.

I drop my basket to the floor, then look over my shoulder to find him standing in the middle of the space, watching me.

"You don't have to stay here, you know," I say.

"Why? Afraid I'll see your panties?"

I roll my eyes. "I meant you probably have work to do."

"Actually, I'm a quite free man this morning," he says as he walks to the four-top dining table and lets his body drape over one of the chairs. He scrunches his nose. "Disappointed you won't be able to look through my stuff while I'm away?"

"Very. I was looking forward to finding a collection of weird shit you keep. Miniature Winnie the Poohs? Nudie mags, maybe?"

He laughs as I start unloading my basket into the washer, the majority of the load just leggings and tank tops. And then, my hands land on my competition leotard, and for a fraction of a moment, I freeze.

Apparently, that's enough for Finn to pick up on it.

"What's wrong?"

"Nothing."

"I have eyes, Lexie. What's wrong?"

I huff, then answer, "Just a bad luck leotard." Lifting it back in front of me, I add, "Maybe I could leave it here, actually."

If only that competition had only been due to bad juju. I know well enough the leotard has nothing to do with it, and by the way Finn's face turns serious, he does too.

"What happened?" he asks.

"My first competition happened." I put it aside, to be hand-washed at some point. Can't waste a perfectly good one, no matter how many bad memories it may bring. I might just wait a week or six before getting to washing it.

"I gather it wasn't good?"

"You gathered right." I close the door, then pour detergent into the appropriate compartment. It's been days, and I still haven't processed the competition. I don't know how to move on. The feeling of falling from the beam still haunts me at night. The sucker punch of shame I felt at the audience's gasp lives in my mind rent-free.

But I think what's made it so much harder to handle has been my loneliness through it. Before, I would've had a team behind me, comforting me that this was just a hurdle in the road. But this time was different. I had no one to talk to, utterly alone, and it was proof that maybe I deserved to be.

Maybe it's all that loneliness that gets me to tell Finn, "Came in sixth overall. Got bronze for vault and silver for floor." I don't bother mentioning the fourth spot on bars and the horrible beam ranking.

Maybe some people would tell me I'm stupid for being somber about this—I ranked in the top three for some elements, after all—but not Finn. He knows what those scores mean for someone who's trying to get to the top. It means I failed. More than failed.

"I'm sorry," Finn says.

My shoulders sink. I'm thankful he's facing my back. I wouldn't have wanted him to see just how much I needed to hear those words.

"Thanks. Me too."

The washing machine thrums from the heavy load as I finally turn to face Finn, then go take a seat in front of him.

"The whole thing sucked, to be honest. I'm competing against girls almost half my age. I have no coach, no sponsor."

"So what does it mean?" he asks. His head is propped on his hand, bright green eyes focused on me.

"What do you mean?"

"Well, are you giving up?"

"What?" I frown. "Why?"

"I don't know. It's probably what I'd do." He shrugs. "If it's not working, just walk away." He lets out a humorless snicker.

"No. No way. I couldn't."

"Why not?"

"Because I can still win." I rub a patchy area on my wrist, over and over. "I'm disappointed—fucking pissed at myself, really—but I'm not discouraged. That was just step one. I'm not done. I can still make it. I know it." It almost feels like a mantra at this point. It doesn't matter whether I believe it or not, so long as I pretend I do.

What I *don't* say is that I don't know how to face the alternative. I can't let this go, because what will I be left with then? It's what my life *is*. Why I moved across the country and abandoned my sister, who's the only person who truly matters to me. How I convinced myself at my lowest points that this life was worth continuing to live. I *need* to succeed. There's no other option.

"And what about the younger girls kicking your old ass?" Finn says, smirking. I can recognize now that what I imagined as arrogance when we met was really just his sense of humor.

"They better watch themselves. I'm coming for them." I stand from the chair and pace around the kitchen, letting out the pent-up energy I've been harboring since my drive back from Mississauga. "They might have the best coaches and all the skills in the world, but I have something they don't."

"And what's that?" Finn asks.

I lean over the table, my gaze on his. "I *want* it."

Slowly, almost catlike, his lips curl up, a wicked glint in his eyes. Then, he lifts a glass of water that was sitting on the table and says, "I'll drink to that."

The next day, Shelli offers me her choreographers for new routines before New York, and as much as I want to brush her offer aside, I remember my discussion with Finn and what I need to reach my end goal, and I say yes.

Chapter 13

Finn

"Look who it is!"

I can't stop myself from smiling wide as I watch my best friend and his wife climb out of their SUV, their two dogs in tow. The moment Molly, the bigger of the two, is out of the car, she starts running my way, her dark fur rustling in the wind as she jumps on me.

"Ah, good girl," I say as I rub her ears. "Yes, you're a good girl."

"Don't you get kinky with my dog now," Aaron says as he walks my way with two carry-on cases in his hands, grinning.

"Fucker," I say before embracing him tightly. He drops the bags to the ground and taps my back twice, then hugs me a little longer. "I've missed you, brother," I add. "You don't visit enough."

He pulls away. "I know. I'm sorry. Work's been crazy, but we couldn't miss this weekend."

Martina, his mother, is celebrating her sixty-fifth birthday tomorrow, and my mom is organizing a party with our two families and a few friends from around town.

"Hey, Finn," Wren says as she joins us with Woody, her smaller and calmer dog, following her heels as closely as is physically possible.

I give her a quick hug. "Was just telling your husband how much I miss you guys."

"We suck, Aaron," Wren tells him over my shoulder, then turns to me with a frown. "Last month's been crazy at work, but I promise we'll be around to help soon," she says.

"I'm not talking about the farm. I miss my friends."

"You getting sappy, Finn?" Aaron says.

I punch his shoulder as an answer. God, it's good to have him here. We text and call every now and then while he's in the city, but it's not the same thing as having my best friend around. When I was traveling, it was easier to forget how much I missed him, but it's been much worse now that I'm in our hometown and he isn't around.

"All right," Wren says, "I'll go see if Martina needs help with dinner and take the dogs to Callie," Wren says. "She'll kill me if I don't."

"See you soon," Aaron says, then gives her forehead a kiss. It's an act that's so mundane, one I've seen my father do with my mother countless times while passing her in the kitchen, but it still makes me envious. I wish I could be so at ease with someone that kissing them becomes an automatism, a given. My parents have been a prime example of love that's as natural as breathing, and seeing Aaron finally live the same thing only makes me sadder that it might never happen to me.

Wren walks to the main house with Woody, then whistles for Molly to come inside with her. After spinning two times around a tree, the dog finally listens. Aaron chuckles at the sight of Wren, who was clearly getting ready to trudge through mud after Molly, heeled boots be damned.

"So, married life still good?"

Everything in Aaron's face softens as he keeps his eyes on Wren and says, "Yeah, man, it is."

We both start walking toward the row of fir trees that lines the beginning of the farm. Even if he loves his life in the city, I'm sure Aaron misses the calm of this place sometimes. I sure would. Nothing like a walk through the forest, where branches crunch under your feet and birds' songs keep you company, to decompress.

"Good. I'm happy for you," I say.

He turns to me. "What about you?"

"Do I have a wife I don't know about?"

"Dumbass. I mean anyone new?"

I shake my head. I'm not even sure why he uses the word "new." I haven't had someone in my life since before I left town at twenty. Chrissy was the last. There've been plenty of girls around me—more than I'd like to admit—but never for more than for a few nights in a row.

"Interesting," Aaron says.

"What?"

"Well, a little birdy, aka my mom, told me she's seen you spending some time with the cabin girl." He waggles his dark brows.

"Nah, that's..." I search for words to explain what Lexie is to me, but it's surprisingly difficult. She used to be a girl who hated me. But now? It's kind of fuzzy. It's been a while since I've spent as much time with someone apart from Aaron and Lil, and while it was often luck that brought us together at first, now I'm pretty sure we do so knowingly. "It's not like that," I decide on.

"What's it like, then?"

"She's a friend, I think. Not a hundred percent sure."

Aaron pauses his gazing around to give me a weird look, then asks, "Did anything happen between you two?"

I kick a large rock away from the path. "God, no."

"Why are you saying it like that?" He snickers. "Never saw you make that face about a girl before."

Why *did* I say it like that?

It's not like I wouldn't have looked at Lexie that way if we were in another context. But with the way our relationship started, and then with the time we've spent together afterward, giving away candy and messing with each other in the gym, I couldn't see her as someone I could have a one-and-done with. Maybe at some point I could have, but not now, when I've seen so many sides of her that getting together would definitely mean something.

"It's just not like that between us."

"So there *is* an us," Aaron says.

"Don't you have anything better to focus on?"

He smirks. "Not at all."

The temperature has plummeted in the past week, and with only my fleece jacket, the wind is getting to me. I cross my arms in front of my chest, continuing our trek through the trees that are almost ready to be cut down to decorate warmly lit and festive living rooms.

"So what's different about her, then? Not your type?"

"No, it's not that." Images flash in my head of Halloween night, when her hair was pulled half up and the rest fell in loose curls over her shoulders, her smile so damn bright against the night sky. Who wouldn't see that girl as their type? "She's just..."

"More?"

I swallow. Is she? More?

My next breaths feel harder to take. As envious as I am of all the loving couples around me, I don't know that I'll ever truly believe in *more*. The last person I fell in love with dumped me because she didn't think I could ever be enough to make her happy and give her a good life, and that shit doesn't ever go away.

"I don't know," I answer as I tug my hat lower on my head, three words that scare the shit out of me.

Aaron jumps on this. "Does my little Finn have a crush?"

"Fuck off," I say, still stuck on the word *more*.

He laughs. "All right, I'm done."

I don't answer, my head somewhere else. I don't usually mind Aaron's intrusiveness—I'm the same with him, maybe even worse—but that's because his questions don't typically send me spiraling.

"But seriously, you know I'm always here if you need to talk, huh?" he says.

I nod. He might not be in town all the time, but he really is only a phone call away.

Aaron must notice the change in my mood, because he drops it. We continue strolling around the place that's beautiful now, but that will become magical when the snow arrives, and as much as I love catching up, spending time in silence feels just as nice.

"You've done a really great job with the place, man," Aaron says.

"Thanks." We stand in the part of the farm that's accessible for customers to cut their own trees starting in two weeks, and while it's still mostly the same as it was when Aaron was managing the farm, I've added a few elements. A photo booth for families, handmade wooden Christmas decorations made by local artisans, a sugar shack booth to grab maple taffy while tree hunting.

"So it's going well?" he asks. "The farm, I mean. Ma and Dad don't tell me much about it."

"Yeah, it is." I tell him about the first edition of the Halloween event and what I've planned for this holiday season, and Aaron's eyes widen with each new element.

"Look at you, Mr. Business Man."

I smile, my gaze on my boots. I *am* proud of what I've done with the place, but I'm not done yet. I have big plans for the farm. In fact, the idea of going back to school to get a business degree has started to run around in my mind. I wouldn't mind having schooling that'd help me make this place reach its full potential.

But just as I'm about to say the words out loud, they stay locked in my throat. I don't think I have the guts to take that step yet. The logical part of me knows that Aaron's a good person and would be supportive, but there's this other voice that tells me maybe he'd think the idea's stupid. Maybe he'd laugh as if I were joking, and that would knock me down. I don't think I could open up about it to my family either, at least not until it's done. I've shown them multiple times how shitty of a student I was. I disappeared for years to couch-surf and travel the world. I've never held a home or a stable relationship. I flunked out of classes right at the start of college. How could they believe this time's different?

"And how's life around here? Anything new?"

"It's..." I think back to the past few weekends, where I spent my time looking at the clock and wondering why the days were passing by so slowly. I've been lonely before—it's inevitable when traveling solo. But somehow, it's never felt quite like this, where I feel like I don't relate to anyone anymore. Not to my high school friends, who've either moved away to bigger cities or built lives around here. Not to my parents, who are pillars of Sonder Hill, knowing everyone by name and loving to spend time with all of them. Not to my sister, who continuously runs away from us. Not even to Aaron, who has a family of his own now. I can drive around and find stuff to do, go to the gym, visit the library, hang out in clubs, but the feeling never dulls. Not entirely, at least. "It's fine," I conclude.

And honestly, it is. I look around, taking in the place that's become my sanctuary. It's fine to live life day by day, not having anything in particular to look forward to. It's fine to spend most of your time alone. It's fine to have a life that's just *okay*. Not great, maybe, but fine.

"Hey, you okay?" Aaron asks, pulling me out of my daydream.

I shake myself, realizing how crappy I'm being. My best friend's in town for the first time in forever, and here I am, moping about all the things my life is missing.

"Yeah." A gust of wind blows a few fallen leaves through the air. "Although I'm freezing my balls off out here." I smirk. "What do you say I get you a beer and then I beat your ass at *Madden*?"

He gives me a look that's a little too inquisitive, but thankfully, the only thing he says is, "Lead the way."

Chapter 14

Lexie

I wake up feeling like an ice block, my covers up to my chin.

My teeth chatter as I get out of bed and shuffle to the heating control with my duvet in tow, but even when I turn it up a couple notches, everything remains the same. No sound of systems turning on, no gush of warm air, nothing.

I try to look around for something that might be disconnected or for a button that might have been turned off, but I'm no electrician and nothing seems amiss.

Shit.

My fingers can barely move as I get dressed, dropping a curse or two as I put on jeans over leggings, and then another two layers for a top. How did it get so cold overnight? It might be December, but there's barely been any snow yet.

Except when I look out the window, everything is covered in white. My entire body goes lax as I stare at the dreamy setting, and for a moment, I forget about the freezing air, only focusing on the awe-inducing winter wonderland outside. It's embarrassing to admit, but I've never seen snow before. The sight makes me feel like that summer when I was a kid and Arizona was plunged in the deepest drought, until one day, it started pouring and everyone cheered and stood under the rain, laughing and shouting. I just want to run outside and open my mouth to catch snowflakes with my tongue and make snow angels on the ground, feeling like a kid again. The entire forest outside my cabin looks ethereal, the tall trees capped with heavy snow, their branches bending under the weight.

The only thing that gets me to stop smiling excitedly is remembering the issue at hand. The snowstorm overnight must've been intense enough that something in the heater broke. While I'd like to say I'm an adult and can handle the issue myself, there's literally nothing I could do about it.

I quickly build a fire in the fireplace to try and warm the place a little, but when I see this won't be enough to keep me warm throughout the coming nights, I reluctantly grab my phone. I think of calling Aaron, the guy who I initially contacted to rent the cabin, but I don't think Finn would appreciate that. Plus, if I have to bother someone, I'd rather it be the guy I've come to know is a great person.

I select the number under the name Finnick Olsen—one he force-fed into my phone a few weeks ago—then press dial.

"Hello...?"

I find his tone strange, until I realize I never gave *him* my contact.

"Hi, it's Lexie. Um, Tuffin." When there's a moment of silence, I add, "The girl renting—"

"I know who you are, Crabby. What's up?" I can hear the smile in his voice.

Yeah, maybe that was stupid.

"I'm sorry to bother you, it's just that I woke up really cold, and I think something's up with the heater."

"You're not bothering. And all right, I was already on my way so I'll be there in five."

"Thanks."

"No worries. See ya soon."

We hang up, and I realize he's coming here and I just got out of bed, which means I probably look like hell. It doesn't really matter, but I still run to the bathroom to comb my hair and brush my teeth. It's the polite thing to do.

Just as I finish tying my hair in two low buns, a knock comes from the door. I rush to it.

"Hey, thanks for coming so fast."

"Lex, stop thanking me," he says with a shake of his head, and without hesitation, he steps inside. He removes his work boots on the welcome mat, then heads to the heater control.

While he's not looking, I take a moment to scan him while trying to ignore the way it felt to hear him call me *Lex*—something I don't remember anyone except Josie ever doing. He's wearing a long-sleeved thermal turtleneck that hugs his sculpted arms and his typical work jeans, roughened up but fitting him to a T.

He messes with a few buttons on the control panel, then stands before it with his hands on his hips and stares.

I step to his side. "You don't know what you're doing, do you?"

Without looking away from the control panel, he says, "Not a fucking clue."

Before I can control it, I burst out laughing, the sound so loud and clear it almost startles me.

Finn turns to me with the biggest grin on his lips. "Lucky for you, though, I have the number of someone who does know what they're doing, so just give me a minute." He points at my closet. "Pack your clothes in the meantime."

"What?"

But he doesn't have time to answer, already slipping out of the cabin, phone to his ear. "Hey, man…"

Maybe he got confused and thought I'd be going away to a motel. Sadly, I don't have enough in my bank account to afford the daily fees for a hotel, even if Finn gave me a voucher for the cabin, but if the repairman can come in the next few days, I can stay here and figure something out. Worst case, I'll sleep in my winter jacket and get up every hour to put new logs in the fireplace.

I start a pot of water on the stove and grab instant coffee from the cupboards. My drink's ready by the time Finn steps back in, the spring door smacking close behind him.

"So?"

"He'll be able to come around tomorrow to take a look."

"Great. Thank you."

He eyes me with an annoying expression, then looks over my shoulder to the unmade bed. "Where's your bag?"

"What bag?"

"The bag I asked you to pack."

"I'm staying here, it's fine. I'll just bundle up."

"Over my dead body." He chucks his chin up. "Come on, go pack something."

I pop my hip and cross my arms. "Finn, I have nowhere else to go."

"The hell you don't. You're coming with me."

Thank god I'd already swallowed my sip of coffee because I would've sputtered it all over him.

There's no way I can agree to that. Spending two hours there doing laundry is one thing, but sleeping there? Eating there? Showering there? I can't. It's way too intimate, too domestic. I wouldn't do it with a boyfriend. With someone I barely know anything about would be crazy.

"That's not necessary," I start, but Finn interrupts me with a hand up.

"You can either pack your bag and come willingly, or I'm picking you up and bringing you like I did with your laundry."

"You wouldn't dare."

He quirks a brow in response. His eyes are a dark green this morning, reminding me of a forest basked in moonlight, and while they're usually sparkling with glee, right now, they're telling me he'd actually make good on his threat.

And when I imagine him actually picking me up, his fingertips digging into the soft skin of my hips, heat creeps up my neck and my cheeks. I look down, not wanting him to notice it.

All right. It's not like I have that many options available. And if it's only one night, what's the worst that can happen? I'm not scared of Finn. If he'd have wanted to hurt me, he'd have done so already during one of the countless times I was practicing at night and he was alone in the gym with me, and regardless, he's never made me feel uncomfortable. I could say yes, go to work today, then practice until 1:00 a.m. and spend the last few hours of the night on his couch. It wouldn't be the end of the world.

Resolute, I face him and say, "Fine. Thank you."

His face lights up. "Crabby, I am so proud of you."

"Shut up before I change my mind."

He chuckles. "Well, then, let's go."

☙

I don't know what to do.

This morning, I entered Finn's apartment with him, and after dropping my bag to the ground in the living room, I escaped to the gym to coach my first group of the day. I didn't come back all day, but now it's almost 6:00 p.m. and I'm starving, but I forgot to bring something to eat. So I'm stuck having to go back to Finn's across the street, and I've just knocked twice with no answer. My car is still at Evermore where I left it, so I can't go back there to grab some food.

Shit.

I go through my options. On the one hand, he could be in there with a girl, and I might walk in on a scene I very much don't want to see. On the other hand, if I don't get something in my stomach soon, I might die. Literally.

Well, I guess I'll let hunger win.

Careful to make as much noise as I can to give him time to slip back into his pants if he was getting down to business, I push the door open and say, "Hey, it's me!"

No answer, but loud country-rock music is playing, so he might not have heard me.

Risking another step inside, I look up to find Finn alone in the kitchen, full-on dancing to a song with a foot choreography that seems too complicated to be spontaneous. Lips pinched tight to keep myself from laughing, I stand there and watch as he shakes his ass and moves around the kitchen, using a pair of tongs as a microphone.

When I can't take it any longer, I walk to the kitchen, but the music is so loud that he doesn't hear my steps.

"Hey," I say right next to his face, making him jump three feet high.

"Jesus fuck," he shouts with a hand on his heart as he goes to turn the music off. "Didn't think to announce yourself?"

"I did. You were just too busy with your one-man show to notice."

He purses his lips, then lifts one side of his lips into an annoying smirk. "Good, wasn't it?"

"I will decline to answer this."

He shakes his head, then turns toward his stove. "I was just making dinner. Want some?"

"Sure. I can help."

"Oh, that won't be necessary." He grabs a pair of oven mitts from an orderly cupboard, then opens the oven and pulls out...

"Are those dino nuggets?"

"Uh-huh."

"What are you, five years old?"

"Excuse me, I didn't know there was an age limit to enjoying these babies."

I hold it together for all of three seconds before laughing out loud. "You want me to go get you a Fun Dip while at it? Or maybe a Happy Meal?" I snicker again.

"I'm a little bit of a picky eater, okay?" Finn says.

"A little bit?"

"Fine, a lot."

"It's good you're very self-aware."

"Shut up and grab your dino nuggets," he says, and with a smile, I indulge him.

We fill our plates with literally just that—veggies are probably a no-go for him—and only once we're both seated face-to-face at his dinner table do I dig in.

God, this is good. It's been years since I've eaten one of those, always focusing on fueling with the cheapest and leanest protein while training or while prepping for the upcoming season. My mother rarely did the groceries at home, so I usually went by myself and got everything I needed. Josie was usually happy with my healthy meals, and if the rest of them weren't, I didn't care.

"See? It's good," Finn says after swallowing his mouthful of nuggets.

"I never said they weren't good, I said you were eating like a child left alone for the weekend."

"Don't people say children always speak the truth?"

"Sure," I say. "It definitely applies to that."

"Thanks for agreeing."

I snicker as I bite into another nugget.

"So now that you know what my very adult diet looks like," Finn starts, "imagine my picky ass when I was traveling to foreign countries and had to find something to eat."

"Not a big culinary adventurer?"

"Nope." He gets up to fill two glasses with water. "Didn't stop me from traveling, though. I just got used to surviving off rice and bread."

"Nutritious."

"Absolutely," he says as he hands me my glass and sits down.

"Thanks." I take a sip. "So you traveled a lot?" I'd started to figure as much when I saw his office was filled with all kinds of items that looked like they came from foreign places, just like the ones by the window in the kitchen here.

"I did, yeah. Wanted to visit every continent by age twenty-five, and I did."

Wow. I can't imagine living that kind of life. The trip I made to Italy with my team—where I first met him—was the first time I'd left the country. Other than for major competitions, I never traveled abroad.

"You were gone for a long time, then," I say.

"Seven years, on and off."

My eyes bug out of my head. Seven years away from the place he's always known? I'd never have been brave enough to do something like that.

My weight shifts back in the chair as I watch him. "Didn't you miss being home?"

"Sure, a bit, but mostly I was happy to escape this place."

"Escape," I repeat.

"Yes, escape."

He stares back for a second, our dinner forgotten.

"You haven't grown up in a small town," he says. "Everyone knows everything about everyone. It made me nuts. When I was in Bangkok or Brisbane or Helsinki, I was just a face in the crowd. It was amazing."

"So why'd you come back if you liked it so much?"

He puffs his cheeks then blows out a breath. "My friend Aaron needed my help with the farm, and it was time, I guess."

"Were you happy to be back?" I ask. I'm not sure why I'm being inquisitive—if the roles were reversed, I wouldn't want him to be—but I want to know more.

I freeze for a moment when I realize it's the truth. I do find myself wanting to know more every time we speak and collecting all the little nuggets of information in some part of my mind. I don't remember when was the last time that happened. Finding someone I didn't want to see only as a distant acquaintance at best. Someone I could know, and who maybe could know me.

"Yeah," Finn says, bringing me out of my thoughts. "I mean, I started traveling because I felt empty, but after a few years, I realized being in another country didn't make me feel any fuller."

I blink as I replay his words. This man has just said one of the most vulnerable sentences I have ever heard, over dino nuggets, not holding anything back. I'm so blown away I need a minute to find the appropriate words. I wish I could be more like him, open and trusting.

"I think we all feel a little empty sometimes," I say, allowing as much honesty in my voice as I can. "But I do hope you'll find what fills the void for you."

"Me too," he says with a smile that's so different from the cocky, humorous one he wears on a daily basis. This one is soft, almost shy, and it makes my throat feel tight. I like this one best.

Except I have no place thinking about how much I like his different smiles.

I clear my throat, then stand and take my empty plate to the dishwasher, once again finding it neatly organized. "Well, thanks for dinner, but I have to get back to it if I want to make sure my next competition isn't another shitshow."

"Sure," he says. "But you'll be back to sleep, right?"

"Yes, I will." For four hours, maybe, but that still counts.

"All right. I'll leave you the bed and take the couch."

"No please," I say. "Keep the bed."

He smirks. "So you want to share?"

"Aaaaand the creep is back!"

With a chuckle, he says, "I'm kidding. But I'm not budging on the bed."

"Me neither. I'll be back late anyway. I'll wake you if you're in the living room."

I know I've made a good point when he keeps a straight face and says, "You're the worst, you know that?"

"Same goes to you, Finny."

Chapter 15

Finn

"You're really secretive."

Lexie lifts her forehead from where it was anchored on her knee. "Huh?"

She's currently in a position I call the "extra-splits." On a yoga mat, her front foot is propped onto a foam block, which means she's doing more than the regular splits. She came back a half hour ago from her practice session and has been stretching in my living room since, her round ass in full display in those tiny shorts. I've tried to busy myself in the apartment, I swear, but short of locking myself in my room and ignoring her, I can't stop staring. It's pathetic. So the only thing I found to do was distract myself by making her talk.

"You are," I say from my spot at the kitchen table, an ignored newspaper app open in front of me. "It practically feels like my roomie is a complete stranger."

"We're not roomies," she says as she switches sides in her splits, not even getting back up and down again, but simply twisting her torso so she faces the opposite leg and it's her back one that's propped up now.

Goddammit. *Get a grip.*

"Are we not sharing an apartment?" I say.

"Temporarily."

She's officially been living here for four days now. The day after her heater broke, my electrician contact did go see what was up, but he told me the problem wasn't electric, it was with the heater itself, so I had to wait another day to get a heater repairman there. Then, that guy said the problem was a broken piece, and he'd need to order a new one, so it would be another couple of days at best.

Surprisingly, Lexie didn't make a big deal out of it, not even when I made it clear that if she didn't want the bed full time, then I wouldn't agree to anything less than fifty-fifty. She grumbled a little—that wasn't surprising—but when she looked back at the couch, which I bought on sale when I moved in here and know for a fact is pretty damn uncomfortable, she agreed. I then told her where the clean sheets were, thinking she'd want to switch them between us, but the only thing she said was, "Has there been someone other than you in them recently?" The meaning of the question was clear as day. I shook my head, not lying, and that was that. And I'll be honest, it felt good that she didn't doubt me.

I didn't mind that she had to stay either. Having her crabby self here, even for a few moments every day, has given me a boost I didn't know I needed. I've had a few guys who work on the farm ask me what was up my ass because I was singing to a Christmas carol while finalizing the outdoor arrangements of the self-serve part of the farm. I don't know when it became a crime to sing out loud in public, but that's beside the point.

Of course, the one downside is that I have to smell her shampoo on my pillow when I wake up, and I have to see her in clothes that make it pretty fucking hard not to get a constant boner, but other than that, everything's sweet.

"We're still roomies," I say, propping my feet on the chair in front of me. "And it seems weird to not know anything about the person sleeping in the room next to mine. You could be an ax murderer for all I know."

"And you think I would've told you if I was?"

"Maybe?"

She snickers before dipping her face once again onto her forward-facing knee. "You do know stuff about me," she says, the sound muffled by her skin.

"Like what?"

"Like more than most people do."

I can't help but feel a glimmer of pride at that. I was serious—I *don't* know that much about her—but if it's more than most, it has to be a good thing.

"I still need more."

She straightens. "Curious, are we?"

"Very."

A pause, then her lips curl into the most devilish smirk I've ever seen.

"You know, I might have a deal for you," she purrs.

It sounds like bad news.

I grin. "Tell me."

～ eℓe ～

"Fuck no."

She bats her lashes before pushing the plate closer to me.

"I'm not eating that," I say.

"But I thought you wanted to get to know me."

"Lexie."

 She slowly twists the plate clockwise. "I guess you're not as curious about me as I thought, then."

My jaw is clenched as I look down the table, once again fighting a painful gag.

Lexie's amazing idea consisted of going to find all the possible foods that would make a picky eater like me die, and for each bite, I get to ask whatever question I want. She asked me to close my eyes as she prepared the plate, and once it was brought out, she started enumerating what everything in it was. I had to stop her midway because I felt like dying.

"You truly can find all sorts of uncommon stuff at the grocery store."

Hand on my mouth, I steal another glance down. "I can't."

She shrugs. "All righty, then. No information for you." In one swift move, she gets up from her chair and leans forward to grab the plate.

"No, wait."

Her eyes light up. The brat knows what she's doing, and damn me, it's working. Too well, if I'm being honest.

"But if we do this," I say, "I can ask anything."

Her nostrils flare, only once. "To the limits of reasonableness, yeah, I guess."

"Fine."

God, I can't believe I'm even considering eating this. Pork testicles. Chicken liver. Cricket-protein muffin. A funny-smelling yellowish smoothie that makes me want to puke just looking at it.

At the speed of a snail, I crumble part of the muffin so I can pick the tiniest bit in my fingers. Keeping it far away from my face, I dig through my brain to find what I want to ask. It has to be worth it.

Finally, I land on, "Why did you really come to Vermont?"

Her smile dims, eyes dulling, but after a while, she nods, then points at the muffin.

Fuck my life.

Without giving myself the time to think it through, I push it into my mouth and swallow without chewing. It tastes like a regular muffin, I think, but just imagining what's in it gives me a whole-body shudder.

It takes all of one second before Lexie bursts out laughing. "Oh my god, I never thought you'd actually do it. Good job, Finland. I'm proud of you."

"Answer, heathen."

"All right, all right." She leans on her elbows, bringing her hair dangerously close to the pork testicles. I don't know how she does it.

"A bit more than a year ago," she starts, "I had an accident at the gym. Injured myself pretty bad. Needed treatment, yada yada." She rotates the plate again. "And then I tried to get back to where I was, but it wasn't working. I was scared, and I kept choking on my movements, so my coach decided I was too old and uncoachable and kind of fired me. I didn't want to let go of my dream so fast, so I looked for another opportunity and found your mom's offer." She scratches her hand. "And if I'm being completely honest, I was also happy for the excuse to leave home." She smiles, but this time, it's a little sad. "You're not the only one who's dreamed of escaping, you know."

I nod. "Thank you."

She inhales deeply, then claps her hands. "Okay. Number two." I nod, then take a moment to think about my second precious question—I won't be able to ask ten of these with the stakes here. Once I'm sure I got a good one, I pick up my fork. Steeling myself with a breath, I stab it into the tiny liver, then close my eyes, take the tiniest bite and swallow it whole once again. I choke on my acid reflux, but still, I do it.

Don't think about what's in your mouth, Finn. Don't you dare do it.

"I'm honestly so impressed," she says. The little shit thought I wouldn't do it.

"Why are you single?" I ask.

Her face pulls into a deep frown. "Why are *you* single?"

"Did you eat a liver? No, so suck it, and answer the question."

She laughs. "It's just such a random one. I'm not sure why you'd think I *wouldn't* be single, actually."

"Don't go fishing for compliments, Lexie Lou."

"I'm not, I swear," she says with her hands up in defense. "I'm genuinely confused."

"Come on," I say, giving her a look that says *stop fucking with me.* "You're beautiful, you're funny, you're smart. It doesn't make sense that you wouldn't have someone."

Her cheeks turn a deep shade of pink, just like they do every time I say something that is even remotely close to a compliment. I like seeing the color on her. I like it even more when I put it there.

Leaning back in her chair like she's putting herself at ease, she says, "I've never had time for it—or I guess I never *made* time for it. I've spent my life practicing and hustling and no one ever seemed worth what precious time I had for myself." She takes a long sip of water, as if she was the one who'd just eaten part of a liver. "Plus, men suck, and as you've so nicely pointed out, I can be very crabby."

"Facts."

"Shut up," she says before throwing a piece of bug muffin my way. I duck just in time, thank god.

"All right, thanks for answering."

In a piss-poor imitation of me, she says, "Stop thanking me."

I laugh, then open my mouth to ask something else, but she says, "Actually, I want to ask you something. What—"

My brows climb on my forehead. "Uh-uh. You know the rules."

She gives me the harshest stare before saying, "Give me the damn testicle."

"Talk dirty to me, baby," I say as I push the plate her way with the tip of my index finger.

"Oh my god. You're honestly one of the most fucked-up people I know."

"Is that supposed to be a compliment?"

"No." She lifts a shoulder. "But I like it."

I think I might like it too.

Clearly not as afraid as me, she picks up the testicle and takes a bite that's big enough to make me gag just at the sight. She even dares to chew.

"I think you're my new hero," I say.

She nods, but suddenly her chewing slows, as if she's finally realized what she's eating. With her eyes shut, she forces a swallow.

When she opens her eyes, she clears her throat and pulls her shoulders back. "Well, now that that's out of the way." With her hands crossed in front of her like a stiff judge, she asks, "Were you promiscuous as a young adult?"

The sip of water I just took sputters out of my mouth. "What?"

"First of all, that was disgusting." She wipes a drop of water from her arm. "And second, answer the question."

"Where is this coming from?" I ask, already feeling the tips of my ears heating.

"Something Lilianne said that stuck to me."

I'm going to kill my friend. "Which was?"

"Something about not wanting to be 'one of your girls.'"

Jesus Christ.

"I ate the testicle. 'Fess up. Were you a slut?"

My only answer is to laugh, although I have the decency to be a little sheepish about it.

"God, I knew it! You *were* a slut!"

"I had my fun, okay?"

"Had?"

"Yes, had." I drag a hand over my head. Why the fuck did I agree to play this stupid game? "Apparently, spending every night with a different girl doesn't fill the emptiness any more than traveling does." I'm not going to pretend like I've been a saint since I came back to Sonder Hill, but the interest isn't as present anymore. I want something real, or I want nothing at all.

Lexie simply hums before she pushes the plate back my way. "Or are you done?"

My gaze lifts to hers, earth-colored eyes open, earnest.

"I have one more," I say.

"Go right ahead, then." She leans forward and whispers, "Want me to tell you what's in the smoothie?"

"Nope." I don't give myself time to think about it—I really want the answer to that question—so I close my eyes and take a sip.

I definitely vomit a little in my mouth.

Lexie laughs. "I can't believe you just drank that. It's full of—"

"Don't." I wipe my mouth with the back of my hand and gulp the rest of my water. "That's probably as close to death as I'll ever get until the real thing."

"You deserve your question."

Yeah, I hope so.

I can tell she won't like it and might refuse to answer, but I still risk it.

"Why do you always flinch when I touch you?"

Her entire face drains of blood. On the table, one of her hands balls into a fist while the other starts scratching the excoriated skin on her opposite wrist. I don't think she even notices it. Surely, if she did, she'd try to mask it. That's how unnerved I made her.

I hate that I'm triggering this kind of reaction, but I also think I need to know this. If I'm doing something wrong, I won't be able to stop until she tells me what it is.

Her throat bobs once, twice. Then, she looks up and says, "It's not just you. It's everyone."

Something coils in my stomach.

"What happened?" I croak.

She doesn't answer right away, and when she does, what she says is, "It's not a funny story."

"I didn't ask for funny. I asked for the truth."

Her eyes flutter shut as she seems to steel herself for something, and that only makes the ache in my stomach grow.

Finally, eyes still closed, she begins.

"Something... happened to me when I was younger. I can't tell you what or when exactly, because I'm not sure myself. But I remember being a normal kid before, and then my mom started dating this guy who moved in with us and..." Her words stop as her jaw moves back and forth. Meanwhile, I feel so fucking heavy. I want to tell her to stop, that she doesn't have to tell me after all, but I have this unhealthy craving for the truth.

When her eyes open, they're blurry. She blinks and looks to the ceiling as she forces the emptiest smile I've ever seen. "I don't know what he did to me. I don't remember. The only thing I do remember is one day waking up and hating the feeling of being touched, especially when I don't expect it. Flashes come to me sometimes, but that's it." She clears her throat. "Some therapist in school told me I might have repressed some painful memories and that's why I don't remember, but I've never worked on getting them back. I'm fine not remembering, you know?"

No, I don't know. I can't imagine a word of what she's saying because that's something no one should ever have to visualize, let alone experience.

And suddenly, I feel like breaking something. Throw the forgotten plate against the wall and hear the porcelain shatter. Smash the chair I'm sitting on into the wall and watch the plaster fall off piece by piece. Kill a certain man I don't even know.

But I won't do any of that because what I'm feeling doesn't matter here.

"I'm so sorry," I tell her, the words too simple but also the only ones I can find.

She shrugs, then puffs out a breath. "So, anyway, that's why I'm not a fan of touchy jump scares."

Mouth dry and smile tight and plastic-like, I tell her, "Noted."

And then, as if saved by the bell, a phone rings. Hers.

"Sorry," she says, then gets up and goes to answer it in the living room. I watch her as she answers the call, the dimple in her chin shifting with each word, a toned arm stretching behind her neck. She might look small and sweet, but she's one of the strongest people I know, hands down. Every new thing she tells me about her reinforces that belief. Even through everything, she continues to choose to move forward, and that requires a strength of its own. She didn't let what happened to her crush her down. She decided to take life by the balls and make it her bitch.

Right this moment, I promise myself that what she's just told me won't change a thing about the way I see her. She didn't want my pity, she wanted to gift me with her trust, and that, I know, is one of the hardest things to do. I won't waste it.

"Okay, see you soon," I hear from the living room, and then she's walking back toward me. I paste on a smile, ready to take her mind off things and bring back the lightheartedness from before, but when I see her wide eyes and tight mouth, I know that's not happening.

"What? What's wrong?" I ask, already up on my feet.

"That was my little sister." She looks down at the phone as she says, "I have to go back home."

Chapter 16

Lexie

"Are you sure this is a good idea?"

I don't look up from my weekender bag, which I'm filling with whatever clothes I can put my hands on. To be honest, I haven't taken the time to think this through. My hands shake as I push a SHGC sweatshirt into the bag.

"I don't have a choice, Finn," I say. It doesn't matter that I want to go home as much as I want to get back-to-back root canals. Josie needs me, so that's that.

"I don't like this," he mutters, standing stiff as a rod next to the couch where all my clothes are spread out. I haven't even checked whether there's any red-eye available for tonight. I'll just show up at the airport and hope for the best. Chaotic strategy? Sure, but I don't have the brainpower to think further than this.

"Why?" I ask, flicking my eyes from the pairs of socks in my hands, finding a long crease between Finn's eyebrows.

"Have you seen your face since that phone call?"

"I'll try not to be insulted."

He rolls his eyes. "You look scared, Lex."

Something moves through me at that damn nickname, and it needs to stop. I can't have that sort of feeling happening right now.

Not after I randomly decided to open up to him about my biggest trauma and somehow didn't feel horrible afterward.

I don't know what made me tell him the truth. I always told myself this would be a secret I'd take with me to the grave. Sure, my mother knows, and I think Josie might have guessed some of it, but it's never been something I wanted to broadcast. I don't want people to see me as less than because some fucker put his hands on me. It doesn't define me, even though it does have repercussions, even years later. But when Finn asked, I didn't consider lying. It was natural, even, to tell the truth. I ask, he answers. He asks, I answer. This type of relationship has always been mysterious to me, yet here I am, spilling my secrets because, for some reason I can't pinpoint, I trust this man. And while I'd have thought sharing my darkest truths would've made me more vulnerable, it hasn't. I even feel better now that he knows. I don't know if I'll ever be able to comprehend it.

And once again, he proves how well he can read me by saying what he just did.

When I don't answer right away, Finn steps forward and takes the balled-up jeans from my hands, dropping them softly to the couch. "What's back there that you don't want to see?"

My mouth twitches. In a low voice, I say, "Everything?"

"What does that mean, exactly?"

I meet his eyes, but after a moment, I need to look down and get back to my packing. It's almost intolerable to be stared at by him. It's like he can read into every crook and crevice of me, see all the ugly parts I'd rather keep hidden, and drag them out of the shadows.

"My mom's not winning any mother-of-the-year award anytime soon," I say, which is a true euphemism. "And I have an older brother... Well, half-brother, and he's the worst mother-effer you could imagine." I don't know what other words I could use to describe Kyle. At thirty-one years old, he still hasn't figured out how to live without begging my mother for money. "No job, crappy friends, thinks he's the king of the world," I add.

A sound comes out of Finn's throat—a groan or a sigh, I'm not sure.

I walk toward Finn's bathroom to pick up my toothbrush and toothpaste, ignoring how strangely domestic it looks to have our two toothbrushes side by side, my hair ties next to his deodorant, his contact lenses container pushed on top of a T-shirt I forgot to pick up after my shower this morning. Once I've packed all my stuff, I get back to the living room, where Finn is still waiting, on his feet, with arms crossed.

"And then there's also my mother's new boyfriend," I add, hating the way the words taste in my mouth, "who's apparently kind of a—"

"Fuck, Lexie," Finn interrupts as he rubs a hand over his head, the hair longer than it was a month ago. He'll probably need to go buzz it soon. "Why the fuck would you go there?"

I drop my toiletries in my bag, then turn to face him. "Because my little sister is there and was just crying over the phone because that fucker has been mean to her and she'll need to spend the holidays with him and the rest of my crappy family." I shake my head, fighting the lump building in my throat. "I don't have a choice, Finn. If someone's going to aim at her, then I'll let her use me as a shield every single time."

A muscle ticks in his cheek. "I should go with you."

Laughter spills out of me before I can contain it. When I see his expression hasn't changed, I say, "You're joking, right?"

"Not one bit." His frown deepens. "I would go if I could, but it's the farm's biggest season, and I can't—" He drags a hand over his mouth. "Fuck, I couldn't do that to them."

I pause my packing. "Finn, it's okay. I'm a big girl. I wasn't able to defend myself before, but I can now."

My words don't seem to reassure him, but I have too much to do in too little time to spend more thoughts on this. I turn back to my luggage, going over a mental list, then say, "Leotards. I need leotards." I run to the washing machine and grab two that are still damp, then push them into my bag.

"Why do you need those?"

"Competition season's coming fast. I can't afford to miss two weeks."

"So what are you gonna do?"

"Not sure yet. Maybe beg Andy—my old coach—for some gym time. Worst case, I'll go outside, run through my routines and work on cardio and conditioning." It wouldn't be ideal, but if push comes to shove, it'll be the best I can do.

I look down at my watch. With all that messing around, it's almost 9:00 p.m. I need to get to the airport ASAP if I want to have the best chance at finding a last-minute flight.

"Okay, I think I'm good," I say, then hook my bag onto my shoulder and turn to him.

I don't think he's moved an inch in the past twenty minutes.

"When I come back," I add, "the heater will probably be repaired, so I guess this is goodbye, *roomie*." My lips turn into a smile, although there's something heavy in the air that prevents me from actually finding this funny. I'm going to miss this, I realize. We haven't shared the space for long, but it still eased the deep sense of loneliness I've felt ever since coming here. Maybe even before then.

Voice low, Finn says, "You have my number, right?"
I nod.

"I want you to call me every day."

"Afraid you'll miss me too much?"
"Something like that, yeah."

He still doesn't move, but for a moment, I have the sense he's going to lean forward and hug me. And not some soft one either, but a big bear hug, fingers digging into clothing and face pressed into the crook of my neck.

I have never particularly appreciated hugs. In my experience, they usually come from people I'd rather stay far, far away. Drunk men in clubs, high school acquaintances I did not keep in touch with for a reason, family members that have never been present for me, people who say they missed me but mean the opposite. And yet, I think I wouldn't mind this one, especially after what he's just said. Because even though he hasn't uttered the word, I'm pretty sure it means he cares.

Only a small lamp is alight in the living room, accentuating every curve of his face, the slight downturn of his lips and the sharpness of his jaw. He really is good-looking. Too much, almost.

Jesus, what is happening to me?

Even when I move toward the door, he stays still. Like he's not ready yet.

"It'll be fine, Finn." I don't say *I* will be fine, because the likelihood of that is pretty slim, but I don't think he'll notice that.

His eyes lock with mine once more, the forest green almost midnight in the dimness of the room.

Finally, he exhales and says, "All right, then. Get in the truck before I change my mind and lock you in here."

"Oh, no, you don't have to. The airport's hours away."

"I don't care."

"Finn, I won't—"

"Don't finish that sentence or I swear I'll lose it. Let me *at least* do this one thing for you. Okay?"

A fist wraps around my heart, twisting it in a thousand directions. It's painful, and fuzzy, and overwhelmingly thrilling.

"Let's go, then."

Chapter 17

Lexie

"What's up with you?" Josie asks from where she's lying prone on my old pink bedspread. Most of the stuff in this room was inherited from me at one point or another. Dark hair spills onto the pillows from her long ponytail. We've been told a few times growing up how much we look alike. Personally, I don't see it. She's much prettier than I am. Her brown eyes are soft and warm, her face heart-shaped and sweet. She looks as nice as she is.

"Nothing," I say, picking popcorn from the bowl sitting in my lap and dropping it in my mouth. The first thing I did after getting out of the airport yesterday was go to the grocery store for a haul. I didn't need to see the empty cupboard and fridge to know how they likely looked. The way she's been eating anything and everything since makes me certain I made the right decision. "Why?"

"You've been staring out that window for five minutes."

As she says it, I steal yet another glance outside. We're two days to Christmas, and yet there's nothing that would indicate this when looking outside. The grass is rock-dry as if we were still mid-July, with neighbors playing outside with water hoses and torn-down bicycles.

It's a view I'm used to. Except for the rare occasions when rain or even a few snowflakes came down over the winter, this is what I've grown up with. And yet, as I look at the bright sunshine and at people sitting out on patio sets, smoking cigarettes in mini skirts and sleeveless shirts, I feel a deep sense of longing for Vermont, and more specifically for Sonder Hill. I don't know why I'd miss a place I was in for less than three months after only being gone for a week, but I do. I miss going outside and being hit with the fresh scent of pine trees and earth, and seeing snow drift over the trees and thicken the air, creating an almost soundproof space around my head. I miss running for miles through forest without meeting a single other soul. More than that, I miss the girls I'm used to teaching multiple days per week. I miss being able to practice as much and as long as I want in an empty gym. I miss living in a town where I'm not the daughter of Cynthia Tuffin. And, as crazy as it would've sounded a few months back, I think I miss Finn most of all.

This morning, as I waited to cool down from my heatstroke-inducing run, I scrolled through my Instagram notifications. I'd added a photo the day before of me throwing a front aerial on the balance beam, one I was proud of having taken by myself, using a makeshift tripod, and a comment caught my eye. I don't usually go through the comments section—I've learned my lesson—but this time, I did, solely because Finn's name was in there.

@bigboyy66: Do you think anyone thinks your hot? Loose the shoulders and than well talk

@FinnTheGreat: @bigboyyy66 If I were you, I'd spend less time online and more time learning how to spell. Now kindly fuck off.

If I were a better person, maybe I'd have felt bad that the guy had gotten severely humiliated on a public platform, but I'm not. Instead, I laughed out loud and liked Finn's comment. I still can't believe he did that. I can't even find it in me to be embarrassed that he saw all the crappy comments people have left on all my posts. The fact that he thought it was necessary to defend me... It makes me feel warmer than the Arizonan heat.

"Josie!" a male voice shouts from the other side of the hallway. My mother's mobile home is far from large, and the walls are paper-thin, so even if he's not in the room with us, we can hear Kyle as if he were shouting straight into our ears. "Turn that shitty music down, or I swear I'll come do it myself!"

In one swift move, Josie's on her feet and turning Harry Styles's voice off from her portable speaker.

"Jos, leave it," I say.

"No, it's fine."

"It's not fine. It wasn't even loud."

"Doesn't matter," she says, hiding her gaze behind her bangs. I feel like getting up to pull her hair back and tilt her chin up. "I don't want to make him mad."

"Why?" All the muscles in my body have contracted, and I'm still as a statue as I wait. When she doesn't answer, I get up from the windowsill I was sitting on and join her across the room. "Josie, why?"

She drops back down onto the bed. "You don't know what it's like when he's here. Everyone's fighting all the time. I just do whatever I can to keep away from trouble, that's it."

I breathe out. I don't remind her that I've lived with him for far longer than I would've wanted to, even though he'd been away from home for a few months before I left. I do remember what it was like to live with him. I guess the difference is I didn't mind stirring shit up if I thought he was acting like a dick, but Josie's much younger than him and a much sweeter person than I am.

"Have you told Mom?" I ask.

"She can't do anything about it," Josie answers as she opens one of my old *Seventeen* magazines, telling readers what type of highlights they should get and how to score as many dates as possible in high school.

I open my mouth to say she's wrong, but deep down, I don't think she is, or at least not completely. Mom *could* do something about it. She could tell Kyle to shove it if he doesn't want to be nice to her daughter. She could kick him out. She could decide to finally take a stand. But she never will, because I don't think she even realizes what could possibly benefit her daughter.

Josie's still browsing the magazine, not even looking up when I approach her spot on the bed. I guess she's done talking about this.

"I'm going to go grab a drink. Want anything?" I ask.

"I'm good," she says. Her sock-clad feet are crossed in the air as she flips through. It hasn't been that long since I left Arizona, and yet it feels like she's grown so much in the short period I was gone.

I'm not sure if the change is physical or emotional, but I feel like my little sister is not so little anymore.

I drop a kiss to her head, then leave the room and walk straight outside the house, where I find my mother sitting on a plastic chair, smoking a cigarette while scrolling through her phone. I grab a seat next to hers, making her glance up.

We've barely talked since I got here. I don't think she even knew I was coming for the holidays. When she opened the door and found me standing on the front porch with my small duffel bag and hands full of groceries, she only said, "What are you doing here?" I explained Josie had invited me, and that was that. No *I'm happy to see you* or *I missed you* or *How has it been going?* She just opened the door for me and went to grab a beer in the kitchen, her yellow hair hanging limply down her back.

Today, she's wearing a Corona tank top and tiny jean shorts, her nails chipped as she pulls the cigarette away from her lips and blows smoke out.

"Hey," I say.

"Hey."

I chew on my bottom lip, wondering how to go about this, then say, "I was wondering what you were planning on doing with Kyle."

"Jesus Christ, Lexie, can't you give me a fucking break?"

I grind my teeth. *Calm. Stay calm.* "Mom, I—"

"No, I think it's time *you* listen." She takes a drag of her cigarette. "You're real fucking selfish, you know that?" Clumps of mascara hang from her lashes as she blinks. "You left here like you were so much better than this life, then you come back and try to take control of the place."

"That's not what I'm trying to do. I just want—"

"I gave you everything you could possibly want," she spits, a finger pointed in my direction, "and you still want more. You're never happy."

Pressure builds behind my eyes, in my throat, in my chest. She gave me everything except love and security. The two things I wish Josie could have.

"Look, I don't want to fight," I say. "I just know Kyle hasn't been nice with Josie and—"

"If *Josie* has a problem, then she can tell me. As for Kyle, he's found a job, and he's bringing money in. We're all doing good here. I don't need you to tell me how to live, okay?" She shakes her head and looks away. Her cheeks cave around her cigarette. "I don't even know why you're here. If you're too good for us, you should've stayed wherever it is you live now. We'd all have been better off."

Don't break. It's nothing you haven't heard one way or another before.

"I came for Josie," I say. "Because she wanted me here, and despite what you think, I do care about this family." I stand on wobbly legs. "And I don't think I'm better than you are. I just want her to be happy."

"'s there a problem here?"

I look up to find Jim—Mom's new boyfriend—stepping toward us. He's wearing a stained white T-shirt and dark jeans, a blond mustache curling over his upper lip. I met him yesterday, and while he won't win stepdad-of-the-year anytime soon, he doesn't seem dangerous, although you can never really know with that kind of thing.

"We're good," I say.

"Cyn?" he asks. I fight an eye roll. The man has been dating my mother for all of ten weeks, but apparently, he should be protecting her from her own daughter.

"We're good, Jim," I repeat.

He chucks his chin at me. "You causing trouble again?"

Oh, Jesus. And what does that *again* mean? I wasn't even here for months.

As I look at the two of them, a heavy, dreadful fatigue hits me. I don't think I even have it in me to fight anymore. It won't change anything. Without another word, I turn back toward the house.

"We're lettin' you live here, but we don't have to," Jim says behind me. "Remember that."

For Josie. You're doing this for Josie.

I reach the spring door, then run to the bathroom and lock myself in. I don't know how I'm going to survive another week like this.

I force myself to take deep breaths. It doesn't matter that my own mother doesn't want me here or that my family seems straight out of a drama series. I'm happy. I'm safe. I'm going back to training soon. Competition season's starting.

I'll be okay.

Once I feel calm enough, I reach for the door, but something pulls at my attention. My phone's vibrating. I pick it from my pocket and see Finn's name on the screen with an incoming call.

Shit. I can't talk to him now. I still feel like my throat's about to close up. He'll hear in my voice that something's wrong. Somehow I know he will. I wait until the call goes to voicemail.

Not even thirty seconds later, a text message comes in.

Finn: You said you'd call every day.

Me: I'm okay, just not in the mood to talk.

Of course, he doesn't leave it at that.

Finn: What's wrong?

I answer honestly.

Me: Everything?

Finn: Please answer my call?

Me: I'm okay, I swear. Just in a crappy mood.

Finn: I could make you smile if you answer. Bet

Finn: What about if I ate something really disgusting while on the phone and you heard me gag? Isn't that your favorite thing on earth?

I smile. He doesn't need to call me to succeed.

Me: I know you could. Later?

Finn: Fine.

Finn: I don't like it.

Finn: But fine.

Finn: Call me whenever. I mean it, Crabby.

Me: I know you do. x

Chapter 18

Lexie

I'm woken up by a sharp sound.

I jump up in bed, hair matted to my cheek and heart hammering out of my chest as I wait to hear whatever startled me up again.

And there it is. Another rap at the door.

I unplug my phone from the wall and see it's barely 6:30 a.m. I don't think my mother has ever been awake at that hour, so she couldn't have invited someone over this early in the morning.

The house remains quiet, as if no one has heard it yet. Kyle would probably have thrown a fit if the sound had ruptured his precious sleep. Not wanting to deal with that kind of crisis anytime soon, I jump from bed, throw a hoodie on to cover my tank top and sleeping shorts, then rush to the door.

Another knock.

"Yes, I'm coming," I whisper-shout, as if the person on the other side of the door could hear me. The house is still dark, only illuminated by the sliver of sun that has started to rise, creating a honey-colored glow over the television and leatherette sofa.

When I reach the door, I pause. I haven't lived here for a while. What if the person on the other side isn't here for friendly reasons?

I don't think my mother has gotten into anything shady, but what about Kyle? Or Jim?

I rub at my eyes with the meat of my palms. Better me than Josie, I guess.

Steeling myself for the worst, I open the door.

And freeze.

It takes me a long moment to process what I'm seeing, as if I need to go through all the details to make up the whole. The muddy black sneakers. The tall build and wide shoulders. The dark five o'clock shadow on the strong jaw. The most dazzling green eyes.

"Hey," Finn says with a corner smile, as if we've just crossed paths outside of my cabin while I was leaving for work and he was coming in.

I blink. I'm probably still dreaming. I must be, because why would Finn Olsen be standing here, in front of my childhood home, on the other side of the country, smiling like he was supposed to be here all along?

"Is this your crabby way of saying hello?" Finn asks, adjusting the strap of his backpack on his shoulder.

"I..." I rub at my face once more, thinking maybe the image will change if I wake myself enough. It doesn't. "What are you doing here?"

"I'll try to act as if this is not the shittiest welcome I've ever received."

"Finn," I say. I can't even think of proper words. This can't be happening.

His smile dims as he says, "I didn't like the thought of you having a rough time here, and I figured you could use a friendly face around."

Instantaneously, my eyes fill with water. I'm not a big crier. I learned from a young age that showing my pain wouldn't get me anywhere. If I landed badly on my ankle after a dismount and cried, I'd still be hurting. The only thing different would be the way my coaches looked at me. If I cried at my mother because Kyle had stolen my coaching money from under my mattress, it still wouldn't get me my hours back. It would probably only make things worse in the house.

And yet here I am, tearing up because this might be the first time someone has thought of me this way. With so much care.

In a thick voice, I say, "W-what about the farm?" It really doesn't matter at the moment, but it's as if my brain needs to focus on the logistics if I don't want to break down.

"I gave as many hours as I could over the week, and I asked Aaron and Lil to do me a favor and cover for me today and tomorrow. I'll be back after that."

I squeeze my hands tight at my sides, trying but failing to control myself.

"You're really here?"

His grin is butter-soft. "I'm really here."

I don't know what takes over me, but one second I'm standing in front of him, his body towering over me, and the next I'm in his arms, my fingertips clinging at his gray T-shirt, so tightly I think for a moment I might tear it.

His own arms slowly come down over me, then wrap me up with a gentleness I think might cause me to tear up again. He holds me as if I'm breakable, and yet it's probably the most comforting touch I've ever felt. I'm surrounded by the smell of moss and clean detergent, by the softness of his shirt and the warmth of his body around mine. For a moment, it's enough to make me forget where we are. We're alone in the world. In the entire universe.

His nose tickles my neck as he says, "Are you wearing my hoodie?"

I don't need to look down to realize that yes, the shirt I picked up in my bedroom was indeed Finn's. "Shut up. It landed in my laundry by mistake." I'm not even lying, but what I'm not saying is that when I found it in my things, I was happy to put it on, engulfed in the stretched, over-washed fabric.

He snickers, sending soft puffs of air against my skin that make me shiver. "That's what they all say."

When he pulls away, I sniffle and look away, knowing my early morning face is probably not something Finn should be seeing.

"Well, this weather's much better than in Vermont," Finn says as he looks behind his shoulder. We're still on the broken-down front porch, and while the sun isn't fully up yet, the air probably feels like summer to Finn.

"I'm not sure I agree," I say, finally looking up. Whatever, at this point. He's already seen me looking all kinds of fucked up. "What—"

"Lexie, shut the fuck up!"

I jump at the sound, immediately recognizing Kyle's needle-scratch voice. I grind my teeth. That guy will force me to go to jail at some point.

If this were any other time, I'd go to his room and rip him a new one for talking to me that way, but not today. Not in this moment that feels so precious, so fickle. I'm not letting that asshole ruin it.

From the corner of my eye, I spot movement.

"Don't," I say as I grab Finn's forearm, stopping him from going further in. "Let's just go."

"That your brother?" he says, his face redder than it was a second ago.

I don't answer his question. Instead, I pull him back toward the porch and say, "Come on. Let me buy you breakfast."

"No way."

"I swear! This guy just came in with an actual pet llama and didn't understand why I was staring at him. Said something like, *'There a problem?'* Um, yes, sir, I'm not sure llamas are appropriate animals to bring to a Christmas tree farm. Jesus."

My stomach hurts from how much I've been laughing. Finn's on fire this morning, and after the past few days, it feels amazing to be able to relieve the bomb-like pressure I was feeling and just have fun.

"But how could he have known?" I say.

"Yeah, I guess it was a valid assumption." Finn bites into a tater tot and releases a moan. My lips twitch at the sound, which I feel all over my body.

Get a grip, Lexie.

I pop a grape into my mouth, trying not to look too envious of Finn's plate of greasy goodness as I eat the only healthy thing I could find on the menu. I wish I could enjoy a breakfast like his, but with the competition season around the corner, I can't afford to let myself go. It's bad enough that I don't have a regular training schedule right now. If Andy could see me, he'd shake his head and pat himself on the back for dropping me. At least, with it being the holidays, my old gym was almost empty, and an old teammate of mine did me a solid and let me in when no one was around so I could use the equipment for a few hours. Maybe she took pity on me, being coach-less and all, but I took whatever I could get. While training in the place that holds so many bad memories wasn't ideal, it was better than nothing. Still, I missed Sonder Hill's gym more than I could explain.

I look up from my plate. Even though Finn acts energetic and in a good mood this morning, the dark circles under his eyes tell me a different story.

"When did you decide to come here?" I ask him.

His chewing slows, then he swallows. "I didn't like those texts, Lex."

My brows crease. "So, what, you packed up and left overnight?"

He shrugs, then returns to dipping his toast into his egg yolk as if making that decision was the most unremarkable thing in the world.

"You shouldn't have." When he freezes, I realize how that sounded and add, "I mean, I'm really, really glad you did, but I feel bad. What about your family?"

"They're fine. Christmas is probably going to be tense with Francesca anyway, so I'm not missing much."

"Your sister?"

He nods. "She's... It's not always easy with her, and I have a feeling the holidays are not going to be any exception."

"I'm sorry," I say.

"All good." He smiles, then drops his sunglasses from his head to his eyes. They hang from his nose, but he still gives me a goofy grin and says, "Pretty happy to be enjoying that sunshine anyway."

I laugh. "That why you came?"

"Sole reason." Finn bends to engulf two pieces of bacon at once—the man acts as if he hasn't eaten in four days—and as he does, I spot on his scalp a patch where the hair's almost gone.

"Why are you staring? Want some?" he asks as he extends a piece of bacon my way.

I accept it and after taking a delicious bite, I ask, "What's that on your head?"

"What?" His hand jumps to his shortly-cropped hair as if he thought there was a spider on there, then says, "Oh. That." He wipes his hands with a napkin, then crumbles it. "It's just a patch of alopecia."

"Alo-what?"

"Alopecia areata. It's an autoimmune thing. I lose my hair sometimes."

"Like all of it?"

"Usually not, but I get these patches often. That's why I keep my hair short."

It doesn't matter that he says it in this careless way. Something in my stomach twists at the thought that his buzz cut is there to hide a medical condition. And that thought brings me to an even worse one, which is that at some point, he was much sicker.

"Lilianne told me something when we hung out last time. She said something about dialysis?"

He snickers and shakes his head. "She really spilled all the beans in one short ice cream run, did she?"

"Were you really sick?"

His interest snags on his piece of toast, which he eventually drops in the puddle of yolk. "For a while when I was in high school, yeah. Autoimmune stuff often comes as a group, and I was blessed with both this," he says as he points at his head, "*and* the kidney thing. I was lucky enough that it went away with medication and I only spent a few months on dialysis."

"I'm really glad you're okay now."

"Me too. Dialysis sucks."

"I bet," I say. My hand drifts to my fork, but I find my appetite gone. Even if Finn's healthy now, the thought of him being ill and bound to a bed with no energy is impossible. It's like thinking of an ocean with no water. It makes no sense.

"So if the alo…something happens often, why haven't I seen it before?"

"It doesn't happen that often, that's the thing. I have some loss here and there, but my last true flare up was more than a year ago."

"So what caused it?"

"There're a few possible triggers. Usually it's mostly stress."

"What are you stressed about?" I ask.

He leans back in his chair, elongating his already-tall body. "A lot." After a pause, his eyes drift to the other side of the restaurant and he adds in a low voice, "And I guess this past week had me a little worried too."

It takes me a moment to figure out what he's talking about, and when I do, I feel my entire body become aflame.

It's terrible that I'm even thinking this, but I can't help myself: someone stressing this much over me must be one of the nicest things I've ever felt.

Chapter 19

Finn

"**I** can't cook this."

Lexie gives me a look as if I'm the dumbest person she's ever met before saying, "Yes, you can."

"I might be sick," I reply.

"Oh my god, you're such a drama queen. It's just stuffing."

"Just the word makes me gag."

"Would you rather some testicle, then?"

"You're a witch," I say.

Lexie rolls her eyes, smirking, while Josie giggles, sitting at the countertop next to her.

Even if I hadn't known those two were related, I would've guessed it within a minute. Yesterday, when we came back from breakfast and Lexie invited me in to introduce me to Josie, the first thing that came to mind was, *Look, a mini Crabby!* Except she isn't actually crabby like her sister, mostly shy and quiet. I think I've gotten to her, though. Last night was Christmas Eve, and surprisingly, the three of us were alone in the house. Lexie didn't seem surprised that her mother didn't come home all night, so we didn't make a fuss about it and we simply ordered pizza and played Monopoly—a ruthless game, might I add. While Josie barely said a word all afternoon, by the time we'd finished the game, she was right there with Lexie, shouting at me to stop stealing their money.

What can I say? I'm pretty fucking good at Monopoly.

I left for my hotel well past midnight and came back this morning, once again finding the girls alone. Yesterday, Josie might've taken their loneliness well, but today, she was clearly sad not to have her entire family with her on Christmas Day. So Lexie decided to recreate a typical Christmas as best she could with what she had on hand, which is why I'm now stuck cooking some of the food I hate most in this world. Gravy, dry turkey, and whatever *yams* are, were all invented by the devil.

"Give it to me, then," Lexie says as she grabs the stained white plastic bowl from my hand.

"My lord and savior," I tell her.

She moves past me to get to the other side of the kitchen, but since the space is small and I'm leaning against the counter, her ass grazes my front, all the while her smell surrounds me. I grit my teeth as I feel my body immediately react to her, just like it has the bad tendency to do these days.

Think of something else. Anything not to get a boner, especially in front of Josie.

Eventually, the thought of stinky hockey gear does the trick, but not fast enough for me not to become aflame. At least both girls seem too busy to notice.

This has got to stop. I can't continue thinking about her like that, especially after what she's shared about her past, but easier said than done. It's like she has the power to turn me on with a single glance. I hate it.

"Lexie's recipe is good, actually," Josie says, thankfully bringing my attention elsewhere. "Much better than—"

The sound of the front door opening stops her in her tracks. We all turn to see who I can only assume is Lexie's mother wobbling inside, accompanied by some older guy and another man who looks about my age. Immediately, the house fills with the smell of pot and cheap liquor.

"Mom!" Josie says, a heartbreaking smile on her lips. Even though her mother looks like she's just stepped out of a rave and likely doesn't even remember what day it is, Lexie's sister is happy to have her around.

I don't miss the way Lexie doesn't acknowledge anyone. In fact, if I had to guess, I'd say she's probably pissed at all of them for not being here earlier or even yesterday. I get that. If it were my parents that had broken Francesca's heart, I would've already blown a fuse. Not that that could ever be our reality. No, in ours, my parents are the heartbroken ones, wondering why their daughter won't let them in. Mom and Dad called this morning to say she hadn't showed up for their scheduled dinner yesterday, even though she still technically lives at home. And the worst part of it all is, there's nothing I can do about it.

Lexie's mother steps inside the house with her high-heeled boots still on, the other two, who I assume are her boyfriend and son, following close behind. I expect for her to notice the food we've been cooking or the strings of tinsel we wrapped around one of the windows and wish her daughters a merry Christmas, but what she does is settle in front of me and say, "And who the hell are you?"

"I'm—"

"You got a boyfriend and didn't tell me?" she interrupts, this time addressing her question to Lexie.

"No. Of course not," Lexie says, and I won't lie, the way the words come out of her mouth does sting. For a second, I'm thrown right back to Sonder Hill ten years prior, the same feelings of dread bubbling. Obviously, we're not together, but I wish it wasn't such a shameful thing to be associated with me.

"He's a friend." She wipes her hands on her form-fitting jeans. "Finn, my mother, Cynthia. Mom, this is Finn. I train at his family's gym in Vermont."

Despite not wanting to, I paste on a smile and walk to Cynthia, offering my hand. "Pleasure to meet you, ma'am."

"Oh, for Christ's sake. Don't call me that."

"Mom," Lexie growls.

"It's okay," I say, making sure my smile is still intact. "I just wanted to thank you for welcoming me today."

She sucks air through her teeth as she looks me up and down, then simply says, "I need a cigarette. Jim?"

The older man behind her pulls out a pack out of his pocket, then hands it to her. "I'll come with." The two of them disappear outside, taking with them all the warmth we spent the day creating.

Silence ensues. I turn to look at Lexie, but her face is pointed down at the mixing bowl in her hands, clearly avoiding my gaze. Still at the counter, Josie smiles at me, but it's nothing like the one she wore an hour ago. In a single minute, her mother destroyed all the hope Josie had built that they might have a normal holiday after all.

As if reading my mind, Lexie glances at her brother, who sprawled himself onto the couch in the living room, and says, "We've made enough food for all of you, if you want to join us for dinner." The body I've seen being agile and flexible time and time again is now rigid, as if going through something that's not natural.

"Least you could do," the guy says without looking up from his phone.

It's my turn to stiffen.

Lexie must feel it because she moves closer to me and brushes my arm with hers, the touch as calming as it is electrifying.

But then that asswipe goes on by saying, "Actually, while you're at it, why don't you clean up around here? Make your trip worth your while."

Lexie drops the bowl, which causes a clinking sound as it bounces onto the laminate countertop. "All right, Kyle, that's enough." There's fire in her eyes, probably because this is happening in front of Josie.

He looks up from his phone, a can of beer in his hands. "What? You're too good for that too, now?" He takes a swig of the drink that's probably been hanging around the couch for a while.

"Will you all stop with that? That's not why I left, and you know it."

"Right. Little Miss Usain Bolt and all."

I remember vividly this one time in New Zealand, three years or so after I'd left home, when things got out of hand with this other tourist who was hitting on a drunk girl and touching her when she was clearly too wasted to say no. I pushed him off her and told him to get the fuck out before I destroyed him. He must've seen how serious I was because he did leave. Before then, I'd never felt the urge to be physically aggressive with someone. I'd been angry, sure, but never in this sort of primal way.

Today officially tops that time at the bar.

I tighten my fists by my side as Lexie remains calm and goes for another tactic this time: ignoring him. She turns toward the stove and continues reading the stuffing recipe on her phone, not uttering a word.

I hear footsteps coming from the living room, and then he's there.

As much as Josie and Lexie look alike, he couldn't be more different, with his brittle hair and too-intense blue eyes. I know from what Lexie's told me that they all have different biological fathers—all out of the picture—so he must look like his father while the girls take after their mother. Even from here, I can smell the sweat and cheap alcohol emanating from his clothes.

"What?" he says. "Cat got your tongue?"

"Jos, help me with the cranberries?" Lexie says. Even through her nonchalance, I notice the way the muscles in her neck are strung like a bow.

Josie scrambles from her stool to her sister, just as Kyle steps forward and spits, "Answer me, you bitch!"

His words are the hatchet to the cables that were holding my temper in check.

Moving in his way, I lift a hand to his damp chest and say, "You take another step and we're gonna have a problem, pal."

He snickers, his rancid breath making me want to puke. "Are you supposed to scare me, skinhead?"

Pots clang behind me before Lexie steps in between the two of us, steam practically billowing out of her ears. "I think it's time for you to shut the fuck up, Kyle." She moves even closer, her chin lifted so her brother can see every angle of her beautiful sneer. "And if you ain't scared of him, then be scared of me. I *promise* I will fuck you up. Understood?"

Kyle huffs, not moving an inch.

"I'm not above going to the cops with what I found in the basement," she says, and Jesus Christ, I don't think she's ever looked hotter.

His face drains of blood. "You wouldn't."

"Try me."

A second passes before he says, "Whatever." Then, he disappears down the hall, and I'm pretty sure we collectively release a giant breath.

It's only when he's out of sight that Lexie's shoulders fall and I notice she's shaking from head to toe.

"Lex..." I start.

"How about a picnic?" She turns to her sister, a serene expression back on her face. "We could show Finn around town. What do you think, Jos? Wanna get out of here?"

Josie's nod is almost too eager.

"Okay, then," I say. "Let's do it."

It's close to midnight by the time we get back to the house. Lexie wanted to make sure Josie had the best Christmas celebration possible, and all in all, I think we were able to give her something pretty nice.

"Goodnight, Jos," Lexie says after kissing her sister on the forehead. "I'll be right in."

"Night," Josie tells us both with a wave, then disappears inside the house. Lexie waits for the door to close, then slumps against it, falling to the ground. I join her, once again thankful we're in Arizona and not in wet and cold Vermont.

"God, what a shitshow," she says, eyes closed. "I'm so sorry about tonight."

"I'm not."

She opens one eye.

"Don't get me wrong, your brother's a Grade-A dick, but I still had a great time with you girls."

"You did?"

"Yeah, I did." I lean back on the porch and gaze at the almost full moon. "It's been a long time since I was able to picnic at Christmas. Last time was probably in Jordan, years ago." I have great memories from that day. I'd spent the day sand-surfing in the desert and ate the best food I had in months, a world of stars over my head. The world seemed so big then, so full of possibilities and hope. Still, I'm pretty sure I'd take tonight over it.

"I do have a question, though," I say.

She glances at me, the porch creaking as she pulls her legs to her chest and wraps her arms around them.

"What *did* you find in the basement?"

Amusement taints her face. "I haven't stepped a foot in that basement in years." She shrugs. "Just a hunch."

"You little minx."

She snickers, then sighs. "It's all so messed up."

"Yeah, it is." Making sure she sees me moving, I slowly bring a hand to her sneaker and squeeze it. "But you did good, Lex. You really did."

Her lips twist to one side as she looks at me. "Thank you, for coming. I don't think I'll ever be able to tell you what it meant to me."

"Had to make sure you came back to me safe and sound. You're not done helping me bulk up." I add a laugh for good measure. I can't tell her the truth, that thinking of her alone with her family was literally driving me insane. That I didn't sleep for two days straight, and that I ended up calling Aaron in the middle of the night to ask him for help. That she could've been on the other side of the globe and I probably would've come anyway, not for her sake but for my own.

Yeah, I can't say that.

"Right," she says. "Almost forgot."

I squeeze her foot once more. "I told you you'd accept my help one day."

She snickers, then shoves my hand playfully. "You know you've helped me more times than you could even count, don't you?"

I shrug. "What can I say? I like it."

It takes a long, long time for her to answer. But when she does, it's in this small, almost airy voice that sends shivers down my spine.

"I think I might like it too."

Later that night, I wait for Lexie to go to bed, then remain outside for a while. It doesn't take ten minutes before my wish is answered and Lexie's mom comes outside, a cigarette ready between her fingers.

Shock overtakes her features when she sees me. "What are you still doing here?" She lights the cigarette, then returns her gaze my way.

"I'm leaving," I say, standing. "Just wanted to have a little chat beforehand."

She lifts her brows, taking a drag.

"This girl right here?" I say, pointing toward the house. "She's probably one of the best people I've ever met."

Cynthia still doesn't say a word.

"She works her ass off day in and day out to achieve something most people couldn't even dream of doing, and yet she dropped everything to come here the minute she was called. She didn't even think twice about it. She would do anything for her family, and you don't even have the decency to show up for the holidays."

"I don't—"

"I'm not finished," I interrupt with a hand in the air, then inhale deeply. I need to breathe, or else I'll blow up.

She looks at me, boredom written in her gaze, but I don't care. I have something to say, and I'll say it even if it falls on deaf ears.

Hands in my pockets, I take a step in her direction and say, "I won't pretend I know all about your history because I don't. But what I do know is that Lexie doesn't deserve the way you and your son treat her." I shake my head. "Josie doesn't either."

"Who do you think you are?" she spits, but there's no intensity in her words.

"Someone who cares about her."

Cynthia doesn't respond, and I think that's my cue to leave. But just before I can reach my rental car, I turn back to the rail-thin woman still watching me and say, "You have gold on your hands. It's time you treat her that way."

Chapter 20

Lexie

Time off has never done me any good.

It's something that doesn't make much sense, but it's always been that way for me. It's one of the only things that made me happy not to have typical family vacations over the summer as a kid. Of course, the actual breaks are good, but the return to normal? It's actual hell. While I was in Phoenix, I was able to practice only a fraction of the time I should've, and for the three weeks since I've been back, I've tried recuperating from that short break, to no avail.

Seventy-two, seventy-three, seventy-four,...

My core is on fire as I try to finish my fourth set of crunches, feeling like I might pass out from either pain or exhaustion at any moment. The gym is quiet, save for the low music I put on an hour ago. I needed a little extra motivation, so Beyoncé it was.

I should probably go to bed, but with the first competition of the Cup a short two weeks away, I don't want to take a luxury that might cost me a win. Especially not one I need more than ever.

Ninety-eight, ninety-nine, a hundred.

I let my back drop to the ground and breathe rapidly, the fur-like surface of the mat tickling my bare arms. I'll need to up my game if I want any chance at a podium in New York. Practice nonstop until then, probably.

"Is it me, or are you getting slower?"

I jump at the sound of the deep voice coming from a dark corner of the gym, followed by the squeak of the wheels on the cleaning cart.

"Is it me or are you just getting creepier?" I say, stretching my back from side to side. "Doing the cleaning at 2:30 a.m. is a new low for you."

Finn finally comes out of the shadow, his usual smirk in tow. "What can I say? The company's better at night."

"Oh my god, do you have to be this cheesy?"

"I don't *have* to, no. So that must mean it's the truth."

"Sure." He probably got swamped at the farm today and had to come here much later than usual. Even though the peak season has passed, maybe he had accounting to do.

Ever since we came back from Phoenix—him a week earlier than me—things have been different between us. He's seen a part of my life I'd have rather kept hidden, but now that it's done, I'm glad for it. It almost feels like we went to war together, and we came out on the other side with something that only belongs to the two of us. Something I couldn't have put into words if he hadn't been there.

"How long do you plan on being the gym's maid anyway?" I ask as I move into a plank, my stomach burning the second I get into position.

"Show off much?" he says before joining me in his own plank. I grin at the floor. With the amount of times he's done this with me, he's gotten much better—not that I'll ever admit that to him. "And I don't know. As long as Mom needs the help, I guess."

"You think she'd give me the job?" I ask.

"Always dreamed of being a midnight Cinderella?" he teases.

"Sure, why not."

"Wait, you're serious? Why?" he asks, looking at me funny.

"Wouldn't mind the extra cash," I admit. Earlier today, I got a call from my bank that the interest rate on my loans needed to be recalculated, and that single sentence made me shiver. I'll now owe the bank an even bigger shit ton of money than I already did.

Without my surgery, I wouldn't currently be in so much debt. My mother thought it was stupid to spend money on a body that would recover on its own. And sure, it might have recovered *enough*, but never to a point that would have allowed me to compete again, and that was a loss I wasn't ready to face. So I had the surgery, and the weeks of rehab, and it paid off, I think. It also put me in a situation that's so precarious I could cry.

"How much?" Finn asks in a strained voice. "Maybe I could—"

"Finn, stop," I interrupt, looking up from my plank. "I'm not looking for a sugar daddy."

"What the fuck, Lex?" he says with a bark of laughter. "I never said you were."

"Just making sure."

"You're too much," he says. "And your plank times are too much too."

"Shut up and hold it."

He groans but does as I say.

"So what do you need the money for?" he says after five seconds, probably to distract himself from the pain. I know that strategy well.

"A whole lot of medical debt."

"Right. I'm sorry," he says.

"It is what it is." I flick my eyes up. "Get that butt down."

"Tyrant." He puffs out air.

"Want those abs or not?"

"I *have* abs."

He does.

"Keep telling yourself that," I tease, and he snickers, knowing I'm full of shit.

After another few seconds of silence, Finn says, "So what's the plan?"

"Not sure." If I got my sponsors back, things would be different, but right now, my options are winning the lottery or selling an organ. "But don't worry. I'm used to hustling." I don't remember a single day in my life when I wasn't worried whether we'd be able to pay the bills at the end of the month. I used to have nightmares about my mom pulling me out of gymnastics so she could afford groceries and cigarettes. She did cut me off for a few months when I was ten, but thankfully, my coaches saw something in me and let me train with them for free, until I was old enough to work for them.

"So why didn't you try to get a college scholarship?"

"I didn't want one. I sucked at school, and I never cared for it anyway." Sure, it would've paid for my gym fees, but at what cost? I would've had to spend hours on end in a classroom, studying something that was useless to me, all to be able to train. It felt like a waste of my time.

"Even when you were younger?"

"Even then." I snicker. "I barely passed my classes all throughout high school because I couldn't focus on anything other than my training. Didn't care about the rest."

He grins. "Haven't changed much, have you?"

I shrug, knowing he's right. Do I wish I could be any other way? Of course, I do. I wish I could've been strong enough to stay in Phoenix. I wish I could've done whatever it took for Josie. But I'm selfish enough to still want it more than anything. To have that goal take control of my life, because it *is* my life.

I glance up, but his gaze already on me. "Have you never wanted anything like that?"

He shakes his head, arms trembling under his weight. "Not really, no. I've always kind of...bounced round, I guess? Looking for the next thing to do."

"Is that why your apartment still looks like you're ready to move out at any moment?"

One of his knees falls to the mat.

"It's okay, let's switch to a side plank," I say.

He hums, and only once he's in a position says, "Maybe you got a point."

For some reason, it doesn't make me happy to be right.

"I mean," he starts, "I do have some short term goals, but—"

"Like what?"

We're facing each other, so I can see the bob of his throat. "I've started considering maybe going back to college, actually. Get a business degree, or something. It know it sounds stupid, but—"

"Do you want to do it?" I ask.

"Yeah," he says without a moment's hesitation, which gives me even more proof that his mind is made up.

"Then it's not stupid," I answer simply. "Not at all."

He doesn't say anything as we move on to the other side, then back into a midline plank, but I can tell that his silence is reflective. His mind is likely as loud as he is quiet.

The heating system kicks on, creating a whirr above us that mixes with the music and the sounds of our breaths.

"All right," I say, bringing my knees down and sitting on my heels.

Finn goes down less gently, letting his entire body drop to the ground. He groans, then sniffs. "It's only with my face this close to the mat that I realize how much it smells like ass."

Laughter spills out of me at the sudden break in tension. That's Finn in a nutshell. "You've only just realized this?"

"It's horrible. I feel like I'm stuck with a thousand kids' stinky feet in a bouncy castle with no way out."

"Is that what your nightmares look like? Bouncy castles?"

"Among other things."

"What else?" I can't imagine Finn having nightmares. He's always so chirpy, I can only see him having sunshine-and-rainbow dreams.

He sighs, seriousness immediately permeating the air. "You wouldn't want to know."

"I'm pretty sure I would, actually." When he doesn't answer, I bump him with my toe. "Tell me or I'll make you smell my own stinky feet."

"Kill me now."

I shift on the floor so my foot moves closer to his face.

"All right, all right." He rolls from his stomach onto his back. "Jesus, I thought torture was illegal in the States."

"Ha, ha. Now spill."

His face sombers, and even if he could choose not to tell me, I have a feeling he will. The gym at night feels different. It's so quiet, so personal, that every time we're here alone, it almost feels like a different universe. One where it's safe to share secrets.

Finn sits cross-legged, reminding me of a little boy as he plays with the laces of his sneakers. "I have a few dreams that come back often," he says without looking up. "One's of me, but like, old as shit. Everyone around me has kids, a family, this perfect life, and I just have to stand there and watch them have it all while I remain alone."

My brows furrow despite myself. I don't understand this man. He could have whoever he wants, whenever he wants, and yet he keeps showing sides of himself that are at odds with his confident persona. I don't know who the real Finn is. The one who teases and smirks, or the one who thinks he needs to be embarrassed about wanting to go to college. Or maybe he really is both, all at once.

"I don't think that's likely to happen," I say.

He gives me a half smile.

"What else?" I ask.

"Hm, let me see." He closes an eye. "I'm not scared of clowns or dolls, but I did dream once of a huge-ass snake that ate me and forced me to live my life inside his belly, and it was pretty traumatizing."

"Be serious."

"I am! It was scarily realistic." He laughs when I roll my eyes. "Okay, what else." His teeth drag over his bottom lip, and I force my gaze away. The sight is a little too tempting. "I guess sometimes I dream about the people I love getting hurt. Of Lilianne getting sicker. Of Francesca..." He shakes his head. "Yeah, those dreams suck."

"I bet."

This time, it's him who taps his foot against mine, although I notice the slowness he uses to move toward me. It turns my heart upside down.

"What about you? What do you dream about?"

Immediately, my body stiffens. Images hit me of the nights I wake drenched in sweat with the feeling of unfamiliar hands imprinted on my skin. Those nights when the nightmares don't have a clear image, but feel like moist breath and a sense of wanting to disappear.

I fight a shudder, then stand up. I need to get to bed if I want to be at least semi-functional tomorrow. Plus, the kind of thoughts I was starting to have toward him needed to stop.

With a hand extended in Finn's direction, I say, "I don't really dream."

Chapter 21

Lexie

I'd forgotten just how packed the first event of the competition season could be.

As I pass group after group of athletes, my duffel held close to my chest, I become overwhelmed. The stands are already getting filled as gymnasts and their coaches walk out of the locker rooms and onto the different mats, stretching while chatting about the hours to come. Young girls with the same team uniforms giggle as they start warming up in a slow jog.

I used to love seeing this camaraderie in sports events, yet today, it makes me want to disappear. I've never felt as much like an odd duckling in a sea of swans as I do today.

I focus by remembering the luck I have at simply being here. I could've never walked again, let alone competed. This is what's important.

As I put my stuff into my assigned locker and change into another one of my favorite leotards, this one maroon with a deep V in the back outlined by ruby-red rhinestones, I try to get my mental game back into place. I'm here to perform. To win. It doesn't matter whether I have zero or a hundred people here to cheer for me from the sidelines or the stands. I can do this.

To remain in the right headspace, I grab my earbuds and put on my favorite rap album, then head to the warm-up stations, going through the motions and focusing on the details. Sharper shoulder push in that front handspring. Faster twist in that second rotation. Looser jaw during that jump. While Andy isn't here to shout the words at me, I can still hear them.

I feel ready. As impossible as it sounded a few months ago that I might be confident going into today, I think I am. I did what I had to do. Even without a coach, I've disciplined myself to get the hours in. My cardio's better than it was, even before my accident. I think I can actually do this.

The competition started in full swing a good half hour ago, with gymnasts taking the mats left and right on the different apparatuses and presenters announcing their names and their scores with booming voices through the speakers. I try to ignore it as much as possible, to focus on me and only me, but when a familiar name is called, I have no choice but to turn and watch.

Clara Popov hasn't been in the roster of potential Olympic gymnasts for long. She was probably still in diapers by the time I started competing, but that doesn't mean anything now. For the past four years, she's been winning competitions left and right, sponsors at her feet for an opportunity.

And she deserves it all.

I've seen her perform a few times, and when you watch her, it's easy to forget gravity applies to her too. Her movements are so elegant in their power that sometimes, it looks like she's actually flying. She's obviously one of my biggest competitors, both today and for the rest of the season, and while she's going to give me a run for my money, it's an honor to be in the same category as her. She'll push me to do better than I think I can. Already has. Through social media, I've seen the routines she performed last year, and that pushed me to rethink some of my own, with the help of Shelli's choreographer. If I want any chance at winning, I need to be at least better than she was last year.

She's starting on vault, just like I am. I'm on in less than thirty minutes, so I shouldn't be watching her, but I can't stop myself. Today's the first time I'll see what she has in store for this year—what I'll need to beat.

Clara's completely in her element as she walks to the start of the runway and salutes the judges, her dark hair combed in a perfect bun, shoulders straight and chin high. Confidence emanates out of her. It's clear in her posture that whatever happens, she's convinced she'll win. Something very similar to doubt settles in the pit of my stomach as I watch her get into position.

My unease only grows when, from the corner of my eye, I spot a familiar face. I do a double take, but I don't know why I didn't expect it. Of course Andy's here. By his side are two gymnasts I used to train with. And while everyone's eyes are on Clara, his are on me. My teeth clench tighter. Before, when he looked at me, it was with excitement, with conviction. Now, it's the opposite. Like he wants me to fail. To prove him right for dumping me. Then, as if remembering he should be cordial, he smiles, one that's tight and uncomfortable. I don't bother returning it, instead turning toward the vault as if I haven't seen him.

As I wait for Clara to start running, I decide something: today's performances won't be for myself, or even for a medal. They will be entirely to spite him.

And then Clara moves, and my entire focus goes to her.

The good thing about gymnastics is scores are posted almost immediately after a performance, so you don't need to wait for the end of the event to know what the podium will look like. Even before competing, you know which score you need to beat.

The bad thing about it is when you see that score and know there's no way in hell you can top it.

She went for a roundoff onto the spring board, half turn onto the vault table, followed by a tucked front salto with a 540-degree twist. It's a move I've rarely seen in competitions. She doesn't land it perfectly—she takes a step before stabilizing and saluting the judges, which tells me this move must be somewhat new for her—but it's still going to give her a score that's too high to beat.

The numbers appear on the screen a minute later, and yep, that's too high. I want to look away from the red neons burning the score into my retinas, but I can't. And even if I wanted to, the announcer shouts the score, creating a roar of applause throughout the stadium as people call out her name and cheer for her with large signs elevated above their heads.

Fuck.

Vault is one of my strongest elements. If I can't win gold for it, how am I supposed to get a chance at an overall podium?

I shake my hands in front of me as I crack my neck left and right and think of what I could do. I've had vault performances with higher scores than Popov's. For instance, a Cheng—which is similar to her move, except that the front salto is straight—would allow me to top her. I've done it in the past, and done it well. I'd just need to change my plan at the last minute and go for a move I haven't practiced in more than a year.

Minutes pass as I move on to new stations, juggling different ideas in my head. Cheng or not. Gold or silver. Land something confidently or risk doing something that could potentially send me to a hospital, or leave me paralyzed or even dead.

When my name is called, I barely hear it, too lost in my head. On one hand, we always have two turns at the vault, so I could count the first one as a practice shot and make sure my Cheng is good on the second run. On the other hand, if I miss the first one completely and hurt myself, there might not be a second one.

My smile is not as confident as I'd like as I salute the judges. When I turn to face the vault table, I can still feel my mind raging like a storm.

Focus, Lexie.

I breathe in, and on the exhale, I start running. It's only when I'm one step away from the spring board that I make my decision. I chicken out and go for a sure silver. My roundoff is clean, my shoulders use just the right amount of force to propel me, and my spins are clean. When I land, there's no wobble. It's a brick thrown onto a mat, strong and sturdy. And yet even as I smile and salute once again, I know that score will never beat Popov's.

Polite applause comes from the audience as I walk off the mat. I try to keep a collected air and stare at my feet, but something makes me look up.

A loud whoop, followed by a "Let's go, Lexie!"

I need to squint and blink a few times to make sure I'm not imagining things. It's only when a few moments pass and the image does not change that I feel myself break into the giddiest grin in the world. Because up there in the stands is Finn, cheering for me with a homemade sign that says "Crabbys do it better." Next to him is Shelli, who's clapping so hard her hands must be hurting.

I've never felt like crying during a competition. When I lost or fell or fucked up, I was overwhelmed with anger, not sadness. A bronze medal wouldn't fill me with sorrow; it'd fill me with fire. It would push me to practice harder, to get to the gym earlier and stay later.

And yet looking at these two people in the stands cheering for me, I have the strange urge to fall to my knees and sob like a baby.

My cheeks and neck are warm as I give them a quick wave, then turn to the panel so I can see my score. My foot is tapping the floor repeatedly as I wait with bated breath. When the numbers finally come out and I get the answer I expected—I'm in second place, and will likely remain so—I feel a mix of embarrassment and relief. Maybe Finn and Shelli haven't seen me give my best performance, but this is still better than anything anyone could've expected when I got injured and started my rehab journey.

I'll settle on the positive for now.

Looking over my shoulder one last time, I give my two supporters another thankful smile, then get ready for the rest of the competition.

"Lexie!"

The sound of the voice I could now recognize anywhere makes me turn around, and when I see Finn's face, full of so much happiness and excitement, all the negative feelings I had about today disappear. People are filing out of the stadium, both from the seats section and from the floor, but Finn must've found a way to get to me because he's here, mixed in with all the gymnastics professionals and not looking the least bit worried about not being allowed down here.

He's still on the other side of the floor mat, but the second he starts walking my way, I drop my training bag to the ground and run toward him. I stop abruptly once I'm inches from him, my heart beating faster than it has all day.

"I don't understand," I say, beaming. "What are you doing here?" While New York isn't on the other side of the country, it's still a more than four-hour drive from Sonder Hill.

"Wanted to see if all that training had been worth it," he says. I laugh as he plugs his hands into the front pockets of his jeans. "And I didn't want you to celebrate that first success alone."

His words grip my throat and make it so tight I can barely swallow. Without him saying it, I know that's the real reason he's here. Not to see me, but to make me feel less alone.

It's the most beautiful gift I've ever received.

His eyes crinkle at the corners. "You were amazing, Lex."

And in this moment, it doesn't matter that I choked the dismount that would've given me the highest difficulty points, or that I only won bronze in the all-around category, because when he says it, I believe it's the truth.

"Thank you," I say. For believing in me, for being here, for becoming some kind of pillar I didn't know I would ever find.

People are still swarming toward the exits around us, but we stay rooted in place, two sequoias in a tsunami. I can't imagine moving from here. No words are exchanged as we stare at each other with the dumbest smiles on our faces, and with the adrenaline still flooding my body from that last performance, the moment feels otherworldly. My hands shake from the thrill of it all, and I don't hide it. I don't hide anything.

Finn wets his lips before saying, "I really want to hug you right now."

"Then do it," I say, the answer blurting out of me.

"You sure?"

I nod. How can he not see this? There's no one I trust more than him, I realize. This man who I didn't know a few months ago, but who is here today, for me.

Once he finally decides to move, he still looks hesitant, which only shows just how right I am to trust him. Not wanting to wait a second longer, I take that last step between us and climb on my tiptoes to wrap my arms around his neck as tight as I can.

This hug is vastly different from the one we shared in Phoenix. While then he seemed hesitant to touch me, this time, he squeezes me as hard as I do him. I can barely breathe from the tightness of his embrace, and hypoxia has never felt so good.

His arms remain circled around my waist, until he lifts a hand to caress my hair, then to cup the nape of my neck. My eyelids flutter against the warm and sweet-smelling scent of his neck, goosebumps covering my entire body. Compared to other times when being this close to someone made me lock up or disappear into a memory I don't even have, I enjoy everything about this. The way his stubble scratches the top of my forehead. The feel of his heart beating against my nose, the *thump-thump* almost as loud as mine. The way his arm is tugging at my hair, a pain I don't mind one bit because it means he's here, hugging me.

"I have to be honest about something," he says in a gravelly tone, making me pull my head back with my arms still around him. I'm not ready to let go quite yet.

It's only when my eyes meet his that I realize how dark his gaze has become, his pupils so wide they've overtaken almost all of the green. Around us, the sound has decreased, most athletes and coaches having left the space. Or maybe they're still there and I can't notice them anymore, my focus pinpointed on only this.

"Yes?" I barely recognize my voice as it comes out. It's airy and low. It shows everything I'm feeling.

Finn's Adam's apple bobs before he says, "Hugging you's not the only thing I want to do."

My lips part, a wave of want hitting me. I *want* this man. I don't remember ever experiencing this feeling before, and yet the moment the thought occurs to me, I realize it's true. I might even have wanted him for a while.

My fingertips dance against his shoulder blades, alternating between soft touches and centering grips. I feel him sway on his feet, the movement bringing him even closer to me. From here, I can smell the mint of his breath, see the small acne scars decorating his cheeks. He's the most handsome man I've ever encountered, and the outside doesn't even account for half of it.

Shifting on my feet so the tips of my toes touch his, I say, "You can do whatever you want, Finn."

Once again, he moves as if he has all the time in the world, giving me every chance to change my mind.

I remain firmly in place, breaths coming in fast, every cell in my body bursting with anticipation.

And the moment his lips finally land on mine? It makes all the wait worth it.

Finn kisses me like he doesn't belong anywhere else. It's slow, and confident, and with so much purpose it makes me weak in the knees. My hands grip his neck as his climb up to my cheeks and hold me like I'm made of gold.

I let him take the lead as he explores every inch of my lips, pressing kisses that make me ache for more. It's almost too slow.

I want it all, yet he continues giving painstakingly slow nips at my bottom lip, then gripping the top one between the two of his.

His hands never stray from my face, and it's still the most sensual moment I have ever experienced.

Feeling like I'm about to catch on fire, I move even closer to him, and the hardness I feel pressed against my belly is proof that he's into this just as much as I am.

I move once again closer to him, and a groan erupts from his throat.

"Jesus, Lex," he whispers, gulping in a breath. Then, he's back on me, this time with his tongue teasing the entrance of my mouth. I open for him, ready for him to ravage me whole.

The moment I taste him, I know I'll never crave anything more than this.

"Finn?"

We both jump away from each other a second before Shelli appears at the end of the hallway, looking around the room before she spots us. "There you are! I was looking for you." She walks our way, and with each step, I try to get myself to calm down.

"Congrats on today, Lexie," she says before leaning in for a hug, which I return.

"Thank you. And thank you so much for coming. It truly means a lot." I hope she doesn't notice the way my hands are trembling. I might be here, talking to her, but my mind is still stuck on the softness of her son's lips. Behind her, I spot Finn's shit-eating grin, which lets me know my thoughts are probably written all over my face, at least for him.

"Of course," she says before returning her attention to Finn. "You ready soon?"

"Yeah. Meet you out in a sec."

"All right." She glances at me. "I'll see you in two days? Take tomorrow off. My treat."

"Thank you," I say with yet another grin. I don't remember a competition I didn't win where I smiled this much.

Shelli leaves, and then it's just Finn and me. Still wearing that smug look, he takes my hands in his and says, "Let me take you on a date."

"Now?"

"No, dummy, not now. Back home. Whenever you want."

I don't even have time to think about whether this is a good idea or not, because then he adds a "Please," and the decision is made for me.

"Okay."

Chapter 22

Finn

I don't think I've ever been this nervous in my life.

It's almost comical—no, not almost. When Aaron called me this morning and asked me why the fuck I was this much of a babbling mess and I told him the truth, he burst out laughing. According to him, being this much of a wreck because of a date was exactly what I deserved after teasing him endlessly about him and Wren before they got together. Serves me right.

I'm standing in front of the mirror after having switched back and forth between a black dress shirt and a dark gray sweater fifty times. Is a dress shirt too much? Does Lexie want me to be too much?

I change back into the sweater, then examine myself again. I still have the alopecia patch on the top of my head that started appearing the day after Lexie told me she was going to Arizona, and a new one has appeared since, hidden behind my left ear. As I rub a hand over my short hair, I consider putting on a beanie but decide against it. I can't imagine wearing one in a restaurant would be better than showing my bald patches. Lexie has already seen one anyway, and that didn't stop her from kissing me.

And what a kiss it was.

For the past four days, I haven't been able to stop thinking about it. How her skin felt under the pads of my fingers. How her tongue tasted in my mouth, like the electrolyte drink she'd just had and something uniquely hers. How her body pressed against mine and made me want everyone in the stadium to disappear so I could have her all to myself. At the same time, I was thankful for everyone around us. I don't know where my limits lie with her. At first, I thought any kind of touch would be a no-go. Then, when I saw she didn't seem to mind my touch when she expected it, I explored further, always careful. I'm a touchy-feely person, always have been. I've greeted Aaron with hugs since we were in daycare. I cannot pass by my mother without giving her a quick embrace. It's how I show my appreciation and love. I would've found another way with Lexie if she'd hated every kind of touch, but I'm starting to realize there are rules that, once respected, can make her feel both comfortable and safe with me. I just wish there was a textbook that came with her. I'm so afraid of crossing a line I didn't know was there. What if a brush of her hand was fine, but a hug was too much? And what if a hug was good with her, but a kiss sent her back to a memory I'd give everything to eradicate from her mind?

The only solution I found was to follow her lead. I'll do whatever she wants me to, so long as she shows me she's okay with it first, and I'll hold back from anything that might be a trigger for her.

I spritz some cologne on my neck, feeling myself starting to sweat under my arms. This is crazy. Both my reaction to the date and the date itself. I have never gone on a date for the purpose of actually dating since I was in high school. After that, it was seeing a girl because I knew that sooner or later, we'd have sex, maybe for a night or maybe for a month, and then we'd part ways amicably. I was fine with that, and the girls I was with were too. But tonight's the total opposite. I will not have sex with her tonight, and I might not ever. This might be a hard boundary for Lexie, and after what she went through—whatever it is—I would understand it. And the weirdest part is, I don't mind. Not one bit. Of course, I got hard when she kissed me and pressed her body against mine. I'm only human. But as much as I want her, I'd be okay with never having her that way. I like her body, but I like her mind way more. I wouldn't have invited her on a date if I wasn't sure of that.

My body feels the same way it did an hour before a playoff game. Ears buzzing, hands tingling, stomach hurting.

Jesus, get a grip, Finn.

I don't know why I'm this nervous. This is just Lexie, after all. Lexie, who's threatened me with her stinky feet and who's seen me gag over food. Lexie, who knows some of the ugliest parts of me and still, for some strange reason, wants to spend time with me.

Giving my cheeks two slaps to keep me from freaking the fuck out even more, I exit my room and go to grab my keys. If I want to be at her place at 7:00 p.m. sharp, I need to leave in five minutes. Then, I'm bringing her to my favorite Italian restaurant a town over, and once we're done eating, I'm driving her to an ice skating path through the woods, where twinkling lights shine over the ice and create a cozy, romantic experience. Maybe if I'm lucky, that'll earn me another one of those earth-shattering kisses.

I feel like a teenager, lusting over a kiss, and surprisingly, I love it.

As I start zipping my coat, my phone buzzes on the console next to the door. For a millisecond, my heart stops. What if Lexie's changed her mind? Then I remember once again that she's Lexie and she wouldn't do that to me. If anything, she'd call to tell me not to pick her up because she doesn't need me to.

I grab my phone, surprised and relieved at the same time when I see it's an unknown number calling.

"Hello?"

"Finn?"

Immediately, everything in my body tenses, ice filling my veins. "Fran?" I say.

My sister doesn't answer, but the sound of her crying both confirms it's her and scares the living shit out of me.

"Fran, what's wrong?"

"I—" She hiccups. "I messed up."

I'm already out of the door when I ask her, "What's wrong?" Then, "Tell me where you are."

She sniffles. "I'm at some party Cam brought me to."

My vision turns red. Of course it's got something to do with that Cameron fuckface.

"Do you have an address?" I ask her before the sound of my truck door slamming shut fills the line.

"I...I think so."

I notice my hands are shaking when I try to insert the key in the ignition and can't align it with the hole. I force a breath in my lungs, and when the call connects to Bluetooth, I pull the phone away from my ear and say, "Are you okay? Are you hurt?"

She starts to answer, then breaks down into sobs so hard I can barely hear anything she says.

"Fran, I need you to calm down and tell me what the fuck's going on." I can't handle this. All kinds of terrible thoughts cram into my head, from her having been drugged all the way to Cameron having lifted a hand to her.

I guess tonight's the night I finally go to jail.

"He brought me to a party," she repeats, "but it wasn't the type of party I expected."

"What does that mean?" I look over my shoulder to pull out of my parking spot. I don't know where I'm going yet, but I can't sit still any longer.

"There were other guys here," she says in a squeaky voice, and everything inside me stops.

No.

I feel like I can't breathe as I ask, "Did...anyone touch you?"

"N-no. I got out..."

I don't hear the rest of her sentence as my blood pressure falls, and I thank every possible god out there.

"Give me an address, please," I say as calmly as I can, which is not fucking calmly at all. The worst might not have happened yet, but it doesn't mean she's out of the woods. She ended up moving in with this guy a month ago. Maybe she even thinks they're in love. This might just be the beginning.

My phone pings with a location about an hour south of here.

"Don't move, I'm on my way," I say, immediately heading toward the highway.

"Thank you," she says. "And Finn?"

"Yeah?"

"Don't say anything to Mom. To anyone. Please."

"Fran, this isn't fair." I can't hide anything from my parents, much less when it's about Fran. I'm a terrible liar, and more than that, I hate the idea of keeping secrets.

"Please," she repeats, and the thickness of her voice is what finally gets me.

"Fine," I grit out. "Stay safe. I'm coming."

I hang up, then push on the gas.

Chapter 23

Lexie

He's five minutes late.

It's not a big deal. I'm used to getting everywhere on time because being late for practice when I was part of a team meant everyone had to do extra conditioning and no one forgave you for it afterward, but most people don't associate a ticking clock with physical pain. Still, I can't help but feel it's not like Finn to not be there on time. He's texted me every day since New York, even with updates about tonight's date. He's kept the majority of it a secret, only giving me a few directions on how to get dressed.

The brisk January wind ruffles my hair as I look down at myself. After an embarrassing half hour of debate, I settled on dark jeans and my favorite burgundy cardigan. When I asked him if wearing a skirt would be a good idea, he told me, "Only if you'd like to freeze your ass off," so I crossed that idea out.

The cabin's porch is covered, so I am protected from the slow drift of fluffy snowflakes, which land on the tall trees covering the estate. The view is idyllic and peaceful, yet it doesn't tame the anxiety bubbling inside me. It doesn't make sense.

When an extra ten minutes pass, I go sit on the frigid swing that decorates the porch. Ice coats its surface, but I need to busy myself with something. I rest the cookies I baked in my lap and fidget with the red ribbon I tied the translucent bag with. I tried to recreate the recipe we tasted in Phoenix. It was on Finn's last night in town, and I'd brought him over to my favorite bakery. He'd sworn they were the best cookies he'd ever had, and while I'm not a great baker, I could imagine him lying to my face later tonight and telling me mine were even better, just for the sake of making me smile.

My knee bounces as I wait to hear the sound of his truck's engine. And wait.

Maybe he got into an accident? His place is less than five minutes away from the farm, but it *is* snowing. What if he's hurt?

Feeling myself getting more and more antsy, I pull out my phone to make sure I haven't received any texts, and when I see I haven't, I dial his number. Fuck it. If I look like a control freak, then so be it. At least I'll know where we stand.

After six rings, I realize he's not going to pick up. I end the call and grab my mittens out of my purse. The sun has long since set, and the cute spring coat I decided to wear was a bad idea.

I'm not sure why I tried this hard tonight. Maybe because it's my first actual date. I've never had a guy come pick me up and try to romance me away. Never wanted one to either. But when Finn asked, it didn't even occur to me to say no. Not when my body felt featherlight. I could actually envision this night. Imagine him sliding closer in a restaurant booth or a movie theater, trying to steal my warmth or pass me some of his. And when I saw those images, it wasn't dread that filled me, but excitement. Like this might actually be something I'd want.

Yet the longer I wait outside this porch, the stupider I feel. When have men ever proved me wrong? My father left. My siblings' fathers didn't last long either. Some of my mother's exes are the definition of earth's scum. My own *brother* treats me like crap.

But then there was Finn. Caring, sun-warm Finn.

The bite of the cold on my cheeks and nose tells me maybe I was disillusioned about him. Maybe I only had to wait until he showed me his true colors. I can't imagine him being disingenuous with me all those months, but the truth might sit somewhere in the middle.

This is painful, and I hate that it is. I hate that I got my expectations up, only to have them smashed under his fist. I shouldn't have given him this kind of power over me. As a friend, he wouldn't have been able to make me feel this small, I'm sure.

This is what I get for thinking things were starting to look up after all these years.

I try his phone another time, and when it goes to voicemail again, I end the call and turn my phone off, then walk back inside. The face I see in the mirror after locking the door behind me makes me angry. It looks pathetic. Made-up eyes, red lips, frostbit nose that ruins the look. After removing my coat, I open the cookie bag and go to grab one, but I realize I'm too nauseous to eat anything. I end up dropping the bag on the kitchen counter, then go lie in bed, clothes and all.

This is all my fault. If I hadn't gotten my expectations up, I wouldn't be feeling this crushed. Pressure builds in my chest, and while I know it would be relieved by a good cry, I don't allow myself to.

Once again, I only have myself to rely on, and that'll have to be enough.

Chapter 24

Finn

I wait until 7:00 a.m. before knocking on the cabin's door.

There was a chance when I showed up fifteen minutes ago that she could already have left for work, but her car is still in the driveway, so I guess the odds are in my favor. Minus that part where the only thing that could've kept me from our first date actually happened.

I almost jump at the sound of my own knocks against the door. Sniffling, I plunge my hands back into my coat and wait. Honestly, I'm not sure what I expect Lexie's reaction to be, and I'm not even sure which one I'd rather receive. She might refuse to talk to me out of anger. She might be deeply hurt. I think the former would probably be better.

Ten seconds pass, and still nothing. I consider knocking again, but figure I'll give her a little more time. I owe her that, after all.

Looking at the porch's ceiling, I rub a hand over my face, wincing where I touch the fresh bruise on my right eyebrow. I don't know how it's possible for so much to have gone wrong in a twelve-hour period. I feel like a week has passed since I was standing in my room, figuring out what to wear on that date.

It's been thirty seconds now. Not that I'm counting. Figuring she might not have heard me, I lift my hand and knock again.

When another period of thirty seconds has passed, I ball my hands into fists and turn around. Either she's sleeping, she's not here, or she doesn't want to see me.

I wouldn't blame her.

When I think back to last night, I know I should've done a lot of things differently, but when panic overtook me, I could barely think straight. I just wanted to get Francesca safe, and I didn't even consider everything else that was at play. The thought of calling Lexie escaped my head, simple as that. I barely remember how I got to the address Fran sent me. The drive must've been close to an hour long, and I don't have a fucking clue how it went.

And then I got there, and hell ensued.

Even without an answer, I wait a little longer to leave the porch, as if I don't want to give up just yet. I really hoped I could talk to her this morning. I don't want her getting the wrong idea for even a second longer, but I guess that's not up to me.

Chest tight, I turn and I stumble down the steps, the cool wind cutting my face. I round the corner to my truck and think of places where I could find her when suddenly, she's there.

I don't know why I didn't think about it in the first place. Of course she was on a run. I'm such a mess, functioning on three hours of sleep and two cups of coffee, and my brain is only half working.

She doesn't spot me right away. Her breaths are short as she slows to a halt, her eyes fixed on her digital watch, earbuds in.

While she's distracted, I grab the opportunity to watch her, just for a minute. Her hair's up in a short ponytail, and even with a simple black windbreaker and leggings, she looks absolutely stunning.

My staring is cut short when she tenses and looks up, as if she felt me there. The moment her dark gaze meets mine, I know this will not be good. The affection that used to reside there is gone, replaced by blocks of ice thicker than those hanging from the roof, drip-dripping onto the porch behind me.

"Hey," I say like a dumbass.

She takes her earbuds out and studies me from head to toe before saying, "Hi."

The sound of her voice is almost enough to make me lose my balance. It's so...wrong. I feel like I've stepped back to that night in September, when poison spilled out of her eyes every time they met mine. The velvet-soft tone I earned over the months has vanished.

I go to ask her how she's doing, but change my mind before a word comes out, feeling like that might detonate a bomb. Instead, I jump straight into it and take a step in her direction. "I feel like apologies aren't enough at this point, but I swear I can explain."

The corners of her mouth tighten, but still, she remains silent. I don't miss the way her gaze catches on my bruises, yet she doesn't ask me where they came from. Maybe she doesn't care anymore.

"Something really important came up, and I was called away. I swear I didn't mean to leave you hanging."

She crosses her arms in front of her, almost like she's hugging herself. I wish *I* could hug her. "And you couldn't call? Text?"

"I..." The words die in my mouth because I could've. I *should've.* "I was fucked up. It was a really nerve-racking thing, and I could barely think straight."

She bobs her head slowly, still standing way too far. I take a small step her way, but that only forces her to pull back. I freeze.

"So what was it?"

"Huh?" I say.

"What was it, that important thing that made you forget everything?"

My jaw clenches at the one question I feared was coming. The truth is, there's nothing I want more than to tell her everything. To let her know the way I felt when I heard my sister's frightened voice on the phone. To tell her how, when I got to the mansion my sister had sent me to, I knew things were bad. How I didn't even knock at the door, just stepped inside the house and started shouting my sister's name until she dashed out of a locked bathroom and jumped into my arms, her entire body shaking like a leaf, a thin satin robe covering her barely-dressed body. How she told me not to go find Cameron and to just take her home, but how he came out of the basement right that moment, two middle-aged men with him. How I didn't need to know the details of what had gone on because wrongness was thick in the air. How I jumped on him and started hitting left and right, not caring how many punches he was getting in, until one of his friends pulled me off. How I thought of finding a way to actually kill the guy, but Francesca grabbed my hand and pleaded with me to leave. How she fell asleep almost instantly in the car, and how I spent the drive back home lost in rage and grief and sadness. How I brought her inside my apartment and laid her down in bed before falling asleep on the couch myself for a few hours. How by the time I'd realized what had happened and what I had missed, it was way too late to call or text.

But the only thing I do say is, "I'm so sorry, but I can't tell you."

A soft snicker comes out of her mouth, and she turns toward the cabin.

"No, Lex, wait. I swear, if I could tell you, I would, but I promised."

"It's fine," she says, looking so fucking *not* fine.

"Please, you have to believe me."

"I do. I think," she says.

I take a careful step closer. "So we're good?" My heart speeds in almost-relief. "I'll make it up to you, I swear."

"Yeah, we're fine." She doesn't meet my eyes when she adds, "But there won't be any making it up."

"I'm sorry?"

"We're good, but I think friendship's probably where we should leave things."

My heart splatters to the ground.

"I don't... I don't get it. You said you understand."

Her nose twitches before she stabs me with her words.

"I've been an inconvenience my entire life."

"Lexie, that's not—"

"I know it probably wasn't your intention, but it just reminded me that I'd rather have no one than be a second thought again, you know?" She rubs her nose with the back of her hand. "And it's not on you to change those expectations. I'm sorry if I put that on you. You don't owe me anything." She gives me the saddest fucking smile. "I just don't think I'll risk it again."

"Lex," I say with a sigh, but I can't follow it with anything because what the fuck am I supposed to answer to that? I made her feel like shit—the one thing I'd promised myself never to do to her. She deserves the world, the entire fucking universe, and no one was good enough to make her feel that way. Not even me.

"It's okay, really," she says. "Whatever happened, maybe it was for the best." I blink, stunned. How can that be for the best? "You're forgiven. Let's just move on from this, okay? Friends?"

I feel like someone is squeezing my throat in their fist, crushing the cartilage until I can barely speak or breathe. Still, I force a smile and say, "Sure. Friends."

"Good." She points behind her and says, "Okay, well, I better get ready for my shift so..." With a wave, she turns and leaves, not even giving me the time to say anything before the door closes behind her. When I hear the sound of the lock turning in the door, it feels like the final blow. She doesn't trust me anymore.

The hardest thing to get, and the easiest one to lose.

Chapter 25

Lexie

I know the moment Finn has entered the building even before seeing him.

It's like something in the air changes. Electrons shifting, every cell in my body tuning in to him. I'm on the balance beam, practicing my new routine—even harder than the previous one—and while I'd like to say his presence doesn't change a thing, it does. I land poorly after my aerial, almost falling off the beam but catching my balance at the very last second. However, that mishap is enough to get him running my way, the thuds of his boots loud against the mats. Shelli would kill him if she knew he'd walked in with outdoor shoes.

"Jesus, you scared me," he says, sounding out of breath.

I didn't expect the sound of his voice to have that effect on me, but after six days of not speaking, it's like the first ray of sunshine in spring and an icy rain storm at once. My back is still to him, so I have the time to steel my face and prepare before I slowly turn around and continue my routine as if nothing happened.

"Sorry," I say in a tight voice as I get into position for my double spin, gaze fixed on a point on the opposite wall. "I'm not at my best today," I lie. Things were going great before he came, but I'm not about to admit that his mere presence threw me off-kilter. I'm not that desperate.

He remains silent as I finish my routine, landing my double pike perfectly. I exhale, then turn to him as I wipe my chalk-covered hands on my thighs.

"Hi," I say. The moment I take him in, I feel underdressed. Sure, he's seen me in old leotards and shorts dozens of times, but today, he looks sinful in a tight black T-shirt and jeans, his jaw covered in just the right amount of stubble. I hate the way my stomach flips over at the sight of him. Hate how I feel like stepping closer just to know whether he wore that cologne I love. Hate how I haven't been able to stop myself from thinking about him even after the worst possible almost-date in history.

I hate it all.

"Looking good," he says, and for a second, I think he might be talking about me. That is, until I notice how he's nodding in the direction of the balance beam to my right.

"Oh, yeah. Thank you."

Finn's stare feels empty as it stays on me. "Haven't seen you in a while."

It's at that moment I realize he doesn't have the cleaning cart he usually uses around here. As if he's forgotten he needed an excuse to be hanging out around here at 1:00 a.m.

"Been pretty busy. Competition season, you know." I add a smile, but he doesn't return it.

"You didn't come for laundry day," he says as if we have a routine of laundry. We had a few weeks of it, sure, but I didn't think he'd notice that I missed one week.

"Martina let me do it at the main house."

His cheeks cave in, as if he's biting them from the inside. A long silence ensues, and just as I'm about to return to my training, he says, "Lexie, I hate this."

I jolt at the sound of my name, which I haven't heard from him in a week. The way he says it is so different from the way it sounded all throughout my childhood. My mother made it sound like a reprimand. My brother made it sound like an insult. My coach made it sound like a sigh.

Finn makes it sound like the easiest thing in the world.

"Hate what?" I say, although I know what's coming.

"This," he says, pointing at the two of us. "The awkwardness."

I force a swallow down. I could pretend I don't know what he's talking about, but that'd be another lie, one that would be much harder to hide.

"We're good, Finn. I told you."

"Then why are you like this?"

"Like what?"

"All...formal and shit." His lips twist to one side, and for a moment, the emotion in his eyes almost makes me break. He looks...sad. Not like Finn. "I don't like it. I want my old Lexie back."

"I *am* here," I say. "We're good. I swear."

And, really, it's only half a lie. I do believe his side of the story. Despite being hurt, I know Finn's not a liar. He's a good person, and if he says he had somewhere else to be, then that's what I'll believe. There was also the black eye that corroborated his version of things.

Still, it doesn't mean that night wasn't a wake-up call for me.

There's a reason why I barely have anyone in my life. It's not because I enjoy spending my time alone. It's because being alone is better than expecting someone and ending up disappointed. My loneliness is a cocoon I've found ways to make comfortable, and getting out of it didn't bring me any good. It's also why I decided from a young age to bet everything on gymnastics—because it can't hurt me. It can't make me feel less than. It can't leave me alone. It's not dependent on someone else showing up. It's there 24/7, on good days and bad, and if I work for it, I can have it all. And while I deviated from that thought for a little while, this sting brought me back on track.

Plus, Finn is the first good friend I've made in who knows how long, and I'm not just talking about friends to chit-chat with and train together. I'm talking about someone I actually trust with myself. Someone I know will listen to me and who will be there for me when I need him. Dating is not worth losing that person in my life. I need a friend much more than I need romance. It doesn't matter that I see him as more than a friend. If we can have that and preserve it, that piece of gold in a mine of coal, then I can live with not having it all.

"We don't feel good," Finn says.

The distraught look on his face kills me. If he can't recognize his Lexie, then I definitely cannot recognize my Finn without his annoying smirk. Realizing I'll need to be more convincing than that, I walk to him and grab his arms. I pretend I don't notice the way his muscles tense under my fingers.

"Finn. We're fine." When he still doesn't blink, I go for the big guns and pull out a teasing smile. "Now stop being a cry baby and help me get good pictures for my socials, will you?"

His expression remains tight for a moment, but I know I finally convinced him when he cracks a smile, sunshine spilling through a blanket of clouds. "All right."

In all honesty, I had no plan of doing that tonight, but now that he's here, might as well make the best out of it. After New York, I got a few of my sponsors back, and while I've been trying to grow my platforms as much as I can, it *is* hard to get good pictures by myself. Makeshift tripods don't always do the trick.

Finn goes to turn on all the lights in the gym while I walk to the mirror lining the walls, to make sure I don't look like an absolute troll, and once I think I'm good, I get back to the beam.

"Ready?" I ask

He nods, his phone already held up.

I try to pretend he's not there as I go through my routine again, but now that I know he's staring, it's much harder to focus. I can almost feel his gaze on my skin.

"Stick that pose for a second," he says as I climb on one foot with my other leg held to my nose, almost like a ballerina. I do as he says, and after a few seconds, I resume my routine.

"That's pretty," he says after one of my favorite jumps, and despite myself, I smile. Complimenting me is one thing, but complimenting my skills always feels so much better.

"So, when's the next competition?" he asks after I've finished my first combination of acrobatics.

"Two weeks," I say tightly while I go through a turn, focusing on not making a strange face for the pictures. "In St. Louis."

"You feel good about it?"

"Sure," I say. I've worked on the things I could have done better in New York, but even with routines that are more difficult, I don't think they can get me to the top, as clean as they are. Not if Clara Popov stays in the running.

"Wait," Finn says as I get into position for my double turn, the one where I'm almost seated on the beam. He jogs in my direction, and when he reaches me, he lifts a hand and says, "May I?"

I have no clue what he's about to do, but I nod, almost in a daze. I both anticipate his touch and fear it might be too much.

And yet when his knuckles graze my cheeks as he places a stray strand of hair behind my ear, I need to fight every instinct inside me not to let my eyelids flutter.

It only lasts a second, but I still feel like his fingers stay in my hair longer than they need to. And while it might not be appropriate for friends, I still want to lean further into his touch, keep it there just a little longer.

It's in this moment, with his fingertips barely touching me and his sequoia green eyes melting on my skin that I realize just how deep in shit I am.

Chapter 26

Lexie

"**I**'m not winning."

I'm staring at the ceiling, sprawled over my bedspread like a starfish. Meanwhile, Finn's sitting on the small couch by the large cabin window, slouched just like I am in a "I'm done with life" position.

It's been three weeks since we decided to keep things friendly between us, and while we're not quite where we were before, I'd say we're as good as can be. Proof in hand: he just walked into my cabin without knocking and let himself drop onto my couch, a single "Hi" coming out of his lips as an explanation.

He did that for the first time two weeks ago. I was folding some clothes, having come back only minutes before from doing laundry at his place. He opened the door, dropped his huge body on my bed, and stayed silent.

"What are you doing here?" I asked.

"It's boring at home without my roomie," he said.

"We were roomies for four days."

"So? I miss you. Sue me."

And that was that. Since then, we haven't questioned why we keep popping into each other's places. We just do, whenever we feel like it, and it feels almost too natural, if I'm being honest. Like we're getting too comfortable. But what's done is done, and we both seem to enjoy it, so I try not to question it too much. I also try not to think about what would happen if I stepped in one day and he was with a girl. The chances of it happening are high if I believe what I've heard about him, and seeing that would be more painful than I care to admit.

I think I'll start knocking from now on.

"I know," Finn says as he throws a stress ball in the air and catches it, again and again.

I turn my head his way, cheek squished against my pillow. "Wow, thanks."

"What? I can't lie to you."

I groan. "I don't know why. I'm doing everything I can think of."

Last week's competition in St. Louis didn't go as planned. Or actually, it did go as planned—I hit everything I was supposed to, didn't miss a single landing, performed my routines as well as I possibly could—but it still wasn't enough. I got third place overall, gold on floor, and a couple other podiums, but that's it. Meanwhile, Clara Popov aced performance after performance. A few other girls I didn't know should be on my radar also stepped up their game and made me actually doubt whether my Olympic dream is only a kid's fantasy at this point.

I hate to think like this. Winners can't think like losers, but the thought has infiltrated my mind, and it's hard to kick it out once it's taken root.

"I do. Know why, I mean."

One of my brows stutters up. "Then why don't you inform me, oh Great Knowing Finn?"

"Sure." Sitting straighter on the couch, he leans forward and rests his elbows on his knees. "You're not winning because you're scared."

I freeze.

"I saw you in New York. There was fear in your eyes, and that's holding you back. You're a better all-around gymnast than Popov. She's just more fearless than you are." His eyes narrow in on me as he adds, "To win, you'll need to want it more than anything. More than your fear of failing."

"I'm not scared of failing," I grunt. "I'm scared of dying."

Once again, I'm hit with images of lying on the ground after my fall, unsure if I'd ever walk again. Of looking up as the anesthesiologist gave me a drug to inhale so I'd fall asleep before my surgery. Of pain that was almost unbearable while in recovery, day after day. Of feeling like I might never get what I'd worked for my entire life.

Finn gives me a sad smile. "As much as it kills me to say, it doesn't matter. Judges don't care about that."

I clutch my pillow tighter as he asks, "Is it still the one thing you want more than anything?"

I nod. As I told myself after our failed date, gymnastics is what I need to keep focusing on. Nothing else.

With a grunt, Finn pushes himself off the couch and walks to me, then extends his hand.

"Then let's make you fearless."

"Are you out of your mind?"

"You want to win or not?" Finn asks.

"That's totally unrelated."

"Is it?"

"Finn, come on," I say, pointing at the ominous train track behind him. It's currently empty, save for the few snowflakes blown from the neighboring trees onto the rusty metal. The sky's a soft gray this afternoon, blending with the pale, icy ground. Yet, even with no train in sight, the tracks scream *danger* from a mile away.

"You want to stop being scared of death?" He tips his head to the side. "Then you need to actually face it."

"I did face it. Very closely, in fact." Falling onto one's neck is an easy way to say goodbye to your life.

"But you need to face it again," Finn says.

"How are you still alive?" I ask.

He shrugs, an irritating smirk on his lips. "Guess death doesn't want me yet."

"Not funny." I don't like imagining him being reckless. Not caring whether he lives or dies. I want my friend around for a long time.

When I see he starts moving backwards, I say, "Where are you going?"

"Where do you think? Facing death."

Then, the dumbass goes smack dab in the middle of the tracks and lies down.

"What the hell are you doing?" I hiss. "Get up."

"Nah," Finn says with a smile like everything's fine in the world.

"Finn, I'm being serious. Get up."

"Come on, Lex. You gotta do this."

"No." My arms are crossed in front of my chest like a petulant child, but I don't know what else to do. Even with no train in sight, seeing him lying there is giving me hives. I scratch the back of my hand.

He pushes himself into a seated position and goes for the killing blow. "Do you trust me?"

I grind my teeth so hard it hurts. For maybe thirty seconds, I stand there while he stares at me, his face never transforming into irritation, only calm happiness.

"I hate you," I mutter as I come to a lying position next to him.

He lies back down. "That why your face got all red up there?"

"Shut up."

For a while, nothing happens, and my thundering heartbeat calms down. That is, until I jerk and say, "You hear that?"

"Yep," Finn says, popping the P.

"Then let's get up!" I move to do as I say but his hand on my arm stops me. "What the hell?"

"You haven't faced it, Lex."

"Finn, there's a train whistle that just sounded maybe a mile from here."

"I know."

"And it's headed right toward us."

"I know. What do you think 'facing death' means? Playing Risk at home?"

"This is stupid," I say, my hands trembling in my lap. Still, something keeps me in place. Poor survival instinct, probably.

"Just try to relax. Close your eyes. Feel your breaths." He's doing exactly that, his hands now crossed over his belly, beanie-covered head leaned back against the fallen leaves frozen on the ground.

"I feel like that dumb girl in horror movies who goes straight toward the murderer without anything to defend herself with."

"Not the same thing," he says. "We're not dying today. Just getting close to it."

"Sounds like an incredibly sane plan."

I try to relax, but the louder the sound of the train becomes, the harder it is to stop myself from bolting out of here. It's like I hear it in every crevice of my body, a thrum that's shouting at me to do something.

"I can hear you overthinking from here," Finn says.

"How are *you* not scared?"

"Death doesn't scare me."

I turn to him with my brows drawn, but he doesn't see me, eyes still closed. He's not lying. I can see it in the looseness in his body, in the soft pulse in his neck.

How is it possible to be so careless about death? The one thing that would end everything?

I don't have the time to question it because soon, the rattle of the tracks becomes so overwhelming, I can barely hear my own thoughts.

"Is this close enough?" I shout over the din.

"Almost."

Jesus Christ. I can't wait much longer. When I open my eyes, I see the train coming toward us at a speed too fast for me to even comprehend. It's maybe a few hundred yards away.

Finn's breath tickles my left ear as he says, "See how that feels? That thrill? That anxiety? Take it in. Remember it. And then you'll see that it's not the end."

I try to do as he says, but right now, the only thing I can think about is RUN, YOU DUMB GIRL!

"Finn, I can't," I whimper, body tense and ready to bolt.

"Soon, darling. Just hold on a few seconds longer."

It doesn't feel like we have that many seconds longer. The air now smells like diesel, almost as if the train itself is whispering at me to get out if I want to live. But now that I'm here, I don't want to give up, and as scared as I am, I do trust Finn. He wouldn't hurt me intentionally.

Still doesn't mean this wasn't a stupid fucking idea.

"Okay, almost there. I'll count to three, and on three, you roll to your right."

My breath is shaky as I nod, my eyes shut firmly. I can't see. The vibrating ground under me and the eardrum-piercing sound is enough to let me know just how close it is.

"One."

A sharp horn blares, making me whimper as I stutter.

"Two."

Wind rushes onto my face, freezing my lashes in place. It's there, right there...

"Three!"

I launch myself to my right, expecting Finn to do the same on his own side, but instead, I feel him throw himself on top of me and push me out of the way as we start rolling away from the track. A millisecond later, my hair is blown all over the place as the train crosses the exact place we were just lying in, horn tooting again.

"Oh my god," I shout, forcing my eyes open to find Finn sprawled on top of me, his green eyes bright like morning sunlight, his breaths now coming as fast as mine.

And then, I burst out laughing.

Snow has made its way into my coat, my jeans are thoroughly soaked, and I don't think I've ever laughed as hard as I do now. Finn joins me, and soon we both have tears streaming down our cheeks.

"I can't believe you made me do this," I say, my belly hurting from all the laughter.

"You should've seen your face."

"A-asshole," I get out.

It's a long time after the train has come and gone that we finally start to catch our breaths. Only then do I fully realize Finn is lying on top of me, our bodies entangled, his face only a few inches above mine, close enough that I can feel the soft puffs of air on my nose and mouth.

"See? You did it," he says, a grand smile on his lips.

"Yeah, and I almost died."

"But you didn't. That's what matters."

And as I nod, I realize he has a point. I did do it. Faced my fear. Came close to death, and made it on the other side.

And felt as alive as I ever have in the process.

"Thank you," I say sincerely, unable to stop myself from glancing down at his mouth. Just once.

His eyes search mine, pink lips parted in a soft exhale. With the snow and the light sky surrounding him, he looks almost angelic, something I know for a fact he's the opposite of.

"Of course," he says, and I don't miss the way his gaze also drops to my lips. I lick them, feeling like destroying the space between us and tasting him again, even just this once.

But that would be a terrible idea. My heart is too fragile for that, no matter how much I like to pretend otherwise. So I use all the self-control I can muster and softly push him off me, then get to my feet.

"All right, daredevil. What next?"

He blinks, as if taken aback, then sits up and grins. "Thought you'd never ask."

Chapter 27

Finn

"I'm drained," Lexie says, slumped against the window of my passenger seat, her eyes half closed. Outside, the sky is a lavender canvas, turning darker by the minute.

"Is my lifestyle too exhausting for you, Crabby?" I ask.

"Your lifestyle? Like you let yourself fall backward from roofs into the snow all the time?"

"You need to be precise. It was from a *shed*'s roof."

I feel her gaze on me, but I keep my attention on the road ahead. We're almost at the farm, where I'll drop Lexie off before heading back home.

After our adventure on the train tracks a few days ago, I've invited Lexie along on a couple of weird activities, including, yes, dropping backward from my parents' backyard shed into the thick, fluffy snow, the way I used to do with Aaron when we were kids. We also went jumping from the highest diving board at the public pool—an easy one for Lex, but much harder for me—and hiking one of Vermont's steepest mountains, all of those activities interspersed into the few free spots in Lexie's schedule. That girl is always busy, whether because of work or because of practice. Mom said she's one of the best coaches the gym has ever had, and if she puts the same amount of effort and dedication into it that she does with her own training, then I have no doubt about it.

"Shed or not, it was high," Lexie says.

"And I bet you'd love to do it again."

She huffs, then turns my way. "Life's never boring with you, is it?"

"Just figured that out?"

She shakes her head. "It was pretty obvious that night in Rome, actually. After speaking with you for a couple hours, I was convinced no one could be bored with you around."

I grin, flattered that she's remembered even one positive thing about me from that night. Then, I throw her a wink. "I thought you were pretty cool, then, too."

We spend the next minute in silence, and as I turn onto the driveway that will lead to the small cottage, I notice she's rubbing at her neck while wincing.

"You okay?" I frown as I add, "Did you hurt yourself?" Jesus, if she did while going through one of my stupid plans, I'd never forgive myself. Not when there's only one thing she really wants in this world and it's dependent on her body being at its best.

"No. Well, not recently anyway." She shrugs. "Just typical gymnastics aches coupled with past vertebral fractures." One of her eyes closes as she seems to hit an even more tender spot. "A shitty mix if you ask me."

Gravel crunches under my tires as I slow down in front of the cottage. I hate seeing her in pain, and I have the strongest urge to replace her hands with mine and try to ease the hurt there. Only one of the thousand instances since New York—even before then, if I'm being honest—where I've wanted to touch her in one way or another.

Before I can think through my words, I blurt out, "There's a hot tub at the main house."

Lexie's head snaps my way. "I'm sorry?"

"I mean, it's good for muscle pain, I think? And Martina and Dennis are visiting Aaron and Wren in Boston right now, so they're not there."

Her chocolate eyes are wide. "We can't. Well, *I* can't."

"They don't mind," I say, insisting for some strange reason. "I use it all the time after work. In fact, I'm pretty sure I'm the only person who uses it."

She tucks a loose piece of hair back into her short ponytail. "I don't have a bathing suit."

"It's fine. Me neither."

Her brows climb her forehead.

"I mean, I don't have any here. But lucky for you, I never go commando." I wink, but her face seems even less amused than before.

"I don't know," she says, and only then do I realize I must look like a fucking creep to her, trying to get her naked in a remote place where we're alone.

"Lex, if you're uncomfortable—"

"No, I'm fine," she says while avoiding my gaze, and after a sharp exhale, she adds, "Let's do it, then." Her answer comes a little too fast, but before I can question her further, she's getting out of the truck.

I follow her out, the freezing air suddenly feeling like a sauna.

"I'll go change. Meet you there?" she asks.

"Sure."

And then she disappears inside the cabin, and I realize just what a dumb idea I had.

Fuck. Fuck, fuck, fuck.

We're supposed to be friends. That's the only way I can have her in my life, and it's something I've accepted. But nothing will scream "friendly" like the giant boner I'll get when I'll be stuck in a hot tub with her barely covered body.

What a dumbass.

As I start walking toward the main house, hoping the wind will cool the heat on my face, I grab my phone and dial Aaron's number.

"What's up?" he says as he picks up.

"I'm in trouble," I answer.

"Mrs. O'Connor finally realized it was you who stole from her pumpkin patch in fifth grade?"

"Fuck off, I'm being serious."

He chuckles. "What'd you do?"

"Where do I even start?"

I briefly go over what happened since our ruined first date, the forced friendzone that ensued, and what things have been like between us since. Once I'm done, I'm breathless, and Aaron is quiet, so I add in a rush, "And I just invited her in your parents' hot tub, and I don't know how I'm supposed to survive it."

Aaron hums. "I love that hot tub."

"That's fucking disgusting," I say. There's only one thing that tone can mean, and I'd rather not think about it.

He laughs. "But seriously, though. What happened that made you skip on her?"

"I can't tell you." If I couldn't say a word to Lexie about it and ruined what we'd barely started, I'm not going to break Francesca's trust with Aaron, no matter how much I'd like to tell him the shit I found out about my sister's ex-boyfriend. If he's still her ex-boyfriend.

"Fine. But even without knowing, I can imagine how she'd feel. You ditch her and don't offer a good explanation. Maybe if you gave her *something...*"

"I can't. Besides, that's not the point. The point is, I'm about to get real close to a girl I'm... A girl I like, and I don't know what to do with myself."

"Man, I feel you. That sucks."

I rub at my scalp. I'm sure this situation alone will give me another bald patch in a few days.

"Give her some time," Aaron says. "That's the only thing you can do at this point if you don't want to be fully honest with her about everything. Regain her trust. Make her see you're there to stay."

There to stay. The one thing I've never been good at doing.

"Yeah, okay," I say. I guess there's no other option anyway.

After a moment, Aaron breaks my spiraling thoughts by saying, "I *knew* you were into her."

"Shut up." Having reached the main house, I use the key they gave me a while back, then step inside. "It's not like that." I head toward the bathroom on the main floor where Martina keeps the towels, then put Aaron on speaker phone so I can start undressing.

"What's it like, then?"

I push my tongue into my cheek. "I don't know, man. It's..." The words die on my tongue because really, I don't know what it's like. I can't say precisely what Lexie is to me except that she's *more*. So much more.

"I think I get it," Aaron ends up saying, no trace of sarcasm in his voice. In a way, I think he's right. His path to Wren was so damn rough, and yet they have the most beautiful love story I've ever seen. Two people who fought their feelings for so long but who were always meant to end up together.

"All right, gotta go," I say, now only in my checkered boxer briefs. Thank god they have tiny buttons closing the fly, because the last thing I need right now is flashing Lexie in the hot tub like a weirdo.

"Hey, Finn?"

"Yeah?"

"You'll be fine. She'll figure it out. See you're a great guy."

"Thanks man," I say, his words easing some of the tension in my shoulders. Aaron's the best man I know, so if he has hope, how can I not? "See ya."

I hang up, then see I've received a text while I was talking.

Lexie: Where are you?

Me: Heading into the hot tub. Meet me in the back?

She doesn't answer, but when the "seen" message appears on my phone, I rush out the back door with my towel, then push open the lid of the tub, steam billowing out and making me blink.

I wait next to the hot tub, but after a while, I realize seeing a man standing in his underwear in the cold might be slightly awkward, so I jump in and settle into the scalding water, willing my heart to calm the fuck down. I've seen more naked girls than I can count, for Christ's sake. This is nothing.

I finally get myself to relax, for a while. The jets against my back and the warmth of the water compared to the iciness of the air make me feel better.

That is, until Lexie appears around the house and makes my heart drop not just out of my body, but down a fucking crater.

I see her in leotards and practice gear all the time, but apparently, that was nothing compared to seeing her in actual underwear, her simple black bra pushing her goosebump-covered breasts up, her arms curved around her muscle-lined abdomen—as if she has anything to hide—and that perfect, tight ass in matching black panties.

Aaaaaand here's the perv I promised myself not to be.

Clearing my throat, I pretend to find something very interesting in the direction of the pond in the forest, and only when I feel the water ripple around me do I dare steal a glance her way. Thankfully, she's now submerged in water. Doesn't help the tent in my boxers, but at least the bubbles are hiding it.

Lexie leans back, and as she closes her eyes, she releases a moan that does nothing to help matters.

Jesus Christ, Finn, get a grip.

"God, this feels good."

"Told you," I say, hoping she doesn't notice the strain in my voice.

"Was cold as shit to get here, though. I had to run."

"Why didn't you bring a towel?" I ask, just now realizing that damn towel would've helped me not get images I'll never be able to stop seeing when I jack off at night.

"A question I asked myself with every freezing step I took." Even with just her head exposed, I can see the tension easing out her pores. Calm overtakes her until she starts snickering.

"What?" I ask.

She shakes her head. "Nothing. It just reminded me of one time at a guy's house I would've rather forget."

Everything in my body hardens, but I try to keep it casual as I ask, "What happened?"

She laughs again. "Don't judge me, okay? I was pretty wasted."

As much of a hypocrite as it makes me, I really don't like the direction in which this is heading.

"I was at this bar in Baton Rouge after a crappy competition a few years ago, and I agreed to go back to this guy's house, and just as we were starting to...you know..." Her cheeks turn the shade of the Christmas bows adorning the trails on the farm. "His mother walked into his room unexpectedly, and he threw a stinky bath towel on me. I was so embarrassed I left my clothes there and just ran away with his towel." She covers her face with her palms, still laughing. "God, it's even worse when I say it out loud."

I try to laugh with her, I really do, but the only sound that comes out of my mouth is a choked grunt.

Eventually, she removes her hands, and when she sees whatever expression I'm trying but failing to hide, she asks, "What?"

I shake my head.

"Finn, what?"

"Nothing. I just..." I try to work out what it is I'm thinking and feeling in a coherent sentence. "After what happened to you, I didn't think you'd..."

"Have sex?" she says, a hint of a grin on her lips.

Now it's my turn to become Christmas-bow red. "I'm sorry, that's a fucked assumption. I just thought with your aversion to touch—"

"No, you were right in a way, I guess," she says, making me pin my mouth shut. I don't want her to feel forced to share, but I also want to give her the space to do so if she feels like it.

"I'm not a virgin," she says, then adds with an awkward chuckle, "obviously. But more often than not, I feel like I *try* to enjoy sex more than I actually enjoy it."

Bubbles roam around our necks and Lexie seems to settle into them, taking in their warmth as she drags her hands above the white foam. I remain silent.

"You know, even if I don't know what happened to me, I still *feel* it sometimes. That unwanted touch. And I guess having sex on my own terms has been my way of regaining that power that was stolen from me, no matter how uncomfortable it can feel sometimes."

I feel like hurting someone. Scratch that; hurting them wouldn't be enough.

I force myself to breathe in slowly, then exhale. If she can say all of that so calmly, then I get myself to maintain my composure too.

"It makes sense," I end up saying.

The smile she gives me just about destroys everything in me.

We fall into silence, both of our gazes turned up toward the night sky. When I was away and sleeping in larger cities all over the world, I'd sometimes forget how beautiful the sky is in Sonder Hill, and only once I'd come back would I remember. Without light pollution, every star is sharp and bright, an incomparable sight.

"So you've never actually enjoyed it?" I ask, the question slipping out of my lips like skates on ice.

"Not with others, no." At that, an image of Lexie touching herself fills my brain, and I want it out. It's too much. The thought of her head thrown back, legs spread wide with her small, calloused hands between them is just about enough to throw me over the edge. "But to be fair, it's always been with guys I'd only met a few hours before and who I never saw again, so maybe they didn't find it great either."

I grind my teeth so hard I feel a vein pulsing on my temple. "Maybe sex's not the problem, then. Maybe it was just those selfish assholes you were with." It's an assumption, but I'd bet my left hand it's the truth. Guys like that must've been done in five minutes, barely touching her beforehand.

I'd never make that mistake.

"Maybe." Lexie's face is still tipped upward, giving me the perfect view of the bob in her long, perfect throat. "It's a struggle, you know. I *want* to be touched, but I also don't want anyone touching me."

I shift then, turning toward her just as she does the same. The air around the hot tub is so quiet, so still, as if we're in some kind of bubble separating the two of us from the rest of the universe. And while Lexie might feel shy or vulnerable telling me this, I've rarely seen her look this strong. It's in the glint in her eyes, in the straightness of her shoulders, in the way she still leans toward me even after all that's happened to her.

That's probably what pushes me to say the second dumbest thing today.

"I can't pretend I'm a shrink or anyone who could actually help you make sense of all of that. But what I can tell you is I'm always going to be there for you if you need me." My gaze deviates toward her shoulders, strong and smooth, barely protruding out of the water and covered in droplets. "And if ever you felt like trying...*things* with someone you know, someone I hope you trust, then I'm here too." Her beautiful eyes have become round as saucers, yet she hasn't stopped me. "And that's not me propositioning you. That's me saying that if you want to use me to figure things out, then I'm giving you permission to do so."

For a moment, I expect her to shout at me, to tell me I'm out of my mind and I've ruined everything. But when she finally speaks, the only thing that comes out of her mouth is, "Just for me, huh?" Her grin comes back full force, making me chuckle.

"Just for you, my crabby."

"So generous."

"You know me," I joke. "Always there to lend a hand." Pun only half intended.

She laughs, then says, "Well, if ever I want to be added to that world-famous list, I'll be sure to let you know."

I smirk even though every single one of those words have felt like tiny needles pricking my skin. Is that who she thinks I really am? Who I *still* am?

She'd trip if she knew I haven't touched a soul in months. My longest dry streak since I was a kid, and I can't even explain it. Just that I don't feel like fucking left and right anymore.

She glances at her phone lying on the side of the tub, then moves out of her seat. "If I want to make it out of tomorrow alive, I better get going." In one quick move, her body is out of the tub, dripping water and reflecting the bright shine of the moon. "Thanks for everything, Finn. This was great."

"Of course."

I'm too busy focusing on not staring at her that I miss the way she gets out. Only when she says, "And thanks for the towel," do I realize I got duped. She even throws in a wink to make me feel even dumber.

Fuck. Me.

She walks away from the tub and turns the corner of the main house with my towel wrapped around her body, the same way she's got me wrapped around her fucking finger.

Chapter 28

Lexie

Sweat drips down my back as I stare at the set of bars, a mix of fear and anticipation coating the air.

"I don't think it's a good idea," I mutter.

"You said the same thing about the tracks and everything else."

"Yes, because they were all objectively bad ideas." The hot tub probably being the worst of them all. If I thought I could pretend he was just a friend before, that evening murdered this concept entirely.

"But did you die?" he says from where he's leaning against the bars' supporting structure, his arms crossed over his chest, muscles almost bursting under his T-shirt. I've grown up around male gymnasts with massive arms and thighs, and yet I can't help but ogle him.

"Probably more due to chance than to your great ideas."

"Stop being crabby and just do it."

"Did Nike hire you for a commercial?" I say, cocking my hip. "You'd be a great motivational speaker."

"I know I'd be. Now stop stalling, and get up there."

I turn back to the bars, my body tensing at the thought of what I'm about to do.

The moment I felt my neck crack under me a year and a half ago, I swore to myself I'd never try that dismount again. I'd lose every competition before I'd come this close to dying again.

And now here I am. Making past me look dumb as hell.

I contract and release the muscles in my thighs as I try to go over the movements in my head, step by miniature step. I can do every single one of them separately. I'd even done that dismount countless times before, both in competitions and during practices. The logical part of me knows I have the physical skills to do it, but the emotional part of me sees this as my personal nightmare.

"I'm scared," I say in a voice that makes me sound three feet tall.

Finn's entire demeanor changes, his face loosening, losing all the fake edge it was wearing a second ago.

He's the one who suggested I do this. We were eating dinner in front of the television earlier—I'm not a big series fan, but he recently got me hooked on a zombie show, and I can't stop myself from taking a break every day at dinner time to watch it with him—and suddenly, he pressed pause and turned to me to say, "I think you should try your double twisting double back again for San Francisco."

I paused my forkful of roasted chickpeas midair and gaped.

"What?" he asked, as if his question was nothing out of the ordinary. "You've faced death so many times now. It'll be a piece of cake."

I didn't want to. *Really* didn't want to. But Finn being Finn, he somehow found a way to convince me, except now I can feel my salad coming back up, and I'm *this* close to saying hell no and walking out of here.

"Lexie."

Finn's voice is coming from much closer than it was before, but I don't turn to him, my gaze stuck on the tall bar, the one I'll eventually need to let go of and pray for the ground not to come at me too fast.

"Lex, look at me."

I do.

He's not just closer than before; he's *really* close. His hands are lifted midway between us, as if he wanted to touch me but thought twice about it.

I hate that he had that reaction. It's not like it's not justified—it is—but I also wish I'd never jumped from his touch. I wish I could've embraced it right away, could've felt somehow that it wasn't the same as anything I'd ever encountered before, something not to balk from, but to linger on, to melt into and to wrap myself around.

Instead of saying this, I shift to my right so his fingertips have no choice but to graze my skin, all the while keeping my gaze fixed on his. *Don't you see?* I want to show him, *This is okay. It's you, so it's okay.*

The squeeze he gives my elbow tells me he gets it, or at least part of it.

"I'm right here," he says. "You think I'd ever let anything happen to you?"

I twist my lips to one side, trying to pretend like his words haven't just lit a fire inside my chest. "You think you can stop gravity?"

"No. But I know I'd throw myself under you and take the brunt of your fall if it ever happened, so gravity isn't relevant here."

"I'd crush you."

"It'd be an honor to be crushed by you, Alexandria Tuffin."

The way he pronounces my full name is like gasoline being thrown onto the blaze, turning it into an inferno. I don't even know where he learned it from since I never use it—your mother telling you you were named after the town in Virginia where you were conceived will do that to a person—but coming from his lips, it sounds...reverent.

I don't trust my voice to sound steady, so I simply answer with a curt nod, then turn my entire body toward the bars. To my right, I catch him moving away, but even without seeing him, I know he won't go far.

With my eyes closed, I go through three sets of deep breaths. Only when I feel collected do I look up and begin.

The first part of my routine is the same. A combination of pirouettes, releases, flips, and transitions from one bar to the other. To a spectator's eye, it always looks so easy, as if the gymnast is simply letting herself fall in the direction the wind carries her, but no other element requires this much out of me. It's a heady blend of strength, agility, precision, and graceful power, and the gymnast who makes it look easy is one who's mastered it all.

"Come on!" Finn shouts from the ground, the same way I do with my own students. Even through a pirouette, I have to fight my grin. He must've observed me at some point, or maybe we just have that aggressive way of encouraging in common. "Push!"

It feels just like being back in the gym with Andy, his rude remarks and loud calls only driving me to do better.

"That's it," he says when I catch the bar after having done a piked Jaeger, where I swung backward before releasing the bar in my rotation and catching it again after having done a forward salto. It's a move I love, and also one that reminds me I'm almost at the end of the routine. "Easy."

I start my second-to-last full rotation around the tall bar, forcing myself to breathe. It becomes hard as I complete that rotation and get to that last one.

Time moves in slow motion as my body completes that last 360 degrees. *I can't do it,* I think over and over again. *What was I thinking? I almost lost everything by doing it once, and suddenly I want to tempt fate again?*

I'm about to release the bar and do a simple double back dismount, the same I've been performing during my last competitions. But then I spot Finn from the corner of my eye, standing right where he promised he'd be, his body on high alert.

He won't let me fall. The realization comes to me as easily as my next breath. He's there, and he's not going anywhere. It's a fact I believe in, even more than in my inability to perform the dismount.

Which is exactly what makes me decide to start twisting to the left while rotating into my first backflip. I don't think. I don't even blink as I let muscle memory take over my body and lead me to the right place.

The moment I feel hard ground under my feet, everything goes blank for a moment, as if I've landed in some other dimension, one that only exists in a dream. I still can't breathe, not yet realizing what happened.

Finn's the one who gets me out of my trance when he says, "Holy fuck."

I blink, getting my bearings as I examine my surroundings. In a whisper, I say, "I did it." Then, I turn to Finn, who's gaping at me like he's just seen a miracle take place.

"I did it," I repeat louder. This time, Finn's face splits into a huge beam. "Fuck yeah, you did it." And then he's there, and I'm running even closer, and the smell of earth and trees envelops me, and I can't help but throw myself into his arms and hope he catches me.

Of course he does.

"I can't believe that just happened," I say against his neck, soft and warm, like a blanket I just want to wrap myself into.

"I can," he says, squeezing me so tightly against him it's almost painful. I love it. It's nothing like the careful way he was five minutes ago, and it makes me feel so much better. So alive. "You're a star, Lex. A goddamn supernova."

I smile even bigger, and when he starts twirling me around, I can only yelp and hold on to him.

The last time we hugged like this, it was after New York, and just like then, I feel this immense sense of euphoria at being embraced by him, like he's holding together all the pieces of me I thought would never fit again. For this moment, it doesn't matter that I'll never have him as anything more than this. I can live with it. Not everyone gets the chance of meeting someone this wonderful and having them be a part of their life the way Finn is for me. It doesn't matter what he is to me. The only thing that matters is that he remains here.

When he finally stops turning, my head continues spinning, a carousel of glee and thrill, one I never want to get off of.

Pulling back, he lets me see those gleaming green eyes and says, "Those Californians need to prepare themselves. They won't know what hit 'em."

Chapter 29

Lexie

"You need to leave that guy." Finn's voice is firm, leaving no room for discussion.

Lilianne, who's sitting on the seat opposite ours at the table outside the ice cream parlor, shakes her head and laughs. "You don't get it," she says before dipping her spoon into her cookie dough treat.

Today's the first day that gives me hope that spring is around the corner, with temperatures in the high sixties and a bright sunshine that puts everyone in a great mood, my Arizonian ass included. So when Finn came to get me at the gym and asked if I wanted to go with him and Lilianne for ice cream, I didn't hesitate. Cold weather has never stopped those two from going on their weekly dates, but while I've only agreed to accompany them a few times, I wouldn't have passed on it today.

It's been an exhausting couple of weeks. First, there was San Francisco, where I got my highest scores of the season to date, with a gold medal on floor and bars, and an all-around silver. Landing that dismount at the bars certainly helped, but more than that, it felt like finally, I was back to where I used to be. I was ecstatic about it, but while it was a step in the right direction, it still wasn't enough. Next, I need to get that all-around gold. If I don't win it at least once before the World Championships, I can pretty much kiss the idea of winning at the final competition goodbye. The moment I stepped off the plane back in Boston, I started training with a new fire, but also with a new level of discipline. Days off are a no-go now. It doesn't matter that my body feels like it's made of thousands of different cogwheels that don't fit together, old and rusty, and that every morning, I'm in more pain than I was when I went to sleep the day before. If that's what it takes to get my place at the Olympic trials, then I'll endure it all.

This afternoon's break is the first one I've taken in weeks, and I'd be lying if I said it doesn't feel like a week-long vacation in the Bahamas. My frozen yogurt tastes like heaven, the scratchy music coming out of the cheap speakers sounds like it's been composed specifically for me, and I've probably smiled more in the last half hour than I have all week. The only other occasions I've felt myself laugh were when Finn visited me at the gym or when he had me over for a quick dinner, and even then, those moments never felt like enough.

Things got a little less fun, though, when Lilianne mentioned how much of an ass her boyfriend is.

"Lexie, a little help here?" Finn says.

"I have to admit, I'm on Finn's side," I say, offering Lilianne an apologetic smile. "You deserve better than that, but *obviously* we don't know everything." At this, I kick Finn under the table. He needs to lay off her a little. He's been hammering at her for the past ten minutes to dump her year-long boyfriend on the spot.

She rubs a spot between her eyebrows, and for the first time today, I realize just how tired she looks.

"It's not as bad as it sounds," she says.

"Lil, he dodges your texts all the time, he leaves you alone to play video games like some kind of twelve-year-old, and he forgot to pick you up yesterday," he says, putting air quotes around the word "forgot." I have to say, I agree with Finn that he probably didn't forget, and if he did, that doesn't make it that much better. The guy didn't go pick up his girlfriend at the hospital after a four-hour dialysis session when he'd promised he'd be there. Thankfully, Finn was free and could be there in twenty minutes, but I can't begin to imagine how that must've felt for her.

"But he loves me," she says, breaking my heart into a million pieces.

Finn doesn't answer, simply grabbing her hand over the table.

The mood has changed drastically, now somber even in the sunlight, our ice creams melted and forgotten on the table.

"I need to go to the bathroom," she says with a smile that doesn't look natural, then disappears into the grocery store next to the ice cream stand.

"It kills me to see her like this," Finn says. "It's like everyone can see it but her."

"I know. But we can't make her do something she doesn't want to."

Finn rubs at his scalp before getting up and scooping the bowls from the table, then throwing them in the trash can so hard that some of the melted ice cream flops onto the ground. "I'm so done with all those fucked-up men."

"What have other men done to you?" I ask. I know I'd have my fair share of names to give if I'd been the one asked, but apart from Lilianne's boyfriend and maybe my brother, he doesn't seem to have other assholes around him.

He opens his mouth, but it's as if the answer is trapped in there. My brows crease.

He goes to start again, but before he can answer, someone calls his name behind me. A feminine voice.

I notice the multiple emotions going through Finn's face as he looks over my shoulder. First, there's the confused narrowing of his eyes. Then, there's the stiffening of his entire body as recognition seems to hit him. Then, worry, or maybe it's anger? And finally, his expression slackens, shoulders stooping as if he wants to be swallowed whole. I didn't recognize the voice, but even without knowing who this person is, I hate them with a passion.

"Chrissy, hey," Finn says, having regained his smile in the last second. He's a fabulous actor. If I didn't know him like I do, I couldn't tell he's faking it.

Slowly, I turn to see who that Chrissy is. She looks to be around our age, or maybe older, with a toddler on her hip and a baby in a stroller —a gadget that looks like it cost more than my car. Her pale red hair is pulled back into a bun, and she has a full face of makeup.

She's really, really pretty.

Behind her stands a tall, skinny guy with long brown hair and a boring face. He's staring at his phone and doesn't even look up at whoever Chrissy's talking to.

"Oh my god, it's been so long!" she says, throwing her free arm around Finn's neck and squeezing.

"Yeah," he says, giving her back a few taps, nothing like the hugs I know he can give. That tells me all I need to know about how he feels about her. "How are you?"

"Oh, I'm great. How are you? I didn't even know you were back in town!"

"Yeah, for a little more than a year now."

"I can't believe it," she says as she pulls back, and the way her hand lingers on his chest tells me something else: they were more than friends at some point. "Little Finn, all grown up."

He tenses under her touch.

I clear my throat. "Hi, I'm Lexie." I extend my hand, and as she takes it and starts shaking it weakly, I blurt out, "His girlfriend."

I don't know what makes me say it. Maybe the discomfort written all over Finn's face. Maybe jealousy. Or maybe just that I want her to stay the fuck away. I've never seen Finn this shaken, so she must've done something to him at some point.

From the corner of my eye, I spot Finn spinning my way with wide eyes, but I pretend as if I haven't noticed it and hope he just goes with it.

She gasps theatrically, then smiles. "Well, well, well. Who would've thought you'd end up settling down?"

A muscle ticks in Finn's jaw. Meanwhile, I struggle not to glare. Why would she say something like that? Finn's one of the most mature men I know, caring for everyone around him and as responsible as can be.

"I don't find it surprising," I say.

"That's because you didn't know him before." She winks at him. "Guess you've changed."

What the fuck is her problem?

"I'm pretty sure he would've settled down with anyone he thought was good for him," I tell her with the bitchiest smile I can muster.

She ignores me, instead saying, "I remember when all you'd talk about was hockey and partying."

"Yeah," he says, chuckling. "I was also seventeen."

She laughs as if he's said the funniest thing she's ever heard, then starts bouncing her kid on her hip when he starts crying. She also tries to shut him up with a pacifier, but when that doesn't work, she turns back to us, wincing. "Well, duty calls," she says. "It was really good to see you, though."

"Yeah, you too," Finn says. I don't bother faking niceties and simply stare as she and her little family turn toward the ice cream stand to order.

"You never told me about her," I say once she's out of ear shot.

"Yeah." He scratches his neck, then looks at his wristwatch. "Hey, I have to go, uh, help Mom with the lock-in tonight, but I'll see you later, 'kay? Tell Lil I said bye."

I look him up and down. He's never mentioned anything about needing to go help with the preparations. Sure, we're both supposed to spend the night at the gym with a few of our athletes for their yearly sleepover party, but from what I'd understood, everything was already organized.

"Um, sure, okay?"

He nods, then turns and jogs toward his car.

"What was that about?" Lilianne asks, back from her trip to the bathroom.

"No clue," I say, staring at him speed out of the parking lot and onto the street.

Chapter 30

Finn

I'm amped up.

My body feels like it's been boosted by hundreds of electric cables, making me restless. All evening, I've been running left and right, passing down snacks to the kids, then hosting a few games, and finally helping them all get ready for bed. Some are as young as seven years old, so they need quite a bit of help, and I'm all the happier to provide it. Anything to keep me occupied. Because if I stop, then I'll start thinking about what happened this afternoon, and I don't know what I'll do if that happens. Probably have the breakdown that's been looming over me all day.

Another reason why I've been so antsy: I can't look Lexie in the eye, and avoiding someone in a closed gym takes a lot of effort.

It's not that I'm mad at her. More like the opposite. I think the only thing that made the meeting with Chrissy bearable was Lexie's lie. I'm still not sure why she pretended we were a couple, but I don't think she'll ever realize how much I appreciated it. She saved me from proving to Chrissy that she was right all along about me, even though she might have been.

I *should* be thanking Lexie for having my back and not hiding from her, but the truth is, this afternoon was probably one of the most embarrassing moments of my entire existence. Worse than the time I got food poisoning in Thailand and made myself a bus full of enemies, and worse than the time my dad walked in on me and some girl I'd picked up at a bar, who was in a very precarious position on her knees. Because today, it was about something that actually matters, but more than that, it was in front of *someone* that actually matters.

I don't know why I think this specific moment might have been eye-opening for Lexie. It's not like she's blind. She doesn't need someone to tell her I'm a loser. She could see it for herself. And yet, when I'm alone with her, it always feels like she sees me as someone better than I am. Not anymore.

"Okay, everyone, lights out in five minutes," I shout over the dozens of high-pitched voices. Boys and girls have been separated in two sections of the gym, and everyone has selected the mat they want to use as a mattress, draping their pillows and sleeping bags over them.

I love lock-ins. Because both my mom and dad had to be present when they happened, I always got the chance to attend as a kid, and even though you'd be way more comfortable at home, it feels special to be in this space with friends at night and sleep on the mats used for training only. Kind of like camping. With it being Lexie's first one, I'd planned on bringing booze and making margaritas in the staff room for her so she could enjoy her night off even more, but with what happened, my head hasn't been in it.

"Hey, stranger."

It takes me a long moment to steel myself before looking in her direction. I'd thought seeing her anger and disappointment after our failed date was the worst thing that could happen, but I think seeing Chrissy's pitiful and belittling expression on Lexie would be an actual stab to the heart.

Of course, it doesn't happen. When I finally gather all my courage, the only thing I see on Lexie is a casual smile. She wouldn't do that to me. That doesn't mean she can't pity me in her head, but I'll take what I can get.

"You okay?" she asks.

"Yeah, why?"

"You're acting weird."

"No, I'm not," I answer too rapidly, in a weird tone. She cocks her brow as if to say, *see?*

"I, uh, have to get the kids to bed," I mumble before walking in the direction of the floor section, where rows of all types of mats are spread out, covering the blue floor. I feel Lexie following me, and once we've made sure everyone is settled and ready to go, I send my mother a thumbs-up at the other end of the gym, telling her she can turn the lights off.

The moment we're basked in darkness, Lexie makes her way back to me. "Are we going to bed too? It's only 9:00."

I want to say yes. If we stay here, then we have to stay quiet, and if we sleep, then we can't think of the shitshow that was this afternoon. However, she'd guess something was actually wrong, and then I'd never hear the end of it.

"We can go hang in the back for a while," I whisper. That was the initial plan, after all. My parents are going to stay in the offices closest to the floor so they can help the kids if they need something, which means Lexie and I are off the hook for a bit.

Without answering, Lexie heads in the direction of the staff room, and I follow her.

"Oof," she says once we've both walked inside and turned the lights on. "What a day. Handling fifty kids on a sugar high is harder than I'd thought."

"Yeah," I say.

Her eyes are on me as she lifts herself and settles her butt onto the lunch table, her lips pursed.

"So, are you going to talk to me now?"

"Huh?" I say.

"Don't play coy. You think I don't know when you're avoiding me?"

"I wasn't," I lie.

"Finn, you walked away when I went to offer you food, grabbed a slice of pizza that'd fallen on the floor, and said you were good."

Yeah, maybe that wasn't my smartest move.

"So, I repeat my question: are you okay?"

I swallow.

"Is it that girl?" she asks.

A huge breath leaves my lungs. "I didn't want you to see that."

"See what? Her being shitty?"

I slump in the chair facing Lexie.

"Who is she anyway?" she asks.

And there it is.

Scratching the back of my neck, I say, "A girl I dated a while ago."

"Did you do something to her?"

"No. She left me."

"Why was she speaking to you like that, then?"

"Like what?" I ask, knowing precisely what she means.

"Like you were some kind of dumb jock." Her nostrils flare. "I hated it."

I quirk my lips up. "It's fine."

Lexie's eyebrows meet as she says, "No, it's not."

My foot wipes the floor between us, sneaker dragging a plastic bag that was left on the ground.

"Finn, it's not."

I wish she'd drop it. The longer this conversation goes on, the more chances she'll have of figuring out what made Chrissy see me this way. I'm the guy girls want to be with only for the night. The one who still lives in his hometown and who never went to college. The one women like Chrissy would never have considered starting a family with.

"Look at me," Lexie says in her coach voice, and despite the fact that I want to get out of here and never speak about it again, I do as she says. I don't think she could ever ask something of me I wouldn't give her.

"You can pretend all you want that everything's fine and that you're some casual guy who cares about nothing, but I see right through you, Finn Olsen. You're not." She pushes herself off the table and shakes her head, her mouth twisted in a frown. "In fact, if one of you is dumb, it's her for making you feel that way and then going for some fucking Keanu Reeves wannabe while you were an option."

I can't quite catch my breath. In fact, my throat is uncomfortably tight. Lexie spoke like she was a history teacher in front of a class of students, like she was stating unarguable facts. I don't think I've ever had anyone talk about me this way. But doesn't that just mean she's the one who's wrong? Even my parents have been ashamed of me at some point or another. They never said so, but it was obvious in their demeanor. *Dropping out of school? Running off to travel? Really, Finn? Have you thought this through? What about us? You're just leaving?* I've heard all variations of these sentences over the last decade, and if that's not disappointment, I don't know what is.

"I'm pretty beat, actually," I say like a real chickenshit, then get to my feet. "I think I'll go to sleep."

Lexie's face is rigid. "You sure?"

"Yeah."

"Okay, then." She steps forward and grabs her bag. We're already in loungewear, but our sleeping bags and pillows are all in here.

"You're coming too?" I ask.

"Is that a problem?"

I shake my head, then indicate for her to lead the way. We walk back to the floor section, and while I unroll my sleeping bag, I start scavenging for a mat. Lexie does the same, and it's only once we both stop in front of a tiny mat under the balance beams that I realize this is the only one that's left.

"You okay to share?" I whisper, the knot still ever so present in my throat.

"Sure."

I don't move yet, but when she drops her sleeping bag and pillow onto the mat, I do so too. It's already dark and silent in the gym, so the moment we lay down side by side, we remain still and silent. I try my best not to think about who it is exactly who's lying a few inches from me, the smell of her pear and vanilla shampoo making me want to groan.

"I can't believe we're voluntarily sleeping on a mat thousands of bare feet have stepped on," she whispers.

I try to keep my laughter as low as possible. "That's the beauty of lock-ins."

"There's nothing beautiful about getting a plantar wart on my ass."

"You naked in there, Lex?"

She glares at me, then says, "The smell isn't so bad when we're upright, but this close to the ground, I might dream of millions of stinky feet trampling me to death."

"I thought you didn't dream?"

Her smile dips before coming back up as if nothing happened. "This smell is enough to awaken all that is dormant within me."

I sniff. "So no cheese-and-sweat smell before falling asleep. Noted."

"When are you planning on having me over?" she teases, and while it's clearly a joke, I'm thankful that the darkness hides the warmth in my cheeks. If only she knew just how much I've dreamed of that over the months. Of knowing she'd be sleeping close to me, safe, and maybe at some point getting up during the night and going to join her on the couch, hoping she'd been thinking of me the same way I'd been thinking of her.

"I told you, I miss my roomie," I say, voice rough.

She snickers. "Well, goodnight, roomie."

"Goodnight."

I would've expected Lexie to maybe feel uncomfortable about sleeping so close to me, but with the way she shifts, then flops onto her belly with her face inches from mine, it's clear she doesn't.

And isn't that something? The girl who used to jump every time I brushed her skin by mistake is now trusting me to fall asleep next to her, leaving herself unprotected and still deciding to do it. A girl who has so many fears but who *decides* to be fearless.

I want to be her when I grow up.

Which is probably what pushes me to whisper, "I know what you said earlier, but what if she's right?"

Lexie lifts herself on her elbows, and even in the darkness, I can see fire burning through her irises. Even without saying who I'm talking about, she knows.

"I'm not some big catch, Lex. You were so embarrassed for me, you had to lie and say you were with me to make me look better, but the truth is, I'm a twenty-eight-year-old who lives in a small apartment next to my parents' house in the middle of bumfuck, nowhere. That's not the epitome of success."

I don't expect the whack to the chest she gives me. "Ow!"

"You're so freaking dumb, Finloo. That means jack shit. You *are* successful. You manage a great business. You're there for everyone around you. You are loved by so many people, and you're a great freaking person." She shakes her head. "Don't you get it? It doesn't get better than this."

Once again, I'm speechless. I don't have the mental capacity to process everything she's just said. Mostly, though, what sticks to me is she didn't mention that what I'd said wasn't true. I *am* still in Sonder Hill, and I *do* live in an apartment close to my childhood home, but what she said was that I could be valuable not despite of it, but *because* of it.

"Are you going to get that into that thick skull of yours now?" she says.

I laugh. "I'll try. Thanks, Lex." The words feel too easy, too empty for everything I'm feeling, but they will have to do.

"Just telling the truth," she says before letting her head drop back onto her pillow. "And for the record, I didn't lie because I was embarrassed for you. I lied because I wanted to twist the knife into what a giant mistake she's made."

The biggest smile rips my face, and this time, I don't stop myself when I lean forward and press a kiss to her temple. She's so feral, and I don't think I've ever loved anything more about someone.

"You're the best, you know that?" I say.

"It's what I'm aiming for, after all," she says with a smile.

"Goodnight, Lex."

"Goodnight, Finny."

I wouldn't bet my hand on it, but I'm pretty sure she snuggles closer to me once she falls asleep.

Chapter 31

Lexie

The moment I step inside Finn's apartment, I throw myself onto the couch, boneless.

Steps come from the kitchen, and then, "Well, hello to you too."

My only answer is a groan.

Something clangs as if he's dropped a metal bowl onto the coffee table. I can't be sure because my face is currently crushed against his suede decorative pillow.

"What's up with you?" he asks, laughing.

"I'm dead."

"Pretty sure you're not."

"Yes, I am." I force myself to flip my head sideways so I can see him. He's dressed in gray sweatpants and the thinnest white T-shirt known to man, his hair longer than it's ever been since we met. There are two patches of baldness, and I love how he doesn't seem to give a shit about them. He's hot no matter what his hair looks like, and he seems to have slowly come to realize it. "This afternoon's practice has killed me."

"You couldn't give yourself one day off after yesterday?"

The simple mention of yesterday makes me smile. My first all-around gold. Sure, it might have been at an overall smaller competition, but it was still part of the official competition circuit, and I'll take the wins where I can get them.

Finn wasn't present at the competition, but the second I was able to get to my phone, I saw a hundred text messages, all from him. Apparently, he'd been streaming the event from work.

Josie called too, right after him, reassuring me that things were fine at home and that she was proud of me. After that, the day couldn't have been more perfect.

"I can't afford a day off. We're two months away from the World Championships." Although with the way my back—actually, my entire body—is hurting right now, it might've been a good idea to take the break. I don't know how I'll be able to train for the next few days since I can barely walk.

"You're the most stubborn person I know," Finn says.

"I prefer the word 'determined.'"

"That's too bad cause 'stubborn' is what you get."

I grumble.

The couch dips beside my feet. "What do you need?"

"A new body. One eight years younger, preferably."

"You act like you're ninety-five."

"Twenty-five is ninety-five in gymnast years."

"Didn't think you had your own metric system."

"The more you know..." As I shift a half of an inch to the left, a muscle spasms in my back, and I fake sob into the pillow.

"What about another trip to the hot tub?"

My face heats instantly at the thought of that night. It's been more than a month, and I still remember precisely how it felt to be this close to Finn's half-naked body. How tempted I was to get closer, even though that's not what friends do. Especially not when one of those friends has feelings for the other.

It's so strange, that I have this physical attraction to Finn. It's never happened to me before. Sure, I could tell when a guy was sexy or good-looking, but never did I feel the need to touch them, to kiss them. For a long while, I thought I might be asexual, but now that I've experienced what my body feels like when it's close to Finn, I think that might have been a wrong hypothesis.

"I don't think hot tub jets are going to cut it, this time," I say. I'm not even sure what *would* help. Daily PT and a hefty dose of painkillers, maybe.

"Come here, then."

That gets me to lift my head from the pillow and glance at him over my shoulder. "Huh?"

He taps his knees. "Come here. I'll give you a massage."

"Um..." That's a bad idea. I can feel it from a mile away. If being in the same hot tub as him was hard, I can't imagine how it would feel to have his hands on me. Just sleeping on the same smelly mat at the gym the other night had me hot and bothered, and that was when we had couple dozen kids around us. Again, I've never experienced anything like this. It's like I've been trying to flick on an empty lighter for so long, and he's the kerosene not only making it burn, but causing an explosion. "I'm fine, but thanks."

"You've been whining for five minutes. Just come here and let me help already."

I grit my teeth. I never thought one day I would avoid someone's touch not because it repulses me but because I want it too much.

On the other hand, the idea of a massage is heavenly. My muscles feel like one tight block of cement, and at this point I'd be willing to try anything to get that pain to diminish.

"I've been told I give very good massages," he says with a smirk.

"Is that supposed to sound as dirty as it does?"

He laughs. "No, that's your filthy mind playing tricks on you."

Yeah, it definitely is.

"Come on, Crabby. Flip over."

I pause as he stands and walks over to the couch. I'd have expected to sit between his knees to give him access to my shoulders, but I guess he wants this to be a full-on massage.

When he sees I haven't moved, he gives me an expectant look.

I gulp but do as he asked.

The second I feel his body approaching mine, I know this was a giant mistake. My stomach tightens as Finn climbs over me and straddles my backside, his knees barely fitting on the small couch. My body somehow finds a way to tighten even more, now for a whole different reason. I should've kept my muscle strain. It would've been better than feeling this urge to turn around and jump my friend.

However, once his warm, large hands land on my shoulders, I let out a sigh of relief. God, this feels good. He starts rubbing with the perfect pressure, not too much that I scream in pain, but hard enough that I feel the loosening of the tensions in my body.

"Relax," he says above me, his deep voice sensual, or maybe that's just my horny mind imagining it this way.

His thumbs rub a little lower, this time at the level of my shoulder blades, digging into the hard knots and making me groan.

"You're really tight in there," he says as he picks at a particularly strong knot, and when I start chuckling, he joins me. "Sorry, that was too easy."

"You're the worst," I answer, not believing my words for even one second.

Once he reaches the level of my bra and massages on top of it, I feel like telling him to remove it so I can feel his hands better, but that would be the dumbest thing I could do, so I stay quiet. That doesn't mean my body does the same. I'm so jolted up it feels like every one of his touches could send me over the edge. Goosebumps cover whichever area he brushes by mistake, my breathing is loud and shallow, and I would be embarrassed if only this didn't feel so good.

Trying to shift my thoughts, I ask, "So who'd you give massages to?"

"Jealous?"

"No," I lie. I can't forget Finn has a past that's probably a hundred times more extensive than mine, but I also can't blame him for it either. He had every right to get all the fun he could. He still does. Maybe he does get it and I'm just unaware of it.

That thought causes me more pain than I'd care to admit.

"Just curious to know where you got those skills," I say.

"You'll be happy to know I only ever give massages to my mom after a hard day in the gym," he says. "Although maybe I should monetize my talent."

"No," I blurt out. "I mean, you're not that good anyway."

"Really?" he asks, reaching a spot in my lower back that almost has me rolling my eyes back. "That why you're squirming under me?"

Am I? Oh god, I think I am. I force stillness into my body, but it's too late. He knows everything he needs to.

"You know what? I think I'm all back in shape now."

"Wait, I still have your legs to do." His gaze meets mine over my shoulder, darker than they were when he started. "Is that still okay?"

I hesitate. Once again, it's not really okay, but only because of how much I want it. Of what his touch does to me. Having his hands rubbing on my thighs would be another terrible idea.

But I must be a masochist, because I nod.

Shifting so he's seated on my feet, Finn's hands land high on the back of my upper thighs, which are as tense as my back was. No movement he does is inherently sexual, the push of his fingers in my skin purely to help with the strain, and yet something clenches in my belly at every new touch. It's like I anticipate him everywhere. *Want* him everywhere.

"You good?" he asks.

"Mmhmm." Too good, in fact. After that, I'll run home to use my vibrator, and I know damn well who I'll be thinking about when I come.

Oh god. I'm the worst "just friend" in the entire world.

He gets to my calves, a zone I had no idea was erogenous but clearly is. My skin is moist, and Finn's living room feels like a hundred degrees. I'm burning up under him, and I pray to all that is holy that he doesn't notice it. Because if he does, I don't think I'll be able to lie. Not about this. Not when my body probably shows just how much I want him.

Once he's done with both of my calves, he clears his throat and says, "Do you want me to do the front?"

I'm a sucker. I really am.

The answer I should give him is clear in my head, but the instinct to go against it is too intense. It takes over everything. The house could be on fire, and I'm not sure I'd notice.

Wordless, I turn onto my back, keeping my half-mast eyes on him as he sits on my legs and starts massaging the front of my thighs.

Jesus. If I thought the backs of my legs were sensitive under his touch, that was nothing compared to this. His thumbs rub into the muscles of my inner thighs, sending lightning through my entire body. This time, I can't stop myself from squirming under him.

"You okay?" he asks, his hands resting above my knee.

No, I'm not. I'm so not okay.

Forcing myself to inhale deeply and to stop staring at his nipples through his thin shirt, I say, "Much better than before. Thank you."

I expect him to take it as a hint to get off and walk away. Leave me be so I can live my horniness in peace. Instead, he stays in place and continues boring holes into my eyes.

"You're flushed," he says, his chest rising and falling almost as fast as mine.

"No, I'm not."

"Yeah, you are." His hands give my thighs a squeeze, making me gasp. He leans forward. "Tell me what's on your mind, Lex."

I can't breathe. Two options stand in front of me, and neither of them seems good. On the one hand, I can lie and tell him everything's fine. I can continue to live as if Finn and I are just friends and will never be more. On the other hand, I could give in and kiss him right here, right now. Live through whatever fantasies have been inhabiting me for months now. While I have no illusion that Finn would fall in love with me and want to have all my babies, he might want to keep being friends while also letting us have our fun.

I could go with the first option. I have enough self-restraint left to go through with it. Except that when I glance back at Finn, I notice I'm not the only one who's flushed. Not only that, but the tent in his sweatpants tells me he might actually want this as much as I do.

And that's what makes the decision for me.

Lifting myself on my elbows so my face comes inches from his, I say in a breathy voice, "Are those practice sessions you offered still available?"

"Yeah," he says on a sigh. "Yeah, they fucking are." And then his lips are on mine, and I forget every reason why this was a bad idea.

As careful as Finn was with me the previous times he touched me, today, he's unleashed. My fingers dip into his scalp as his tongue enters my mouth and meets mine, the feeling so heavenly it makes me moan, which in return makes him release the holiest of groans.

I didn't know a sound could turn me on as much as this one just has. An ache builds between my thighs, and when his body drops between my open legs and his pelvis rubs against mine while he drags his lips down my jaw toward my ear, I almost pass out.

How did I ever think I was the problem when this feels so good? Maybe Finn was right. Maybe the other guys just sucked.

Actually, I know that's the right answer when Finn's hands dip from my neck and he drags his fingertips over my sternum, between my breasts, and I feel like crawling out of my skin from how much I want this.

"God, Lex," he whispers before pressing a warm kiss to my clavicle, the smell of pine trees storming my senses and making me want to bask in it forever. "Do you have any idea how long I've wanted this?"

His words only prime me more. In one quick move, I pull his head down to me and take his bottom lip between mine, my turn to taste him. His tongue curls slowly around mine, as if we have all the time in the world. I feel like devouring him whole, while he seems intent on making this last forever.

"You'll let me know when it's too much, yeah?" he says between kisses.

I nod before pulling his T-shirt up. He helps me take it off, and once his naked chest is above me, I let my hands roam free. If I believe the sounds he lets out, he doesn't mind.

"Can I?" he asks, pulling at the bottom of my top.

I answer him by removing it, leaving me only in my sports bra. Even so, he stares at me like I'm wearing the prettiest lingerie. Like I'm someone who deserves that kind of stare.

"You're so fucking beautiful," he says. I'm still in workout gear, my hair is a mess, I have no makeup on, but somehow, with the way he looks at me, I believe him.

Carefully, he brings his hands up to trace the outline of my bra. Just as I let out another moan, one of his thumbs rubs delicately over my pebbled nipple, making my eyes drift close. My body is flooded with sensations, from the hardness of his length pressing against my soaking middle to the taste of the strawberries he was eating when I came in. It's too much and yet not enough. I want him everywhere.

Making eye contact with me, he grabs the bottom of my bra. I nod, which prompts him to pull it up, baring my small breasts to him.

"Goddammit," he says, kissing between the two before twirling his tongue around my right nipple. "I'll never get enough."

I hope he doesn't.

As I arch my back against his mouth, he starts thoroughly ravishing me, one hand pulling at my hair, the other squeezing my flesh. He begins by licking my nipple before taking it between his lips and sucking on it, all the while playing with the other with his fingers. And then he's switching sides, and I can't do anything except gasp and whimper at the feel of him.

"Finn," I whisper, clenching my thighs together. I don't know what I want from him exactly.

Climbing so his lips are a hair's breadth away from mine, he asks in a raw voice, "Are you wet for me?"

Normally, I'd be too ashamed to answer this question, but now, with the green in his eyes burning and the speed of the pulse in his neck, I feel so wanted I don't even care.

I nod.

"I knew you would be." He then lets one of his hands move lower, and lower still. Everything in me that wasn't on high alert yet turns alive, my body hot and cold at the same time, full of anticipation and wanting, but also full of nerves. The last few times I did this, it was painful or somewhat uncomfortable, and I ended up telling the men to stop trying to get me off and just get on with it so we could be done. This time feels like the opposite, but I also don't want to be disappointed if the same thing happens.

With the single tip of his middle finger, he draws circles around my navel and above the hemline of my shorts. "You know what I really, really want to do?" he asks, and Jesus Christ, is his voice made of crack? It's almost enough to make me combust.

"What?" I ask, nipping at his earlobe. He trembles beneath my touch.

"Taste you." Just as he says it, he breaches the band of my shorts and slips his hand inside my panties, and I freeze. He's so attuned to me that he immediately senses it and pulls his hand away, then pushes himself off.

"No, no, please," I say, pulling him back down to me and kissing him. "I'm good."

"Lex…" he says, his voice back to its serious form.

"Finn, I want to." I don't even know what happened. It's like for a second, my body remembered that maybe it shouldn't like this. That maybe what would follow would be painful and would be going against its wants and needs.

But even if my body has its reticence, I *want* this. I don't think I've ever wanted anything as much as this. Because no matter what, I trust Finn with everything I have.

His face contorts in pain. "I don't want to push you too fast." Leaning forward, he drops the sweetest kiss on my lips, so far from the fire from before.

"Please," I say. If we stop now, I don't know that I'll ever get the courage to start again. Not when my logic will kick in and remind me that doing this with him might mess up one of the best relationships I've ever had with anyone.

His eyes alternate between mine, then explore my body, examining every inch like it's priceless.

When he comes back to me, his face has perked up. "I have an idea." Then, he lifts himself and shifts our bodies so my head is leaning against the armrest of the couch and he's lying sideways next to me, getting an unobstructed view of all of me.

"Touch yourself with my hands."

My eyes almost pop out of their sockets.

"I—"

"I know what you're going to say, and don't. You'll get to have what you want while remaining in full control." He licks his lips. "Use me, Lex."

My heart rate increases as I look down at his fingertips tracing shapes on my belly.

"And don't for a second think about being embarrassed about this." He brings his lips so close to my ear that I shiver from the warmth of his breath when he says, "Let me see how gorgeous you look when you come on my hand."

How is a girl supposed to say no to that? She can't. That's the answer.

Pretending I have all the courage in the world, I nod and take the back of his hand under the front of mine. Then, I slip both of them into my panties, and the second we both feel just how wet I am, Finn mutters a "fuck" and lets his forehead drop to my temple.

"I think you might be the death of me," he mutters.

"Likewise," I say before I start to circle his fingers above my throbbing bundle of nerves, the sensation so strong I gasp.

"That's it," he says, kissing along my jaw. "You're doing so good."

His words push me to become brazen and to rub his middle and index fingers faster against me, the exact way I would with my own if I were alone. Except I'm not alone, and this is as far from what it's like at home as can be. Having Finn's long fingers on me, but mostly knowing they're his, makes all the difference in the world. And as he continues to whisper praise in my ear and to give every inch of my face slow, tender kisses, I start to feel pressure build between my legs. Thighs shaking between our hands, I find the perfect pace and let my eyes flutter shut. Finn never once tries to take control or to change things up, and even so, he's still so damn hard between us. Like just the idea of me getting off is enough to get *him* off.

"Are you going to come for me, Lexie?"

"Yes," I say.

"Good." Then, he grips my chin and turns my head to pull me in for an earth-shattering kiss. His tongue moves at the same rhythm as his fingers, and his free hand remains on my chin and neck, making me feel protected and cherished.

The pressure between my legs is too much, but I continue rubbing myself until finally, my core starts clenching and I moan into Finn's mouth as my hips buck from the couch.

"Shh," he says before kissing me again, his hand never letting go of me, letting me reach the full length of my orgasm. It feels like it's never going to stop until finally, I pull my and Finn's hands away, too sensitive to even think about continuing a second longer.

"I was right," Finn says as he removes his hand from my shorts.

"Hmm?"

"You do look fucking gorgeous when you come."

I burst out laughing, but stop when I see him bring his fingers to his mouth and suck them clean. The sight makes my throat dry at the same time as it makes me want to go at it once more.

"Perfect," he says. Then, he pulls me to him, hugging me close as he rubs my shoulders and back for what feels like forever. It's rare that Finn's quiet, and I'm not sure whether I should take it as a good sign or a bad one.

Lifting my head up so I can meet his eyes, I say, "What are you thinking about?"

He gives me the biggest shit-eating grin I've ever seen. "How I can't wait to do that again."

Chapter 32

Finn

"I can't believe you know how to do this."

"Who do you take me for?" I ask.

"*Not* someone who can do crown braids like an expert."

"I'm full of surprises," I say, then press a kiss to the back of her neck. She arches into the touch, always wanting more.

That girl gives me every reason to feel like a smug bastard.

It's been a week since we finally gave in to our urges, yet every time I get to kiss her, to touch her, it feels brand new.

We've been taking it slow. If I'm being honest, this is as slow as I've ever been with anyone, and I wouldn't have it any other way. Taking each thing step by step allows me to appreciate them so much more. Every new opportunity I get to discover her body and make her see how sex can be a positive experience makes me so damn happy. I can't erase all the fucked up things that were done to her, but I can make sure the only thing she feels from now on is pleasure.

Lexie giggles in my arms. "You're going to mess up all your hard work."

"I'll make you another one later," I say as I completely let go of the short hair I'd braided almost all the way around her head and flip her over so she's lying on her back, the white pillows on my bed crowding her. After we woke up, I didn't care to make the bed since I knew that after making her breakfast, I'd be dragging her back in here, maybe make her come once or twice more.

I'm a man of my word.

She's wearing my T-shirt—*only* my T-shirt—and I never would've thought a white undershirt could be this hot until now.

I drag my hands down her chest until I reach the hem of the shirt, then slowly glide them up her tight belly. She squirms under me, something I've come to gather as a sign that she really likes something. I go higher and higher, my thumbs brushing the underside of her breasts, and just as I get to her nipples, she shifts us so I'm on my back and she's straddling me.

"You've given me too much already," she says, the braid starting to unravel, hair falling over her shoulders. Her mouth is quirked into the cutest of smiles as she rubs a hand on my naked chest, callouses scratching at my skin in the best way. "I think it's only fair I return the favor, no?"

I groan as she rubs her middle on my already-hard cock, then lowers herself so that she's seated on top of my thighs, her mouth coming dangerously close to the tent in my boxers.

Fuck me.

I'm not sure whether I should stop her and ask her to wait some more, but at the same time, Lexie's a big girl. If she does something, it's because she wants to.

Still, the last gentlemanly cell in my body forces me to ask, "You sure?"

She glances up with a fire I should've expected. "Finn, shut up and enjoy."

I smirk. "Yes, ma'am."

Her short nails send shivers down my spine as she pulls my boxers down, the movement so slow it's some sort of torture. When finally she lets me free, the sexiest gasp escapes her lips as she stares at me with some sort of awe.

See? Smug bastard–inducing.

"Touch it, baby," I say, hands behind my head. I know she wants to. I also know she'll want to be the best at it, just like with anything she does.

Losing the shy girl act, she grips me firmly, sending my head back with a curse on my lips.

With a slow drag of her hand up and down, she says, "And what if I want to lick it?"

Jesus fuck.

"Darling, you can do whatever the hell you want with me."

She grins wickedly, giving me another hard pump. I bite my tongue. I need to think about something other than this or else I'll bust in three strokes.

Keeping her eyes on mine, she lowers herself and darts her tongue out, the same way she did when ice cream dripped from her cone last week and she licked the whole of it to catch the droplet, bottom to top. She's looking at me the same way too, like something she wants to savor.

I twitch in her hand. "Goddamn, look at what you do to me." I feel like a teenager being touched for the first time and coming in his pants at the simple graze of a hand, but I guess that's Lexie's power.

Her tongue is now a fraction of an inch from my cock, and just as I can feel the warmth of her breath...

A knock.

Lexie jumps away, and for a second, I think of going outside and punch whoever it is that bothered us.

"Are you expecting someone?" she asks.

"Nah. Must be a package delivery." I do love me some online retail therapy on nights when I'm alone. "They'll leave."

Lexie hums, and after twenty seconds, when it looks like we're in the clear, she relaxes and leans over me again, but just like before, a second set of knocks interrupts her.

"Fucking hell," I mutter, taking a calming breath before shifting so I can get up and throw on a shirt. Lexie follows me out of the bedroom and into the living room, although she remains half-hidden behind a wall as I go to the door. Barely anyone ever comes here. My parents do sometimes, but only when I invite them beforehand. The only other person I can think of is Aaron, and if he's responsible for this, I won't let him live this down.

However, none of those options proves true when I open the door and find my sister standing on my front porch, wearing a sundress and Doc Martens boots, picking at the skin around her thumbnail.

"Fran, hey," I say. "Wasn't expecting you."

"Yeah, sorry." She looks behind my shoulder. "Can I come in?"

"Course." I open the door wider, and only when my sister stops abruptly in the entryway do I remember Lexie is there, wearing a T-shirt that barely covers the top of her thighs.

"Hi," Lexie says with an awkward wave. "I'm Lexie. Finn's...friend."

I hate the hesitation that was there, and I hate that answer even more. Still, I force a smile and pretend this was precisely the answer I was expecting. We *are* just friends, after all. For now, at least. I have hope I'll convince her of trying something more later, but I still think I need to earn more of her trust before that. I might only have one chance to try it, and I won't waste it on the wrong opportunity or at the wrong time.

"Hey," Fran says, giving Lexie an equally weird wave.

"I was actually just going to the gym, so pretend I'm not here," Lexie says, and while I'm incredibly happy my sister came to find me if she needed something, I wish it could've been at any other moment. If Lexie's going to the gym, I can't say when it is I'll be seeing her next. She very well might sleep there to be able to start as early as possible tomorrow. The final stretch of competitions is getting near, and I know she feels that pressure.

Lexie disappears into my bedroom and comes out with her overnight bag hitched onto her shoulder, a pair of leggings added to her current outfit. She stops when she nears Francesca and says, "It was really good to meet you. Finn talks a lot about his little sister."

Fran throws me a look that's half worry, half curiosity.

"Great to meet you too. Hope I'll see you around."

"Yeah," Lex says, and then it's my turn to receive that awkward fucking wave before she leaves. Not even a hug or a kiss. I'm not owed either of those, but after we've spent every night for the past week together and kissed every time we parted ways, I feel like I just missed out on something.

"So," Fran says once the door is shut. "A friend, huh?" She prances to the couch and sits, way too happy to have something to gossip about with my parents. When she wants the conversation to veer away from her at the dinner table, she always finds a way to make it about me.

"It's complicated," I say, joining her on the couch.

She throws a blanket on top of me. "Cover up. I'm afraid I'll see something I could never forget."

I chuckle. "You're the one who came in unannounced. It'd be your fault if it happened."

"Sorry about that, by the way."

I ignore this and ask, "Is everything okay?" I don't want to broach topics she doesn't want to mention, but I also need to know if she's gotten back into what she asked me to pull her out of.

"Yeah." Her fingers find a loose thread in one of my throw pillows and all her attention snags on it. "No. I don't know."

"Has he contacted you again?" I ask carefully, not needing to name him.

She nods, and my hands immediately ball into fists.

"He said he was just joking by bringing his friends home, that no one would've gone through with it."

I don't ask what "it" is. I don't think I'd be able to keep my cool if I knew everything in detail.

"Tell me you won't go back," I say.

Her gaze doesn't meet mine, which is a bad fucking sign. "I don't know. He really does love me, Finn. And I love him too."

Fucking fuck. This is exactly like Lil's speech about her dumb boyfriend, except this might be even worse since I have strong suspicions that Cameron is dangerous.

"Love shouldn't feel like that," I say, and for the first time in my life, I get the sense that I know what I'm talking about. Love should feel like lazy Sunday mornings in bed, sharing coffee and stories. It should feel like constant first times, like careful trust and touches that feel like home.

I think I might also be in deeper trouble than I'd initially thought.

"I don't know," Fran says. As she ties her long brown hair in a bun, I think I might see what looks like a scar on her upper arm, and while I want to ask, I think it'll be better if I remain silent. Getting on her case about this might make her close up and feel like she can't come to me anymore, and that would be the worst-case scenario. She needs to know she can call me any day, any time, and I'll be there.

"Anyway, I don't want to talk about me anymore. What about you? Tell me about her."

I puff my cheeks and blow the air out. Where do I even start? She's the girl I've been thinking about every single day since she arrived out of thin air in September? She's someone I'd see myself settling down here for?

"She trains at the gym and lives at the cabin at the farm," is what I decide on.

Fran's face twists at the mention of the cabin, which had been vandalized by her dearly beloved last year.

"And?"

"And I really like her," I say, the words landing heavily in the living room.

"And does she know that?"

"Kind of? I don't know?"

"What a shitty answer," Fran says as she brings her legs closer to her on the couch. "Tell her, then."

"It's more complicated than that." I then summarize what happened the terrible night that should've been our first date. I know she'll feel bad about it, but I also know she'd hate it even more if she figured out I'd lied to her.

"Oh god," she says. "Why didn't you tell me?"

"It's fine, Fran. I'm glad you called that night, and if Lexie knew, I know she'd understand." I smile. "This was just a small step back," I say, hoping with everything in me that it's not a lie. I need it to be true, especially now that I've had a taste of her. I'm completely hooked.

"Hm."

"You going to see Mom and Dad later?" I ask, wanting to veer away from Lexie. She's like my little happy secret for now, something for me and only me, and I like it that way.

"Not sure yet," Fran says. "They don't understand."

She's right. They don't understand why she'd rather stay with a friend than come home now that she's broken up with Cameron and why she dates someone who doesn't love her the way she needs to be loved. I don't either, but I'm not about to say that.

"You should," I say. "They miss you. Even if they don't understand."

She nods. "Yeah, maybe I'll pass by."

She has no idea how happy my parents would be. Even without knowing what happened the night she called me, they do know their daughter isn't in a good situation for her, and that kills them a little every day. It reminds me of how I felt when Lexie went to Phoenix and I had no idea if she was safe and happy. I can't fault them for being overly protective of Francesca. I'm exactly the same with Lexie.

Another hint that this isn't some simple crush.

Leaning forward, I take my sister's hand and give it a squeeze. "We'll be okay Fran, yeah?"

She squeezes me back. "We'll be okay."

Chapter 33

Lexie

Wind blows my sweat-ruffled hair as I walk back to the gym from Finn's place. He might not like the place he lives in, but it sure is useful for me—it couldn't be closer to where I spend most of my days and nights. We wouldn't be able to spend nearly as much time together if that weren't the case, and that would be a real shame.

Mostly, our dinner dates are the same as they were a month ago. We watch TV and talk and joke around, except that now, when we tease each other, it always ends up with him on top of me or me on top of him. And every time, I wait for the sensation of dread and horror to crawl over me, but it never does. The only thing Finn makes me feel now is pure lust and comfort. He remains careful—almost too careful—with me, which means we've taken things slow and haven't actually slept together yet, although we've done pretty much everything else. I'd like to say he's the one who's the most eager to be with me, but that'd be a lie, or if it's not, then he hides his game well. I can't get enough of him. I want his smell to be imprinted on my skin at all times. I need his hands on me, whether it is to make me reach bliss or to comfort me after a crappy day, rubbing my back and kissing my shoulder. It's like his presence alone is enough to center me. I count the hours until I can have the excuse to visit him for dinner, and the second I leave his place, I start missing him, which is exactly what's happening right now.

Quite pathetic, if I'm being honest.

And what's worse is this shouldn't be happening, especially not now that we're on the last stretch of the competition season and the World Championships in Anaheim are less than four months away. I've still got big competitions coming before then, including the US championships. My entire focus must be on gymnastics, but so much of my mind has drifted to the man with the buzz cut who makes me feel more alive than ever. It's wonderful and frightening at the same time. I'm not sure what this thing means for him, but I know I'm falling for him, and I'm not sure what I'll do if it ends up that he only wants to keep this a friendship.

I swallow, brushing the thought away. That's a concern for another time. For now, I'll keep enjoying him, and I can only hope the heartbreak that might one day happen won't be too devastating.

As I round the corner of the street that leads to the gym, I pull out my phone to answer messages and emails. Ever since my gold medal in San Francisco, I've gotten thousands of new followers, which has led me to get most of my old sponsors back, and even gain some new ones. I now don't have to worry about how I'll pay for flights and for the next few months of rent, which has eased a huge weight off my shoulders. Since it's mostly thanks to Shelli and Finn that I've gotten here, I've organized a few clinics for gymnasts to thank them, and apparently, the gym has been at full capacity since.

On Instagram, I find a few notifications that weren't there yesterday. I open the picture in question, one where I'm stretching, my back arched to allow me to grab my back leg while doing the front splits. Finn took that one a few days ago, then proceeded to make me hope there weren't any security cameras in the gym. That man is wicked.

The usual comments are there, most from younger gymnasts and fans who are encouraging, and a minority from assholes.

@franky69: Ugly bitch.

I snicker. They never get more original, do they?

But the thing that actually makes me laugh is the comment below it.

@FinnTheGreat: @franky69 Why don't you fuck off with your sixth grader username and crawl back into the hole you came out of,   yeah?

I reread it five times, finding it funnier every single time. While the comments about my body and my face used to hurt me in some way, now, with Finn's expansive array of creative insults, I've come to find them entertaining.

Opening my texts app, I go to his name.

Me: You don't have to respond to every online troll, you know?

He sees my message right away and doesn't waste a second to answer, as if he was waiting for it.

Finn: I know. Difference is, I want to. Fuckers :)

My heart does ten handsprings, which is definitely not a good sign for me, but how can I fault it?

Me: Don't let me stop you, then.

Finn: Wasn't planning on it, darling. xx

I smile like a giddy teenager as I walk into the gym, the dark room faintly illuminated by the lilac sky outside. There are no classes or practices on Friday nights, which means I can start my own training earlier than I do the rest of the week. My next competition's in North Carolina in two weeks, and I want to try a new vault. If I can up my game on that event and make sure I execute it well, then that'd be an almost guaranteed gold.

After connecting my phone to the speakers and putting on Rihanna's *Anti* album, I get into my stretches and think about tonight's practice plan. I might start with a few reps of the vaults I currently have mastered before getting to the new one. It'll be the first time I try something I've never done before without a coach there to guide me through it, but at this point, there's no way to avoid it. Plus, I feel better than I have in months. So much better than when I experienced Andy's growing disappointment every passing day, feeling like a weight was dragging me down while I kept trying to fly.

I shift into my shoulder stretches on the floor when my phone vibrates on the ground next to me, Josie's name on the screen.

Jos: Hey! You're still planning on coming home for my birthday, right?

"Fuck," I mutter as I close my eyes. I'd completely forgotten about this. When I first arrived home at Christmas, she asked me if that was the only time I'd be coming for the year, and I told her

I'd try to fly back for her birthday, which is in a month. It never crossed my mind again.

My phone buzzes again.

Jos: Kyle's been stealing money left and right this week, so things at home have been pretty shitty.

And here it is. The other shoe I expected to drop.

I stare at the phone for a minute, not knowing what to write. I know what she needs me to say. I also know that I can't say it.

I go deeper into my stretch, relishing the pain. I have the money to book flights now, so that's not a problem. The actual problem is the fact that I'd rather stab a pen in my eye than feel again the way I did when I was there. I barely survived the Christmas trip. Finn being there was probably the only thing that saved me. Just imagining being frightened by my brother and feeling my mother's resentment again is too much. I don't know that I can do it.

But if I say no and leave Josie to that nightmare without any support, that makes me the biggest coward on earth. I'm surprised she even asked—she rarely calls or texts, I think out of fear of worrying me—so why did she today? What if something more than the thefts happened to her?

"Fuck!" I repeat as I hit the bouncing floor with all my strength. Once again, I'm faced with the fact that I can't protect myself *and* be there for my sister, and that rips my heart to shreds. I could never explain how it feels to be in that house that brings so many memories, some of which my own mind hid from me. How the sheets in my old bedroom remind me of unwanted touches, and the glow-in-the-dark stars on the ceiling make me think of feeling pressure on my wrists and being trapped. The house itself was bad enough, but add to that my brother who's a real asshole, and the last thing I want to do is go back there, and sans Finn this time.

I look back at the phone, then figure I'll answer tomorrow, when I've had the night to think it through. Maybe a genius idea will come to me in the meantime.

I finish my stretches and warm-up, then head to the vault table, where I practice some hand placements and try to visualize the rotations I'll have to do. Usually, I'd have someone spot me and even hold me on the table so I could get a feel of the position before throwing the new skill, but I'll have to do without. I was never good with that anyway, considering having Andy's hands on me always threw me off.

I shake my shoulders, then wiggle my arms. Something's gotten into me tonight, and I don't like it. I need my mindset clear. "Kiss It Better" is blaring through the gym as I walk to the end of the red aisle, rolling my shoulders front and back.

Get out of your head, Lexie.

I'll start with something simple to get me in action. A straight Yurchenko with a single twist. It's been a while since I've done it, but I mastered it at eleven years old, so I should be able to throw it with my eyes closed.

Staring at the table eighty feet away from me, I breathe in as I climb on my tiptoes, and on the exhale, I start running.

Lift. Roundoff. Push. Blocked shoulders. Twist.

The words circle around my head with each step I take, and yet something's different. They seem to be fighting for space that's already occupied, images of my sister and my mother blending with the movements, creating a tornado that wrecks everything in its path.

The jumping board comes faster than I anticipated, even though I think I've taken the same number of steps I always do. I try to regain my momentum, going through the motions I'd visualized before, but again, something is off. I have an inkling of it when my hands come in contact with the table after my roundoff, and it's clear as a day when I get into the rotation.

I'm all off.

The gym around me becomes a blur as I twist more than I'm supposed to—or maybe less than. At this point, everything becomes white, and I don't know up from down and left from right. My body takes over until I meet the ground.

And then, pain.

A scream tears through my lips as my head hits the thin mat, but that's the last thing to make contact with the floor. My foot did first.

Fire lances from my toes all the way to my right thigh. I scream again, this time a mix of agony and of despair.

No. No, no, no.

My vision becomes blurry as I scream for help, but of course, no one hears.

I try to catch my breath, but the air has been stolen from my lungs during the fall, and the anxiety overwhelming me prevents me from getting any more oxygen. I don't want to look down at my foot, afraid of what I'll see.

Not again. Please, god, not again.

The pain is so sharp that for a moment, I fear I'm going to pass out. Or maybe that's the hit I took to the head.

A tear finally falls as I try to get up and fall down when it feels like my foot is about to be ripped in two.

"Help!" I scream, spit flying out of my mouth. "Finn! Someone help! Please!"

A sob tears through me then. So this is what true loneliness feels like.

I try to get up again, but it's useless. There might be a bone popping out of my leg and I wouldn't know. Not wanting to stay at the far end of the gym, I flop onto my stomach and start crawling, pain lancing through my entire body with every movement, dizzying me. Breathless, I drag myself off the small mat, my nails digging into the padded floor. I crawl and crawl, tears, sweat, and snot covering my face.

I can't think about what's happening. If I stop and take the time to think about the fact that I might've just ruined my career for good, I'll never be able to get back up.

Eventually, my arms give out, and I lay in the middle of the floor section of the gym, almost at the spot where I'd left my phone, but I'm too delirious to move an inch more. Instead, I let my head drop to the floor and stare at an electrical outlet with my tilted gaze.

Minutes pass like this, or maybe it's hours, until I hear the front door of the gym open.

"Lexie?"

I don't have any strength to speak or look up anymore. The only thing I can do is squeeze my eyes shut as another set of tears leaks out of me.

"Lex?" Slow footsteps, then, "Oh my god, Lexie!"

Finn gets to me in a single breath, dropping to his knees hard enough that it makes my body bounce from the floor a little, sending another string of pain in my leg.

"What happened? Oh god. Oh Fuck." His hands are on my face, on my arms, touching me as if he needs the reassurance that I'm actually here. "Jesus Christ, say something."

"My foot," I croak, then sniff. "I think I need to go to the hospital."

His eyes close as he lets out a long breath. "Thank god." He leans down, then presses a kiss to my forehead, my cheek, my jaw, and my shoulder. "Let's go."

Carefully, he brings his arms under my knees and shoulders, then lifts me. I wince at the pain but feel like finally, I can let go.

"I got you," he whispers above my head as he jogs outside.

I let my head drop to his shoulder and allow my eyes to drift close. Yes. He's got me.

Chapter 34

Lexie

The ceiling of the cabin's main room is made of 173 slats of wood. I know because I've counted them, over and over and over.

It's been a week and a half since I broke my foot, and while that might sound short, it's 14,440 minutes of not knowing what comes next. I've never had so much time on my hands, and I've never not known what to do with it quite like I do now. Shelli told me to take as much time off work as I needed, but I should probably quit altogether. I don't see myself going back to that gym, knowing it's only to coach.

I shift on my pillows as I bring my attention back to the left end of the ceiling.

One. Two. Three.

On the small kitchen counter, my phone vibrates, like it has again and again since my accident, which is precisely why I've left it back there. The last thing I want to do is scroll through Instagram and see the girls who used to be my competitors showing pictures of their training and their journey to the World Championships in Montreal. I'm in enough pain as it is.

My foot feels better than it did when Finn brought me to the hospital. Apparently, listening to the doctor's orders to rest it and take painkillers has helped. Killed my morale, sure, but helped nonetheless.

I'm only a little embarrassed to say I've stared at the X-ray of my right foot more times than I can count, every day since I left the emergency room with a walking boot—no cast, thank god—and a broken heart. I had asked Dr. N'Diaye to give me a copy of the imaging and got it printed at the library, and while I'm no radiologist, I haven't been able to stop staring at the little crack she pointed at. Two tiny millimeters that have cost me my career.

Once I'm done counting the ceiling slats for the millionth time, I switch to the X-ray, staring and staring again. I can't cry about it anymore. I'm all emptied out.

My phone vibrates once more, and again, I ignore it. Even knowing it might be Josie who's calling can't get me to stand up. I called her from the hospital right after I was seen by the emergency room physician, and after making sure she wasn't in immediate danger, I told her I'd have to think about her text and would get back to her soon. Since then, I haven't even looked to see if she's texted or called. What I don't know can't hurt me. I still don't know what I'll do about her birthday or about the Kyle situation because I can't think of a scenario that would solve all our problems. I'm useless to her, as much as it kills me to admit it.

A sharp knock comes from the front door a single second before light pierces the room and makes me squint.

"Jesus, are you trying to become a vampire?"

"Not funny," I tell Finn as he walks my way. When he's close enough, the clean scent of his shampoo hits me, and I realize I don't remember the last time I showered.

"Don't come too close." I sniff. "I think I smell."

"Damn right you do," he says before dropping a kiss on my forehead. "Lucky for you, I don't give a damn."

I groan. I should probably feel embarrassed, but I don't have enough energy to care.

"What are you doing here?" I ask softly as I curl myself into a ball, tucking the covers closer to my chin.

"I came to bring you food," he says, the same thing he's told me every time he's visited since my accident, meaning every single day. I'm not sure I wouldn't have starved to death if it weren't for him, but again, too tired to care. "Martina made *sancocho* for you. Said nothing makes her feel better than when she eats this."

As he says it, the smell of the Dominican stew reaches me, and my stomach grumbles. From the few times I've had the chance to taste Martina's cooking, I know this will be as delicious as it smells.

"That's nice of her. Tell her thanks for me?"

"Why don't you tell her yourself?" Finn says, his hand clutching my thigh and rubbing in slow circles.

"Maybe," I lie. We both know I'm not getting out of this place. Maybe ever.

He smiles. "I also came to tell you that's enough."

"Huh?"

"You're done with this," he says, gesturing at the entire cabin. "I gave you ten days, and those ten days have come and gone."

My brows furrow. I lift myself on my elbows, wincing when I move my foot too fast. I'm still supposed to wait another four-and-a-half weeks before I can freely weight-bear.

"I can't do anything, Finn."

"Yes, you can." With a swing of his legs, he's on his feet, dragging all the curtains open, blinding me with the early summer sunlight. "You can get out of this cabin and have dinner with me. You can get some fresh air. You can stretch so getting back to it in a few weeks will be easier."

I was about to answer that I could have dinner with him here, but the words die in my throat with his last sentence. I lift myself even more, so I'm sitting, my swollen, purple foot dangling off the bed.

"Finn," I say. He halts with the half-full laundry basket in his arms. "I don't think I'm going back."

"Of course you are," he says, then resumes his decluttering of my place.

"Finn," I say, jumping on one foot while trying to locate my walking boot. "You don't understand." Once I find my boot, I lean against the wall and put it on. I have a feeling he's going to make this difficult, and I need to be able to run if he does.

"I understand enough to know you're not quitting."

"We're a little over three months away from the World Championships, I can't walk, let alone do basic training for weeks, my foot will probably be all stiff and screwed up by the time I start using it for high-impact again, and I'm too old to tell myself I'll just try again next year." I blink repeatedly, hoping it'll make the emotion in my eyes disappear. "Maybe it's time to come to the realization that gymnastics is over for me." I bring my fist in front of my mouth to hold in a sob. I've been thinking about this from the second I felt my foot crack under my weight, but saying the words out loud hurts more than I could've imagined.

Finn's gaze is blank as he straightens and says, "No, it's not. Those are just excuses."

I sigh. Of course he has to be unreasonable about this.

Wobbling to him, I grit my teeth against the pain and say, "You're not listening to me."

"I *am* listening, Lex." He lets the laundry basket fall to the floor and bounds my way. "But you told me you needed this. Winning. And I'm not standing there and watching you give it up. Fuck no." His head shakes, determination etched into every pane of his face, then he puts his hands on his hips like I'm a kid in need of a scolding. "You're getting back out there, and you're doing this shit, so help me god."

"I can't! I told you I can't." Getting back to training after six weeks off and trying to win a competition two months away would be pure stupidity. I'm not delusional like he is. This injury means the end.

"Yes you can," he says, his face so close I can see all the different shades of green in his irises. "You're just going to fight for it."

A ball of lead drops into my stomach. I glance up at the familiar wooden slats as I try to catch my breath and control my emotions. Why is it that everything I try to undertake becomes an Everest? Just as I was getting over an injury, another one hits. When I move away from the place that inspired all my nightmares, it feels like I've abandoned the only person who's ever loved me. When I get all my sponsors back, I have to lose them all over again and figure out how I'll continue paying for my ever-growing stack of bills.

I exhale shakily, like the weight of the world has fallen onto my back and I cannot straighten up anymore. "I've been fighting my entire life, Finn. I'm so *tired* of fighting." My voice catches on the last word, and all the hardness in him disappears before he wraps me in his arms, the touch familiar and warm and safe.

"I know you are. Fuck, I know." He kisses the top of my head, then grasps my cheeks and tilts my head so I'm looking at him. "But it still isn't a reason to quit. You need to get back and do it because you deserve every fucking good thing that's going to happen to you, and that's one of them." His thumbs caress my cheekbones, a move so soft it makes my eyelids flutter. "You'll win, and you'll throw it in the face of all the fuckers who didn't believe in you. *I* believe in you, and you'll believe in yourself, and that's all that matters."

I let my eyes fall closed, absorbing his words. He's right. I'm right too, but his point is better. I can't give up without at least trying. The clock hasn't run out of time yet. There's hope, even if it's small and rumpled. And yes, my life might've been filled with Everest after Everest, but I climbed all of those damn mountains. I made it to the other side every single time. Winded and halfway dead, maybe, but I still made it.

Finn drags his hands down my arms before taking my hands in his and pulling them to his mouth. His breath is warm on my skin and sends goosebumps all over me. He kisses my knuckles with all the tenderness in the world, then says, "My girl's not quitting. You've fucking got this. Yeah?"

I let my forehead drop to his throat. "Yeah. Yeah, I got this."

Chapter 35

Finn

"Come on, five more," I say as I clap my hands. I never thought I'd become a sports coach one day, but here I am. Thankfully, all the men who trained me while I played hockey taught me well.

"I can't," Lexie grunts, letting her body fall like a rag doll over the yoga mat I placed in the center of my living room. "I think I'll die if I do one more."

"Such a drama queen," I say, poking her thigh with my toe.

Her eyes narrow. "Try doing five sets of twenty reps of weighted squats with a half-broken foot and let me know how it feels."

"The magic word here is '*half*-broken.'"

What can I say? Riling Lexie up is still one of my favorite pastimes.

It's been three weeks since she decided she wouldn't give up on the sport she loves, and because of her keenness to get back at it as soon as possible, her doctor agreed to some weight-bearing earlier than was originally planned, so long as she respected certain limits and waited a few more weeks before getting back to high-impact training. She's even started coaching again, something I know she missed when she was away, even for a few days.

"Have you always been this much of an asshole?" she says from the ground, sweat plastering fine hairs to her forehead.

I smirk. "Have you always been this bratty?"

She sends me another murderous glance, and in a beat, she pounces, pulling at one of my ankles so I trip backwards and fall onto the couch.

I burst out laughing. "Oh my god, and murderous on top of it!" This time, she joins me in my laughter, but too soon, her smile disappears, replaced by a groan. "Ugh, I hate this." The meat of her palms digs into her eyes. "It feels like being a pro musician, only to start doing scales again."

I let an arm fall off the couch so one of my fingers can rub her arm up and down. It's something I haven't been able to stop doing for the past two months: touching her. It's like as soon as she's in my vicinity, she's a magnet and I'm a weak sheet of metal. Most of the time I don't even realize I'm doing it until she looks up at me and smiles. And what a goddamn smile it is.

That need to be close has even intensified after her injury. When I stepped into the gym that night, it was because she hadn't answered a couple of my texts, and even though that wouldn't be unusual if she was training, I had this feeling in my gut that something wasn't right. And when I saw her lying there... My heart stopped. Simple as that. She was still as a rock, and for a moment, I thought maybe she wasn't there anymore. Anything can happen with gymnastics. I've known that since I was a little boy and my mom talked about a new injured athlete every single week. The image of her lying motionless is one that still haunts my nightmares sometimes, and it's something I never want to experience again. I swear it gave me at least a dozen gray hairs.

A part of me wanted to protect her after that, tuck her into a bubble-wrap-lined box and keep her there, safe next to me, but that would've been selfish. I meant it when I said I wanted her to make her dream come true, even if seeing her on vault will probably send me into cardiac arrest. I'll encourage her to do all the dangerous shit she needs to, but no one can blame me for touching her every chance I get, maybe only to remind myself that she's there, that she's fine. We might not be a couple, but every day I spend by her side is a reminder that she means more to me than she'll ever know. I'm waiting for the right moment to tell her—if I ever get the guts to do so—but with the injury, that was the last thing on both our minds. We've barely even kissed since then. It's been all about her recovery and maintaining her fitness, which was a struggle with an unusable foot, but we made do.

"You'll get back to where you were in no time," I say. "Give yourself a chance."

She scratches at the irritated patch of skin on her hand, and I gently pull her hand away. Sometimes, she'll get lost in her anxieties so much that she'll make herself bleed. This time, though, she takes the opportunity of my available hand and drags me off the couch and onto her. I brace myself just in time not to squash her under my weight.

"Jesus, Crabby. You really are an animal tonight." Even so, I can't pretend I don't swell painfully in my jeans. She has that kind of effect on me.

She smirks as her fingernails scratch softly at my head. "You mind?"

"Not one bit." My gaze dips to her lips, and before I can try to stop myself and let her get back to business, she pulls me down, and I give in.

Her lips are soft under mine, tasting like minty toothpaste and *Lexie.* I can't get enough. Leaning onto my elbows so I can get even closer to her, I drag my fingers through her hair, untying her ponytail so I can have her hair everywhere. She moans, the sound almost enough to make me lose the ounce of self-control I have left. We still haven't had full-on sex yet, and while I'm more than happy to respect whatever pace she needs, I'm only human, and I dare you to hook up with Lexie Tuffin for months and not feel like crawling out of your skin from how much you want to be inside her.

"Don't think I don't know what you're doing. Bamboozling me."

"Is it working?"

"Fuck yes, it is."

She smiles against my mouth as her hands glide under my shirt. I lift myself so she can easily pull it off my chest, immediately returning to our kiss once she's done. I'm rock hard against her middle, and when she grinds her hips against mine, I groan.

"Goddamn, Lex," I say, my kisses dipping to her jaw, to her neck, and then to her collarbones, licking a path against her salty skin that just makes me want more.

Careful of her injured foot, she gently pushes me off so she can sit up, then pulls at her top, baring herself to me. My mouth dries as I take the time to just stare, just like I do every time I get the chance to see her. She's my personal eclipse: I know I should look away, but I can't help myself.

"You're the sexiest thing I've ever seen."

She grins, then pushes us to our knees so she can kiss me with all the fire she possesses, her tongue dueling with mine, fast and exploratory all at once. I pull at her so she's stuck to my body like glue, her hard nipples rubbing against my chest, and when she brings one of her legs around my pelvis, I grab her ass and lift her so she can climb on me.

With one of my hands in her hair, angling her head so I can kiss even more deeply, I drag my other fingers from the back all the way to the front of her shorts, finding her warm and wet even through the material.

I don't remember the last time she flinched when I touched her. It's the most wonderful fucking feeling in the world.

Her lips part on an inhale as I start rubbing her, gaze locked on mine. I never look away, only biting my bottom lip when I move her shorts and panties to the side and find her thoroughly soaked.

We both sigh as I sink a finger into her. Hands gripping at the skin at my neck, she lets her forehead fall to my shoulder and starts riding my finger. Even though I'm the one inside her, she's fully in control, hitting the spot exactly the way she needs to, and I'm only there to enjoy the show.

When she moans my name, I almost come in my pants. It takes all my self-control to keep pumping her pussy with the same rhythm, using my thumb to rub her clit at the same time.

We're both panting when I ask, "Think you can handle another finger?"

She nods, her coffee eyes meeting mine before drifting closed. Her breath is warm on my chest as I softly insert a second finger, getting off on the small gasp she lets out. With my free hand, I tilt her head so I can claim her mouth with mine and swallow every single one of her sounds, the soft whimpers and breaths tasting like heaven. She's dripping all over my hand; no hiding her enjoyment.

I can't get enough of it. Of her.

"Jesus, Finn," she whispers against my skin, the soft hitch in her voice a telltale that she's close.

I lean forward to bite one of her nipples, then climb to her ear and whisper, "Come for me, Lex." A second later, she does, her pussy clenching around my fingers as she lets her weight fall onto me, boneless and quivering. "That's it."

When she stops spasming against me, I pull my fingers out and bring them to my mouth so I can suck them clean, mostly because I enjoy the way her pupils dilate when I do it. Then, I lean forward and kiss her once more. "See how good you taste?" I say in a husky voice.

Her only answer is to bring my lips back to hers. Like she can't quite get enough of me either.

With her thighs still wrapped around my hips, I get to my feet, but just as I move to set her on the sofa, she grabs my cheeks and says, "I want you, Finn."

It takes a moment for my brain to settle on what she's actually saying, and when it does, I freeze. It's not like we haven't done everything other than this, but sex still feels like some kind of line in the sand I don't know we're ready to cross. Neither one of us knows for sure what happened to her when she was younger, but my biggest fear is that I start fucking her, only to realize she's lost to me, imagining it's someone else touching her. Someone she wishes would stay away.

"I don't know, Lex."

Her face drops, and I immediately cup her face so she doesn't get the wrong idea. "It's been an emotional couple of weeks. I don't want you to do something while you're not thinking straight." Especially since what's left of my restraint is pretty fucking thin, and I know I won't be able to say no if she insists.

"I *am* thinking straight," she says, determined. "In fact, I've never been more sure of anything. I want this." Then, the little heathen reaches between us and grabs my hard cock, squeezing it and making me grit my teeth. "Now, will you touch me or not?"

Those seven words are my undoing.

My lips latch onto hers, a renewed intensity in our kiss. Without looking, I leave the living room with her in my arms, and in six long steps, we're in my bedroom. The moon is lighting a sliver of the bed, but we're otherwise bathed in darkness. I lean and carefully drop her onto the bed, then straighten so I can look at her again.

Without the full light, she's all angles and shadows, looking good enough to eat.

So I drop to my knees on the bed and prowl toward her. Her eyes glint in the darkness as I remove her shorts and panties in one swift move, then grab her thighs and lift her middle to me. She tenses, but not in fear.

Gaze remaining on her, I lick my lips, and when I see the hitch of her breath, I know she wants this as much as I do. Smirking, I bring my tongue to her cunt and stroke it once. The sound she lets out is out of this world.

Jesus, she tastes so good. I give her restless body another lick, then reach into my bedside table for a condom.

"Wanna do the honors?" I ask, half because I want to test whether she still wants this and half because being touched by her is my kryptonite.

Panting, she lifts herself to her knees, tears at the foil packet, then wraps the condom around my length, all the while giving me slow, delicious strokes.

"I know what you're doing," I groan.

"Is it working?" the wicked thing asks, parroting her earlier words.

I push my rock-hard erection against her hand. "What do you think?"

She continues touching me, watching my every move and sound, as if she wants to learn all there is to know about me. She feels amazing, but when I feel like I won't last long if she continues, I lay her down on the bed, spreading her thighs and kissing both of them, long enough to get her squirming under me. I want to get her begging for it.

I let my tongue dart out to lick around her clit once again, and when her legs start shaking, I look up and say, "Think you're wet enough?"

"Yes," she moans.

Hands clutching her thighs, I say, "Well, just to be sure." And then, never breaking the eye contact, I spit on her pussy. Her lips part, eyes aflame.

Grinning, I say, "Now I think you're good."

I climb her body so we're face-to-face. As much as I liked getting her ready, I feel like stopping for a moment. Tucking a strand of hair behind her ear, I say, "You still sure about this?"

"Finn?" She pulls me closer, and in my ear whispers, "Just fuck me already."

Now, how am I supposed to say no to that?

With a wolfish grin, I grab myself and align with her center. "As you wish."

Then, I push inside, and everything inside me blanks out. Nothing remains but her and me. Nothing but the fruity smell of her damn shampoo and the taste of her lips. I don't think I could tell you my name if you asked.

She doesn't just taste like heaven; she feels like it too.

Slowly, I pull out and thrust back in, never looking away from her face. I fear noticing some sort of disconnect, but the only thing I see is her head thrown back, bottom lip clenched between her teeth, a beautiful blush on her cheeks.

"You entirely with me right now?" I say before biting her shoulder.

She nods, her hips bucking under me.

"Say it, then." I drop a kiss under her earlobe, earning the softest sound out of her. "Tell me who's fucking you."

"You are, Finn."

I up the pace as I bring a hand to her clit and start rubbing in tight circles, just as she likes. "That's right, baby. I am."

I shift forward so I can hit a spot that makes her eyes roll back, and to help me reach at an even better angle, she lifts a leg onto my shoulder, stretching around me like it's the easiest thing in the world.

I guess the rumors were true: gymnasts *are* the shit.

No, not just gymnasts. *Lexie*'s the shit. Not just because of her flexibility, but because of the small crease in her chin, and the sound of her laughter when I hit my elbow against the headboard and curse, and the way she looks at me like I just hung the moon.

My thrusts are jerky now, the orgasm building in my groin. I fight it off as I rub faster at her clit. I can feel her close again, and finally, when she claws at my back and moans my name loud enough for the neighbors to hear, I let go, and my mind disconnects.

I am nothing, no one, just this one sensation that could never be compared to anything else. No one will ever feel this good.

It feels like forever until I come back to myself. Spent, I let myself fall to her side and cradle her body with mine as I try to catch my breath.

"That was..." she starts.

"Yeah." I don't think I could find the words for it even if I searched for days. Already, I'm craving more. If Lexie was addictive before, she's suddenly topped the strongest drug in the world.

"You feeling okay?" I ask, rubbing her shoulder. Her skin is so soft, I want to bury myself against her forever.

"Yeah." She looks up, sparkles dancing in her eyes. "Yeah, I'm okay."

I grin like a fool, then dip to kiss her, and when I feel like she's going to drag me down again, I push myself away and say, "All right, let's go."

Her forehead creases. "Go where?"

"Living room. You owe me another set of reps."

Her bottom jaw drops. "Are you actually kicking me out of your bed after hooking up with me?"

"Yep," I say, getting up to discard the condom in my trash can, then putting on a clean pair of boxers. "But I'm kicking myself out too, so it doesn't count."

She still hasn't moved from her spot on the bed, so I kneel next to her and take her chin between my fingers. "As much as I'd like to keep you here and fuck you mindless for hours, you have dreams to reach, and I sure as hell ain't holding you back." I drop a kiss to her lips, then go grab a white T-shirt from my drawer and throw it at her. There's nothing I like more than seeing her wear my clothes, save maybe for watching her with no clothes on.

She catches the shirt, a shocked smile on her lips.

"Now come on, Crabby. We've got work to do."

Chapter 36

Lexie

The day couldn't be more perfect.

With Finn's official birthday in three days, Shelli asked me if I'd help her throw a last-minute surprise party for him, to which I of course gave an enthusiastic yes. And with an August birthday, we have the perfect weather on our side.

It's almost 4:00 p.m., so Finn should be here in a minute. Shelli pretended to invite him over for dinner, and I asked all the guests to arrive before then.

"Everyone, get ready," I shout to the small crowd gathered in the Olsens' backyard, the pool glinting in the sunlight behind everyone.

People's voices go down as we wait for Finn's arrival. Meanwhile, I walk toward the barbeque and ask Gil, Finn's dad, "Do you need anything?"

I've met him a few times before, but today's the first time I noticed just how much he and Finn look alike. Similar close-cropped light-brown hair, with sharp noses and forest green eyes—the prettiest shade there is.

"I'm good, thanks," he says while flipping a beef patty, then another. "Go sit down, will you? Don't want to put too much strain on that foot." He smiles, and it has the same warmth as Finn's. Even without knowing him much, it feels as if I do.

"I'm also good," I answer, not even lying. It's been a hard couple of weeks—months, if I'm being honest—but I got through it, and it finally feels like I'm getting to the other side of this thing. I'm able to tumble again, and even though I'm in pain all the time, I'll take it. My doctor wasn't sure starting high-impact training this rapidly was a good idea, but I couldn't care less at this point. Otherwise, he said my foot has healed surprisingly well considering how I broke it and how short my off-period was, so it's almost a miracle I'm here. I'm never going to take feeling like this for granted.

With the injury, though, I've had to skip a big portion of the competitions this season, and since I don't want to get back to it until I'm sure I'm as good as can be, I won't be participating in any other competition before the selection camp for the World Championships—if I even get an invite based on my previous performances. It's nerve-racking to think my big return will be during one of the most important moments of my life, but at this point, it's not like I have much of a choice.

When I hear tires roll down the driveway, I gesture at everyone to stay silent. Then, we wait in a crouched position until Shelli brings Finn out the back door and everyone screams, "Surprise!"

Finn stands still for a second before exploding in the most magnificent smile. Looking at the pure glee written across his face, so honest and open, it feels like my heart is *this* close to bursting. I never knew someone else's happiness could be so closely tied to mine.

Finn's immediate reaction is to go hug everyone he can get his hands on, starting with his best friend, Aaron, and his wife, Wren. Then, he moves on to a few of his high school friends Shelli took care of inviting, followed by Lilianne—minus her asshole boyfriend—and then to my personal favorite: Josie.

After weeks of reflection, I finally came to the conclusion that if going back to Phoenix made me feel sick, then I shouldn't do it. Actually, Finn made me come to that conclusion, and I'm so thankful he did. However, I still wanted to be able to celebrate my sister's birthday with her, which is coincidentally next week, so I decided to get her plane tickets and make her come to us instead. I think she was even happier with that plan. She's going to be spending the week with me, getting all the time in the world to visit the town I've been living in for close to a year now.

Once he steps away from the bear hug he gave my sister, Finn finally meets my eyes, and the emotion I see in them is palpable. He's the kind of person who doesn't need much to be happy, and when he is, everyone around him can feel it. He emanates this joy that can only brighten the days of those he comes in contact with. I know it firsthand. Sometimes, when I have a tough practice or a shitty conversation with my mom on the phone, I go to him, and it's as if I get plugged in and have my batteries recharged. I don't know how I'd live without it anymore, which is what makes the feelings I have for him so damn scary. Losing him would be one of the worst things that could happen to me, and while I wish I could tell him everything I'm feeling, I can't find it in me to do so. Not when there's a risk it could fuck everything we currently have.

"You did this?" he says once he arrives close to me, his hands buried in the front pockets of his jeans.

"Most of it's your mom."

"She just told me the opposite," he says with a raised brow. Then, without preamble, he picks me up and hugs me so tight it steals all the air from my lungs. "Thank you, Crabby," he says before pressing a subtle kiss to my head. We haven't told anyone about whatever's going on between us, and while I'd love to shout from the rooftops what he means to me, I also love that it's him and me against the world.

"My pleasure," I say as he lets me go, and the way he looks at me sends all my hormones out of whack. It's like being doused in sunlight, burning but embracing the pain because it feels too good.

"Who wants some burgers?" Gil says, his "Kiss The Cook" apron stained with grease from all the grilling he's been doing. The smell is heavenly in the backyard, and Finn's stomach's grumble is loud enough to make a few heads turn.

"Go," I tell him, not wanting to take too much of his time. Not when I get him to myself so often and Aaron is looking at Finn like a sad puppy who just wants to hang out with his best friend.

Finn grins. "'Kay. See you later." He mimics an air kiss, then goes to Aaron, who already has his hands full of food.

"The dynamic duo's finally back together," a feminine voice says to my left. While I've heard a lot about her, today's the first time I finally got to meet Wren. The moment she introduced herself and said she was married to the guy who couldn't stop himself from dancing to the music I'd put on, stars in her eyes, I knew I'd like her. "People who say teenage girls are the biggest gossips clearly have never met Aaron and Finn."

I grin. "I'm pretty sure I saw tears in Finn's eyes when he saw Aaron."

"Oh, there definitely were," Wren says.

Next to her stands Lilianne, who, despite the smile she wears, seems even more tired than the last time I saw her.

I bump her with my hip. "You okay?"

"Yeah."

I don't believe her one bit, but I don't push it. Whatever's happening in her life, she deserves a night's rest.

Wren gives her a look, and even though today's the first time they're meeting, something passes between them, as if they understand something only the two of them can. Wren gives her shoulder a squeeze, and Lil smiles in return.

"Anyway, enough about that," Lil says, bringing her attention back to me. "I'd rather talk about what's happening here."

"Meaning?"

"Meaning all the lovesick glances you and Finn have been exchanging since he got here," Wren answers, again as if she and Lil are able to speak telepathically. She takes a sip out of her glass of sparkling water, her navy eyes boring into me like she can see every single one of my secrets.

And of course, my reddening cheeks aren't helping.

"No, there's nothing." As soon as the lie slips past my lips and Lil and Wren look at me like I'm the dumbest person on earth, I realize there's no way they'll believe that. "Okay, there might be something, but really, we're friends."

Their dubious expressions don't move an inch, but I'm not sure what else I can say without exposing everything I'm feeling for him.

"Lexie, I'm sorry to say this, but you're a terrible liar," Wren says.

I laugh, although there's a hint of nervousness in there. I'm losing every bit of control I have here.

"I think you two believe you're more subtle than you actually are," Lil says with an apologetic expression.

I take a sip of my rosé to help me deal with this interrogation. I could continue denying it, but these two girls seem trustworthy, and I can only hope that if I ask them to keep something quiet, they will.

"Look," I say, "we've been having some fun for a while, and yes, I may have a thing for him, but that's where it ends."

Their expressions remain serious for all of a second before their lips twist as they hold back laughter. Then, they turn to each other and start snickering for real this time.

"What?" I say.

"Oh, honey," Lil says at the same time as Wren asks, "You really don't see it?"

"See what?"

"How he looks at you," Lil answers, smiling as she throws a quick glance in Finn's direction, where he's eating his burger with Aaron, Josie, and Callie, my gym student and Aaron's sister.

"I don't..." How *does* he look at me? The same way he looks at all the people he cares about.

"I've known him for a few years, and Lilianne for longer than that, and I think we can both say that we've never seen him like this."

"Like what?" I ask.

Lil grins even wider. "In love, Lexie."

My breath catches in my throat, and for a second, all my senses dim, as if I've stepped into a fishbowl, the sounds muffled and my vision blurred. Then, everything comes back into focus. The word "love" is so often used yet so rarely understood. What they see as love might only be affection, and the glances they think mean longing could simply be a deep sense of appreciation. They can't know what he truly feels.

"It's not like that." I'm not sure if I say it because I believe it or because I don't want to get my hopes up.

Lil shrugs, although she doesn't seem to believe me for one second. "I can't make you see it, but what I can do is tell you I've never seen Finn look this happy in his life. Not when he was traveling, and not when we go out, and not even when he took over the farm."

"And I'm probably the worst person to try to give you advice, when I didn't notice my husband's feelings for months, but from an outsider's perspective, it's different. Trust me."

I swallow against the knot in my throat. Could they have a point?

I'm about to answer something—anything—when someone taps my shoulder. I jump a little, then turn to find Finn's sister.

"Hi," she says. "I don't know if you remember me, but I'm—"

"Francesca," I say. When we met, I didn't take the time to take a good look at her, but now that I do, I notice she has the same eyes as Finn, with a similar chin and cheekbones. "I'm so glad you're here." Shelli wasn't sure whether she'd be here today, but I know nothing will make Finn happier, even if she arrived late.

"Me too," she says. Then, she greets Lil and Wren, and once she's done, she asks them, "Would you mind if I steal this one for a minute?"

"Go ahead," Wren says before leaning forward and whispering in my ear, "Think about it, hmm?"

I pause, then nod and follow Francesca toward the pool area, where it's quieter and we can dip our feet in the warm, blue water.

"I guess now's the time to say sorry for that awkward first encounter," I say once we're settled.

She chuckles. "Please. Embarrassing my brother is my favorite thing to do." Her waist-long brown hair flies into the wind and sticks to her glossy lips, so she picks it up into a ponytail. "Although I do wish we'd had the chance to talk then." Shifting closer she says, "Finn's told me about your ruined first date."

My back straightens. I never thought that story would get out, and especially not to his sister.

"And I wanted to tell you that it's my fault."

Francesca proceeds to tell me about the absolute horror of a guy she was with, who she's finally dumped for good, and how Finn dropped everything to be there for her the night of our first date, when she called him in sheer panic.

"I'm sorry," she says once she's gone over everything. "If I'd have known it would ruin things for him, I would've let him tell you, but I'm the one who asked him to keep it a secret."

I gape at her, all the while feeling terrible. To think I chastised him for not being there for me when he was helping his little sister with something like that... Now that I know, I'm actually happy he ditched our date. It brings him even higher in my regard. In fact, I should've known it was something like that. When else has Finn disappointed me?

"That's not your fault," I say. "And I'm glad he was there for you."

"Me too." She smiles, then glances at Finn, who's now chatting with Aaron's parents, Martina and Dennis, by the patio table, moving his arms animatedly and making everyone laugh. "You know, I wouldn't say this if I didn't fully believe it, but my brother's one of the good ones."

Flashes of moments bombard my mind in an instant. Finn showing up on my mother's front porch in Phoenix when he knew I didn't want to go in the first place. Him being there during my competition, even when I didn't ask him to. The relentlessness he used to get me to hold on to the dream I was ready to let go of. The care he's taken with every single one of his touches, like I'm made both of glass and diamond.

And it's with those images I realize something: he's not just one of the good ones. He is *the one.* I've never been happier than during the months I've spent by his side. Never been this excited to make someone laugh or smile or even simply look my way. And while that scares the living hell out of me, it also brings me back to the conversation I just had with Lil and Wren, and again, I wonder if there's a fragment of truth in what they said.

I'm not sure I've ever wanted anything more.

Chapter 37

"**N**eed a hand?"

My mother's hands drip in soap suds as she twists in my direction and presses them to her chest. "Jesus, you scared me."

"Sorry. Didn't think you were so entranced by your dishes." I grin as I give her a quick side hug. "So, need a hand?"

"I'm fine. Your dad will help me later." With a wave, she says, "Go with your friends."

It's too late, though. I already have a rag in hand and a plate to dry off. She rolls her eyes but smiles. She probably already knew what I was about to do.

"Thank you for tonight," I say over the soft music playing in the background. At the end of the night, when the wind got brisker and people started asking for blankets by the fire, we brought the party inside and Martina, Callie, Aaron, and Wren led everyone to start dancing in the middle of the living room. I'm not a dancer, but even I wasn't able to resist.

"I'm glad you had fun. It's not every day my boy turns twenty-nine." She waggles her brows as she hands me a dripping wine glass. "Big thirty next year."

I'm not sure whether the tightness in my chest at hearing those words is normal, or even healthy. I don't want to be frightened of getting older, but I don't know how to help it. It's as if while you're still in your twenties, you have the right to be messed up. To still be looking for who you are or what you want to be. But by thirty, you're supposed to be an actual adult, to have your shit together, and that's not close to how I feel about my life.

"Yeah," I say, then flick some water her way. "That make you feel old?"

She bursts out laughing. "Damn right it does." As she rinses a pot, she adds, "But I always remind myself that it's a privilege to grow old. Not everyone gets that chance."

"You're right." My mom's obviously smarter than me, and once again I feel dumb for being scared of turning thirty. So what if I never become a fully accomplished man? There are worse things that could happen. So long as my parents aren't too embarrassed of me, I think I'll be all right.

Plus, Lexie made a point during the lock-in, one that's been running through my mind ever since. Maybe I feel like a fuckup because that's how I was taught to think about a life like mine, and not because of what I actually feel about my life.

I start humming to the music, and we spend the next couple minutes washing and drying in comfortable silence, until Mom turns the faucet off and faces me.

"Finn, I have a question for you, and I want you to be painfully honest."

I stop drying, the plate half-wet in my hands. My mother is one of the easiest people I know. She's a happy-go-lucky woman who never complains and mostly goes with the flow. Sure, she was able to discipline us when Fran or I did something stupid, but otherwise, the mood in this house has always been relaxed. So to hear the severity in her tone right now makes me stiffen.

"Sure," I say, depositing the plate onto the counter.

"Are you happy?" Her eyes crease. "Here, I mean."

I stammer a couple of sounds before getting out, "What kind of question is that?"

"You weren't before, and while I never fully understood your need to leave and to always be in a different place, I love you and I accepted that it's the way you are." She picks up the rag from my frozen hands to wipe hers. "But then Dennis and Martina needed help with the farm and you decided to come back and stay for Aaron, and while I think it's admirable and I'm so incredibly proud of you for it, I keep wondering if that's you settling into a life you don't really want."

My mouth is dry, even when I lick my lips. "I don't... Where is this coming from?" I know I'm avoiding the question, but I think I need some answers first. I've been back in Vermont for almost two years, so why now? Do I *look* unhappy?

Mom shrugs. "I was just looking at your friends tonight, and... I don't know. I'm afraid you decided to come back to make all of *us* happy but that you forgot yourself in the process, and as much as I love to have you around, I wouldn't want that." She braces herself over the sink, but even turned away, I don't miss the glassiness in her eyes. "I know you could be fine here, but I also want your life to be as wide and strange and wonderful as you need it to be." She pauses, then takes hold of my hands, hers trembling. "It's okay if you need more. If you need to leave. Martina would understand." She squeezes. "*I* would understand."

I've never been one to break down, but this? It fucking gets to me, because I know that she's not lying. She believes every single word she's saying, and I know if I said I needed to move on to something else, she'd help me pack my bags and find a new home away from her, even if it killed her in the process.

Because of that, I take my time to answer. She's offered me an opportunity for honesty on a silver platter, so the least I can do is be sure that once I tell her how I feel, the truth is what comes out.

As if knowing I might need some time, she turns the faucet on and resumes washing. However, once I really start thinking about it, there's only one answer that comes to mind.

I step forward and turn the faucet back off.

"Yeah, Mom, I think I'm actually happy." My back meets the countertop as I face her. "Maybe when I was younger, I needed *more*, but now, everything I need is right here." I have a good job, one I love. Sure, I might live near my parents' house, but that also means I get to be close to my family, in all senses of the term. I don't have a life that's fully settled yet, but I get by. And if that makes me small-minded and embarrassing, then so be it. I tried time and time again to find the most fulfilling life possible, and I thought that could only happen far from home, where things would feel otherworldly every day, but a little life can be so good if you pay attention to all the small, beautiful things around. What good is seeing the seven wonders of the world when you're alone through it all? There's beauty in novelty and magnitude, and I've experienced it, but there's equal beauty in a shared dinner with family or a slow, lazy afternoon with the right woman.

Mom's face brightens, as if she were bracing for a storm and I've unleashed sunlight. She's small but mighty, and when she hugs me, it's with a strength I didn't know she had. Probably one that comes from the remnants of her gymnastics days.

"You have no idea how happy you've just made me," she whispers against my chest. I smile, then hug her tighter.

When she pulls away, she rubs her fingers over her eyes, then says, "I probably have someone I need to thank for this."

"What do you mean?"

She lifts both brows. "Please, Finn. We both know you haven't been the same since Lexie's been around."

Color rises to my neck and cheeks, which is stupid, because what am I, five years old? My mother knows I've been with women before. Multiple women, if I'm being honest. But it's different with Lexie, and the look in her eyes tells me we both know that.

"How long have you known?" I ask, not bothering to circle around it.

"Since the moment I looked at the security cameras months ago and found out you'd started doing the cleaning in the middle of the night. That told me all I needed to know."

I pinch my lips, but can only resist all of two seconds before I start laughing. Mom joins me soon after.

"That was pathetic, wasn't it?"

She grins, then pats my chest. "Don't worry. I love you anyway."

I chuckle again, then get back to my drying, a new lightness in my chest.

"So if you haven't told all of us about it, I assume it's because you're not together?" Mom says, acting like she's being sneaky.

"Not really, no."

"Then why don't you tell her how you feel? There's no time to waste." She smirks. "You're not getting any younger."

"I know that, but..." I drag my tongue over my teeth as I imagine what it'd be like to be fully honest with Lexie. How her pink lips might part on a gasp. How her pupils might dilate.

How she might run away and disappear from my life.

"I'm scared," I say. "What if I tell her how I feel and she says she doesn't see me that way?" I wouldn't survive it, I think, if she let me down easy. Not with the way I feel about her, like mountains could move under me and I wouldn't notice if she was holding my hand.

"Well, that's always the risk, isn't it?" Mom says. "But I never took you for a scaredy-cat."

I snicker. "Excuse me?"

"Come on, Finn. You've bungee-jumped and swam with sharks before. I think you can do this too."

"It's not the same." Sharks couldn't break my heart.

"Maybe, but I also know you won't get anywhere if you don't try."

She's right, I know she is, but she also doesn't know how good things are with Lexie right now. She makes me happier than I've ever been, like finally, I'm right where I belong. It would be foolish to risk it all because I was greedy and wanted it all.

"Whatever you decide, I know it'll be the right decision. But for what it's worth?" She throws me a side glance. "I don't think you'd be disappointed if you tried."

Chapter 38

Lexie

T he second I finish zipping my training bag shut, the door to my hotel room opens.

"Oh, good," Finn says, his grin already spreading to my lips. "I was afraid you'd be asleep already."

"No chance." I sit on the bed and lean back, stretching my neck. "Never sleep well the day before a competition."

It feels surreal to even be in Anaheim right now. I never thought I'd make it to this year, let alone to this day, especially after my foot so gracefully let me down. Yet against all odds, here I am, competing in the World Championships first thing tomorrow morning.

And even luckier than that: I have this man by my side. I didn't think he was coming, until he showed up at the airport yesterday morning, suitcase in tow and a custom "Team Tuffin" shirt on his back.

I honestly don't know how I didn't ask him to marry me on the spot.

He told me then that he was only here for support and not to be a bother, so he got himself his own room and found a way to busy himself today while I went through my last practice sessions. In fact, now's the first time I've seen him since we got here.

"My mom wanted me to ask how you're feeling," he says as he takes a seat next to me and twists me so my feet rest in his lap and he can gently massage the one currently wrapped in an elastic bandage.

A smile tugs at my lips. Shelli's been nothing short of extraordinary to me these past few months. Not only has she accommodated my work hours in order for me to practice as much as possible, but she's also acted as my coach more times than I can count. When she initially started hanging around late at night, she said it was for *safety reasons*, but the moment she gave me a correction on a double layout and I applied it on my next pass, she stopped holding herself back. I know she'd been wanting to do that for a while—she'd even offered to help me with some skills a few times before, but I hadn't wanted to feel like I was taking advantage of her generosity—but once she decided to be all-in no matter what, there was no changing her mind.

Having her around has been amazing. My skills have improved, but more than that, I've discovered someone I now deeply care for. I was with her when I learned I'd made the Worlds team after the selection camp, and while I almost passed out from shock, she celebrated for the both of us, jumping around and shouting like she'd just won the lotto. Having a person I look up to be happy for my happiness was something I didn't know I needed until that very moment.

It makes sense that she'd ask for updates today. Still, I like to tease Finn, so I say, "Your mom, huh?"

He rolls his eyes, then rubs harder. "Yes, my mom. Now answer the question."

I snicker, then lean back against the plush pillows of the bed. "Tell her I'm doing okay, all things considered." This freaking foot hurts like a bitch, but today went well, so I'm carefully optimistic. I release a groan when he hits a sensitive spot. "God, has anyone ever told you you have magic hands?"

"I think you have a few times."

I return his smirk, knowing damn well he's not talking about massages.

"And how are *you* feeling, Mr. I'm-Hot-and-I-Know-It?"

He gasps, his thumbs pausing on my foot. "You think I'm hot?"

"Shut up," I say, hitting his hard chest with my foot, chuckling. I don't think I've ever laughed as much as I have this past year, and I don't need to look far to find the reason.

"Seriously, though," he says, resuming his massage, "I'm so proud of you. You did the damn thing, Lex."

"I haven't yet."

"Yes, you have. You've faced all the hurdles life could possibly throw at you and still got here, with better technique and skills than you've had all year. To me, that's doing the thing."

My heart swells, and swells, and swells, and I don't know how it hasn't burst yet. I keep telling myself I couldn't have stronger feelings for this man, and every day, he proves me wrong.

"You're right." I let my head fall to the side, the bed soft and smelling like detergent. "A podium to get to the Olympics would still be nice, though." It's not a hard rule, but usually, the three all-around medalists at the World Championships get a sure invite to the Olympic trials of the following year.

"Oh, of course, but I have no doubt about that, so it's not even worth mentioning."

"Don't jinx it."

"Sorry," he says, lifting his hands in surrender. "You're going to be terrible and everyone's going to laugh at you."

I narrow my eyes, then jump to my knees so I can tackle him to the bed. "Not funny, Finny."

His nose brushes mine as he lifts his chin and says, "I think you still like me."

Oh, how close to the truth he is.

Eyes boring into mine, I'm sure he can see it all. Emotion after emotion, written all over me, pouring out of my skin. I don't know how I could hide it.

He presses a kiss to my lips, so tender I nearly melt, before he asks, "And after this weekend, what next?"

"Let's not get ahead of ourselves."

"Humor me," he says. My body is lined on top of his, but despite this, he doesn't make a move to bring things further. Instead, he lays his hands on my lower back and waits.

"Hopefully, training with Team USA, and then the Olympics." Again, I'm tempted to keep quiet in order not to jinx things, but I'm also not a big believer in all things astrology and luck. I believe we make our own chance.

I do believe in karma, though. I like the sound of it.

"What about you?" I ask, tapping his chest twice.

"I'm not the one competing in an international championship. It'll be the same old for me." A pinch at my hip. "Please don't forget about me when you get all rich and famous, yeah?"

Finn's grin falls as he sees I don't return it.

"Wait here," I say, then get up to go grab my phone, which I left on the minibar. Finn's in a seated position by the time I walk back to the edge of the bed.

"What's up?" he asks.

I scroll through my tabs to find what I'm looking for. I wasn't planning on showing it to him yet—I thought I'd probably try to ease him into the idea first—but I can't stop myself. Not after what he's just said, like I'm moving on with my life while he's staying behind.

"I did something," I tell him after thirty seconds of silent searching, "and while you might be mad, I want you to promise me you won't hate me, okay?"

He still has a confused look, but manages to say, "I could never hate you."

"You sure?"

"Yes, you tease." He grabs me by the waist and flings me onto the bed. "Now show me before I steal that phone from your tiny hands."

"My hands aren't tiny."

"Lexie."

"Fine." I shift my position so I'm sitting on my heels, then go to pass him the phone but change my mind midway, bringing it close to my chest. "So I know you'd been thinking about going back to school for a while, but you haven't talked about it in a long time, and it really bothered me that you didn't trust yourself enough to do it, so, um…" I trail off, not finding the right words to say, so I hand him the phone, then squeeze one eye shut as he starts looking at the page displayed onto the screen.

His brows lift, then scrunch, then move again. "What's this?"

"I…" I clear my throat. "I registered you for some classes at the local college, with your mom's help." When he stares at me like I've grown two heads but remains silent, I add, "It would be part time, of course, so you can keep your job, and if you've changed your mind, we still have time to cancel and it wouldn't be a problem, but I really think you should consider it because—"

"I love you."

The room falls silent as I force my brain to focus. It feels like I've just run my car into a tree.

"What?"

Finn's gaze is focused on me as he says, "I love you, Lexie."

I blink. Blink again. I'm suffering from whiplash, but I also think I might be dreaming, or maybe I'm not hearing quite right.

"I wasn't planning on telling you this now, before your big day, but fuck." He rubs a hand over his short hair. "You just had to go and give me this…this piece of trust and understanding and I'm so fucking in love with you, Lexie Tuffin." He shakes his head, then licks his lips. "I've become damn good at pretending, but honestly, I don't remember what it's like to wake up and not feel overwhelmed by the amount of love I have for you. It's almost too much sometimes."

I'm still gawking when he gets to his feet and starts pacing the room. "I love your fire, and I love your crabbiness, but I love your softness too. All the shades of you." He shrugs, as if to say he can't help it, then gives me the smile that's the dart to my heart, finally making it explode. "You're my best friend, Lex. And that course registration?" he says, pointing at the phone resting on the bed, the screen still bright. "It makes me feel *seen*. It's like..." One of his hands climbs to his chest, as if holding on to his heart, and he stops in the middle of the room to face me. "You make me believe that maybe I'm not alone in this world anymore."

My vision blurs, and it takes everything in me not to let the tears flow. He deserves for me to be able to express myself without being a sobbing mess. Just as I open my mouth to answer, he lifts a hand.

"Don't say anything yet." Rubbing his lips softly, he says, "I'm so sorry, I really didn't want to drop this bomb on you tonight, so I'm going to let you sleep it off. Just focus on your competition tomorrow, and we'll figure things out later. Okay?"

I don't know why he's so nervous. Doesn't my face say it all?

I try to speak again, but he interrupts me the same way as before.

"Please. Give us this time, okay? I don't want you to make a decision before something as important as the championship."

I almost laugh. As if I ever had any choice in the matter when it came to him.

"Okay, I'm going," he says, and as much as I want to jump from the bed and hold him back, if he thinks I need to be fully focused on this to tell him I want him too, then that's what I'll do. What's one more day?

"You're going to be amazing tomorrow. I'll be cheering you on from the stands."

Since I can't speak, I only watch as he goes, hoping what I'm feeling is written across my face.

Finn starts making his way to the door, his wide back looking so incredibly good in his flannel shirt, but midway there, he looks over his shoulder.

"Oh, and Lexie? Try to have some fun out there." He grins. "Your stubbornness might have led you here, but tomorrow, try to let your passion win."

And here it is: proof that he sees me just as much as I see him.

"Yeah," I say. "I think I will."

Chapter 39

Finn

I might have made a mistake.

Actually, I'm pretty fucking sure I did.

I didn't sleep a second last night. Instead, I turned and turned, the sheets tangled at the bottom of the bed, all the while replaying my dumb word vomit. It wasn't supposed to come out like that. It wasn't supposed to come out *at all*. Not yet, at least. Especially not before one of the most important days of her life.

But after I saw those registration papers... How was I supposed to hold it in, as if she hadn't just given me the most beautiful gift I'd ever received? It was impossible. She'd gone ahead and taken the step I was too scared to take, and fuck if that wasn't the best thing anyone had ever done for me.

After scrubbing my face with water, I look up from the bathroom sink, finding my eyes sunken and my lips pale. "You'll be fine," I mutter.

That's where I'm at: talking to myself in hotel bathrooms.

It's barely 10 a.m., but already the hallway is noisy with gymnasts and attendees, all heading to the first day of the women's individual event. Sunlight filters through my room, and as I look at the mussed bed, I picture what it would look like if Lexie had been here with me. After months of sleeping by her side most nights of the week, I've gotten used to seeing strands of brown hair on the pillows and untucked covers from how roughly she sleeps. I don't like seeing this bed without those things. It seems...empty.

Yeah, I'm way too much inside my head.

After getting dressed in my Team Tuffin shirt—fucking cheesy, but it made her smile, and I'm not sure what I wouldn't do to see her smile—I grab my wallet and key card, then open the door to go grab a bite before I head over to the stadium where the competition will be taking place. Lexie's not up for at least two hours, so I'll be able to get there on time.

Except I'm stopped in my tracks when I open the door and an envelope falls right onto my sneaker. It must've been tucked in the tight edge between the door and the wall. My knees crack as I squat to grab it, and when I see my name scribbled in Lexie's messy writing, my heart stutters. Jaw tight, I fold the envelope and stuff it in my back pocket before exiting the room.

I can't open it now. Whatever she needed to tell me the morning before her competition couldn't be great. If it'd been good news, she'd have waited until after her performance, which means whatever is in this letter must be an easy letdown.

I try to stay calm as I fill my plate at the brunch buffet, but the simple sight of food makes me want to puke. I settle for an apple, which I eat three bites of before calling it a day and walking over to the neighboring stadium, all the while trying but failing to ignore the grenade in my pocket.

Fucking hell.

I knew there was a possibility she wouldn't see me the way I see her, even though with all the nights—and days—we've spent together, I'd started to think that maybe, just maybe, the two of us could work. She'd agreed to go on a date with me at some point, after all, so would it have been that ludicrous to imagine she could one day fall for me?

I guess that letter will let me know, and because I have a bad feeling about it, I can't get myself to read it.

In a daze, I go through security and pass photographers and reporters, then wade through the chaos of the stadium to find my seat. The previous competitions I attended were packed, but nothing could've prepared me for the World Championships. This is wild. Noise, people, media. Girls of all nationalities are spread out all around ground level, stretching and getting in one last rehearsal before go-time. Since this is the individual portion of the competition, no one is wearing team leotards, different flashes of color all around. Loud pop music is blaring through the speakers as attendees take their seats and all the competing athletes finish arriving and settling in.

It doesn't take me long to find her. In fact, the moment I start looking, I know where to turn, as if she was calling to me all along.

With large headphones covering her ears, she does some jump rope, still in her sweatpants and SHGC gym sweatshirt. A presenter takes over the speakers for a moment, announcing that the first of the performances will start in five minutes. Lexie's starting at the uneven bars, and even though she's not the first one to go according to the schedule, she still stops her jumping and walks to her bag, picking it up and going to a spot closer to the bars to remove her warm-up clothes. Once she's in just her leotard, a perfect ponytail high on her head, she starts scanning the stands while adjusting her chalky grips, and as if she too has that inner tracker, her gaze finds mine almost instantaneously. Even though I'm high and far away from her, I'd swear I can see a smile touch her lips before her focus returns to the competition ahead.

Lexie's not a cruel person. She wouldn't smile at me if she'd just given me the "let's stick to friendship" talk on paper, would she? Unless that was an "I'm sorry I broke your heart" smile?

Fuck. I need to grow some balls and read that damn letter to get some answers.

Faintly, I hear the presenter announce the official start of the competition followed by loud jazz music that's probably accompanying someone's floor routine, but now that I have the letter in my hands again, I can't bring my attention to anything else. In fact, if I continue like this, I might miss Lexie's performances altogether, stuck staring at this envelope for an entire day.

Telling myself that Aaron, Lil, and Lexie would probably tell me to stop being scared and just open the envelope, I take a deep breath, then listen to their imaginary voices and do as they say.

Finn,

You didn't give me the chance to talk yesterday, and while it was a very nice idea in theory to wait until after the competition to talk, I couldn't imagine waiting an entire day to tell you my own truth, so I decided to write this. (I also didn't want to risk having you do something dumb like ask me to stop talking again, so this way, you have no choice but to listen to everything I have to say. You're really stubborn sometimes, you know? Maybe even more than me!)

Even with my hands trembling, I snicker at that. Not a fucking chance in the world, Lex.

As I'm writing this, I'm just about ready to leave my room and get to the stadium. And you know what I realized while I was getting ready an hour ago? That I'd never been this calm before a competition. Not even when I was a kid and the biggest prize to win was a high five and my mother's smile. And that made me see that, for the first time in my life, winning is not my number-one priority. I have something else in my life I want even more.

I have you.

I pinch my top lip between my teeth as I try to keep the emotion in, because bawling like a baby in a packed stadium is not something I'd be very proud of, but hell if that ain't a challenge.

I can't remember the last time someone made me feel like I was a priority to them and didn't just say it, but proved it too. I was wrong to say you couldn't make me a priority after that night in January. No one is better at it than you. And that's worth more than all the medals in the world.

Don't get me wrong, I'm still going to win this thing. Only, it won't be because it's the only thing I want, or the one thing that defines me. I'll win it because I deserve it, and then I'll come home to the most important thing. I'll come home to you.

This time, I feel wetness gather in my eyes, and knowing it's a lost cause, I simply let it fall and continue reading.

Because I love you too, Finn. Of course, I love you too. How could I not? I don't know a single person who could meet you and not fall head over heels in love with you. You're pure sunshine. You remind me of all the good things in life, and you never let me forget that better things are coming. I used to dread waking up in the morning, but with you, I <u>want</u> to live.

So I have a deal for you: Let's stop pretending. Let's put curtains up in your place. Let's hang some picture frames and get you to buy freaking furniture so your apartment doesn't feel so empty. Let's settle you in and make this thing permanent. I'm ready to make Sonder Hill my home, and I'd really, really like it if you were too. In exchange, I can't promise never to be crabby, because we both know that would be a lie, but I can promise to always be by your side and give you all the love I have—and that won't be hard, because loving you is like breathing. Like leaving the ground and knowing there's nothing to be afraid of because you'll always land on your feet. It's so damn easy.

I'll see you later, and this time, if you don't want to talk, I'm all for it.

Love,

Lexie

My cheeks are wet as I read her words again and again, trying to wrap my head around the fact that she means it. I fell in love with the most amazing woman, and by some miracle, she fell for me too.

When I finally lift my head from the page in my hands, it's because her name has been called over the speakers, and even in my lovestruck daze, I couldn't have missed it. Tucking the letter safely in my pocket—if you think I'd ever get rid of that proof, you're dead wrong—I lean forward and brace my elbows on my knees, fingers resting on my lips, whispering a prayer to whoever's listening that this goes well.

She's starting with her most difficult event, and after her foot fracture, her landings have been rougher and less stable than before, but I know she can do it anyway.

My girl's as focused as can be as she closes her eyes to take a deep breath, then exhales and begins.

Her mounting is flawless, just like the pirouettes and transitions that follow. I may not be a gymnastics expert, but I can't see a single thing to correct as she releases the bar and does a flawless piked Jaeger. Even though multiple gymnasts are competing at the same time, I'd swear all eyes are riveted on Lexie and everyone in the stadium holds their breath as she lets go of the bar and exhales when she catches it again.

She spins and turns and flips, all the while keeping a good flow and a tight technique. Even without seeing her face, I can tell she's having a good time, and what better moment to enjoy her sport than when she's on the verge of reaching the top after a hell of a comeback? She must be over the moon right now, almost there, only having to get through the dismount that's coming soon.

When we were talking about it in her bed a few days ago, she said she still wasn't sure which dismount she'd use. On the one hand, she could go for an easier one that would mean sure points and a straightforward routine. On the other hand, she could do her double twisting double back again and try to get as many points as possible, even though it still brings her anxiety and it's hard on her foot, which means she might not stick it. Even yesterday, she wasn't settled on an idea.

I know her routine by heart now, so I can tell when it's almost over. She gets into her first full swing, then the second, providing her with as much speed and momentum as possible, and when she releases the bar for her dismount, I'm pretty sure my lungs are about to burst in my chest. I stare with bated breath, and the moment I see the beginning of her spin, my face splits into the widest grin because who was I kidding? Of course, she went in for the kill. She wouldn't have been happy with herself if she'd gone for the easier option, and I think she knew that too.

It feels like she spins forever, and when her feet finally touch the ground and she sticks the landing like it's the easiest thing in the world, I jump to my feet and start shouting, my fist pumping the air like there's no tomorrow. If people are offended, they can fuck right off because the woman I'm in love with just did the damn thing.

I wish I was closer to see the pride in her eyes, but even from here, I can tell she's happy with herself. Her smile is bright and her back is straight as she salutes the judges at different angles.

There's always a short gap of time between the end of the performance and the displaying of the scores, when the judges take the time to revise their numbers and share their final results with the administrators. I've gone to see Lexie compete enough times to know what her routine is during that time. She'll walk over to where her tin water bottle is, take back-to-back swigs, crack her neck left and right, then turn to the score board and softly scratch at the irritated patch of skin on her left hand while waiting for the results. She's never done it any other way, except for the one time I distracted her with my shout. Her attention won't waver until she knows how she did and whether it should be enough for a podium.

But for the third time today, she rocks my world by ignoring all her usual habits and gazing straight in my direction instead, keeping her eyes and her grin connected with mine. Even when the scores appear, we don't immediately look away, as if we both want to enjoy that peace and happiness for a second longer.

"I love you," I mouth, and even if she can't see it, I'm sure she feels it.

At the same time, we turn toward the score boards.

Lexie might need to keep her composure, but the second I see what I know will be the highest score of the day, I let myself jump and shout again.

It turns out she was right after all. The other girls around here might've had all the talent and chance in the world, but she had the secret ingredient: she wanted it more.

When I force myself to calm down after receiving too many nasty looks, I gaze back down at Lexie, who's now striding toward the beam, her next event. One I'm sure she'll ace.

I notice the moment she stops in her steps in front of a middle-aged man. I squint, and when I recognize his face, my hands curl into fists. Andy Lockwood, that fuckface who coached her and then proceeded to let her go. She never outright showed him to me, but a few minutes of research were enough for me to find him.

From what she's told me, she'd only seen him once since he'd dumped her out of her old gym in Phoenix last year. They were close before her first injury, but afterward, he treated her like an old rag, and even though she didn't say the words, I know that hurt her more than she'd care to admit.

Her pause in front of the man doesn't last long. In fact, with what I imagine is her nastiest look, she steps past him, not uttering a single word to the man who thought he was better than her. After the performance she just did, he must be cursing repeatedly. That's all he deserves. Lexie completely ignores him as she moves on to her next event.

Then, she proceeds to show the world what a fucking superstar she is.

Chapter 40

Lexie

"**F**inn, I stink!"

Carrying my body over his shoulder like I weigh twenty pounds, he slams the hotel room door shut behind us and gives my butt a light slap. "I literally could not give less of a fuck right now. I've waited long enough."

That he has. After the competition ended, I had to go attend a press conference and answer questions with multiple media outlets, and by the time I was able to get out of there, it had been more than fifteen hours since Finn had read the letter I'd drafted in five minutes before leaving my room, a last-minute decision. That is, if he did read it when I dropped it off, or if he's even read it at all. The second he saw me, he cradled me into a bear hug that lasted so long it felt like Finn had absorbed all the nerves I'd been carrying for the past year. He didn't need to say anything. I could feel how proud he was just by the way he was squeezing me. Then, he asked me if I was ready to go back to the hotel, and I gladly agreed.

And now here we are, me on his shoulder, the stupidest grin on my lips and the weight of the world suddenly off my shoulders. After twenty-something years of training, I did it. I earned my spot at the Olympic trials. And while I didn't win like I'd intended to, I've never been happier to carry silver on me. So long as I got to go to the Olympic trials next year, whatever rank I got didn't matter for a second. I shook Clara Popov's hand and meant it wholeheartedly when I said I was happy for her.

In this moment, I don't think anything could make me unhappy, and that's not only due to the medal around my neck. In fact, it's mostly due to the man carefully letting me onto my feet, his support unwavering throughout this whole thing.

This man who *loves* me.

I might have been too shocked to properly digest it yesterday, but this morning when I woke up, for a second I forgot about the competition I was supposed to attend because *Finn Olsen loves me.* And not just that, but he loves me in a way anyone could only dream of being loved. With full understanding and acceptance.

Finn's hands caress my cheeks as his eyes switch between mine, his silence so damn loud. I take it all in, wanting to bask in his touch forever. And maybe now I can.

"I'm trying to find words to say what I mean, but somehow, they all fall short," he says in a soft voice.

"I understand the feeling."

"You were so goddamn amazing out there, Lex." He inhales shakily. "And that letter? I still haven't processed it." His forehead falls to mine as he says, "I think I need to hear you say it out loud."

I'm all too happy to oblige. "I love you, Finn."

The only comparison I can find to the smile that blooms on Finn's face is the sun setting behind the Grand Canyon, creating a halo of golds and reds you feel right through your veins.

"I might ask you to say it again. You know, to be really, really sure," he says.

"Go for it."

Before he can, though, his lips are on mine, and while we've kissed hundreds of times, this one is different—*feels* different—because nothing's hidden. And with each brush of his tongue against mine, I wonder how I could be so stupid not to have seen it before. His love is in every nip of my lips, in every hum in his throat, in every scrape of his nails against my skin.

As he moves us toward the bed, he angles my head back so he can deepen the kiss, and while landing that double back double twist this morning felt incredible, it was nothing compared to the heat of his body and the taste of his lips on mine right now.

Just as we fall onto the mattress, my hands under his shirt in order to take it off, something vibrates in Finn's pocket. I don't mind it, but Finn freezes, so eventually, I push away.

"What is it?" I ask as he pulls his phone from his pocket.

"Fuck, I was supposed to call them." His eyes flick my way. "You got me distracted."

"Call who?"

He doesn't have time to answer because right then, he answers the video call, and I gasp at what I see.

"What's going on? Is she around?" Aaron asks, surrounded by a table full of the people I've gotten to know and love throughout the year. Wren is sitting next to Aaron, and beside her is Lilianne, the Scott-Perezes, Shelli, Gil, and even Francesca. Behind them is a rustic living room I recognize as the Scott-Perezes', with its wooden floor covered with cushions and blankets, the television tuned to ESPN.

These people who I didn't know when I arrived in Vermont a year ago just spent the day watching me compete and waited until the late hours to get on a call with me. Somehow, that brings tears to my eyes for the first time today.

I didn't have many friends growing up, and even fewer when I graduated high school and pursued professional gymnastics. I didn't think I'd ever find somewhere I'd fit in.

For the first time, these people on the other side of the screen make me feel like maybe I just hadn't met the right people yet. My family isn't here today, and I realize it doesn't make me sad like it would have before. I might not have a great biological family, but I have an amazing chosen one. Finn's people have become my people, and I couldn't be more thankful for it. Isn't that part of what love is anyway? To merging your life with someone else's, keeping your individuality while becoming part of a whole?

I really, really love that whole.

Finn turns the phone my way so everyone back in Vermont can see me, and I can't help but giggle like a schoolgirl when they all start cheering, Lil jumping up and down in the back. "We're so freaking proud of you," she shouts before blowing me a kiss.

"You're my new idol," Wren says when she steals the phone from Aaron's hands.

They then proceed to pass the phone from one person to the next, each of their congratulations making the knot in my throat tighten. I didn't know it was possible for one person to feel this loved.

When Shelli gets her turn, she says, "I'm rarely speechless, but that's what you made me today. I really wish I could've been there. Your hard work paid off." She grins. "When you get back, let's talk about getting you a proper coach before the Games' trials, yes?"

"Sounds good. And thank you, Shelli. For everything." I hope she can hear all the gratitude I hold for her. If it wasn't for her help, I'd be nowhere today.

"All right, everyone," Finn says as he takes his phone back. "I'm hanging up now because I want my girl all to myself."

My cheeks warm, especially when no one on the call seems surprised, save for Lilianne's "whoop" in the back. Were we that obvious?

I guess we were.

"Congratulations again, Lexie," Aaron says, his face now the only one in view. Then, he leans even closer and whispers into the phone, "And thank you for making my friend so damn happy."

Finn doesn't appear the least bit embarrassed, and I think I might love him even more for it.

"Trust me," I say, my cheeks hurting, "the pleasure's all mine."

Once Finn has said his final goodbye, he ends the call and pulls me closer so I'm sitting in his lap. As I wrap my arms around his neck, I say, "Your girl, huh?"

"Damn right you are." His bright greens soften. "I think you might always have been."

"Even when you were creeping me out?"

"Even then, darling."

I hug him tighter, and now that I'm closer, I notice a new patch of hair loss I hadn't seen before, right at his nape. Tapping it, I say, "Stressful week?"

"Yeah."

I lean forward and kiss the spot. "Sorry."

"It was all worth it." He brushes a strand of hair away from my forehead. "And there's someone else we need to call, but before that, I wanted to talk to you about something."

I lift a brow.

"I know you don't like Josie staying in Arizona, so I was thinking maybe you could ask her if she'd want to come stay with us for a while? You know, since we're settling." Color rises to his cheeks. "I'd be there to help, and we have people around. We could get a bigger place. Maybe she could at least visit the schools around, see if she likes—"

I stop him in his tracks by kissing the words out of his mouth. When I pull back, I say, "Have I told you how much I love you?"

"Yes, but I'm not against hearing it some more."

I kiss him once more, but just as it deepens, I pull back with my eyes narrowed and say, "Did you just sneakily ask me to move in with you?"

"Hoped you wouldn't notice." He shrugs. "But it's not like you have much of a choice, Crabby. I'm not spending one more night without you, and I'm not above kidnapping."

I laugh. "I don't think you'll need to."

We spend the following twenty minutes talking with Josie over the phone and making her the offer. As I'd expected, she says yes in a heartbeat, but I still tell her to take a few days to think about it and be sure it's what she truly wants. I'm pretty sure that's what she'll decide anyway, but it doesn't hurt to give her some time. I'll call my mother tomorrow to introduce the idea, but my guess is she won't put up too much of a fight.

When we hang up, I let myself fall back onto the pillows, completely spent yet buzzing with energy.

"This whole day's felt like a dream," I say.

"I know," Finn says, tucking me under his arm and kissing my forehead. "And it's just the beginning."

I sigh, both in exhaustion and happiness. "It is."

"So what's next?" he asks like he did yesterday, but this time, the answer comes easily.

"Well, tomorrow, we get back to work." To get to the Olympics, I still need to have a successful performance at the trials, and that won't happen by relaxing.

His index finger traces the line of my neck, then dips between my collarbones and my breasts. "What about now?"

"Now?" I shift so I'm straddling him, finding him hard against me. I smile against his lips, then slide my hands under his shirt and say, "Now, we celebrate."

Epilogue

Lexie

I'm so exhausted I could probably fall asleep on my feet.

The practices I've had all year to get here were no joke, but the ones with Team USA the day before our individual events at the Olympics were something else. Still, it felt like a dream to be there, so I embraced every second of pain I went through.

Not even caring to undress or shower, I let myself flop onto my hotel bed. Skincare can wait until tomorrow. All my muscles loosen as I feel sleep tugging at my conscience, yet the second my phone vibrates next to me on the bed, I jump up, a new buzz coursing through my veins.

"Hey," I say without even needing to look at the caller ID.

"Lexie," Finn says, my name always sounding like a compliment, like a reverence in his voice. "How are you doing? Missing me yet?"

"You know I am," I say, fighting to keep my yawn silent.

"I wish I could be there with you right now."

"I know, but it's fine. That meeting's too big of a deal." Since I'm up, I pad to the bathroom to brush my teeth. "Plus, you get to have a break from me, and you should enjoy it cause it won't happen again anytime soon."

Ever since I earned my spot as one of the five gymnasts who'd represent the USA at this year's Olympic Games, the plan was for Finn to come with me. But with the expansion he's been doing on the farm—the degree he's still working for turned out to be the thing he needed to turn full businessman mode—he had to meet with potential investors, and sadly, one of those meetings had to fall this week.

"I don't need any day off from you, Lex. Trust me."

I smile. Even after a year together, he still succeeds in making me giddy in that lie-on-your-back-and-kick-your-legs-in-the-air kind of way. Even though we've technically been living together all this time, I've been traveling all over the place for competitions and events, so we've had to deal with a lot of time apart, and while I can't speak for him, I can say that if I never have to spend another day without him, I'll be the happiest woman in the world. It's almost embarrassing to think, but it's the truth. When I'm with Finn is when I feel like my best self. A little smilier, a little brighter, a little happier. Together is where we belong.

I pull my toothbrush out of my mouth to ask, "Josie still doing okay?"

"Yeah. She's with Martina and Callie right now, I think."

"What do you mean, you think?"

Ever since Josie moved in with us, she and Callie have become like sisters. When I have to travel away, she sometimes comes with me, and she always helps me with the organization of the clinics I host at the gym, but most of the time she stays either with Finn or with the Scott-Perez family. I've never seen my sister happier.

When she first moved to Vermont, I was apprehensive that she would find it hard to be away from everything she's ever known, including her mother, but the truth is that she's been blooming ever since. It's as if she felt like she shouldn't take too much space in Phoenix, but here, she feels comfortable to be as wide as she wants to be. Our mother calls her every week or so, and that seems to be a convenient arrangement for the both of them. As for me, I've given up on trying to have a healthy relationship with her and Kyle, and the simple act of letting go has been like a breath of fresh air.

"I mean I'm not with her right now so I can't say for sure," Finn says.

I spit in the sink, then rinse my toothbrush. "I thought your meeting was only tomorrow morning." With the time difference, that's in about twenty hours for him.

"Yeah, it was."

I frown when a knock comes at the door.

"Gimme a sec," I tell Finn, already walking to the door. "Someone's knocking."

Without another thought, I undo the lock chain and swing the door open, expecting to see my coach, Trudy, or maybe a hotel staff member, but the second I see his face, I drop my phone to the carpeted ground and take a step back.

"You're not even going to let me in?" Finn says, grinning like a fool.

"Wh— I don't..." I can't find logical words as I try to wrestle with the idea that he's actually here. This feels like Phoenix all over again, except that this time, I don't have to hide anything of what I'm feeling. "Oh my god," I finally say before throwing myself into his arms. He catches me and easily carries me back inside, squeezing me tightly against his body as he whispers in my ear, "Hi, darling."

"What are you even doing here?" I gasp, inhaling a gulp of his clean, woodsy scent, one that always fills my dreams.

"You really thought I'd let my girl compete at the fucking Olympics and not be there for her?" He pulls his head back so our gazes can meet, the green of his reminding me of that first bloom of April in Vermont. "Not a chance in the world."

"But what about your meeting?"

"Canceled it a while ago." He shakes his head. "Was never gonna happen."

I bring my hands to his face so I can trace his nose, his sharp cheekbones. "I can't believe you're really here." I'm a big girl. I would've been fine on my own. But damn if I'm not relieved he showed up. Tomorrow—and the week to come—is going to be one of the biggest days of my life, and going through it with the man I now consider my pillar will only make the experience smoother.

"Good surprise, I hope?"

I smile before kissing him again. "Very."

"I won't keep you up for long." Gently, he sits me down on the bed. "I just need to say a few words first."

I lift my brows.

"What? I was supposed to be here earlier, but my plane was late, so I'll do this quick." He takes my hands in his and presses a kiss to my knuckles. "I want you to know that whatever happens tomorrow, it will never change the way I feel for you. You're one of the strongest people I know, and I'm so fucking proud of you. A medal doesn't mean anything."

"Honestly? It doesn't matter much to me either." I shrug. "I only ever wanted to get here, and I did it. A podium would only be icing on the cake." My head tilts to the side. "Really freaking tasty icing, but icing nonetheless." I never thought I could be this serene the day before the Games, but I'm glad I am. I also know that I'm officially retiring from professional gymnastics after this, focusing instead on coaching, so whatever happens, I want to enjoy every second of it.

"Good." He kisses me, and when he pulls back, there's a new emotion on his face. It looks like...nerves? "And there's something else." He swallows roughly. "You know how much I love you, Lexie, right? Like the entire universe could fit in my chest when I'm with you. And I can't imagine ever getting enough of that." A sharp exhale. "So I wanted to know if you would do me the honor of— Oh fuck, I forgot to kneel."

My smile is so big it pulls at all the muscles in my face as Finn drops to his knees in front of me and drags a hand down his face. "God, I'm sorry. I'm a mess, but only because just thinking about the possibility of spending my life with you sounds too good to be true."

I feel tears cloud my vision, and I don't try to hold them back.

"Let me try again, okay?" he says.

With a thick voice, I say, "Go ahead."

"Lexie," he says, his hands slightly trembling in mine. "I never expected you. For a long, long time, I thought I'd spend my life alone. And then, one random September day, you showed up. The one who understood my loneliness and helped me tear it down. And since then, not a single day has passed when I haven't felt part of something bigger than me."

He inhales shakily. "I think a part of me fell in love with you the moment you threw me onto my ass out of that cabin."

I guffaw. "I didn't throw you out!"

"Semantics," he says, then winks. "And if I'd been smarter, a part of me definitely should've fallen for you in that small alley in Rome. Still sorry about that, by the way."

I laugh even as tears stream down my cheeks. Who knew being stolen from meant the chance at finding the love of my life?

"But more than that, I lost all of my heart to you when I discovered the funny, smart, amazing person you are. You showed me what it meant to be loved in your entirety, and I'll never be able to thank you enough for that."

I'm shaking too now, too many emotions coursing through me to begin to name them. Finn lets go of one of my hands in order to wipe the tears off my face, then rests his hand on my cheek. "You asked me once if I had a dream like yours, and I told you no, but that's not true anymore. *You* are that dream for me. Spending my life with you. That's what I'll give anything to get. So once again, let me ask you one thing." He opens his mouth to repeat his question, but stops before saying a word. In a quick gesture, he gets to his feet and scrambles to the backpack he just dropped to the floor, then returns to me with a small velvet box.

"Really need to work on that proposal game," he says.

"Who needs smoothness anyway?"

He smirks, then kneels once more. "Alexandria Tuffin—Crabby—I love you more than time and words could ever express, and I'd be really, really honored if you agreed to become my wife."

He pulls the box open, revealing a delicate gold ring, adorned with multiple small diamonds, the sight reminding me of a starlit sky. It won't catch on anything when I'll be exercising or coaching, and I'd bet everything I have that this is partly why he picked it. I bring a hand to my mouth, once again overwhelmed by it all.

"Yes." I nod, another set of tears leaking from my eyes. "Yes, of course I'll marry you."

His entire face lights up, brighter than the diamonds on the ring. He doesn't even take the time to make sure the ring fits before his hands are in my hair and his lips are on mine. He then proceeds to make love to me and prove his words with every single one of his touches.

When we're done, we lie in bed, our naked bodies tangled in the sheets, and I feel just like he said: part of a whole. Like I'll never be all of me without him. I can't even be nervous about the amount of sleep I skipped because I'm stuck in a lavender haze.

"You picked your night, didn't you?" I say, chucking him under the chin.

"I'm pretty sure I was your lucky charm that night before the World Championships, so I thought, why not test fate again?"

I shake my head, laughing against his warm chest. I couldn't have imagined this man even if I'd tried. And now, I get to spend my life with him.

Propping myself on my hands so I can see him better, I say, " I do have a question for you, though."

"Shoot."

"Do fiancée privileges come with knowing what 'Finn' really stands for?"

He laughs, the sound traveling all the way to my toes. "You're insufferable."

"You love me anyway."

"I really do." He presses his lips to mine, and I wonder if I'll ever get tired of this. It seems that after a year, I should be done wanting more and more and more of him, but maybe that's what happens when you're with the right person. You can never get enough, always craving, greediness taking over.

With my nose pressed against his neck and his lips on my temple, I whisper, "I never thought I could ever be this happy."

Finn's hands grasp at my cheeks and level my face with his so I can see the glimmer in his eyes when he says, "Oh, darling, but this is just the beginning."

Acknowledgements

Here we are again! Five books in, and it never fails to feel surreal. And once again, I have a huge team of people working by my side who I need to thank because, without them, I couldn't do it!

First and foremost, I'd like to thank Melissa, someone who began as a collaborator and ended up becoming a true friend. Your unwavering support through the process of writing and publishing this book has been nothing short of a gift, and I feel so grateful to have you around. Please never stop sending me weird Reels.

Then, I want to thank Lil, who gave me all her precious gymnastics insight and welcomed these characters with open arms. I hope this book did your sport justice.

To Clara, who never fails to remind me that she will support whatever I publish, no matter what.

To Gab, best friend and reader extraordinaire.

To Émilie, who gave me the chance to convert her into a lover of romance novels. I know you started reading them to make me happy, and be sure that I love you endlessly for it.

To Charles, dear colleague turned reluctant proofreader! The fact that you never shut up about my books makes me both very embarrassed in public and incredibly grateful.

To my love, always. I can't wait to marry you.

To Jackie, who remembers my past books better than I do and who reminds me with every line edits that I don't actually know how to use commas and prepositions, but that's okay because you're there to correct me!

To Murphy, who once again outdid herself with this cover. Your talent will never cease to amaze me.

To Taryn, the best foreign rights agent who made sure my books could be read all over the world. (You guys keep your eyes open for more news coming soon!)

And finally, I want to thank you, my lovely readers, for having taken your precious time to read this book. Whether this was the first book of mine you've picked up or the fifth one, know that I couldn't be more grateful for you all. You make all the work worth it.

Want to learn more about Wren and Aaron? Read their story in **WHERE TIME STANDS STILL!**

Twenty-six-year-old Wren Lawson knows she will soon forget who she is. With early familial Alzheimer's disease written in her genes, it's a fact she's wrapped her whole life around; to indulge in friends or romance is a risk for everyone around her—one she's not keen on taking. Throwing herself into her work as a lawyer is the only thing she can do.

Aaron Scott-Perez was happy with his quiet life in Boston, but when a doctor's mistake leaves his father unable to run his Christmas tree farm, Aaron has no choice but to move back to the small Vermont town he used to call home. He never saw himself managing the business, but since it is so dear to his father, Aaron has given up everything to do it. To get his father the justice he deserves, he hires none other than Wren. She's emotionally blunted and secretive, but her kindness and competency provide something his family hasn't felt for a long time: hope. So much so that Aaron starts to think the life he didn't want might not be so bad when she's around.

Yet Wren cannot let him in, too haunted by her future.

As the two get closer and the lines become blurred, Wren and Aaron find themselves at a crossroads. But their attraction is un-yielding, and together they must decide what risks are worth tak-ing, and if love is better to lose than to never have at all.

Also by the author

A RISK ON FOREVER

THE INFINITY BETWEEN US

WHERE TIME STANDS STILL

OUR FINAL LOVE SONG

About the Author

N.S. Perkins lives the best of both worlds, being a resident doctor by day and a romance author by night. When she's not writing, reading, or studying, you can probably find her trying new restaurants, dreaming about the next beach she'll be visiting, or creeping the cutest dogs in the parks near her house. She lives in Montreal with her partner.

Find her on:
Threads: @nsperkinsauthor
Instagram: @nsperkinsauthor
TikTok: @nsperkinsauthor
Website: www.nsperkins.com